~ **Myster**

**Asylum **

Independent Pu

~ Early Praise ~

"Dark deeds in shadowy halls haunt generations in Kathryn Orzech's
Asylum. A must-read."
— *Marian Lanouette, thriller author*

"An intricately woven mystery with well-developed characters, *Asylum*
pulls in the reader on the first few pages. Kathryn Orzech skillfully
unfolds the story along separate timelines, seamlessly moving between
centuries, in a search for clues on two continents. Take *Asylum* to the
beach or in front of the fireplace … or anywhere. Just don't go down
the dark tunnel alone."
— *Penny Goetjen, mystery author*

"Family secrets from the 19th century send shockwaves through time
in this suspenseful multi-generational saga. You're gonna love it!"
— *Rhonda Lane, author and blogger*

~ A Book Club Favorite ~

"We read *Asylum* for my book club and we loved it! I read it in two days.
It had everything from intrigue, romance, and suspense."
— *C. Bernhardt, Ladies' Book Club*

"I think of the small child mysteriously sent away and her father's search
to bring his cherished daughter home. A strong plot and plenty of
subplots weave through two time frames and kept me thinking about
what the characters might do. I really enjoyed reading *Asylum* with my
book club and many others will too."
— *K. Berube, Southington Book Club*

"A well-researched suspense thriller, *Asylum* leaves you waiting to turn
each page until you come to a well-written resolution."
— *K. Webster, Ladies' Book Club*

"If you like suspense, *Asylum* is a great read and I had difficulty putting
the book down! The character development, the unfolding story, the vivid
descriptions! I encourage mystery fans and book clubs to add this exciting
mystery to their schedules!"
— *N. Moore, Rocky Hill Book Club*

Asylum

a dark suspense saga

~ • ~

Kathryn Orzech

Best-Wishes

Kathryn Orzech

DREAM
WATCH
PRESS

Meriden, Connecticut

DreamWatch Press
Meriden, CT 06450
www.DreamWatch.com

Dreamwatch® is a Registered Trademark of Kathryn Orzech
Cover photo by Laura Fogarty

This book is a work of fiction. All characters, places, and events are either products of the author's imagination or are used fictitiously. Any resemblance to actual events or locales or businesses or companies or persons, living or dead, is entirely coincidental.

ISBN 978-0-9892261-2-7 print book
ISBN 978-0-9892261-3-4 ebook

Publisher's Cataloging-In-Publication Data
(Prepared by The Donohue Group, Inc.)

Names: Orzech, Kathryn.
Title: Asylum : a dark suspense saga / Kathryn Orzech.
Description: Meriden, Connecticut : Dreamwatch Press, [2017]
Identifiers: ISBN 978-0-9892261-2-7 (print) | ISBN 978-0-9892261-3-4 (ebook)
Subjects: LCSH: Family secrets–Fiction. | Rich people–Northeastern States–Fiction. |
    Asylums–Connecticut–Hartford–Fiction. | Women executives–Northeastern States–
    Fiction. | Inheritance and succession–Fiction. | Betrayal–Fiction. | Suspense fiction.
Classification: LCC PS3615.R94 A89 2017 (print) | LCC PS3615.R94 (ebook) |
    DDC 813/.6–dc23

Produced in the United States of America

~ A Heartfelt Dedication ~

To my widowed father,
a principled man, who without complaint,
shouldered a heavy burden
with dignity and forbearance.

I was his sunshine.

He was my North Star.

~ Acknowledgements ~

Life, career, and travels often interrupted
writing *Asylum*, sometimes shelving it for years.
The untimely passing of three pivotal friends
lit a fire in me to finish it. Marcia, a force since
childhood; Geri, an adulthood ally; and Liz who
gave more than I deserved, enhanced my life
and I miss them. Their absence left me lost.
My heart cold. My drive extinguished.

New friends with shared interests entered
my life and when enthusiasm limped, they were
my crutches. I'm grateful to Roberta, Louise,
Ann, JoAnne, and Martha.

I appreciate the professional support
that evolved into valued friendships with fellow
Sisters in Crime, Rhonda, Marian, and Penny
whose encouragement continues to poke
my embers.

~ ONE ~

1974 • October

MARGARET ROSA DELITO should have known the day would come to a grim end. She had a sense about things like that, important things; life-and-death things.

She lived a deliberate life centered on one purpose—to erase the memories of her dark days.

From the second floor of Delito, Inc.'s home office, Rosa descended the grand staircase with quiet grace, like she had nearly every day at 5:20 p.m. for more than sixty years. She paused at the atrium, sighing with a hypnotic stare through the lobby's wall of glass. Wispy clouds, blushed scarlet, drifted across a clear New England sky. The low sun warmed her face.

Her fingers tightened around the scrap of paper clenched in her disfigured hand. The newspaper masthead, dated 1900, had been left on her desk during the night ... a cryptic message from someone connected to her past—someone employed at Delito. Secrets were bound to surface. Something wicked was sure to follow.

She'd sent her granddaughter to a meeting at their New York sales office and wondered how she fared. She had hoped to protect Laura, but if someone at Delito knew of its tarnished past, of the family's complicity, and the source of her shame, she had to tell her everything. And she would. Tomorrow.

Rosa stashed the torn newspaper into her purse before buttoning her favorite cashmere coat. Outside, dried leaves clattered across the sidewalk in a gusty wind. The American flag fluttered like a beating heart, like her heart, pumping faster in a rhythm gone bad. Pressure in her chest forced the wind from her lungs like when she slammed to the ground that day long ago—that day when it all began.

As her heels tapped across the lobby's white marble tiles toward the exit, Rosa's recall skipped through memories of those times, in that place, that had tormented her life and haunted her dreams, like a phonograph needle scratching across damaged vinyl … walk cold … cold … cold …

My feet walk cold stone floors. I wear no shoes.

I feel my way along a wall. Fingers scrape its gritty surface and sand sprinkles on my feet. I sense a tunnel though I see nothing but darkness.

Dampness veils my skin and a foul taste, musty and bitter, settles in my throat.

I sneak toward a distant line of light where a door is cracked open. Voices inside. Moaning. Sobbing. Fear tightens its choking grip as I stand alone, knowing I must look into that room.

A chill crawls up the back of my neck. Cold. My hands tremble. My knees weaken as I creep toward the door to see … Oh God … Oh God …

Be silent. Mustn't scream.

Gray ghosts … Gray ghosts …

Shhh … They'll see you.

Pain burned through Rosa's left arm and her purse slipped from her fingers, landing with a thud. Her hand stretched out as if seeking support as she stumbled toward the sofa set against the wall.

I feel my way …

Light dimmed as Rosa's skin grew clammy …

Dampness veils my skin … I hear voices …

The receptionist bolted from her desk. "Ms. Delito, what's wrong?"

I stand alone … My knees weaken …

Clutching her chest, gasping for air, she collapsed to the floor in a dizzying yet elegant spiral. Her back braced against the sofa. Her legs sprawled before her like a rag doll propped against bed pillows.

Panic distorted the receptionist's features as she screamed, "Help! We need help out here!"

The girl advanced toward her, seeming to move in slow motion as if wading against wild water.

Is this how it ends? ...

Gray ghosts ... Gray ghosts ...

WITH THE NAME LAURA DELITO, my ego should have been bruised when the trades slammed Delito's new line of costume jewelry as "mediocre," but I was prepared for defeat. I'd lost my battle months ago when our COO Sam Bender, my stepfather, rejected my designs which made me wonder why I'd been "invited" to a marketing meeting.

Our Manhattan sales office was the last place I wanted to be, but Gram had insisted. The office depressed me even on a good day. Nicks and scratches scarred the conference table. Chairs were lumpy and hard. A whitish rectangle framed by decades of grime marked the wall where a painting once hung. Something beautiful had been there, but now it was gone, like the short history of Delito, Inc. With an antiquated thermostat stuck at eighty degrees, coupled with last night's restless sleep, I could hardly keep my eyes open.

As much as the trades had tainted my company pride, I had to agree that "mediocre" pretty much summed it up. Our fiercest competitors—Napier, Monet, and Trifari—had to be gleaming. The best news today? It wasn't my responsibility to sell the stuff.

I glanced at Michael Bryce who sat beside me. It wasn't his responsibility either. As Gram's right-hand man, he knew her daily routine better than I, though no relationship came close to the connection I shared with Gram. Michael had accompanied Sam and me from the home office in Barrows, Connecticut, and he was the only excitement in my mediocre life.

He leaned against me and whispered, "You look like you're somewhere else."

Even after a year of knowing him, his touch sparked fire. "Just wishing I were."

I had been content in Chicago, working at the museum with my career poised to soar. Then Gram phoned, demanding I return. We didn't even talk long—fifteen minutes at most. Her ambush challenged that I'd wasted enough time "finding myself" and if she didn't find me back at the plant, she'd sell the business. Done deal. I returned within the week.

Another ten years away would have been fabulous—twenty, even better—but I couldn't risk that she might actually sell. Someday, in the far future, I wanted it if only to prove myself to Mother and my stepfather. Gram seemed to be in a different time zone. A different zone. Period. Wanting everything done now. Her urgency escaped me because even after a year, my role remained unclear. Everyone had a title except me, and at twenty-eight, almost everyone thought of me as "the owner's kid." And far too many people were calling me Del, a name I reserved for those closest few, except Gram who was too proper to adapt to casual mores. The sixties damn near scared her to death.

Honking horns and traffic noise drifted from the street twenty stories below. An emergency vehicle sped by, its siren faded into the distance. The alarm switched my thoughts. Something was wrong and my muscles wrenched tighter than twisted sheets after a bad dream. I squirmed in my chair—a hard, lumpy chair—and accidentally bumped Michael's arm.

"Del, what's up with you?"

"I should be home." I clipped an urge to cry out and ask if anyone has heard from Rosa? The hollow cold in my chest warned that something bad was about to happen ... had happened. "Did you talk to Rosa, today?"

"After lunch." Michael adjusted his Bulova. "Around two. Why?"

"Just a feeling. Anxiety, I guess. I resented that she had insisted I be here, so I didn't call..." I glanced aside and downward as I confessed, "...To punish her."

He rolled his eyes.

"Guilty, I know. Shame. On. Me."

"Anxious about what?"

None of the executives noticed that Michael and I spoke outside of their agenda. No surprise. They rarely noticed me at all. "I should be with her." My neck and shoulders tightened. My fists were clenched.

"Del, chill out. Take a breath or something, geez. I know you can't justify Sam's choices for the line, but we're almost done."

"I'm not doing this again. I don't care what she says. I feel trapped in a bad dream."

He swiveled in his seat to face me. "A bad dream? You had that nightmare again, didn't you?" Determination skewed his forehead as his eyes shot open. "Didn't you?" He checked his watch. Again. "I'm not letting you off easy. We will discuss this later."

Ugh, reluctant agreement. Story of my life. I focused on the pendulum of the grandfather clock in the corner of the room. Ten minutes after six. Its rhythm lulled my mind, my breathing slowed, but last night's dream replayed in my head—the type of dream that Gram and I often shared. No doubt, if I dreamed, she also dreamed …

… A dark dream … Of a dark place … A door cracks open
Voices from inside … I must look into that room
I creep toward the door …
Be silent. Gray ghosts … Shhh … They'll see you.

The clock chimed half past the hour and snapped me back to the worst meeting of my life. Frustrating. Hot and stuffy. I needed space, somewhere high and breezy. Maybe it wasn't a Gram dream after all. Maybe this boardroom was the room I feared to enter. Our senior executives, the gray ghosts. A forewarning of this unpleasantness? Or something worse?

"Del. Hey!" Michael wiggled my shoulder. "Are you ready to go?"

I nodded as Sam rose from his seat. Meeting adjourned. Hallelujah. The men gathered in the reception area leaving Michael and me alone.

He hoisted his briefcase and mine. "You should have told me you were having those nightmares again. I thought they had stopped. Didn't you tell me Chicago cured you?"

With a force that nearly popped a button, I fastened my suit jacket and grabbed my purse. "They did stop, but they've been creeping back since I returned to the business."

"And to your family?"

"A failed attempt at discretion. About four months ago they got bad."

"You've had them all this time?"

Silence. Nothing more to say, and he let it drop.

"We got a lot done today."

I shrugged, not as convinced. "I'm drained. Let's have a quiet dinner in my room or yours and not talk about work. You booked a separate room, didn't you?"

"Of course." A provocative smile curled his lips. "I can be discreet for as long as you want." His hand slipped under my hair and rubbed the back of my neck.

"Mmm, yes. Right there." The turn of my head guided his hand.

"Sam and I are meeting with the ad agency for breakfast at eight. Did you want to sit in?"

"I don't. You can fill me in on the ride home." I scanned the vacant boardroom and tucked the chairs under the table. An evening breeze carried the scent of light rain on concrete. I closed the window that had been propped open with a Lucite ad campaign award from 1968, then turned off the lights.

The room looked better in the dark.

The others were gone, and we were nearly out to the elevator lobby when the telephone rang at the reception desk.

"Let it go, Del."

My hand froze in midair as I reconsidered for two more rings. I snatched the receiver and pushed the button for line one. "Laura Delito."

Vinny Ferro, Sam's second-shift executive assistant rattled words without a breath. "I'm sorry Miss Delito, but I have bad news. She's okay, don't worry, but your grandmother was rushed to the hospital, and they called here when they didn't find you at your apartment. They said she's been asking for you. You should go directly to the hospital."

I set the receiver in its cradle on the third try and steadied myself against the desk. Surprise evolved to fear, then panic before changing to emotions that were all too familiar—new guilt for not being with Gram added to the shame I felt all day for not calling her.

Michael leaned against the doorframe and snapped, "Now what?"

"It's Gram."

He stepped forward. Brow furrowed. Timbre softened. "Rosa? What happened?"

Did Vinny say she'd fainted? Was it her head or her heart? The message blurred, but my gaping mouth said it all.

"Never mind." His hand rested on my shoulder. "We'll leave now. I'll pack and—"

I grabbed his wrist and checked his watch. "I've got forty minutes to get to Grand Central. There's a train at seven forty. I'll get home quicker if I'm on it."

"That's crazy. I'll go with you. We'll take the car."

"It's so late and there's nothing you can do anyway. Go to your meeting. You and Sam take the limo. You'll be back at the plant by noon. Pack my things." I shuffled through my purse. "Here's my room key. I'll catch a nap on the train. This could be a long night."

Did Vinny say her room was 314 or 340? The other day Gram assured me she felt "splendid," and she had agreed to a full physical before Christmas. She had ordered me here. "Get involved, know the staff," she'd said.

I caught the train just in time, but soon regretted I hadn't taken the company car. One hundred miles seemed so far and the ride too long for somber thoughts, and I regretted Michael wasn't beside me.

I should have thought through my plan.

I panicked.

MY FOOTSTEPS ECHOED in the third-floor corridor of St. Mary's Community Hospital in downtown Barrows. My leather pumps danced along the gray-and-white checkered floor though I didn't feel like my feet were in them. Even though Gram could afford the best private care, she had always insisted on St. Mary's, as if she expected the saint to relieve what ailed her. A faint, sick odor escaped the disinfectant as I hurried to her room. Soft night lighting surrendered to the glare of the nurses' station at the far end of the hall.

Cold chills my skin. A tunnel ...

An eerie familiarity from my nightmare rolled shivers down my arms, then someone in a pantry whistled a cheerful melody, breaking the psychic connection.

In a few days, Gram will be home and all will be as it should. The idea tasted like a lie. Something was wrong, and I knew exactly what it was, but if I allowed the thought to form for even a moment, my worst fear would be realized. Don't think it. *Too late. Gram will die tonight.*

A five-foot statue of St. Mary, posed on a pedestal, was the only figure at the nurses' station. Painted eyes and outstretched arms did nothing to soothe me. My pace quickened through the hospital's east wing while I noted room numbers that I passed ... 304, 306, 308.... I brushed against the hallway handrail as I raced toward something grim.

I feel my way along a wall.

... 310, 312. The night nurse stepped out of room 314.

We collided.

She scowled as she peeked at her watch. "May I help you?"

"Laura Delito. To see my grandmother." My tone was polite but firm. Fully aware visiting hours had passed, I didn't need to be patronized by some snooty nurse. I'd had my fill of pompous attitude in New York.

Her stance eased. "She's been asking for you. Your office said you were away on business. We didn't expect to see you tonight."

"I want a doctor to explain her condition."

The nurse wore a gold band on her finger. Black raised letters printed on a white plastic badge read Ida Sturm, R.N. Always get their name right, and you'll gain their respect. Gram had taught me. "Mrs. Sturm, you said she's been asking for me?"

If she's talking, she's alive.

"I looked in on her a moment ago. She's awake."

I see a line of light where the door cracks open. I stand alone, knowing I must look into that room.

I fluffed my hair and tugged my suit sleeves to my wrists to smooth the wrinkles.

My hands tremble. My knees weaken as I creep ...

I eased open the door. A heavy floral scent stuck in my throat like the flowers that had surrounded my father's casket, their smell so thick I'd nearly gagged.

Some foul taste settles inside me.

"Get rid of these. Clearly the office staff overreacted. She hasn't been here four hours." I pointed to two small bouquets on the granite sill. "Leave those and give away the rest. The room smells like a damned funeral parlor."

"I'll see to it myself." She pulled the door closed, leaving Gram and me alone.

A fluorescent light mounted above the headboard bathed Gram's white hair and the white bed sheets in an eerie glow, heavenly bright. I thought I heard angels singing. Maybe Gram was right about St. Mary. Mismatched paint covered the walls with hues of olive green. Water-stained plaster buckled in a ceiling corner where a pipe once leaked. I sat on the edge of the bed. "Gram, I'm here."

She smiled and attempted to push herself upright. "I'm so tired."

"Shall I let you sleep?" I pointed across the room to a brown leather chair, a tuft of stuffing bursting from its split arm. "I'm not going anywhere. I'll sit there while you rest."

"No, stay." Gram smoothed her hospital blanket like she'd fan my skirt when I was a kid, arranging a seat for my guardian angel. With the sweeping motion, her intravenous tube tugged at the pole beside her bed where a fluid-filled bag hung. Bruised flesh ringed the needle piercing her arm. She winced as she picked at the tape that secured it. "This is what tires me. I seem to be withering faster than those cut flowers."

With a gentle hold of her wrists, I braced her arms still across her chest. Her skin felt like cold silk loosely hung on a wire hanger. Where was her vitality? When did this happen? "Stop it, Gram. You'll tear out the needle, and you'll bleed."

"No!" She shot me a clipped, frightened look. "No blood."

She panicked at the sight of it, which was uncharacteristic of one who so fearlessly tackled life. She'd once explained it reminded her of "a wicked time," but I couldn't imagine Gram in such a state. And she wouldn't elaborate. When she calmed, I released her wrists.

"Always remember who you are. Make me proud."

She wouldn't be proud that I'd almost thrown a tantrum at the sales meeting, or that my solution was to tune out, so I lied. "I'm trying."

"Sweetheart, there's something I haven't told you ..." Her words stalled in a timid smile. "You know how neither of us likes surprises?"

I grinned, and shaking our forefingers at each other like we'd done ten thousand times, we said in unison, "No surprises," though her finger barely moved.

She struggled to point toward the bedside cabinet; the hint of a smile was gone. "There's something you should know ... must know...."

"I only need to know you'll recover."

"Something about my past, something a person might use against you."

Don't tell me. I wiped my eyes with the back of my hand. I had to be as strong as she expected me to be.

"A secret I've kept ... about the family ..."

If you confess now, you'll die.

Gram moaned. "Give me a minute." She pushed up on her elbows to sit higher on the bed and again pivoted toward the nightstand.

I spotted a plastic pitcher and filled a cup with water. "Is this what you want?"

She looked long at me before closing her eyes. She didn't open them again. When her last breath escaped, she shook as if chilled and slipped into death so peacefully, it was difficult to realize it had happened. But I knew.

I ran to the hallway and called for help. Shock locked my steps. My arms slumped at my sides. Scenes from Gram's life, of her and me, and the business, flashed in my head. Colored beads, shiny chains, and delicate filigree stampings.

Everything was about to change. I knew days ago when she ordered me to New York and hours ago when I fled. I probably knew a year ago when I ditched Chicago. And she knew it, too.

The nurse rushed into the room, felt for Gram's pulse, and shook her head.

"Do something. We can save her."

"Your grandmother was quite lucid when she requested we not revive her. Why don't you wait in the hallway? I'll call again for the doctor." She left the room.

Was there something proper to do? I needed roadside guardrails and painted lanes. I colored inside the lines. Boundaries and rules maintained my illusion of order, so where were the rules for this?

"Wake up, Gram. You didn't finish telling me." I shook her harder than I intended. "Damn it. Don't you die on me!"

I looked toward the ceiling in a lame attempt to divert tears. I couldn't leave. "You can hear me. I feel you near. We shared dreams and nightmares and knew each other's thoughts." I stroked her hair. She always looked her best, and she'd want that now. From the bedside cabinet, I set her purse on my lap and twisted the clasp.

A crumpled newspaper masthead sat on top. I flattened it on the edge of the bed. The year was dated 1900, the month and publication title torn away. What the hell? Why was she saving this? I stuffed it into my suit pocket.

Her gold-plated hairbrush weighed heavy in my hand as I fluffed her thin hair. It once fell to her shoulders, thick and shiny, with a slight curl; auburn like mine. It's why they named her Rosa. I brushed it for the last time, like I did when I was small and playing at her dressing table with sparkling crystal bottles filled with scented lotions and exotic perfumes from the Far East. "I wanted to be like you and still do. You knew that, didn't you?"

A middle-aged man in a lab coat entered and nodded indifferently. He pressed his stethoscope to Gram's chest. "I'm sorry for your loss." He never looked me in the eye, just checked his watch and wrote on the chart hanging at the foot of her bed. I didn't even get his name.

It was official. Gram wasn't coming back.

Uncapping the moisturizer in the hospital patient kit, I fought not to full-out cry while I massaged each swollen knuckle and finger, including the stub of her left pinkie. Gram had not been self-conscious about it, nor had she explained its loss. She was always there for my falls— my hurts. How did she lose her finger? When did it happen? What were the things in her life that made her hurt? *Was I one of them?*

I laid my hand on her chest where her heart used to beat. "What was your secret?" When Gram pointed to the nightstand, I assumed she wanted water. Maybe she wanted her purse. An idea came to me as if Gram herself had replied—*The newspaper will lead to answers.*

"Rest in peace, Gram. I love you." I removed from the wall a framed print of St. Mary and propped it on the nightstand to guide the soul of Margaret Rosa Delito. Beloved Grandmother. Beloved mentor. Beloved friend.

Now, I could leave. The worst had happened, and I could leave.

Maybe it was Gram's death I saw in my nightmare, her face pale like it was now, her life drained. *A gray ghost.*

Gray ghosts ... Gray ghosts ...

Finally my nightmares would end. I was sure of it.

Falling from a high place. Dark clouds.
A sinking sun slashes red across the horizon.
Field grass sways like ocean swells.
Thunder cracks and hard rain stings.
Falling. Falling.

MY BODY SLAMMED TO THE BED as if it had fallen from a roof or a tree, or that place from where dreams come. For a moment, I wondered where I had landed. My bedroom seemed to roll like a ship in rough seas. Salty sea air had drifted twenty miles inland from Long Island Sound to permeate the room. Gulls squawked as they soared over dumpsters in the parking lot. Cold to the bone and shivering, I rose from the bed and closed the windows.

Seven miles across town from Gram's High Hill estate, my two-room apartment felt more like a hotel suite than my home. No favorite paintings adorned the walls. No family photos posed on my dresser. A set of twenty-dollar dinnerware didn't fill one shelf in the kitchen cabinet. I'd lived here a year and unopened boxes from Chicago remained stored at Gram's. Half my clothes hung in her closets. Neat, classic clothes. Average. Straight skirts across the knee, not minis. Stovepipe slacks, not hip-huggers or bell-bottoms. Herringbone and tweed jackets, not satin or velvet, and definitely not polyester. Wardrobe colors topped out at black, white, gray, navy, camel, and hunter green. Not trendy, but safe, always safe. Not the edge of average, but the smack-dab-middle of it.

Last night, I'd made a dozen or so calls from the hospital until my best friend, Marcia, drove me home. I'd talked to Michael in New York, then I crashed. Clothes on. Windows open. At least, I fell onto my bed.

I awoke feeling alone, not the live-by-yourself-alone that I cherished more times than not, but the singular loneliness you feel when you've lost your grandmother, your father—or yourself. *I wish Michael were here.* He should have insisted on staying with me.

My suit jacket hung over the back of a chair where I'd tossed it last night. While coffee brewed in the galley kitchen, I pulled the newspaper from Gram's purse and laid it on the counter. The title was missing, torn away, and impossible to trace. Not even the library's microfilm archive could help. On the reverse side, a curious diagram had been drawn with a felt-tip marker, a similar stroke weight to markers in Delito's design department and in Gram's office. The crude drawing indicated a large rectangle near the center. Straight lines like wheel spokes connected six scattered smaller boxes back to the middle box. A wavy line scrawled along one edge of the paper, and a bold circle highlighted an X that marked intersecting lines inside the large rectangle. *Great. What do I do with this?* It must have been important to Gram that I see it; she pointed with her dying breath. I folded the paper and slid it into my Buxton billfold for safekeeping.

Today's reality was worse than my nightmares could ever be. Yanked from my Chicago adventure into Gram's grand Delito vision, but without her propping me up, who the hell was I?

Vague dream images lingered in my · head like faces of forgotten friends. I tried not to presume the meaning of the falling ocean dream. I tried not to decipher what Gram had drawn on the old newspaper. I needed to be at High Hill, so I hurried to shower and dress and be with people as soon as I could—even if they were my family.

HIGH HILL WAS LOCATED on the outskirts of the blue-collar town of Barrows. Set on the highest elevation in the area, it offered the finest views of central Connecticut's countryside, though today I didn't notice.

Why Great-grandfather Antonio Delito withdrew from the jewelry capital of Providence to settle in these quiet hills was a family tale learned long ago. He preferred a closer proximity to New York's business opportunities. And High Hill's stunning views had bewitched his young bride. She'd said it would be a grand place to live and a peaceful place to die, though no one could have predicted she would die so young.

I loved this house where I was raised, and even now, had spent more time here with Gram than anyone—more than in my own apartment. A Tudor structure had been added to the original stone and timber house, tripling its size to twelve spacious rooms, plenty big enough for Gram, Dad, Mother, and me without stepping on privacy. Crawling ivy framed the front door and on each side, bright yellow mums filled large wooden planters. Inside, handwoven carpets from Kashmir, Cappadocia, and Iran adorned restored parquet floors. Eclectic furnishings from across the globe graced every room, making High Hill the Delito historical museum. Who wouldn't want to live here?

The family was due to arrive at nine to schedule Gram's wake and funeral, arrange for flowers, food, lodging for visitors, and all the small things that busy a mourning mind. Gram's housekeeper brewed coffee and tea and organized doughnuts and muffins on paper doilies set on silver trays.

I lit a half dozen bayberry candles and sat on an antique church bench in the foyer, staring at my fingernails, with Marcia by my side. We didn't speak, nor did we need to. As different as we were, she and I had been best friends since the second grade. Though I had little interest in local news, I was aware of the daily price of gold and silver, and the political situation in every country, at least the nutshell version. Marcia couldn't distinguish between Cairo and Calcutta, but she could tell you who was married, headed toward divorce, and who had garden tools on sale.

I felt like a Catholic schoolgirl outside Mother Superior's office, a common feeling when Mother came to call. I stretched my knit dress to cover my knees.

A car door slammed and my gaze snapped to the window. A chauffeur stepped out of the black Lincoln Continental and opened the passenger door with precision as if his passengers would accept nothing less. I met them at the door while Marcia stood a safe distance behind me.

"Hello, Mother. Sam." She and I touched cheeks as if it meant as much as a hug or a kiss.

Fragrances of perfume and hair spray trailed Virginia Bender through the foyer, into the parlor, and back, as I dutifully tagged behind. She inspected every corner of the room, chin up, head rigid as her eyes scrutinized every minute detail until her attention fell on me. "You must do something with that god-awful hair. Let me fix it." She lifted her hand to straighten my part.

"Lovely to see you too, Mother." I brushed her hand away.

"Call my salon, dear. I'm sure they'll squeeze you in, considering—"

"Considering what?"

She gripped my arm as if I was five and tugged me back to the foyer away from the others. "That everyone in town will see you at the wake. Don't embarrass me." She nodded at Marcia as if her scolding applied to both and returned to the parlor. I did not.

"Embarrass her?" Marcia rolled her eyes. "You lost your grandmother and that's what she's worried about?"

I said to her, "I haven't lived with her for ten years. When will she treat me like an adult?"

"They never do."

The grandmother clock, partner to the grandfather in New York, chimed Aaron Schaeffer's arrival. As corporate attorney for Delito, Inc., he had been Gram's closest friend for as long as I remembered. Believing he was a blood member of the family, I'd called him Uncle Aaron until my teen years when I discovered he and Gram were also lovers. Oops.

Sam entered the foyer. "Good to see you, Aaron." The clock chimed on. "Now that we're all here, let's get to work."

I interrupted, "Aaron, thanks for coming so soon."

The housekeeper took his coat.

Sam grabbed a coffee and took a seat beside Mother.

Aaron held my hands to his heart for a long time, his eyes puffy as if he'd been crying. "She was dear to me. More than a client and friend, she was—"

"I know she was."

Aaron nodded at Marcia, then greeted Mother.

When I saw the company car, a white limousine, enter the long, straight driveway, I hurried to the door. Michael stepped from the rear seat. Thank God. He draped his overcoat over one arm and carried his briefcase with his other hand. Vinny Ferro exited the opposite side and followed Michael up the gray slate path. Dried crimson leaves cracked beneath their feet. I waited by the open door. Weathered and worn, it looked the way I felt. But Michael was here now. No detail would be overlooked. No mistake would slip by. He would watch my back.

After setting his case in the foyer and balancing his folded coat on top of it, I expected an embrace, but he merely kissed my cheek, no more affectionately than he'd greet an acquaintance—no more than Mother and I had greeted each other.

He leaned closer and whispered, "Virginia and Sam are watching in the mirror."

Vinny scanned the foyer furnishings. "I'm sorry for your loss, Miss Delito."

His condolence acknowledged, I gestured that he should enter the parlor and leaned toward Michael. "Stay until plans are complete, then you should go to the plant. I can't think about business right now. I don't remember my schedule or where I'm supposed to be. It frightens me that I can't concentrate. My mind seems to be slipping away along with confidence to make decisions."

"Don't worry about business, I'm here. I'll see that Vinny is useful, too. He insisted on coming. I hope you don't mind."

As Vinny followed the housekeeper toward the kitchen, I shrugged. A low-level employee didn't belong at an intimate family meeting, yet I realized Gram was also Delito, Inc. and vital to more people than only me.

Michael ran his hand down my back, following me to join the others. I sat across from Mother and Sam, and Michael took a seat next to me, but not too close. The sides of opposition were clearly defined. He recorded the funeral particulars in his ever-present notebook then tucked it into an inside jacket pocket. Now I could be sure everything would happen precisely when it should. The full itinerary was determined within the hour.

"I'm taking a room at the Regency for a few days," he said. "It'll be more convenient than driving from Hartford, and I'll be nearby if you need anything."

My fingers brushed against his hand.

"Sam, come ride with me to the office. I've got the car." He also signaled Vinny to exit and discreetly winked at me.

Sam mumbled, "Exotic flowers, more limos. Too much money. The Old Lady is gone after all."

He always called her that, The Old Lady. Gram never minded, but I did. I bit my tongue.

"You couldn't wait two minutes. You had to say it in front of her." Michael nudged him outside.

"I didn't mean anything by it. It was a joke between us."

I barely heard Sam's half-hearted apology. A joke? They'd no sooner passed through the door when a sudden gust of wind slammed it shut. Its chill swept through me and roamed the house like a familiar spirit.

Gram had just said goodbye.

The limo vanished from sight, and I couldn't help but smile. *Michael, the perfect man, takes out the trash without being asked.*

WITH HIGH HILL EMPTY of guests, the housekeeper tidied up and left for home. I lay on the sofa and pulled a blanket over me. It was nearly four when I awoke and dusk was near.

Wandering from room to room, feeling only the stillness, hearing only silence, I sensed Gram's presence. Are you here? You're in my thoughts. I recalled the things I should have said to her, but didn't. All the things I wanted to say and needed to say, but never could.

You appeared to have everything a person could want, yet when you smiled, your eyes seemed to weep. You thought I didn't notice, but I did. I wanted to ask why. But I couldn't. This thing was always between us—between you and everyone. Did you never beat your demons?

In a bedroom Gram had reserved for my overnight stays, I removed my knit dress, pulled on a cable knit sweater and jeans, and tucked them into knee-high leather boots.

Passing through the den and out the French doors to the rear flagstone patio, I punched my hands into my pockets. Stomping around the perimeter of the grounds, I was angry at Gram for dying, like I had been when my father died. The stone wall dividing the fields was a natural place for separations and farewells. Alone, abandoned, and lost, I sat numb on the largest boulder, hammering my fists against my legs in a rhythmic mantra that wooed me into a trance. My stare locked toward the horizon. Blue and lavender splashed the sky like a watercolor wash. Tendrils of the old weeping willow in the far west field swayed like a forest of seagrass turned upside down. The field's tall, dry vegetation waltzed in glorious waves in a crisp breeze. Golden sun bathed the meadow making it appear more like the sea than the earth—an ocean mirage from another time. Or a recent dream?

Red slashed the skyline as the sun died in dark clouds. The wind smelled electric. Rain stung like ocean spray. I raced the storm back to the main house, bolted the doors, and drove across town to my apartment.

COVERAGE OF GRAM'S DEATH dominated the news for three days. By the time of her wake, the town's sense of loss had reached an unmatched potency. Four patrol officers directed traffic at the funeral home's parking lot and nearby intersections. The line of mourners stretched to the street as community leaders and curiosity seekers arrived to pay last respects. Though my immediate family was small in number, Gram's influence had impacted business and government across the state. And though the Delito fortune was a distant memory, we remained Barrows' royal family.

Marcia and I sat quietly until public entry began. Our high school acquaintances would likely attend, and she seemed eager for a reunion.

When the crowd filed in, Aaron Schaeffer and I joined Mother and Sam in the viewing parlor. Michael was somewhere nearby.

A pleasant scent of lilies competed with roses. People knelt at Gram's open coffin to mutter prayerful farewells, then greeted the receiving line saying how sorry they were, how wonderful she looked, and how much they'd miss her. I didn't mind that their words of sympathy were likely superficial—they eased my pain.

Marcia stood behind me, ready to remind me who was who. Small clusters of guests gathered in various parlors for conversation. After an hour and a half, the steady line of strangers made me realize that outside of business, I had few good friends. Then I saw him. Jimmy Cassella, my first love, and he needed no reminder. We were the couple everyone had envied. "Sure to be married," everyone had said. Marcia still hoped.

He caressed my hands as we spoke. "Need a break? Walk with me, and I'll find some coffee."

Marcia poked me from behind until I consented. "I'd love a cup of coffee ... served with fresh air."

We passed through the outer parlor where Michael conversed with Vinny and other Delito employees. Their contrast was stark; Michael was meticulously tailored—smooth, polished, and perfumed, while Jimmy was earthy and rugged with thick brown hair that needed trimming. What was likely his only suit, fit snugly across his broad shoulders.

"You look great, Laura. Tired, but great. This has to be hard on you." Jimmy rushed the words then turned his head before I could see him blush. It was something he'd done for as long as I'd known him, like calling me Laura. Being near him felt like slipping on worn loafers, marred and scuffed, but broken in and comfortable. The circumstance was wrong, but I couldn't deny our physical attraction, even though I wanted to.

The son of the funeral director delivered Styrofoam cups of strong coffee from a service room. Jimmy and I were soon out the door and strolling down a footpath narrow enough to force us close. We sat on a wrought-iron bench that felt cold against my legs even through my wool skirt.

"Marcia tells me you're in the construction business."

He roared a deep belly laugh. "Yeah, she keeps me up-to-date about what you're doing, too." He slid closer and rested his arm on the back of the bench as if we were still teens at a drive-in movie. "Isn't it funny we never run into each other?"

"I don't see anyone in town. I'm in and out of the office and rarely go out. My small apartment at Victoria Towers is adequate for now with minimal furniture, no pets, and neighbors I've never met." My hand landed on his knee in an automatic and natural motion until I realized what I'd done and jerked it away.

He swiped his chin. "I know the Towers. They're well-built."

At the entrance of the funeral home, another group of visitors had arrived—my cue to remove myself from increasing discomfort. "I should go. It was nice to see you." My words sounded unconvincing, and I didn't want them to be. "I mean it. I'm happy to see you."

Jimmy walked me back to the door and paused, turning the moment delicate. "Laura, I'd like to … Call me … I mean, if I can do anything." He kissed my cheek, lingering a little too long. Breathing a little too deep. Squeezing me a little too tight.

I backed away.

Michael stood outside the door. I didn't know how long he'd been watching. "Del, someone's been asking for you. She said you don't know her, but she must see you."

With his arm around my waist, he guided me through the viewing parlor to a corner sitting area where the woman waited. She appeared to be well into her seventies, maybe eighties, with blue eyes, gold-framed glasses, and a light wool coat that smelled of mothballs.

"Laura Delito, this is Emma Collings," he said.

The woman's gaze shifted from Gram's coffin. Her head tipped upward as she stared. "You have her eyes." Her expression lightened with a hint of a smile. "Can we talk alone?"

"Let's move our conversation to a quiet place." A simple look toward Michael was enough. I didn't need to ask.

"There's a vacant meeting room off the outside parlor." He helped Emma from her chair. After seating us in the private room, he left, closing the door behind him.

"You knew my grandmother?"

"We were close friends. More like sisters."

I slumped backward in the Queen Anne chair. I knew little of Gram's early years. She'd never spoken of them, and I was sure I hadn't heard of Emma Collings. I'd have remembered the name.

"How did you know her?"

Emma remained focused on my features. "It was a long time ago."

I'd often wondered if the cause of Gram's pain was rooted in her childhood. Part of her had been closed. Isolated from everyone. Whatever her secret, it didn't deserve the misery it had inflicted—especially after so many years. I'd often wondered if she had shared her burden, would I have said, "Is that all?" I knew enough about Mother's side of the family, but on the Delito side, all I'd been told, apart from the typical press release version, was that Gram was born and raised at High Hill. Emma Collings might add color to that sketchy picture.

"We were both near twelve when we lived at The Farm. I loved Maggie and cherished her stories. I know it sounds, ah, odd, but I enjoyed our time there."

Her pauses were laced with confusion, and her most conspicuous error was that Gram was called Rosa, not Maggie. Yet, she said the name so definitively. Either she'd wandered into the wrong funeral parlor or Gram's past hid more secrets than I suspected.

"She told stories of her father's travels and the places he would take her one day."

That much was probably true and consistent with Delito's growing business.

"We had great fun milking cows, drawing pictures, dressing up. I remember like it was yesterday."

Gram milking cows? This woman is freaking me out.

"Play was a wonderful escape." Emma reached into the small purse she clutched on her lap. "I kept something that belonged to her. You should have it."

Inching closer, I brimmed with the expectation of new information.

"I had forgotten about it until I saw her obituary in the newspaper."

Fetching the treasure, Emma dropped the bundle onto my open palm. A lace border framed a linen handkerchief. The old woman's eyes encouraged me to unfold the loosely wrapped gift. A three-inch golden key hung on a gold chain. Pinched between my thumb and forefinger, I examined the unusual design. "It's lovely."

She snatched my wrist with unexpected strength. Her voice rang with sudden urgency. "Maggie begged me—"

Her eyes had a faraway look as if she were glimpsing another time, as if she were there, a child again, not hesitating as before, but swept to her past like driftwood torn from a riverbank by spring floods.

"She begged me—to guard it with my life."

With hands trembling, her expression changed as if memories from decades ago surged into her. Her eyes exposed a troubled soul. Same as Gram's eyes. I was lured by them. What had they seen? They'd seen that part of Gram's life never shared.

Grandmother. Someone wonderful.

Something horrible.

A knock at the door startled me and yanked us back into real time.

"Sorry to interrupt." Michael leaned in. "Your mother is preparing to leave."

"Damn." The word escaped my lips before I could stop it. I covered my mouth. "Please excuse me, Emma. I'll be right back. There's so much more I need to know."

Only a few minutes passed, but when I returned, Emma was gone. Perhaps she'd traveled too far into her past, too deep into her mind. Maybe she couldn't, or wouldn't, allow herself to remember. Or perhaps she remembered more than she could bear.

A disconcerted feeling that nothing was as it seemed to be was all that lingered of the old woman's visit. My world turned on end. I'd been doubting my career as jewelry designer and questioning my life's purpose. I was a guest in my own apartment, suffered a dreadful relationship with my mother, and worse with her husband. And I was unsure of how Michael and I fit together. Now, all I had known about Gram, the one person I trusted, was gutted.

The gold chain of the antique key slithered between my fingers as it fell into a graceful swag, swaying like a clock's pendulum. But even time seemed warped as I faced the fog of my family's past and of my future. Guardrails were torn off my road, outlines erased from my story, and my colors were spilling out.

I closed my hand and held tight to the only truth I could grasp —a golden key wrapped in soiled linen.

~ TWO ~

1899 • Spring

MAGGIE DELITO HID in her secret place high above High Hill's west field. The massive limbs of an old weeping willow tree easily held her twelve-year-old frame. Father knew of her secret place, and she peeked through the willow's trailing branches to see him crossing the field toward her. With each step, he planted his walking stick into the earth and pushed it away as if driving a raft upriver. His gait was determined, his path direct. His leather boots crushed a trail in the tall grass, though he spared wildflowers if he could.

Father touched a flame to his pipe until puffs of blue smoke curled up from under the brim of his woolen hat. He tugged at the ends of his mustache, something he did when he was troubled, and twisted them upward to form a deceptive grin, masking what his purpose might be.

Twigs snapped underfoot as he neared. At last, his broad shoulders rested against the tree as he tapped his staff twice against the bark—his signal for Maggie to descend.

Eager arms and fit legs hugged the familiar limb as she eased toward the trunk. A small branch snagged the ruffle of her blue calico dress, but a sharp tug freed the cloth. Father waited below with his good ear tilted as if he listened for the sound of skirts rustling against bark. He braced himself against the trunk when she stepped onto his shoulders.

She slid to the ground and stood before him, hiding the tattered fabric. Father glanced at the dress clenched in her fist and offered a forgiving smile and an outstretched hand.

Not a word passed between them as they strolled alongside the stacked stone wall that divided the east and west fields. Father cherished the open space in the middle of the meadows. It was his secret place. He leaned his walking stick against the wall and snuffed smoldering tobacco from his pipe before setting it on the stone. With his handkerchief wrapped around his forefinger, he wiped smudges from her face. Their eyes didn't meet until he lifted her onto his lap and snuggled his arms around her.

"You're leaving again, aren't you? Like last year and the year before. I don't want you to go." She jumped off his knee, pulled herself free, and socked his legs with her fists.

He let her.

"Business demands I leave within the week, but until then, we will spend all of our time together." The tips of his fingers brushed her tousled hair, nudging curly auburn bangs away from her eyes. "Who is hiding under there?"

Maggie's chin puckered and quivered.

Father angled his head. "Are you about to irrigate the fields?"

She held back a smile to punish him and stifled her tears to please him. "Only you and me, you promise? Not Sally and not Carlotta?"

"Do you call me Antonio?"

The absurd suggestion made her giggle. "Father, I could not."

"Then you must not call your mother, Carlotta. Even Salvatore addresses her properly."

"I don't care what Sally names her."

He rolled his eyes in an exaggerated and comical way. "And you must not call your brother by a woman's name. Address people by proper Christian names."

"He lets me call him Sally." She paused and glanced aside. "So long as no older boys are near."

"Carlotta did not give birth to him, yet he shows her more respect. What am I to do with you?"

When Father traveled, a carefree life had been impossible for Maggie. Carlotta claimed her stern discipline was necessary to "compensate for Father's pampering." Pampering! Normally, High Hill was the family's sanctuary from the noisy, dirty streets of the booming manufacturing town of Barrows. But when he was gone, Carlotta refashioned privacy into Maggie's prison. No tutors. No friends. No visitors. She was locked in her room at night while Carlotta visited the town or tavern. Even servants were sent away. Telling Father would surely worsen her plight. And she did not tell him that Carlotta, during a berating, had admitted she had agreed to bear a child merely to satisfy his condition of marriage. *As long as I mind boundaries, nothing bad can happen.*

"I wish I'd been born to Sally's mother. Carlotta hates me."

Father made the sign of the cross as he did when anyone spoke of his first wife and greatest love. "You are my world. Had Carlotta not given birth to you, I would not have my beautiful Sunshine." He winked. "Even with your childish pout." With the softest touch, his finger raised her chin until their eyes met.

Maggie locked her hands on her hips and demanded, "For how long will you be abroad?"

"Four months. Perhaps, six. Until Christmas, I expect."

A long, slow shiver rattled her.

"Are you cold?" Father briskly rubbed her arms.

"Not cold. I'm … I'm …" Maggie considered the most descriptive language she could recall from her dictionary studies. "I'm fraught with worry."

"Fraught, are you?" Father choked on his laughter, but a broad grin bared his thoughts. "You have been reading too much of somber poets. There is no cause for concern; the servants will care for you. I have made this journey many times and will bring wonderful things when I return."

From an inside coat pocket, he pulled his compass. He was never without it. Fashioned like a pocket watch, a photograph was tucked in its cover like a lady might keep in a locket. "I carry a portrait of you and Salvatore. Yours is the face I see when I feel lost, and I am reminded of where I must return."

He adjusted the shell comb in her hair, a gift from his last visit to London. Since that visit, the combs had been manufactured at the Delito factory. "I will bring something special, perhaps a golden brooch or rose cameo from Florence that you can keep in your treasure chest." The fancy jewelry box from Morocco had been carved especially for her with a strong lock and a key that only she possessed. The chest would be a safe place to hide secret things if she had any. She clutched her father tighter.

"You are my big girl now. Do you remember the time I sailed with Nellie Bly?"

"I remember." Father had repeated the tale many times.

"It was autumn when I left. A season of storms."

Thunder rumbled in the distance as if even nature responded when Father spoke.

"The first night was the roughest." He hoisted Maggie onto his knee and pitched from side to side like a rocking ship.

A sudden current rippled across the fields. Swaying grasses changed to cerulean blue and the fields *became* the sea. Ocean swells tore the horizon. White caps and wind. She took shelter in the warmth of Father's woolen coat and pressed against him; listening to the steady beat of his heart, she felt safe.

"Nellie was there. The young woman exploring the world showed more courage than some who sailed, and her actions helped the weak and the poor and the ill."

Father suggested a broader boundary when he spoke to her of Nellie. *I'm not Nellie.* Though, she wanted to be. Nellie was a model to follow, a friend she could hold inside herself to measure her deeds and weigh their merit. She would make Father proud. Yes, he would leave and return, only to leave again. It was meant to be.

Maggie raised her head. The storm was now upon them. Rain stung her face.

"Salvatore will be joining me on this voyage."

The cold slice of a dagger could not have hurt her more. "NO!" Abandoned and betrayed and far more than angry, a wave of fear swamped her. "Not both of you."

"He is almost eighteen. Time for him to take his bride."

"Sally fears the water, but I love the sea. Father, take me. I'll bring home his bride. We'll become friends. I can tell her what a good brother he is and what a fine husband he will be."

Father gripped her arms and glared into her eyes. "Margaret Rosa. Salvatore will journey with me and that is my final word."

"You can't leave me alone with her. You don't know what she's like when you're gone."

"What do you speak of? What do you fear?"

Maggie pushed and pulled and freed herself from his hold. She slapped the top of the wall and ran as fast as the wind, fleeing his words as if the devil had spit them into her ears. Her footsteps pounded so hard against the earth, they shook her bones.

Father called after her. "Who frightens you?"

Maggie glanced back over her shoulder. "Carlotta Delito." She screamed, "CARLOTTA."

~ THREE ~

1974 • October

THE NEXT MORNING I stood rigid throughout the funeral mass at St. Anthony's Church, fighting to hold myself together. The gray day paled the hues of stained glass windows. Light from candles and chandeliers glinted on gilded religious icons. Aromas of incense, flowers, and woolen coats, damp with rain, filled the space. Organ music accompanied the full Sunday choir. Gram's casket, flanked by six candles, sat perpendicular to the altar in the center aisle as if she was set to lead a board meeting at the home office. I focused on a single flickering flame, trying not to visualize her body in the box.

Michael stood at my side guarding me with gentle strength. At the conclusion of the ceremony, he escorted me down the aisle. Mother and Sam followed. I passed pew after pew without emotion, discreetly scanning the crowd for the old woman who had disappeared from Gram's wake leaving too many questions unanswered, but Emma Collings wasn't there.

Jimmy Cassella was seated in the last pew. His quiet presence comforted me.

Friends, distant relatives, and close business associates were invited to High Hill following the graveside service at the cemetery. Michael had scheduled everything from cars to catering, leaving me free to reminisce with guests. The afternoon was long and filled with more tension than I expected, yet also relief because the worst was at last over.

CLOUDS BLANKETED THE NIGHT, warming it more than normal for mid-October. Only Marcia and I remained in the dining room at High Hill while the housekeeper tended to other areas of the house. Unsure of what I thirsted for, I considered the bar selection, raising bottle after bottle, inspecting labels, sniffing contents, then returning each to its place, unable to make this smallest decision. Nothing would fill the emptiness I felt in my soul. I wanted to run. To be alone with my pain, yet, I needed to be held.

"Seen any good Scotch?"

Marcia squinted. "When did you start drinking Scotch?"

"Since vodka made me sick. It took four years to acquire the taste." I found a fifth of 12-year-old Chivas.

"Four years! That was a stupid waste of time."

I filled two glasses with ice and our drinks, then sat at the dining table where Marcia and I picked at leftover cold cuts and frosted Italian cookies and drank good Scotch and cheap wine.

From the stack of sympathy cards, I snatched an envelope and read my name aloud, "Laura Delito. Whoever she is. Wherever she came from." I sighed louder than I intended; it must have sounded painful.

A crafty expression crossed Marcia's face. "Hey, who was that guy with Michael at the wake?"

"Which guy? What did he look like?"

"Cute, perfect skin, jet-black hair, clean-cut."

"If you're asking about Vinny Ferro, he's Sam's assistant working the evening shift. And barely legal. Moved here from Providence, I think. Why?"

"Just wondering. So he's probably not married?"

"What did I just say? Young!"

Marcia's brow drooped with disappointment before she countered, "He's not that much younger than us."

"Not in years, but he proves his immaturity every day."

"He seems to fit right in with those corporate-type guys. Is he nice?"

"Nice enough, but I haven't worked with him much. So, where were we? Oh, my name. Names." I thought of all the names Gram had trained me to remember. *Would every little thing remind me of her?* It had taken years to stop obsessing about my dad's death, and I didn't want melancholy to absorb my life again. I'd been sipping drinks all afternoon and the hastily downed Scotch pushed me further from sobriety and closer to numbness—exactly where I wanted to be.

Marcia ignored my rambling, opened cards, and read them to herself.

"It was good of your mom and dad to come today. You're lucky to have them."

Marcia agreed. "Listen," she demanded as she waved a condolence card in front of my face. She checked the price on the back panel, then apologized. "Habit. It's just a habit." She read the handwritten message.

"Dear Laura." She raised her eyebrows. "I wish I knew how to tell you how sad I feel for you. It's too bad we had to meet again this way. Call me if I can help you or if you want to talk to an old friend. I think of you often. Always as ever, Jimmy C."

The card whisked across the table like a Frisbee and landed in front of me.

"So, what do you think of that?"

I gulped my drink. "There isn't a person I've seen over the last two days who hasn't offered help."

"I've had major talk time with our boy. I asked why he calls you Laura and not Del like the rest of us?"

"You did?"

"I wanted to know. He told me, 'Del' carries too much Delito baggage, but 'Laura' is his girl next door. He always asks for you. Not just since you came home, but all these years."

"That sounds wonderful, but—I *am* a Delito and I do not live next door." My head sank nearer to the table. "We view those years through different lenses."

"Don't tell me you didn't have a good thing going. It lasted six years."

"We were kids. Besides, six years isn't so long when compared to a lifetime of misery. Geez Marcia, it took me four years to like Scotch."

We laughed.

"You two were perfect together."

"A lot's happened since, and there's more of the world outside of Barrows."

"What's that got to do with Jimmy?"

"I want it, like my dad and Gram. It's what Delitos do." Ice rattled when I wiggled my drink.

"Put that down. We're switching to coffee."

"I'm not going backward to Jimmy. I read that story and know how it ends."

"Yeah, yeah, I know."

"Sometimes I think you don't know me at all."

"Of course I do, because we're so much alike. You think you're different, big dreams and all. Don't kid yourself. You want what I want—a family who'll stand by me, a husband who adores me, and a cushy job."

"Marcia, I'm all I have left."

"That's my point." Her thrusting hands served as punctuation. "That's why I'm worried."

"Well, don't. How did we get off on this anyway?"

"Jimmy Cassella."

"Right. He can't keep up. It's a no-win deal for me, so forget it."

"It's not about winning. It's about bending and sharing your life and not pretending your business will ever be as good as it used to be."

My laugh exploded. "Bending! You're the most stubborn person I know, and you're preaching about bending? One tough divorce and you're a relationship expert? You've been watching too much Phil Donahue."

"For all his flaws, Jimmy's come far and you have to admit, he looks good."

We shook our heads in agreement, murmured lusty chuckles, and sipped our drinks.

"Honestly, I don't know what you see in Michael. He's such a stiff."

"He's smart, witty, and gorgeous. He listens to me. And he cares about me."

"Rarely."

"Mostly."

"Jimmy has a good business, and he just won that downtown renovation project." Marcia's eyes widened. "Everything about him looks good to me."

"Then you go out with him. The last thing I need is another complication." I sighed. "The business may erupt into chaos at any moment. I need my job. Most people don't think so, but I do have to work. Every day brings a new battle with Mother and Sam. He never approves my designs first time around and has to impose his power and bully me to make some crappy change. And I have something important to take care of." The tale of the elusive Emma Collings almost slipped from my lips, but telling a secret to Marcia was like buying a full page ad in the Sunday paper. "Besides, Michael and I are doing fine."

"Yeah, *he's* doing fine, that's for sure."

"Careful. I'm not so drunk I'll forget what you say. And just because I didn't comment, doesn't mean I missed what you said about the business. That hurt."

"Listen Del, the only thing Michael cares about is what you can do for his career. I don't trust him and neither should you."

"You disregard all he does for me? He's strong in a way that's different from Jimmy. He doesn't panic at the thought of going to New York or New Delhi. He's confident and loyal, and I need that now, more than ever."

Marcia slammed her open hand on the table. "He helps you do what you're afraid to do alone. Don't count on his loyalty. He'll take advantage."

"Maybe that's why I need him. When I'm with him, I forget how scared I am."

The stiffness shook from my neck and shoulders when I stood and snatched my car keys. "Maybe, I need some air. Do you mind?

I'll see you tomorrow night. Okay?" When Marcia left the room to get our coats, I reached for the condolence card with Jimmy's phone number and dropped it into my purse.

We met in the foyer. "Here, take this extra key to High Hill. For emergencies. In case we have to meet here again, or I might ask you to check something. Save me a trip across town."

"Thanks. I'll trade your old apartment key."

"Keep it until I've moved out." As we fiddled with key rings, I glanced up. "Hey, have you ever heard of a place called *The Farm*?"

She laughed. "Of course I have. We used to joke about it when we were kids. Don't you remember?"

I shrugged.

"The Farm," she insisted. "You know. It used to be Brookhaven Farm, now it's the Brookhaven Center." Her forefinger tapped circles at her temple. "Outside of Hartford. The asylum."

Goose bumps prickled up my arms.

CLOUDS HAD CLEARED and a full moon lit the night. After a short drive, I arrived at the Regency hotel a few minutes before 1:00 a.m. I strolled through the lobby as if I owned it and returned the desk clerk's suspicious gaze with a brazen, "Hi, how're you doing." The elevator rose to the ninth floor. I knocked on the door of Michael's suite, swaying on my two-inch heels while I waited. They say the full moon makes some people act crazy. I was one of them.

I wanted mind numbness, heart numbness—not this. I shouldn't have come. I must look like hell. God, I certainly shouldn't have driven. Stupid. Stupid. I could accept that at times I wasn't a model of grace and propriety, that I wasn't the perfect Delito, and that I didn't fulfill Mother's measure of an ideal daughter. She reminded me often enough. I could accept that I was flawed, but I couldn't bear that anyone else knew.

Michael's eyes squinted from the sudden glare of the hallway light. His fingers raked through his smooth, chestnut-colored hair mussed from sleep. "Mmm. What a pleasant surprise. Am I dreaming?" He put his arm around me and steered me into the darkened room. "Are you all right?"

My left hand sealed his lips while my right hand grasped the drawstring of his loosely fitted pajama bottoms and tugged. The silky garment slid past narrow hips and dropped to the floor. Then my eyes began a slow journey upward. Soft light from a street lamp, or perhaps the moon, shimmered over the sleek contours of his hips and chest. I buried my face under his chin where a trace of Obsession remained from the day.

In his caress, I felt secure in his arms. "Take care of me tonight."

He lifted me like a baby and carried me to bed where he set me down so gently, I wasn't aware I had stopped moving. *Blame it on the Scotch.* After he peeled off my clothes, hung each garment in the closet, and slipped into bed, I thought I heard his hand glide across the top of the nightstand and drop something into the drawer. He snuggled beside me, stroking my hair, and I fell asleep in his arms.

BY WEEK'S END I was feeling lost and lonely in my apartment. I was the gray ash from a burned out fire, my future dissipating like smoke from a chimney vent—if I had a chimney. How sudden. How shocking. I had no plan to mend my shattered life. I could return to Chicago and beg for my old job though that option seemed to be closed. Too defeatist.

The day was sunny, the air was crisp and fresh, and each breath of it clarified my thoughts. There was something to be said for beige walls, empty shelves, and clean slates. When old plans dissolve, new possibilities fill the empty space.

Mother, Sam, and I met at Aaron Schaeffer's law office because he had urged a quick settlement of Gram's estate. Her death became final when he read her will:

> I, Margaret Rosa Delito, a resident of the Town of Barrows, County of New Haven and State of Connecticut, being of sound and disposing mind and memory, do make, publish, and declare this to be my Last Will and Testament ...

Sam held Mother's hand. Feeling my observation intruded on their privacy, I glanced away.

FIRST: I direct that all my just debts …

Gram and I rarely discussed Delito finances. We did things like visit galleries, discuss art and architecture, and window shop in Manhattan to monitor fashion trends.

> SECOND: I direct that my Executor pay out of my residuary estate, without appointment, the expense of my last illness and all administration expenses together with all estate, inheritance, and like taxes imposed by the government of the United States …

We'd discussed economics, the market, and the price of precious metals and stones. We'd argued politics, Johnson's war policies, and watched Nixon's resignation on TV while eating pizza with mushrooms and sausage and extra mozzarella.

> THIRD: I give all the tangible personal property which I own at my death, including any household furniture, automobiles, jewelry, art objects, and other articles of household or personal use or ornament, to my granddaughter, Laura Delito …

Mother seemed pleased. I didn't believe what I had heard, and waited for the list of conditions I'd refuse to meet.

> FOURTH: I give, devise, and bequeath the property which I own at the time of my death, located at High Hill Road, Barrows, Connecticut, to my granddaughter, Laura Delito …

My throat tightened, and there was hardly a place to aim my eyes without feeling self-conscious.

FIFTH: I give, devise, and bequeath the business and property which I own at the time of my death, located at Delito Circle, Barrows, Connecticut, to my granddaughter, Laura Delito…

My God! Except for Mother's monthly stipend, that's everything. What has she done? No one was more stunned than I that Rosa had left all her worldly holdings to me, except that Sam's grip on Mother's hand appeared to tighten as he glared at me.

My cheeks must have turned red because I felt their burn.

My legs ached to run and never stop.

My heart pounded as if *I had* been running.

Mother had been distancing herself from the business since the day she married into it. She had competed with it for Dad's attention, and she'd lost. She'd come to resent the mere mention of business and rarely wore Delito jewelry for extra sting. She would have sold the business in a New York minute if Sam had allowed. Gram would have known this, too.

I stayed to ask Aaron what he thought. Because I knew nothing about the financial state of the company, he suggested an audit and set me up with a reputable accounting firm.

When I left, I found Sam waiting in the hallway. "Don't start." Oh crap. All I wanted was to leave without more drama. "I didn't ask for this, but I will accept the responsibility, and I'll do my best to exceed Gram's vision."

"If you think this makes a difference in company management, put it out of your mind." He would have grabbed my arm had I not lunged back. "This changes nothing."

My fists tightened as I stepped away. Months of condescension fueled my rage, rage that bolstered my nerve. "I don't care that you married my mother, but I am sick of you treating me like a high school part-timer."

"I've been good to you and your mother. Do you think it's been easy fitting into your family, especially with the business wrapped around you? You have no idea what you're getting into. Without me, you'll lose everything. I don't have a problem with us working together."

"Because we do everything your way."

"The Old Lady spoiled you."

"She groomed me and with proper promotion, my designs will double sales."

He burst into laughter. "Okay, I'm willing to gamble on—"

"You don't have to gamble *my* business on my talent. I don't need you."

Through the glass doors, I spotted his Lincoln parked at the curb where Mother looked uneasy. The business could have been split any number of ways. Wasn't she happy for me? No congratulations. No "I know you can do it, kiddo." More than enough money had been provided for her, but was it enough to keep Sam invested? She never looked more helpless. A stray kitten desperate for care. *I know the feeling.*

Sam exploited weakness. Maybe exploit was too strong a word, but he definitely jumped on opportunity, that's how he became involved with Mother. He was Delito's account supervisor and after Dad died, they met at an ad agency Christmas party in New York. Soon, he was coming to Connecticut for meetings, then staying weekends and Mother melted. Recalling that difficult time infuriated me.

"You took advantage of my mother when she was most vulnerable. Married before Dad's body was cold."

"What are you talking about? I'm suggesting we work together. Your mother has nothing to do with this."

"She passed control of the business to you, but I won't."

"I'm not the only one in a position to sabotage your plans. I may have to wait in line."

Damn him. He's already testing me and we haven't left the building. He'll be a monkey on my shoulder.

I could almost feel his breath on my neck.

I didn't flinch when he called out, "Laura. Watch your back."

HIGH HILL WAS NOW MY HOME. I sorted, packed, and stored some of Gram's personal effects, merging my modest belongings with the rest of her furnishings and the exotic accessories I treasured. Michael's daily calls and frequent visits informed me of events and the mood at the plant. By Friday evening, an important change had become obvious.

"What a yummy surprise. I didn't expect to see you till tomorrow."

"I couldn't wait that long. And I was hungry." He raised a big bag from our favorite Chinese restaurant.

"Mmm. Excellent choice. I haven't had dinner."

"I didn't think so." He scattered pint-size containers on the kitchen table. "It's still hot."

"What did you bring me?" I grabbed two plates from the cupboard and a fork for me.

"The usual. Spicy garlic chicken and vegetables with pork fried rice."

When he leaned forward to fill my plate, I kissed his cheek.

He dug in with chopsticks. "I was tempted to try something different."

"You know I hate surprises." I appreciated that he knew me so well, yet tears welled in my eyes.

He rose from across the table, stooped beside me, and hugged me. "Hey, what's this about?"

"Moments before Gram's death, we said the same thing about surprises."

"The last thing I wanted was to—"

"I know." I wiped my eyes with my napkin. "It's my fault. Emotions are too close to the surface. Sit. Tell me. How was your day?"

"So-so."

"Did something happen at the plant?"

"Not really."

"But, maybe?"

"Nothing I can put my finger on. You should come back to work."

"I'm not ready. I need more time."

"It might help to get away from High Hill for a while, at least a few hours a day. And it's been almost three weeks since Rosa died. The time … it's been … ah…."

"Proper?"

He nodded.

"I need a few more days."

"If you stay away too long … I don't know. Patterns are forming in your absence. New leaders may emerge."

"I understand. You're right. I'll go back sometime next week." Regardless of what he believed, I knew the truth. Half of me hungered to prove myself while the other half struggled in doubt. A precipice was outside the door, and I was afraid of the height.

~ FOUR ~

1899 • Spring

A WEEK HAD PASSED since Father and Salvatore voyaged to Europe. Maggie's disquiet had grown with the passing of each dismal day. Tutoring, cancelled. Visits with friends, forbidden. Church going, ceased. The cook and housekeeper had been sent away and the groundskeeper was instructed to come but twice a month. Most days, Carlotta left Maggie to fend for herself, eating any pantry food from a dwindling stock, then quickly returning outside to play where she remained invisible. She had a sense her clever attempts to evade her fate could not be sustained for the months Father and Salvatore would be gone. Alas, she was doomed.

Early in the second week, she climbed high into her favorite willow tree, scrambling to the clouds, but the weaker branches did not support her. Her body bounced through the tree. Vine-like offshoots slipped through her fingers as she failed to slow her fall. She slammed to earth as good as dead. The impact forced the wind from her chest. Time slowed. The sky darkened. Light dimmed. Her eyes closed as she lay stunned and breathless on the ground, her face buried in grass and soil. Dizzy. Spinning. Burning pain.

Crows squawked in the distance. Maggie gasped as air tore into her lungs like a breath from God raising the dead. Her body wrenched as she anticipated movement, prayed her limbs would move. Fingers lifted one by one, then arms and legs. She cautiously rose, feeling where she hurt, spitting earth from her mouth. Her lip bled. Legs ached. Knees and hands felt afire as blood oozed from raw, shredded skin.

She hobbled toward the house, following the stone wall where Father had bid farewell. Once a tidy boundary, the wall now divided times of serenity from those of abandonment. She hated the lovely damned wall.

Her every thought centered on herself—the stinging palms, her knees, her blood. She needed someone to hold her and mend her. Had Carlotta returned? Would wounds ignite her mother's compassion? There was no one in sight, but Uncle Elias' carriage was tucked beside the house nearly out of view. Thanks to God. Though not a blood uncle, Elias was so often at the factory and a guest in the Delito home, that he had earned the title. He would surely arrange for the physician.

Maggie limped in and out of the foyer and the parlor. Perhaps Carlotta and Elias sat in the library where Father often met with associates to speak of business and weighty subjects. Perhaps he brought news of Father or the factory. Shelves with books towered over the empty silent space. The last of the fireplace embers glowed, yet doled no warmth, seeming it had not been attended since morning.

Maggie heard a thud.

She rushed to the kitchen, then to the pantry. No one there. Another thud and thump. Her head snapped left and right. The sounds came from above, from Father's and Carlotta's chamber.

She faltered up the staircase, stopping once to check her battered knees. Blood clotted and crusted over the dirty scrapes. She winced when she touched them.

Maggie heard moaning from inside the bedroom chamber. She needed someone. Anyone. She eased open the double doors and stared at the bed. There, she saw Carlotta's naked buttocks bounce as she squatted on Uncle Elias. He grunted as if she hurt him, yet he grinned. Maggie watched in silence. Carlotta's round breasts bobbed up and down. Uncle Elias watched them, too.

Carlotta stretched her arms until her hands gripped the headboard of Father's four-post bed. She pushed herself against

Uncle Elias and they bumped and rocked together. The bed knocked against the wall in a deranged rhythm, then Carlotta squealed.

Maggie's eyes gaped. She gasped.

Uncle Elias jerked his head and gawked at the intrusion of her shriek. She stood motionless, her discovery etched into her mind.

Carlotta snatched her dressing gown, draped over a nearby chair, and wrapped it around her body. Her face twisted to an angry scowl.

Uncle Elias pulled on his trousers.

Maggie ran. Down the stairs. Out the door. Across the field. Her heart pumped hard. Her bloodied hands throbbed. Knees stung with a thousand needles.

She ran and ran, twisting her head to look behind. Carlotta and Elias chased after her. Running. Faster. Closer. Closer.

She could almost feel their breath on her back.

When a firm hand gripped her shoulder, Maggie lost her footing. She and Uncle Elias tumbled to the ground and rolled together into the stone wall.

ELIAS CARRIED MAGGIE into the house and dropped her in the foyer closet. Carlotta locked the door, heedless of the girl's screeching and pounding as she stood before the foyer mirror fastening her hair into a loose knot. Porcelain skin flushed from running, she dabbed her face with a dainty cloth.

"I told you Lottie, we shouldn't have," Elias called from the library. "Not with the kid here. She's old enough to know what's going on and too smart to believe an absurd fabrication."

"Shut up, you damned fool." She snatched a bottle from the spirit cabinet, poured a glass of whiskey and paced the room. "I've got to think."

"If she tells Antonio, he'll kill us."

A mouthful of spirit burned down her throat. Arms folded across her chest braced her bosom with exaggerated cleavage meant to distract. The white lace ruffles of her dressing gown danced on her breasts as she stepped toward the French-style doors. At thirty-three, her body was nearly perfect. Only the cursed stretch marks, tokens of pregnancy, scarred her flawless skin. She brushed against Elias like a cat. "He's not going to kill us."

Elias leaned against the stone fireplace facing the piled ash below. "She'll tell him. You bloody well know she will. It's finished. Everything I've worked for. Why did I get involved with you? He'll discharge me from the business if he doesn't slit my throat."

She ignored his worried babble.

"You'll be out of his life, too," he warned.

"A blessed day."

"And cheated of his fortune."

"Shut up!" Carlotta grabbed a poker and jabbed the ashes as she contemplated the grim possibility Elias could be right.

"Think faster, Lottie. We can't leave the kid locked in the closet forever."

The smell of charred wood permeated the room though the fire no longer burned. No amount of poking revived the flames. She tapped the iron tool against the stone, spraying fine gray powder to the floor with each loud clang. "What did you say?"

"You'll be cut from his inheritance."

"After that."

"We can't leave her locked forever."

"Oh, if only we could." Carlotta set the poker down.

Elias' snicker had never sounded so sinister. "My darling, I happen to know just the place."

She bit her lower lip as they contrived a scheme. "I believe we have a plan, Elias Porter. We have a plan."

THE NEXT MORNING, Elias Porter's carriage bumped along a rutted road hugging the Connecticut River. Maggie bounced hard against the horsehair seat. Carlotta sat beside her. Elias sat facing them. They had been riding in a northerly direction for nearly two hours or perhaps three.

"Where are we going?" Maggie asked.

Carlotta didn't answer.

Maggie was dirty, hungry, and hurt. Her knees were swollen

red and blue and thick with scabs. Scraped hands burned. She'd not ingested food since yesterday morn and she still wore the torn dress and stockings soiled with mud and blood. Father would never allow her to be seen in such a state. She tried to brush the dirt with the back of her hand. "Father will be angry."

Carlotta seized Maggie's matted hair and pushed her head hard against the carriage window. "Look. One more word, and I'll drown you in the river, I swear I will."

Maggie crouched on the floor and didn't utter another sound. She pulled a blanket over her head, closed her eyes and hoped when they opened, she would see a better day.

The wobble of the carriage rocked her like Father had parodied Nellie Bly's ship in rough seas. The woolen blanket she clutched felt similar to the coat he wore that day in the field. Then the image of Carlotta's bouncing breasts, the first she'd ever seen, and the sound of Uncle Elias' groaning slammed into her head. *In Father's own bed! There would be hell to pay when he returned.* She drifted into sleep to dream of Father's vengeance.

The carriage struck a deep rut. Blossoms bounced from the posy holder. Maggie woke with a jerk and tossed the blanket from her face. The midday sun momentarily blinded her. Tall spiked rails of an iron fence along the roadside appeared ethereal as they blurred past the carriage window. They rode through an open gate and followed a long, straight path.

An ambulance wagon passed to exit the grounds.

The carriage stopped at a circle of grass in front of the main entrance of a grand Federal-style building. A broad porch with eight fluted columns led to the door.

"Where are we?"

Carlotta grimaced and held Maggie in the coach.

Uncle Elias approached the front entrance and spoke to the man who greeted him. His shoulders meaty, his arms as thick as hams, he was the biggest man Maggie had ever seen. He towered over Elias with eyes gone wide as if Elias was the last man he expected to see. Hair, the color of sand, grew far back on his skull making his bulbous forehead appear even larger than it was. A brown leather apron protected his clean, pressed blouse.

The man glanced at the carriage and nodded several times while Uncle Elias spoke. They looked comfortable together, as if they knew each other—as if they shared secrets. She had often observed Elias at High Hill social functions and thought him to be a bit of a dandy. Most folks, especially the ladies, found him to be charming, which made the man beside him an unlikely comrade. Yet they shared a bond so formidable, the chains connecting them could almost be seen.

Elias reached into his pocket, opened his leather coin purse and counted a certain amount. He handed the money to the man, who wrapped his fist around it and slid his hand beneath his apron, coins clinking as they dropped into his trouser pocket.

The man entered the building then returned to the porch with a woman, who marched to the carriage and pulled open the door. Her strong, stubby hands gripped Maggie's arm. She resisted, burrowing deeper into the carriage compartment, but Carlotta pushed her into the woman's arms.

"Margaret, this is Matron Smythe," Uncle Elias said.

Maggie shielded her eyes from the sun's glare as she first looked to Elias then to the big man next to him. "Steward Heinz Brudolf," the man said, bending down toward Maggie's face. His breath stank of chewing tobacco.

Maggie turned toward Matron. A bun of brown and gray hair, poised atop her head, was tied so tight it pulled her skin upward. Tiny brown eyes hid behind silver-framed spectacles. Flabby cheeks weighed her expression into a scowl, and her chin was as chiseled as a marionette's. She wore a gray striped dress with a white cotton service apron that smelled of bleach.

"You will remain here until your father returns." Elias unloaded a trunk from the carriage and set it on the porch.

Maggie's gaze snapped toward the carriage to Carlotta, but Matron Smythe yanked her up the three steps to the open porch where she read the brass marker beside the door. Etched into the sign, were the words: Brookhaven Farm Lunatic Asylum. All the horrific details of Nellie Bly's newspaper exposé came to mind.

"No!" Maggie jerked her arm from Matron's hold and ran after the carriage. Racing alongside, she tugged at the door with no regard for the torment of her wounds. "Let me in." The carriage rode faster until she could no longer keep pace. "Uncle Elias. Stop. Carlotta, please." She screamed as the carriage bounced down the gentle hill and out of sight. Her hands clenched at her sides. She kicked at the gravel road. "Take me with you," Maggie bellowed. "MOTHER! Don't leave me here!"

~ FIVE ~

1974 • November

MONDAY MARKED THE BEGINNING of my new life—the reincarnation of Laura Delito. I'd spent enough, maybe too much, time alone, but I'd packed, unpacked, moved, and transformed High Hill into my home. I needed to work and returning to the plant felt like the first day at a new job. *Maybe you don't have to die to start your next life.* I'd prove that theory as I shouldered new responsibilities. I had to.

Turning into the parking lot of Delito, Inc. stirred emotions reminiscent of my first factory visit with Gram over twenty years ago, a seventh-birthday treat. We rode in a black limousine with camel-colored leather seats that smelled of lemon. I felt grown up sitting next to Gram even though my head barely reached high enough to see out the window.

We'd arrived at the factory that Saturday morning and Gram held my hand as we entered the mysterious place where those I loved spent their days and evenings. A uniformed man, who couldn't have been that much older than I, unlocked the door. Gram called him Jack, greeting him by name like she did all who worked for her. He pinched my cheek until it turned red, and I didn't like him for a long time after that.

Working summers at the plant through high school, I'd learned every facet of the business, though my interest in the company ran hot and cold. After college and a year at a Hartford ad agency, I put as many miles as I could between me and Delito, Inc., 767 miles to be exact, before Gram lured me back—using

Michael as bait. I glanced toward heaven. *So obvious, Gram.* I took the design job I wanted, but not without a stiff smack of humility, when she forced me to apply for it along with three other candidates. One of her life lessons, it was like ingesting a spoonful of medicine—you knew it was good for you but tasted nasty going down. And I suspect it was her revenge for my leaving in the first place.

Respect from the other designers was earned, and I discovered a preference to leave the responsibility of profit and loss to others, but not anymore. Now it was left to me.

Passing Sam's Lincoln Continental in the lot made the moment seem more real. His car was parked as if this was a normal day at the office, as if he hadn't challenged me or threatened me or even heard me when I spoke, and I didn't like that at all.

The security guard opened the door as I neared the main entrance.

"Good morning, Jack."

"Yes, it's a fine day. Good to have you back, Miss Delito." He winked as I passed.

The heels of my pumps tapped across the floor until I stepped onto the carpeted, curved stairway to the level above the lobby. I peered over the balcony railing. Marble floor tiles imported from Italy had been patterned by Delito's own European designers, Gram had told me. At this height, I was at eye level with a crystal chandelier bigger than a Volkswagen, and through it, a rainbow of color, like sugar granules on Christmas cookies, sprinkled statues posed on white stone pedestals. The grand and elegant vestibule looked like the museum in New York Gram and I had visited only a month ago. And like a museum gallery, beautifully framed paintings hung on both walls of the second floor hallway. In our gallery, the paintings were portraits of old men, Delito founders.

I entered Gram's office—*my office*—the same office where I once sat on Oriental carpets to play with glass beads and gold chains while Gram worked.

I eased myself into the seat behind Gram's desk—*my desk*.

Sam entered without knocking. I hadn't seen him since we'd

argued at Aaron Schaeffer's office. His eyes darted around the office as if searching for something. He flinched with surprise when he spotted me. "Oh, Del. It's great to have you back." He snatched a stack of folders and an unopened overnight package from the coffee table and cradled the paperwork in his arms.

I wanted to retrieve it, but apart from wrestling it from his grasp, what could I do? I took a deep breath. "I made myself clear. I expect your resignation by noon."

"You've been through a lot. You're angry and hurt. Let's cool our heads. Talk to Michael before you make a decision."

"By noon, Sam."

He walked out of the office, but I knew releasing his hold on the business wouldn't be so easy.

I sat with a mug of coffee and the morning paper, reading the headline, masthead, and date. It reminded me of the old newspaper scrap I had found in Gram's purse. Removing the drawing from my billfold, I unfurled it on the desk. Grabbing every marker and pen from the drawer, I drew lines on paper, one by one, until I found the stroke weight that exactly matched the sketch—proof that Gram had rendered the mysterious diagram.

Vinny entered with a bouquet of white roses set in a crystal vase. "Miss Delito, I want to thank you and Michael for bumping me to the day shift. I hope you'll be satisfied with my work."

Since Gram's death, my mind was forgetting a lot and I didn't recall a decision to change Vinny's job description. "I'm sure I will, but you didn't have to thank me with flowers."

"Oh, these? These just arrived." His cheeks fired with an embarrassed blush. "I should have thought of it."

I buried my nose in the fragrance. "Who sent them?"

He passed a small sealed envelope. The card read: You can do it! Love, M.

Mother? Not a chance. Marcia? Wouldn't spend the money. Michael? Safest bet.

"Alert the design department. I want to meet in an hour. Make sure they understand it's a friendly visit."

Vinny was a couple of years out of UConn with a Bachelor's

Degree in marketing. He was six feet tall, a little shy, and sort of sweet. But that's all I knew about him except that Gram had hired him, maybe a year and a half ago, like she'd also hired Michael. But she'd also hired Sam, so that proved nothing about her hiring skills.

"And find Michael and ask him to join me. Now."

No sooner did Vinny leave than Michael crossed the threshold.

"How do you do that?" I shook my head. "We were about to call."

"Good morning." Michael approached the desk. "So do you think Vinny will work out for you?"

"Too soon to tell. I've only been here twenty minutes. Remind me. Whose idea was it to move him?"

"His. But worth a try, I thought. So how does it feel to sit in the big chair?"

Leaning forward, I stretched my arms across the desktop and wiggled my fingers. "It feels like playing office. Scary. Exciting." I pulled my purse onto my lap and removed my billfold, about to store Gram's newspaper scrap.

"What's that?"

I handed it to Michael. "I found it in Gram's purse at the hospital. Turn it over. What do you think the drawing means?"

"Looks like marker strokes. I wouldn't call it a drawing." He slid it back to me.

"Gram's marker, for sure. The strokes match this felt-tip pen she always used."

A twisted look crossed his face. "Looks like she scribbled to get her pen started."

"It does not. Gram drew this and she wanted me to have it. She pointed to her purse on her deathbed, so it must mean something important."

"What do you want me to say? It doesn't look like anything to me." He shrugged his shoulders then turned to the bouquet. "Do you like the flowers?"

"You sent them? I read 'M' and part of me hoped that Mother had."

"Sorry. Next time I'll be more direct." He bent to smell the roses, smiled, and took a seat. "Hey Del, I need to tell you about something."

"I'm listening." I returned the newspaper drawing to my wallet.

"I got a weird phone call last week."

I broke a bud off one of the stems and threaded it through the buttonhole of his lapel. "Okay, but first let me tell you about Sam. I saw him a moment ago and asked for his resignation."

"You what? Kind of sudden, don't you think?"

"I thought you were on my side."

"I am. I only meant a shakeup this soon might make transitions more difficult for you. Sam's been running the—"

"Don't say it." My hands pushed into air as if swatting away the idea.

"I wish we would have talked about it first. He's got friends."

"Who are they, Michael?"

"He's had power here and even more in New York."

"You don't know the whole story. I had to get rid of him."

"How did he react when you told him?"

"Calm, but he had to be seething inside."

He stepped to the window that overlooked our beautifully manicured landscape, the office parking lot, and the forest beyond. Gusty winds slapped a rope pulley against the flagpole. "His responsibilities could be absorbed by department heads, or even myself. We can make it happen."

"I agree. I'm not oblivious to what goes on. We'll be fine." His knowing that I came to my decision while raging in Aaron Schaeffer's hallway served no purpose, so I lied to Michael. "I considered the consequences and this is what I want. He's a problem for me."

As soon as I spoke the words, I recalled Gram's advice, "Use your head," and though she rarely stated the rest, she had also implied, "And not your heart." I'd made my first business decision and had heaved her warning to the winds. Solid start.

"What did you want to talk about? Who called last week? What weird call?"

"Forget it, it's nothing."

"Are you sure?"

"Yes, I'm sure. I'll deal with it."

"I'm meeting with the designers within the hour. I have ideas for the new line."

"Great." He turned from the window.

"Schedule a manager's meeting a week from today. Let's ask for budget summaries from each department and make sure everyone has expenditures to date. I want to know exactly how much money we have left this year. No surprises."

"Del, did you hear me? Yes, you'll be great with the designers so concentrate on that. Try not to worry about money. I'll keep an eye on the budget."

I agreed. "Be sure to invite the guys in New York."

"I'll contact them first. They should get invoices and media contracts from the ad agency. Let's see where our commitments lie."

"Good idea, make sure they bring original contracts not just their summaries. And I want New York's appraisal of the agency's performance over the last three years. With sales figures. Have Aaron Schaeffer review our contract with the agency and figure our cost to get out of it if that's what we decide. Michael, do you have all that?"

"I got it." He jotted a few words in his notebook and left the room.

I buzzed Vinny, leaned into the tufted back of the leather chair, and sipped my coffee. "Did you notice the sender's name on the overnight package that was on the coffee table?"

"It was from our New York sales office."

"Addressed to Sam?"

"Ah, yes, it was." After a brief silence, he asked, "Is there anything else?"

The antique key I'd been wearing on a chain around my neck, since Emma Collings gave it to me at Gram's wake, twirled around my finger—a new nervous habit. "Yes, one more thing. Call the Brookhaven Center near Hartford and tell them we're considering a donation. Tell them I want to tour the grounds with someone familiar with its past. Say I'm a history buff. I don't care, invent something. And make sure they know who I am. This Saturday will be convenient."

I noted the date on the desk calendar and called Michael. "Can you keep Saturday open to accompany me on a personal matter? This weekend. Right. Five days from today."

"Casual or black tie?"

"That's what I love about you." Propriety paired with spontaneity. Exactly what I needed. "I'd like you to wear your most stylish Italian suit so you look sinfully rich."

"Got it. Do you have time for lunch today?"

"I do. Meet me when you're ready. You know where I'll be." From my briefcase, I pulled a package wrapped with plain brown paper and tied with coarse twine, then headed to the design department.

Vinny, concluding his conversation with the Brookhaven Center, signaled a thumbs-up as I passed confirming Saturday's appointment was set.

I strolled the carpeted corridor passing the portrait gallery of Delito's bygone figures. In the style of the era, each cold stare revealed nothing of their personalities. They kind of scared me, and I wondered which of my ancestors shared the secret to which Gram had hinted when she lay dying. Who among them had buried the truth? I was determined to unearth it, but not today.

I had too much present-time ground to cover. My self-indulgence had ignored responsibility, and I was three weeks late to the party. There wasn't enough time today to visit every section, but I had a few extra minutes before my meeting.

Both my talent and pleasure was in creating and manufacturing the costume jewelry. To begin the day with an idea, follow it through each department, and by close of business, hold a finished product in my hand proved most satisfying.

A slow walk through the shop showed everyone I was back. Nothing formal, just—Here I am, like it or not, Delito has a young female owner. I didn't consider myself a feminist, but now that I held the power of change, I was soon going to end a few factory customs that really, really bugged the hell out of me. I called Vinny to meet me in the design department.

THE DESIGN DEPARTMENT was located in the new wing facing a pine forest where fallen needles had formed a permanent brown carpet. A wall of windows and a bank of skylights lit the open studio area. Gray and white mica cabinets set on black and white floor tiles divided work spaces decorated with colored posters and mobiles that twisted in air currents from ventilation ducts. Elton John's *Tiny Dancer* played on a Pioneer hi-fi and the aroma of fresh-brewed coffee filled the room. Not one thing resembled the stuffy New York sales office.

The shelves and taboret next to my former drawing table had been stripped, supplies packed, and moved to the "big office." Michael's doing, I suspected.

Vinny stepped from the coffee nook. "You wanted to see me?"

I tore a sheet of layout paper from a Bienfang designer's pad and scribbled a quick note. "Make sense out of this and distribute a memo to all department managers."

Vinny read the message. "The guys in the shop won't like being told what to do."

"I hate that I have to tell them. Grown men should know better."

"I hear you."

"Yeah, well, you're a new generation. Let's hope they hear the message, too. And Vinny, that's EFFECTIVE IMMEDIATELY. Type in caps. Go. I want this done by day's end."

Four designers and I met at a round table where I had laid my package. Fortunately, I was among friends. If we hadn't worked side by side every day for the past year, this gathering might feel as stressful as a New York marketing meeting. "Thank you for your expressions of sympathy. They meant a lot to me and to my family."

I hung my purse strap around the chair back, took a seat, and folded my hands in my lap to conceal their trembling for what I was about to say. "You've probably heard rumors of Delito's fiscal instability, but I'm promising your jobs are secure for as long as I have a say." The room must have filled with carbon dioxide with the collective exhalation of relief. "I have no doubt our future success begins in this room. Starting today, you'll prepare production estimates for your designs."

Henri, a transplant from France who had been with the company for as long as I remembered, spoke first. "Miss Delito, we have been doing this. We prepare the figures, specify stampings, clasps, and stones, and then make samples for assembly estimates. We can produce cheaper products. Is that what you want?"

"No, but I don't want fat either. Consider alternatives to lower labor costs. If a small design change reduces complex assembly, make the change." I glanced around the table. "Any questions?"

Henri asked, "Do we consult with Mr. Bender before bringing our estimates to the shop?"

"Sam Bender is no longer with the company."

Heads twisted one to the next in stunned silence.

"All right, then." I lifted my package and loosened the twine to unwrap several pieces of Berber jewelry. "I acquired these in Morocco during my buying trip this past spring. Examine them, but keep them intact. Please duplicate them—six samples of each —and note your creative suggestions. I'm considering production this season. We're going to start making money for all of us." My words hung in the air with confident reassurance.

Michael entered the department just as I glanced up. He reviewed sketches at various stages of completion as he passed several drawing tables. When he saw me, he broke out in a quiet laugh.

"What's so funny?"

"I just saw Vinny distributing your calendar memo."

"Not funny, Michael. I'm serious about that." He had no idea how tenacious I was prepared to be.

He rubbed his chin. "I know you're serious. I'm not sure a memo will change shop culture."

"We'll see."

"Are you finished here?"

"Yes, let's go." I collected my purse and briefcase.

"Miss Delito," Henri called. "May I speak with you?"

"Sure, in my office after lunch."

"It is about the necklace you are wearing. It is not important, but you will find it of interest."

I twirled the antique key around my finger. Everyone knew I rarely wore jewelry that wasn't made at Delito, but I'd continue to wear the key until I discovered its significance. "I'll be back by 2:00, let's meet at 3:00." As Michael and I left for lunch, I noted the time on the wall clock and would count the minutes until then.

SAM'S RESIGNATION LAY ON MY DESK when I returned from lunch, a surprise he'd surrendered so readily. I hadn't seen Mother since the reading of Gram's will and wondered how she would react. This final blow was sure to end what little relationship we had, and I wanted to avoid the inevitable confrontation for as long as possible. I paced my office until Henri arrived.

"Am I interrupting, Miss Delito?"

"Perfect timing." I tugged at the chain. "This seems to have captured your interest."

"The configuration of the key is most unusual. I have not seen many like it. I am a collector, you know."

"Of keys?"

"No." He laughed. "Of antique jewel boxes and chests. May I?" He extended his hand and removed a jeweler's glass from his pocket to examine the key in his palm. His brow lifted.

"This is not a copy." His expression of curiosity changed to astonishment. "Is it a recent acquisition, perhaps from your trip to Morocco?"

"Recent, yes, but not from Morocco as far as I know. It was a gift from, ah, a friend of the family. It's not an old door key? I had one like it when I rented a Victorian apartment in Chicago. Tell me about it."

"It is French-Moroccan. See this geometric motif on the top?"

"Yes, I noticed identical designs on brass trays and wall

hangings, and I remember a lattice screen with a similar pattern in a shop Michael and I visited in Agadir."

"It is extremely rare, and for its age, its condition is magnificent. Few of this design have survived. Even in collector's circles, few know about the life chests. Unfortunately, there is not much I can say of its history. It is the chest I must study."

"But I don't have the chest, only this key."

"Pity. Typically it is the key that is lost. You must find the chest."

"I'm working on that."

Henri's inspection continued. "If the chest had been carved by French artisans, it would give indication of the original owner. Chests were often decorated with a scene from the owner's life. Do you understand?"

"Like ancient Egyptian art?"

"Exactly. I'm sure you have seen life scenes depicted in their temple carvings—literal and accurate representations of their culture. We know how they loved, fought, and played. We know what they ate for dinner. So it also was with the artists of old days. Had the chest been consigned by a medical man, the scene might show the physician beside a patient's bed. A caravan of camels or an oasis illustrated a desert trader or nomadic tribal chieftain."

Henri moved to better light at the window and I followed. With the key squeezed between his thumb and index finger, he studied the tip of the shank. "Oh, yes. I see something."

Even stretching on tiptoes, I was unable to peer over his shoulder. "What is it?"

"Can you provide an awl or any kind of pick? A pin will do. And tweezers would be helpful."

I removed a gold cloisonné brooch from my lapel and found tweezers in the desk drawer.

Henri poked and twisted the pin into the end of the key. "Old grime is stuck in here. If I can clear it, the catch might release."

"What catch? It's so tiny."

"Some have a shank hidden inside the outer structure. Some twist open or pop from the bottom, but this is stuck. Perhaps there is nothing after all."

"We can take it to the plating department and dip it in the acid bath, that would eat away the grime, wouldn't it?"

"Acid would help to open the key, but anything stored inside would quickly dissolve. If you do not mind about that, we can try."

"No, continue what you're doing." I put my forefinger to my mouth and nearly bit off a nail, a habit I'd abandoned post-Jimmy Cassella.

Henri's hands shimmied. The pin bowed from the pressure, then he poked harder. The inner shank, freed from years of embedded dirt, slowly emerged from the bottom of the key. The biggest grin crossed my face. I had just seen mama key give birth. Patiently tugging with tweezers, skillfully twisting back and forth, he eased the shank to full length, handed it to me and pointed inside.

Rolled tightly in the tiny cylinder was a piece of paper resembling a twenty-five cent horoscope bought from a vending machine at a highway truck stop. I used the tweezers to extract it, unrolled it, and opened two folds until the aged sheet lay flat in a three-inch square.

A crude, uncomplicated diagram was drawn on the paper with what appeared to be black ink. Everything in me couldn't suppress a gasp. I'm sure my eyes shot wide open.

"How very interesting." Henri stared at the drawing and at me.

I breathed fast and hard. "You have no idea."

"What does it mean?"

"I'm working on that, too." I thanked him, and then practically shoved him out the door.

With a broad sweep, I cleared my desktop scattering papers to the floor. A side-by-side comparison of the drawing preserved in the key and Gram's sketch on the newspaper masthead proved to be a perfect match. Nothing and no one could prevent me from getting to the bottom of this. If this drawing was so important to Gram, that she was able to reproduce it after seventy-four years, I was determined to decipher its meaning—or die trying.

~ SIX ~

1899 • May

CARLOTTA AND UNCLE ELIAS were gone. Their carriage stirred a cloud of dust above the asylum's road to the city gate. Matron Smythe seized Maggie's wrist so tightly her twisted skin burned as she was hauled across the porch. Heinz followed them inside lugging her trunk behind.

Vivid colors of stained glass windows tinted the foyer. Healthy ferns on mahogany pedestals lined the elegant hall where Turkish carpet runners laid paths to important rooms.

Maggie's soles barely touched the floor as Matron dragged her down the hall. The upper half of every wall and door was made of window glass. Some with privacy curtains, some not. She'd never seen so many windows. Or so little privacy. Offices and wards blurred by. One room housed three young women not much older than she, and with curtains pulled aside, they pressed despairing faces against the glass.

Muffled cries, laughter, and then silence as they passed a strong, wide door cracked open where a stone stairway disappeared into a dark abyss. Matron tugged until they reached a scrub room where every small sound bounced off the walls.

White square floor tiles rose four feet up the wall to meet whitewashed plaster. Six sinks, with floor drains tucked beneath, lined one wall. Three common dresses discarded on newspaper were piled in the corner by the door. Matron tugged off Maggie's dress, removed boots and hosiery, and stripped her waist garment and drawers, then pointed to murky water in an iron tub. The three young women had bathed here, Maggie suspected. She remained steadfast, stooping to the floor for her dress and clutching it to her neck to shield her nakedness.

"Get in girl." With smooth, practiced motions, Matron submerged her, grabbed a stiff flesh brush and a cake of glycerin soap to scrub, then rinsed with a bucket of cold water drawn from a sink.

Maggie dried herself when Matron left the room, carefully blotting skin scrapes torn open by the brush. Matron returned with a stack of linens and garments—clean drawers, a gray muslin sacque-chemise, and a blue striped apron—not the fine embroidered Cambric to which she was accustomed, but clean and warm on her skin, and holding the toasty smell of a hot iron.

At the ward where Heinz had stored her trunk, a strange old woman clothed in mismatched garments lingered against the outside wall, moving in slow circles, and mumbling rhymes that made no sense.

Matron, surprised by her presence, called out in a firm tone, "Annie, come with me."

The woman complied. They crossed the hall to a small room where Matron sat Annie at the foot of a bed.

Inside her room, Maggie stationed herself and watched through the hall window. Annie didn't speak, but her gaze fixed on Matron's eyes as if she sought solace. Matron's severe manner toward the woman soon ceased, and she now comforted Annie, stroking her hair, patting her shoulder, and holding her hands. Annie's trembling eased and a calm came upon her. Matron guided her to stand, and they shuffled down the hall toward the main entrance. There was clearly more to their relationship than matron and patient—Maggie was sure of it.

THE SPACIOUS WARD was bright with windows along both the hallway and outside walls; identical to the room where the three woman huddled at the window. Nottingham ecru curtains decorated three large windows on the far wall where crystal vases sat on the center sill. Two rows of beds, ten in all, were equally spaced with pine closets between them, all empty but for one beside the bed where clean cotton sheets had been stacked on the mattress. The white painted bed frames reflected on wide plank floorboards that smelled of recent polish. No dirt. No dust. And not a hint of vermin. Maggie's cashmere cloak hung in her closet alongside a duplicate uniform of the one she wore.

Her trunk had been stowed on the closet floor. She loosened leather straps and lifted the lid, freeing scents of cinnamon and cedar that smelled of home. Inside lay several sets of neatly folded drawers, waists, and hosiery, and a dress pair of French-kid spring-heel shoes that Father had brought from Paris. In her hat box, Carlotta had packed not one of her fancy bonnets, but her favorite plain, straw shade-hat from the Bloomingdale Brothers catalog. *Curious.*

At the bottom of the trunk, Maggie was surprised and relieved to find her most cherished gifts from her father—a French-Moroccan jewelry box and a dancing doll from London. The six-inch child doll was dressed in an emerald velvet gown with a white lace apron. Auburn curls, like Maggie's, draped its shoulders. The doll hung on a stick and with a quick twitch of a tassel, it twirled as if it danced.

Maggie stepped onto the bed to peek at the top shelf where a flannel Mother Hubbard nightdress and cap lay neatly folded. She dropped to the mattress and bounced to test its structure. Landing on the stiff bedding felt a bit like her fall from the tree, and she was struck by the gravity of her circumstance and the events that led her here. She chuckled at her clever thoughts of gravity and falling, quickly allayed by the realization that Carlotta would never free her from this place.

The familiar belongings consoled her. Had that been Carlotta's intention, or did packing her treasures confirm the permanence of her relocation? She spread her arms and twirled in the ward's open space, summoning the eve of Christmas when Father gave her the dancing doll. She had stood atop his shoes as he whisked her around the room, spinning to piano music that Sally played. Dizzy and laughing and singing, she had tilted back her head to magnify her reeling. Ruffled skirts and shining hair flowed while they danced faster and faster. And the Christmas tree towered so high, its star ornament kissed the ceiling. Popcorn and cranberry chains decorated its branches, her weeks of stringing finally worth the effort. *Oh, what joy.*

Maggie returned the dancing doll, along with her other treasures, back to the chest. She hid it under a blanket in the closet and prepared her bed for sleep.

Christmas was months away, and she hoped she would be home by then, though she expected she would not.

DR. JAMESON bent over the new admission report on his desk, scratching his head as he read aloud. "Dementia with delusions of persecution."

"Steward Brudolf's opinion." Matron Smythe fidgeted. "The girl came by fancy carriage. 'Twas this afternoon. When you was out, sir."

"I trusted my last discussion with Heinz would discourage his diagnosis of an inmate's malady, but apparently he remains confused about who cares for the patients and who minds the purse."

Matron's eyes gazed ahead, her hands wringing at her belly.

"Who brought her?"

"Her own mother and father. Said they was from Providence. It was a pitiful sight to see that young 'un run cryin' after their carriage."

"And the gentleman paid in advance?"

"'Til the end of the year. Said annual fees would be paid 'fore year's end."

"It appears her mother holds little hope for Margaret's recovery."

"They call 'er Maggie, sir."

Dr. Jameson turned to the cabinet behind his desk, opened the leaded glass doors, and removed the register. "What was her state when she arrived?"

"Fussin', but she calmed after 'er bath. Skin on the child's hands and knees is scraped bad, and 'er lip is cut and swollen."

Jameson glared over his spectacles with an accusing stare.

"Inflicted by you?"

Matron raised her right hand. "No, sir. I swear."

"By Heinz?"

"No, sir, not by 'im neither."

"Where is the girl now?"

"In the first ward room. Explorin' be my guess."

"She is quite young. It may not be wise to mix her with the other patients."

"What can we do? I placed 'er by me night station. I'll keep me eye on 'er."

"See that you do. Clearly, she is from wealth."

"So said Heinz, by the manner of the folks, and the look of their fine garments. It will take many years to cure 'er, eh?" Matron masked her smile with her hand.

"She is likely to be a delicate child."

"I got me a different idea 'bout that." Matron straightened her service apron. "May I take the girl to supper?"

Jameson looked from his register entry to note the time on his pocket watch. "Yes, of course, to supper. Seat her at a table away from the others until they become familiar. Bring her to me in the morning. I wish to speak with the girl and will examine her then."

Dr. Jameson entered the new patient's Christian name in the register—Margaret Porter of Providence, Rhode Island. Diagnosis: Dementia with delusions of persecution.

"COME ALONG, CHILD." Matron clapped as she entered Maggie's ward. "Doc ordered good care till he sees you on the morrow."

Startled by Matron's sudden appearance, Maggie attempted to swipe her footprints from the bed linens.

The dirty spot didn't escape Matron's leering eyes. "But don't give me no trouble." She extended her arm and waved with her fingers for Maggie to take her hand. Only their footsteps resounded in the dimly lit hallway. They passed a vacant ward where the three women had been housed and continued toward the main entrance. Seated in a richly decorated office, a small man clothed in stylish tweed, and surrounded by the accoutrements of a sophisticated gentleman, peeped from his writing. Their eyes met and remained fixed even as she and Matron turned a corner to the right.

Empty cells lined another long hallway and benches were braced against the walls between the doors. It was too quiet. *Where was everyone?* As they neared the end, the aroma of beef and onions became more pungent. Muffled sounds became clearer.

Double doors slammed against the walls when Matron threw them open. Noise roared with clanging plates, yapping nurses, and screeching women. Chaos eased to a fragile calm as every eye turned toward Maggie. The room became so still she could hear Matron's hose rubbing when she walked. Keys strung to Matron's waist jingled like tiny bells. The deeper into the dining room they moved, the closer she clung to Matron, hoping to escape the curious stares, but there was nowhere to hide. She felt more naked than she had in the scrub room.

Matron pointed to a bench at a vacant table, instructing Maggie to wait while she gathered food from the service table.

Nearby, gray-haired women and two girls older than she were dressed alike in straight gray garments. Four nurses in long white aprons and starched caps sat at a center table.

The three young women she had seen in the ward next to hers clung together in apparent dismay as if they feared the strange surroundings as much as she did.

"Where'd ye come from, girlie?" someone hollered. Maggie spun toward the voice.

"Where'd ye come from?" a woman screeched, her face distorted like a witch as she lunged toward Maggie.

So taken by surprise, she did not recoil, but stood to meet her attacker though her legs wobbled a bit.

Matron bolted between them and halted the woman's assault with a single glance. The woman cowered and sobbed as an orderly led her away.

After setting down two tin plates holding a stew of boiled meat, potatoes, onions, and a heel of fresh bread soaked with brown broth, Matron sat beside her as if nothing extraordinary had occurred.

A girl dressed in a kitchen smock delivered a tray of eating utensils and a porcelain pitcher. She handed a spoon and cotton napkin to Maggie and poured milk into her cup. "Her name is Emma," Matron said as Maggie watched the girl return to the kitchen. "She ain't like them. She won't hurt ya. Her auntie works as a nurse and the girl helps with odd jobs 'cause 'er mum's ailin'."

Maggie tucked the napkin into her collar with a jittery hand, and composing herself, blew across a spoonful of stew.

A loud gong signaled nurses to lead inmates away. "Wash up," the nurses called and clapped hands when further encouragement was needed. Maggie rose to join the march, but Matron held her still. "Finish yur supper." They sat in the empty dining room with not another word spoken between them.

When patients had been secured in their wards, Matron put Maggie to bed. She felt surprisingly safe as she watched Matron cross the hall to her chamber. With clean bed linens, a full belly, and a locked door, she soon surrendered to sleep.

THE CLICK OF THE DOOR LOCK awoke Maggie. She remained still, assessing where she was—a ward in a lunatic asylum. Footsteps entered the room and circled around her bed. A nurse bent over and sweetly shook her shoulder. Dangling from a neck chain, a timepiece marking five o'clock caught the new morning light.

"Wake up. Wash yourself." Her hands clapped twice. "Go quickly before the others if you want clean water." The nurse left and continued down the hall to a staircase that rose to a second floor.

Maggie bounded out of bed and ran to the scrub room where clean towels and basins of clear water sat on counters beside the sinks. Her face and hands washed, she returned to her ward to dress.

A dreary parade of inmates shuffled past her window toward the washroom; their steady path and gray garb reminded her of cows heading to a farmer's barn near High Hill. She wondered how many had come of normal mind and how much time had passed before they became a herd. The three young women from last night were not among them.

Maggie rushed to the dining room where she cracked open the door and peeked inside. A cook looked up from her work and motioned for her to enter.

A short well-turned woman, the cook was not as round as Matron, though she had broad shoulders and conspicuous red cheeks like the St. Nicholas she'd seen on poster art. Two missing lower teeth marred her welcoming smile. "I heard you was here. Pretty thing, ain't ya? We don't much get 'em young as you. Give it here." She called into the pantry. "Emma, bring peaches."

Maggie lifted a tin plate and cup toward the cook who placed two slices of warm bread on the platter. Emma soon appeared with a canning jar filled with the fruit.

The cook shuffled back into the kitchen. Maggie followed and explored.

Cupboards and cabinets lined the kitchen walls. A modern steel range with six burners served as the kitchen's heart. A doorway in the far corner led to a pantry and another opened to a mudroom that exited outdoors. The kitchen felt warm and safe, and the women who worked there seemed neighborly.

From a small jug in the icebox, the cook poured cream on Maggie's peaches. "Listen girl, you call me Cookie. Come before the others, and I'll fix you good."

Emma smiled, waved her arm, and mouthed "farewell," then exited through the back door.

Maggie turned to the cook. "Thank you, Miss Cookie."

"Miss Cookie she says." Another kitchen helper laughed. "Ain't she a dear?"

Midst the morning quiet of the dining room, Maggie sat on the same bench she and Matron had shared last evening. In short time, the inmates marched in, straight and crippled, demure and rowdy, tidy and disheveled. Maggie had rarely been among so many people, not even in church—yet she had never felt so alone.

THE DOCTOR'S OFFICE was small and quiet and smelled of pipe tobacco. With fine furniture and shelves of books protected by leaded glass doors, she could have been in Father's library. She sat on a chair near the door, gripping its curved wooden arms, dangling her feet a few inches above the floor, and waiting as Matron had directed.

Dr. Jameson didn't acknowledge her when he entered. He was a well-ordered man of short stature and respectable appearance which eased her anxiety. Pointing to an entry in a book he read to himself; his lips moved too little for her to distinguish words. *Surely an educated man would see beyond the witless story Uncle Elias must have invented. I might be home by nightfall.*

"Why are you at Brookhaven, Margaret?"

"For no other reason but that Carlotta, my mother, detests the sight of me. My father is abroad and when he returns, he will come for me."

"Show me your teeth and your tongue." He inspected her eyes and ears. "Abroad is he? And what will you tell him when he returns?"

"The truth about Carlotta and why she left me here."

The doctor inspected her scraped hands and wrote in his book. He then waved her out. "Off with you. And bring no trouble."

Maggie suspected that was to be the end of her medical treatment, and she hoped that it was. She wandered out from the office, paused at the main doors, and viewed the far grounds. By the look of the sky, a rain shower was near. Emma secured the doors of a small barn beside a distant pasturage, then turned and skipped to the city gate. Checking that the doctor continued to write in his book, she quietly twisted the knob of the outside door, but it was locked.

Jameson glanced over his glasses. "Do you have more to tell me? Shall I assign chores to engage you?"

Startled, she shook her head and turned from the main entry. *Where am I to go? What shall I do?* Perhaps she did need chores to distract her mind.

Curiosity about the asylum yearned to be satisfied. Desolation begged to be disturbed. She considered all she had come to know. The main building was clean and free of vermin. Fruits and vegetables were fresh from the farm. Cookie and the nurses, even the doctor and Matron, showed concern for her well-being.

The door to Matron's chamber was also locked. She stood on her toes to peek inside. One large window on Matron's outside wall overlooked the front circular drive. Two empty shelves beneath it matched its width. A wardrobe closet towered over a neatly made bed with a six-drawer dresser across from its foot.

Still, no one was in sight, so Maggie returned to her ward and peered out the center window, pressing her nose against it. Spring rain showered against the glass and dripped into puddles off the outside sill, eroding a shallow rut in the ground below. Her breath fogged the pane until she swiped it with her apron's hem.

Grassy hills stretched to a steep bank topped with a row of willows. Maples, oaks, and pines were scattered here and there in the low land where the river snaked beyond.

A sudden rumbling jolted her. The thunder-like sound grew louder and stronger and came not from the sky, but from below like quaking earth. Empty vases on the sill clinked together, sounding like hail pelting glass—even the floor trembled, rattling her bones. The rumbling stopped as quickly as it began.

Maggie scrambled into the hallway expecting to see staff gathered to investigate, but no one came. What was that?

A stairway near the washroom led to floors above. By the wear on the carpet runner, it appeared that a stronger, wider door near her ward was a well-used gateway. Maggie grasped its latch with both hands and tugged, but the door did not budge. Is every door locked? She kicked hard. *What goes down there? What do they hide? Will they need to hide me?*

She slid to the floor, pouting, while contemplating her condition. Pulling her knees tight to her chest, she rested her elbows on them as she buried her face in her open hands and sobbed.

At the far end of the floor, the dining room's double doors slammed against the walls, a clear signal breakfast was finished. She raced toward the noise. Chattering inmates marched out while attendants collected stragglers and led them into a day room. Dare she join them? She hesitated at the doorway.

Inmates settled on parlor settees, chairs, and benches like those in church. Maggie slid around the threshold and eased into a nearby seat where she gauged who might be friend and who might be foe.

The witch lady from last night raved beside a window. Best to stay clear of her. An older girl, who a nurse called Kathleen, held promise. Annie, the old woman mumbling rhymes, clutched Matron's apron while she stared at Maggie with a frozen grin. Hope dimmed of finding a playmate or answers about the rumbling—or the three women missing from the neighboring ward.

Just then, the witch lady seized Maggie's arm. Fingernails, long and curled like eagle talons, ripped into her skin. Maggie squealed. Every eye turned, and the inmates slithered toward her as if she had disturbed a nest of snakes. She was a trapped animal pressed against the wall.

The sudden appearance of Matron Smythe and two nurses halted the attack. Inmates scattered to all the room's corners, screeching and crying and calling on God. Some beat on the walls. Some scratched at each other and themselves. Mayhem.

Matron grabbed a fistful of Maggie's hair, dragging her to the corridor. "Go. Sit. Be still." Matron shoved her away and directed her attention to the fracas.

Maggie glared at fellow inmates as she passed. The mere thought of it appalled her—fellow inmates. Their faces were masks, like half dead castaways drifting numb on empty seas. Blank eyes stared as if seeking lost kin, lost lovers, or lost minds. *Father had better come soon. I will never survive these lunatics.* She ran until the din of rabid women faded. It had taken less than a day to learn that despite the fancy dressings and light of full sun, the asylum was a dark place. A current of wretchedness boiled below its polished surface—and Maggie just got burned.

~ SEVEN ~

1974 • November

MY CAR WAS PACKED, and I'd arrived early at the office where only several cars, including Michael's, were parked in the lot of Delito, Inc. I tried to concentrate but couldn't expel thoughts from my mind of Emma Collings, Gram's map, and the key. Deciphering their meanings proved to be too frustrating.

Michael stepped into the room as I stuffed paperwork into my case. "I'm leaving for a couple of days."

"You just got here!" He flipped past a few pages in his notebook. "Does this cancel Saturday's adventure to the Brookhaven Center? When will you—?"

"Don't worry about it. I'm only going for one night. I'll be back Thursday. Late."

"But where—what are you doing?"

"Nothing. I mean, it's good." I checked the desk clock. "Sorry, got to run. We'll talk when I get back."

Michael shook his head as if he was amused. "Del, you're making me crazy."

He looked stunningly handsome in a charcoal suit, crisp white shirt, and red paisley tie. I could have blown off the day and locked us in my office, but I was committed to something else.

"Follow me. I have to check on something." I grabbed my purse and walked out, stopping at Vinny's desk. "Did you distribute my memo?"

"Yes, Miss Delito. It went out yesterday afternoon before the day shift went home."

"Did you personally hand it to everyone?"

Vinny nodded.

"Excellent."

Michael and I headed down the hall past mostly vacant executive offices and down a flight of stairs to the shop. "I didn't get the memo."

My hand wrapped around his and pressed it against my hip. "You didn't need it."

He pushed open the fire door to the shop assembly area where I scrutinized every wall divider and bulletin board. All sense of playfulness drained from me. "Dammit." I didn't look for Michael's reaction when I said, "Wait here." He stepped back and leaned against the wall.

I rushed from one foreman's office to the next, ripping every pinup calendar and magazine photo of bare-breasted women that littered the walls. My fist clenched a crumpled page and held it high. I must have looked like the Statue of Liberty. "This is trash. It degrades the women who work here." Women at assembly counters glanced from their hand work as I pointed a validating finger in their direction. "It insults and demoralizes them. Don't you understand that?"

Blood surged, and my face burned as I searched the shop, tearing off another photo, waving it like a flag. Several foremen backed away from my fearless glare. "It's crude and vulgar, and it disrespects me." I focused on a stunned molding machine operator and his picture of a pouty redhead wearing only denim hot pants. "How long have you worked here? And you? And you?" I didn't wait for answers. "I asked you to take these down and you didn't. Hasn't my family been good to you? We have more class than this. You have more class than this." I pressed on to the next work area. "Is there anyone who doesn't understand?" Only the light steps of my pumps against the worn plank floor disrupted their stunned silence. I think I scared them.

I circled the entire manufacturing space, and, as I neared the exit, Michael stepped out from where he'd hidden. His lips curled into a faint smile. "Well, that got their attention."

"What's that look on your face? Too much?"

"Too soon."

"Too soon! I've wanted to do that for ten years."

LATER THAT MORNING, outside of Hartford, in a rural branch of a major East Coast bank, I sat in the manager's office filling out a checking account application. Fortunately for the young manager, the forty-minute drive from the plant was long enough for me to chill out, and I admit, savor self-satisfaction.

"How much will you deposit today, Miss Delito?"

I pulled a bulging 5" x 7" manila envelope from my purse and dropped it on his desk.

His eyes widened as he fanned the hundred-dollar bills jammed inside.

"Thirty thousand." Part of Gram's life insurance benefit, though I didn't tell him that.

"It might be wise to deposit a portion in an interest-earning savings account."

"I need it liquid, and I need checks today."

"Of course. It'll take a few minutes." His thigh bumped the corner of his desk so hard I winced from his pain. He soon returned with a receipt and a book of temporary checks. "You'll receive replacements in ten days. Would you like to choose one of our pastel colors for your order?"

I tucked my receipt into the new checkbook and placed it in my purse. Out in the lobby, two tellers whispered while a third counted my deposit. "No, but please alert your people I expect confidentiality regarding my accounts. No one is to know of them."

"Of course. Your privacy is important to us." He tugged at the knot of his tie which must have shrunk too tight.

"Excellent." I stood, straightening my suit jacket.

"Miss Delito, what color checks would you like?"

I couldn't help grinning when I turned toward him. "Green, of course."

"Green." He laughed. "I knew that."

BY THE TIME I PARKED in the short-term lot at Bradley International Airport, north of Hartford, my amusement at the nervous branch manager spurred examination of my anxieties and weaknesses, and how ridiculous they must appear to others. I was about to initiate a business plan I hoped would forever change my view of myself—and that of everyone else. My meeting in Chicago would be the first step and a chance to practice my pitch among friends from the museum. The trades would never again describe Delito, Inc. as "mediocre." I was confident that within eighteen months, we would blow their minds. I grabbed my overnight bag from the trunk.

Inside the terminal, I endorsed the first new check for my round-trip ticket. In the lower left corner, a one-word reminder read—Chicago.

Two Dramamine tablets helped me fall into sleep before the plane reached cruising altitude.

Falling. Falling.

Green ropes. White columns. Dark closets.

Hold tight. Limp green ropes.

Falling. Falling. Falling ...

Jolted by the DC-10's tires striking the tarmac, my arms reached out as if grabbing something from a dream. "Welcome to O'Hare," I heard through my mind's fog. "The temperature is thirty-three degrees with a mix of rain and snow. Enjoy your stay and thank you for flying with us."

The passenger seated behind me opened the overhead compartment. Someone's coat belt and the shoulder strap of my briefcase spilled out and dangled at my head ... Limp ropes ... Weird feeling. Falling. Familiar from a dream? Green limp ropes. A little lightheaded from sleep, I grabbed the thin strap of my purse as if it were a lifeline to the fleeting image. I shook my head, removed my bag from above, and disembarked the plane.

THE FOLLOWING NIGHT, I couldn't have felt better about my life and my future. No one knew about my brief excursion or that I was actualizing the most brilliant idea I'd ever had. Friday passed smoothly and quickly. Everything was falling into place, like it does when you've finally steered onto the right road after you've been lost.

By the time Saturday came around, Michael was irritated by my secretive disappearance. Though he acted as if he believed my lame explanation of needing alone time to think, his cold shoulder betrayed him.

We sat in the rear of the company limousine en route to tour the Brookhaven Center. To avoid his questions, I closed my eyes and faked sleep until the car struck a pothole. For a moment, the sun blinded me. Tall spiked rails of an iron fence along the roadside appeared dreamlike as they blurred past. The railed boundary marked the periphery of the asylum, separating sanity from madness. Beyond the looming bars, the hospital grounds appeared more like a park than an institution. Cottages— reminiscent of a Hansel and Gretel picture book—nestled between sloping hills that surrounded larger, main buildings.

At precisely two o'clock, the gatehouse guard noted our arrival on his clipboard and waved us in. The limousine turned onto a tree-lined driveway where naked branches formed a delicate canopy against a threatening sky.

Narrow access roads split from the main drive with destinations clearly marked for residents or visitors. Manicured footpaths snaked around the grounds, though no one walked them this day.

We stopped near the main entrance where our driver parked beside a round, grassy island. Down a hill, a period-style gazebo looked like new construction.

A man met us on the porch and introduced himself as the director, Dr. Jonathan Clift. His hunching posture made him appear smaller than he actually was. He ushered us inside, occasionally glancing from side to side. It was a cautious habit I also practiced when circumstances seemed twitchy.

Potted ferns decorated the inside entrance hall and stained glass windows lit the foyer. An Oriental carpet runner with worn edges led to the office of Jonathan Clift. The scent of lemon-polished wood made me think of High Hill when Gram prepared for distinguished guests.

I glimpsed something or thought I did. Movement. Flowing skirts. Keys jangling. Then nothing.

Pulling Michael close, I hesitated to ask, "Did you see her? Down the hall, that way. She went right through the door. Not the doorway. The door!"

He shook his head, more than puzzled.

"I'm told you have an interest in our history." Dr. Clift gestured us to sit.

"Oh, ah—yes." My sight locked onto a point down the corridor, but no one was there, and I doubted that I had seen anything at all. "Your hospital and my company were founded around the same time—a fascinating period for which my late grandmother held fondness."

"That's why I keep my office in the original structure." Salt-and-pepper hair framed his brown eyes. His expression appeared sincere. "I've forsaken quiet heating and air-conditioning and adjusted to drafty windows for the pleasure of living with hand-carved wainscot and authentic antique furnishings."

Several men and women in white lab coats conferred in the hallway outside the office, then walked past the spot where I'd seen … something … maybe. "Sounds like a fair trade."

He rose from his chair. "We're in for bad weather, I hear. Let's stroll the grounds to the newer additions before the rain comes."

We chatted as we walked a narrow, paved path with Michael behind us.

"Most of the original structures are unchanged." He indicated where grassy hills stretched to a steep bank. "The Connecticut River flows beyond that row of willows."

"A walk by the water must be refreshing on a hot summer day."

"It's too far for our recreational use, and the spring thaw swells the river as close as that bank over there." He pointed.

I held my hair away from my eyes as the wind stirred earthy smells of dried leaves and damp dirt. From where we stood on top of the highest hill, I tried to visualize the flooding river Dr. Clift described as I studied the land's layout. On some deep level, it struck me as familiar—something I'd seen in a film, or a dream, or in my mind.

"When exactly was the asylum founded?" A quick glance over my shoulder confirmed Michael was paying attention.

"Brookhaven was a recognized leader in the field as one of the first institutions in the country to offer treatment for the mentally ill, and it served as a retreat for widows and children."

"I had no idea your reputation was so, ah, esteemed." I assumed no patient nor staff would remember Emma Collings who claimed to live here with Gram, but I pressed Dr. Clift about timing.

"Is there something specific you want to know about our hospital?"

"When did you say the institution was founded?" Michael interrupted.

"Eighteen twenty-three," Clift snapped, seeming irritated.

I calculated the math in my head. "So that was long before Nellie Bly's exposé?" That was all I knew about asylums, thanks to a documentary I'd seen on public television.

We entered what Dr. Clift described as a recently renovated building. "You're referring to Blackwell's Island in New York?"

"Exactly. Didn't Nellie get herself committed to investigate the inmate's cruel treatment? She's been a heroine of mine."

"Don't confuse us with them. Brookhaven was clean and comfortable, even many years ago. Local farmers and our gardens provided fruits and vegetables. We served fresh milk from our cows. An old barn once stood there." He pointed to the gazebo. "Brookhaven remained a working farm tended by residents and staff. Conditions at Blackwell's never existed here, in fact, rumors claimed a few of the poorest citizens attempted to break into the place."

"Never? Let's be honest, Dr. Clift. Early treatments were gruesome."

"Some might say the same of today's medical research. Besides, that was long ago. Well-intentioned doctors learned by experimenting and observing. Water therapy was popular, and I suppose some bloodletting was practiced."

A chill ran down my back as I wondered how much blood. I turned to Michael with a look of disgust—revulsion at the sight of blood I'd patterned after Gram's irrational fear of it.

"These apartments house our long-term guests. We allow them as much privacy as is safe and practical." Piano music resounded in a great room where "guests" gathered for snacks.

Michael wrapped my shawl around my shoulders as we crossed back toward the main structure.

I asked, "Do you have old photos?"

"Of course. Let's finish over tea in my office. The air is chilling."

When our conversation concluded, I hinted I'd consider a donation to the hospital, but remained uncommitted. "Someone from Delito may contact you if my accountants need more information."

When Michael reminded him about the photos, Dr. Clift selected a book from the case behind his desk. He autographed the title page and handed it to me. "I look forward to hearing from you."

No expense had been spared in producing the cloth-bound volume. I smoothed my hand over its gold imprinted title: *One Hundred and Fifty Years at Brookhaven Farm* by Dr. Jonathan Clift. He tapped his forefinger on the cover. "Everything you need to know is in here."

If only it was.

THE AIR SMELLED OF AUTUMN RAIN. As our limousine departed, I twisted for a final view out the rear window and gaped.

"Look! There she is again." I shook his arm. "On the porch. Michael. Look."

He glanced back. "What am I looking for?"

"Can't you see her? Sitting on the porch in the rocker."

His eyes squinted. "Del. There's no one there."

"An old woman is sitting in a rocker. She's all gray. The same woman I saw in the hallway when we first entered the foyer." I spun around to look again. "She's gone."

"Shall I stop the car?" the driver asked.

"No," Michael snapped.

I glared at him.

"Del, we just walked across the porch. There was no gray woman. There was no rocker. And there was no one in the hallway."

My voice sounding less confident, I shriveled into myself. "I know what I saw."

His arm cradled me. "I'm sure you do."

My elbow nudged his side. This wasn't over. I flipped through the pages of Dr. Clift's book, randomly skimming photos and text. Maybe if I buried my nose in the book he wouldn't bother me.

No such luck.

"Why were you asking Dr. Clift those questions? What do old therapies have to do with pledging a donation?"

"I've been hiding a ghoulish secret." I snarled and stretched upward to bite his neck.

He grinned but pulled away. "I'm serious. Why did you have to see the whole place? It's cold and windy, and you're run down. Are you trying to make yourself sick?"

"Of course not."

"What did you expect? It's an asylum. Did you think you'd see weirdoes dressed like Napoleon?"

"I don't know what I'm looking for, Michael. I don't even know if all these things are connected."

"All what things? What are you talking about?"

"First, Gram was trying to tell me something about her past, but she died before she got it out. Then there was Emma Collings. Remember her at the wake? She told me she and Gram met at an asylum."

"Del, stop." He leaned into the back of the seat, knees apart, trousers perfectly pleated. He pinched a small leaf from his sleeve and dropped it in an armrest ashtray.

"Then, Sam said something strange at Aaron Schaeffer's office after hearing Gram's will."

"What did he say?" Michael's eyes locked on mine. "Did he threaten you?"

I turned and stared out the window.

"Did he hurt you?"

"No, he didn't hurt me. Of course not."

"Well, what the hell happened?"

"I don't exactly remember, but he acted kind of freaky, even for Sam." The last thing I wanted was to tell him that Sam had warned me to watch my back, and that someone in the company would be happier if I'd disappear. I think that's what Sam said, if not the words, I'm pretty sure it was the spirit of what he meant. I had no doubt the family name and the business might be damaged if word spread that Gram had been in an asylum. God, if I wasn't comfortable confiding in Marcia, best friend and confidant, how could I tell Michael? He didn't seem to be especially sympathetic about the subject, about anything, lately. "What about Gram's drawing on that old newspaper? And then Henri spotted the key Emma gave to me." I pulled it from inside my sweater and twirled it around my finger. "Do you think it has something to do with any of this? It can't, right?"

He glared at the key. "Right."

"Emma Collings called Gram, Maggie, but did you know that Gram's full name was Margaret Rosa Delito?"

"And your point is—?"

"Maggie. Margaret. One and the same."

"You don't know that. Why would Rosa switch names?"

"To put the past behind her? To hide the truth from everyone? From me? I don't know. I believe Emma's story about the asylum. She knew Gram as Maggie and I believe her. Maybe someone other than Gram hid that she was confined in an asylum to protect her or the business?"

"You heard 'met' and assumed 'confined'. You don't know that. I need to be convinced, and I'm not there, yet." He pointed to the distant sky where a sliver of sunlight was losing to storm clouds.

"Beautiful." I nodded.

"Scratched lines on a scrap of paper. Some old woman, who probably belongs in an institution herself, gives you a piece of junk and you imagine Rosa in an asylum, and changing her identity. And you associate this incredible delusion with Sam's disappointment about Rosa's will. Listen to yourself."

"Well, when you say it that way, it does seem to skirt absurdity." My head rattled and I sighed. "But I have a feeling it's all related, somehow, if only I could figure it out."

"Figure this. If you keep acting weird and seeing gray ghosts in invisible rockers, Dr. Clift will commit you for treatment. I may send you there myself, so drop it. But while we're on the subject—"

"Which subject?"

"The peculiar behavior of jewelry company owners—like when they vanish without warning. Are you going to tell me where you ran off to the last couple of days?"

"It's a surprise."

"Del, you can't leave like that, not any more. You have responsibilities. We must know where to reach you."

"Next time I'll call." My shawl cinched tight around me as if binding my secrets inside me. This wasn't the time to tell him about Chicago. Gambling my time and my money was enough. I wasn't willing to risk humiliation if my idea failed. Sharing my plan would have to wait—maybe I'd wait before sharing a lot of things with him.

Staring out the window, I didn't dare tell him my nightmares had become even more intense and more frequent. What would he think of me then? I'd never hear the end of it. "Forget I said anything about anything." *Stop asking questions.*

I turned toward him, pushed up the sleeve of his jacket, and ran my finger up and down the vein in his wrist. "But Michael, seriously, how much blood do you think they let out?"

He rolled his eyes. "What a way to spend a Saturday."

We didn't speak much more for the remainder of the ride home to Barrows. Heavy rain hammered the car as we drove through the storm.

THE BLUSTERY SQUALL must have dumped three inches of rain, but it came and went in less than an hour. By the time Michael dropped me at High Hill, the sky had brightened just as the sun was setting. The wind remained fierce.

I didn't invite or encourage Michael to stay. It seemed to be fine with him, but he hesitated before leaving.

It wasn't so long ago we'd be sipping vodka gimlets at a disco on a Saturday night, but a quiet evening home alone was now what I craved. Kneeling at the hearth in the den, I stacked kindling and logs and lit a roaring fire. The room felt cold and more drafty than usual—perhaps the chill was inside me, made cold by visions of a gray ghost.

The French doors suddenly rattled. I jumped to check them. They were unlocked. One door was cracked open. My whole body tightened as I spun around fearing I would face an intruder. Everything remained in its proper place with no sign of disturbance. My diligence about safety seldom wavered, and I was certain I had secured the doors. Absolutely certain. But living alone at High Hill was new to me, and it was possible the bolt had not fully engaged.

A puddle at the base of the door wet my stockinged feet. Wind could have blown the door open and let rain in. I slammed it shut, twisted the locking bolt, shook it to be sure, and switched on outside spotlights lighting far across the field.

Could someone have entered the house while I was at Brookhaven? "Stay calm." I paced and thought. Were they still in the house? *I wish Michael were here. Should I call the police? Is this a paranoid delusion?* "You can handle this yourself." I grabbed a fireplace poker from the rack and a flashlight from the kitchen drawer. The basement door was secure and bolted, so I began my patrol on the ground floor and searched up to the second floor, checking every window and door, closet and pantry—any place where someone the size of an average dog could hide. No one was here except me and my fear. The storm had to be the cause.

By the time I returned to the den, flames raged in the fireplace. Embers sparked and popped against the screen. The scent of burning wood soothed me. I exchanged wet stockings for warm woolen socks and donned cozy overalls. The last time I wore them was in Chicago, perhaps the happiest time of my life, a time when I could fail in private and didn't have to account for my whereabouts or prove anything to anyone, not even to myself.

I loosely tied back my hair and settled in the recliner to read Dr. Clift's book. Its narrative defined the need for a hospital, stating that a thousand "unfortunate lunatics" scattered throughout the state were in need of care. The tedium of fundraising efforts, dates, and facts, along with doctors' biographies, was balanced by engaging personal details about wives or parents, or the religion they practiced. Vivid personalities from the past jumped off the pages.

An absorbing account of a patient's typical day made life at Brookhaven seem a perfect asylum in the truest sense of sanctuary.

I read for an hour or so, through the 1930s, then briefly scanned the balance of Brookhaven's history. Though I didn't know what I was looking for, I knew I hadn't found it.

The fire's popping drew my attention. Flames mesmerized me. Images from the book mixed with scenes from the afternoon. I revisited Brookhaven in my mind, walked the paths and corridors, and overlaid them with pictures from the past. A sense of familiarity struck me during our visit and it hadn't diminished. Did I overlook some connection in the book? Or from my nightmares? Was Emma Collings' story the fantasy of a senile woman? Maybe Michael was right. She was just some old woman who saw the obituary and constructed a fable around the key. It probably locked her own closet door. But if that were true, why had she become so affected? And why did she leave so quickly? A piece of junk? Not likely. And Gram on her deathbed had pointed to her purse and the old newspaper. The drawing must be important.

By eleven-thirty, only the crackling fire disturbed the quiet of the house. Every creak of old wood beckoned me to listen more closely. I'd spent many nights at High Hill when Gram was alive, but then, people were around. Overnight guests often visited, introduced as old friends from across the state or distant cities or foreign countries. Until recent weeks, I hadn't been alone at High Hill nor considered its location to be remote, until now—until I'd stepped in a puddle of rain at the threshold of an open door.

I should get a dog. I'd wanted one for as long as I could remember. A dog would be good company, and if I had one, I wouldn't need to search the house with a fireplace poker whenever the wind blew. Long ago I'd begged, but Gram refused with no consideration or explanation. I didn't understand. High Hill was pet-perfect in its seclusion with no hazardous street traffic and plenty of space. "Gram, we could have two dogs and they could play together," I'd argued. She wouldn't hear of it. She practically went ballistic at the mere mention of a dog. I wondered, but I never asked why.

THOUGH THE DEN WAS COZY and the fire warm, I twisted and twitched in the chair in an uneasy sleep.

The nightmare had begun ...

> *The little girl ran.*
> *No one ahead. Someone behind.*
> *Run faster. Faster.*
> *Footsteps thumped against the ground.*
> *Heavy breathing echoed against dark boundaries.*
> *Closer. Thumping. Gasping. Run. Run.*
> *Run until ...*

The telephone's ring jarred me. A log fell to the hearth. My heart pounded as if I'd been running—pounded as if I'd discovered an intruder in the house. I reached for the phone.

The voice on the line screeched. "Where've you been?"

"God! You scared me." I gasped, pushed myself higher in the chair, and paused to catch my breath.

"Aren't we touchy tonight?" Marcia said.

"No, I'm okay. The phone startled me, that's all. Guess I fell asleep."

"So, where've you been? I've been callin' all week."

"Busy. You have my office number, don't you?"

"Of course I do; somewhere. But you shouldn't be workin' so hard anyway. Relax."

"As soon as I can."

"You're not even eating, are you? Come for dinner."

"I'm eating," I lied.

"Tomorrow."

"Can't. Let's do it next weekend? I'll be better company once I get through this week. I've got an important meeting on Monday with a zillion things to prepare. Senior staff is coming from New York tomorrow evening, so I've got a lot on my mind."

"Next Saturday, then. Be at my house by seven. I'll call Friday to remind you."

"Yes, Marcia. I'm looking forward to it." My tone smacked of *Yes, Mother, I'll be home early.*

"Del, don't bring a date."

"I wouldn't dream of it."

Marcia was right. I hadn't eaten, wasn't eating. I rummaged the fridge and grabbed a hunk of pepperoni and a heel of stale Italian bread. With a glass of Riunite Lambrusco, I sat in the den and returned to browsing the back pages of the Brookhaven book while I snacked. Lists of Officers, Directors, Committee Members, and Executives comprised the epilogue, along with a peculiar dozen of Vice Presidents For Life, By Subscription Of $200 And Upwards. Not a bad idea. I should have my senior executives *pay me.* I'll introduce the Upwards idea at Monday's meeting. Stately names of Comstock, Hubbard, and Porter partnered with their Christian surnames—Amiriah, Jeremiah, and Elias. Poetic sounds like melodies from a simpler time.

Something in the list screamed for attention. I read it again and again. I remembered names. Period. Dare I say, no one was better skilled than I? And there was something I should know—something in the names.

Porter. Porter? I closed my eyes. *Never forget a name. Spell it in your head.* Elias Porter. I knew that name. Porter. Elias. Never met an Elias, yet—I was sure. I remembered spelling it, not now, but years ago. Locking it in memory, somewhere. Some time. How many can there be, an odd name like that? Elias Porter, I *know* you — But from where?

~ EIGHT ~

1899 • May

WAS THERE NOTHING FOR MAGGIE to be cheerful about? Carlotta and Uncle Elias had betrayed Father, and had become the ruin of her life. Even though she had calmed from the witch lady's attack, discontent remained.

A hospital schedule had emerged, and she had observed the times when outside doors were unlocked to facilitate inmate chores. Front doors opened at eight and patients walked in single lines to assignments in the laundry room, making or mending garments, housekeeping in cottages, or tending gardens and paths. No chores had been assigned to Maggie. If left to her, she would choose kitchen duties with Miss Cookie. She ran outside. Perhaps she would ask Matron, but for now she would enjoy the outdoors where sunlit ground fog swirled in benign vortexes as she skipped.

Inviting footpaths curved around gentle hills of lovely grounds. Well-tended gardens framed whitewashed cottages. Early morning dampness from the night's rain smelled of new grass and fresh flowers. Dandelions dotted the lawn and fully bloomed tulips and daffodils edged the asylum's main building. A flock of sparrows perched on its roof.

A light, woolen shawl wrapped Maggie's head and shoulders. Thick, white stockings too large for little legs fell into clumsy black boots that chaffed her ankles when she moved. But despite the blisters sure to come, it felt good to be outside and skipping in the sun—like running through fields at High Hill.

Maggie reached the barn near the bottom of the hill and paused at the door until her eyes adjusted to dim light. Her distorted shadow stretched across a stone floor littered with hay. Its sweet smell filled the shed. Yesterday she had seen Emma in the kitchen, locking the barn, then skipping toward the city gate. She did not see her at supper, inside the hospital, nor with inmates performing outside chores. Determined to find her, she entered the barn.

Coarse ropes and thick chains draped the crossbeams. Rakes, shovels, and sickles hung on rusted hooks mounted on the walls. Remnants of a chicken coop lay in a corner in a tangle of broken boards and wire mesh. Seven stalls along one wall lined the length of the barn. Six white-and-black-spotted cows munched on silage. Tails swayed and slapped flies like the thrash of a bullwhip. A wood-rung ladder rose to a loft that spanned one third of the barn's width. A girl about her age, maybe younger, emerged from one of the stalls, apparently startled when she sighted Maggie.

Maggie moved closer. "Good morning, Emma. I didn't intend to frighten you."

Emma stepped back. Her face was a striking color palette with blue eyes and rosy cheeks on alabaster skin. A limp purple ribbon fastened wavy blonde hair in a loose braid that fell to the middle of her back. The corners of her mouth turned upward into a cautious smile.

"I'm not frightened. Only surprised. I've watched you from the kitchen."

Maggie felt self-conscious and adjusted the apron that nearly concealed her gray hospital dress. "My name is Maggie."

"So I've heard." Emma pointed toward the main building. "Are you one of them?"

"Oh, no. But I live there until my father comes for me."

Emma nodded and continued her duties, first collecting a pail that hung from a nearby post, then a three-legged stool.

"Nor are you one of them. Matron told me." Maggie followed her to one of the stalls. "I'll help with your chores if you show me what to do."

"Why would you do that?"

"I fear it is not safe to be among them, but it is safe to be here with you."

Emma smiled as she took Maggie's hand and led her to one of the cows. She set a second small stool beside the animal, pointed for her to sit, and then wrapped Maggie's hands around the udder's teats. Maggie leaned her forehead against the cow's belly and giggled as she hesitantly tightened her grip. She felt Emma's hand come to rest on her shoulder in a gesture of approval.

An hour later with chores complete, the girls sat on milking stools and scratched silly drawings in the dirt while they talked and laughed.

"I don't mind working here," Emma said. "My mum is quite ill, but will soon give birth. I hope to have a brother."

"I have a brother. He's five years older and his name is Salvatore, but I call him Sally."

Emma laughed. "A curious name for a boy."

"When I was a baby, his proper name was too difficult to say correctly, so I called him Sally and now he prefers it, as long I don't embarrass him in the presence of his friends or strangers." Maggie laughed too, until missing Sally seized her.

"My auntie works here as a nurse and arranged this work until Mum feels better. Do you know the day nurses?"

"Not all, but a kind nurse wakes me so I can wash and eat breakfast before the others. She might be your aunt."

"Yes, it sounds like her. She wears a timepiece—"

"On a chain around her neck."

"I'll return to school when the baby comes. Perhaps. That's my wish." Emma's gleeful expression soured. "I must hurry home to check on my mum."

Maggie nodded. "I hope she feels better. I'll come play with you again if I may."

Emma scratched a smile in the dirt then flicked the stick aside, ran from the barn, and disappeared through the city gate. Maggie reluctantly returned to the asylum where Matron kept vigil from the front porch.

THE DAY ROOM WAS NOT OPEN before supper. With chores completed by late afternoon, the inmates took refreshment in the dining room, then rested in chambers. Nurses gathered on the outside porch to savor tea and biscuits and conversation. It was the time of day when everyone was accounted for and no person could hide, a time when the low sun flooded through windows to light dark corners.

Maggie's morning with Emma in the barn had roused a yearning for structure and normalcy. It was time to do something about it, make a friend, perform a chore—or devise an escape. She roamed empty halls past locked chamber doors, and toward the kitchen to search for Cookie.

On the bench beside the dining room doors sat Kathleen, an older girl who looked enough like Maggie to be her sister. She appeared to be calm enough and if she was getting a cure, she might become another friend with whom to play. Maggie approached. "I saw the nurses eating biscuits and my hunger stirred. I'll find something to eat. Would you like to come with me?"

Kathleen hesitated.

"Come." Maggie urged with her hand.

Kathleen did not reply but rose from the bench. Maggie opened the dining room door, glancing over her shoulder several times to see if the girl followed. Baking bread and simmering chicken stew filled the room with appetizing aromas as the girls entered the area where kitchen ladies chattered.

Maggie secretly listened. "They're gone ... The river barge ..." they said, and "Heinz ..." Even though she hadn't seen Heinz since the day she arrived, his authority held a powerful grip on all aspects of asylum life. As soon as Maggie swung open the door and she and Kathleen came into view, the women stopped talking mid-sentence and stared at the girls. Maggie felt uneasy—she had overheard something she should not have.

After a silence, she clutched Kathleen's arm and pulled her close to share the responsibility of their distraction. "Please, may we have biscuits or fruit?"

"Look at the two of ya. Starvin' ta death are ya?" Cookie laughed. "Come. Sit."

The girls perched at the worktable where a kitchen lady set two plates. Cookie served warm bread and strawberry jam. "Don't eat too much, yul spoil yur supper."

Maggie nodded as she sniffed the bread. "Mmm."

Kathleen hung her head and tore a hunk from the loaf. A lock of hair toppled off her shoulder to settle in the jam. Maggie reached to remove the hair from the dish, but as she was about to touch it, Kathleen jumped from her seat. "Get it off me. Get it off." She slapped at the sticky mess in her hair with deafening shrieks. Kathleen's panicky moves and jerky gyrations launched platters that smashed to the floor. Pots and pans flew off their hooks. The kitchen ladies surrounded the girl, provoking more desperate maneuvers. Louder. Faster. More hysterical. Two women fought to restrain her.

Kathleen grabbed the meat cleaver.

Maggie jumped from her stool and sprang toward the door, frightened, and trembling, remembering how scared she was when inmates had cornered her in the day room.

One of the kitchen ladies scampered into the pantry and bolted the door behind her.

Cookie moved closer to Kathleen with her hands poised to defend herself. "Easy, Kat. Easy. Put down the knife."

Kathleen's shoulders slumped, and she cried. The knife swayed, slicing small cuts in her apron. After a sigh, she lifted the blade to her throat. She appeared helpless and hopeless as if she had surrendered to defeat. Maggie looked at Cookie with pleading eyes.

Cookie kept a distance. "Be careful, Kat."

Kathleen's attention bounced from Maggie to Cookie. Then to the knife. A sudden grin indicated the birth of a brilliant idea. With impossible haste, she raised the cleaver and chopped off six inches of hair sticky with jam. She set the tool on the counter as calmly as if it were a comb and smiled at Maggie. "There. I fixed it."

Cookie and another woman forced Kathleen hard against the

wall. One of the kitchen helpers ran screaming for a nurse. The conflict could have easily escalated to a point where Heinz and the orderlies would be drawn in, so Maggie was relieved to see only a nurse arrive.

With Cookie's help, the nurse tethered Kathleen in leather mittens and a muff, all the while her pathetic gaze conveyed to Maggie, "You did this to me."

Maggie had, she feared. Had she left the girl sitting on the bench, this would not have happened. She had crossed a boundary when she encouraged Kathleen to join her. Tears welled as guilt struck her gut, and she wondered what punishment the girl would suffer on her account.

Matron and another nurse rushed into the kitchen and the nurse assured them that she would secure Kathleen in a private cell. Maggie didn't have to be told to leave. She knew it was time to become invisible, and after a few minutes had passed, she slunk from the dining room unnoticed and tiptoed down the hall.

Stopping at Kathleen's cell, she peeked through the window. Her throat tightened and she cried as she watched the poor girl struggle to escape her restraints. Kathleen sobbed and paced and wiggled her arms and torso to no avail. Her face distorted to a wretched expression of frustration and pain, though it eased when she saw Maggie. The girls stared at each other through the glass, mere inches apart, as proximity gave comfort to both.

Maggie wiped her eyes with her apron. "I am to blame. I am deeply sorry."

Red and teary eyes seemed forgiving, yet pleading when Kathleen pressed her cheek against the window. Maggie spread her hands on the glass trying to soothe her.

Distant footsteps from the direction of the doctor's office interrupted. Firm and steady, they grew louder as they neared. Heinz snatched Maggie's arm. Startled, she squealed. He pointed for her to sit as he shoved her to the same hall bench where she'd found Kathleen an hour earlier. He slammed open the dining room doors as he barked orders for kitchen cleanup, screaming at Matron as if she had wielded the knife. She wasn't even there.

Supper time came and went, and still no kitchen lady had come to ring the bell, which caused great anxiety among the inmates assembled in the hall. The air prickled with the intensity of an electrical storm. *What a mess I've made.* Maggie was embarrassed for Matron; that Heinz had scolded her in the presence of nurses and kitchen help, and she was ashamed to face her. She knew well that it was not Matron, nor Cookie, the kitchen ladies, nor nurses who had permitted the incident with Kathleen to break into pandemonium—it was she.

Maggie remained seated on the bench, unmoved for an hour. No one dared approach until a single brave soul neared her. The old woman who grinned at her on the day of her attack by the witch lady, who Matron had comforted, sat beside her and they waited for the dining bell. Maggie had learned her name was Anne Pierce, but everyone called her "Old Annie." Dare I speak to any inmate?

"Hello, Annie. I am Maggie," Shaking her head, she finally said, "I had quite the day."

Annie sniffed at Maggie's shoulder then reared back.

Pulling her garment's bodice to her nose, Maggie smelled the scent of cow. So much had happened since morning, she had forgotten to wash and dress for supper. "I've been playing with Emma and learned to milk. We cleaned the barn and talked and drew pictures in the dirt."

The milking story made Annie smile with the sweetest look that was as normal as anyone's, even while she glared at the stains on Maggie's apron and her dirty boots dangling above the floor.

Maggie crossed her legs at her ankles and rocked back and forth ignoring the old woman's scrutinizing looks, yet feeling self-conscious she had not properly cleaned herself. "Well." She slapped her hands on her knees. "What's for supper tonight?"

"Chicken stew for me and you."

"You spoke a good rhyme. I like that. I smell hot applesauce, too."

More than an hour and a half past meal time, a nurse opened the dining room. "I hope we have a quiet supper tonight. I've had enough excitement to last a life."

"Last life. Late light. I sit with Maggie tonight."

Matron stood guard at the door, watching and listening, as inmates passed. Maggie looked to her as humbly and apologetically as she could. Matron nodded as if she understood Maggie's intent. And Maggie read her nod to be a signal that Annie was safe to be with.

They came in turn to the serving table and collected their meals. Annie held her cup to Cookie. "Maggie's milk."

"Say what ya want, woman."

Maggie grinned. "I helped with the cows today. She wants my fresh milk."

Cookie laughed as she filled their cups. Her lighthearted temper implied she did not begrudge earlier events.

Maggie and Old Annie sat at a table near Matron's post where they enjoyed a quiet supper. "Talking with you has been quite pleasant."

Annie nodded, and then pointed to the scabbed scratches on Maggie's arm.

"Yes, the witch lady attacked me in the day room, remember?"

Annie plucked a piece of hay from Maggie's hair and set it on the table. Her elbow knocked over her empty cup, which rattled against the platters and silver. The clinking sounds struck Maggie, sounding like the vases clinking on her windowsill the day the floors rumbled.

"You've lived here a long while, I imagine. Tell me about the thunderous noise and the three women who also arrived that day. I've not seen them since."

"Like Maggie, she smell. Annie no tell."

Maggie moved closer and whispered, "Remember when the ground shook and rumbled like thunder? I think the sound came from below."

Annie's eyes shot wide open. She gripped Maggie's wrist with surprising strength. "Ya go dere ... ya don't come back ...." She snapped in a dark, raspy voice, "The dog he gonna git ya ... ya don't come back ... Annie knows."

Maggie tried to slide away to put distance between herself and the fear in the crazy woman's face, but Annie grasped both of her arms and pulled her closer until their eyes were inches apart.

In a moment of clarity, as if years of therapies had suddenly triumphed, Annie was perfectly lucid when she insisted, "Do *not* go down there."

~ NINE ~

1974 • November

AN HOUR HAD PASSED since my last time check. My room at High Hill was too dark to be morning, and I was too tired to have slept an entire night. I rolled to the other side of the bed and closed my eyes—again.

"Are you up there?"

I screamed, startled by a piercing voice. Marcia. Her distinct footsteps on the stairs thumped like an ogre's. Reaching for the clock, I groaned and bolted upright. "Damn. Nine-thirty! I set the alarm for eight." I shook the stupid thing and slammed it down.

Marcia slowly opened the bedroom drapes, her mischievous grin clearly meant to provoke. With my hand shading my eyes, I slid off the bed without comment and stumbled toward the sink.

"I'll make coffee." She poked her head into the bathroom. "I brought doughnuts."

"Good. I was dreaming of food, so I must be hungry." While brushing my teeth, details of the dream returned to mind. "Hot applesauce. Strawberry jam. Milk."

"Nope. Cinnamon with apple filling and other favorites."

Toothpaste foamed around my mouth, bearing semblance to a rabid animal. "A little girl in my dream was holding a tray toward someone round and jolly who put warm bread on her plate."

"Sounds like a Santa Claus wish."

"Go away. It's hard enough to remember without you making fun."

Twenty minutes later, I bounced down the steps and into the kitchen, cheerfully humming. I sat across the table from Marcia and reached for a Bavarian Cream doughnut. "I wasn't expecting you till next Saturday."

"With your mother gone and the housekeeper off, I thought you'd be lonesome and running out of food."

"When have I been lonesome because Mother wasn't around? We haven't spoken since before I forced Sam to resign. And we're not likely to speak any time soon."

"You canned Sam?"

I nodded and sipped my coffee.

"Hot damn! Well, good for you. I knew you had it in you."

"Whoa. Back up. My mother is gone? Where is she?"

"It's Sunday, my guess would be Barbados. She told you she was cruising the islands. I know she did 'cause it was you who told me."

"A cruise? That's strange. I had a nightmare a while back that I was on a ship. It felt so real, it took me a minute to restore my land legs. Weird, huh?"

Marcia shrugged. "I guess."

"Did Sam go with her?"

"Who am I, Perry Mason? How the hell would I know? She's your mother."

"I guess I expected her to cancel her trip out of respect for Gram."

We looked at each other and said, "Naaahhh."

"I thought the cruise wasn't for another few weeks."

"It probably was when she told you last month. You know, what you need is a babysitter."

"I have a babysitter, but she's not very good."

"The housekeeper?"

Cream filled my mouth and powdered sugar coated my lips. I couldn't reply. I stretched to the counter behind me, nearly tipping in my chair, and picked up a small mirror framed in Florentine silver to aim at Marcia's face.

"Me? Your babysitter? Funny. If I wanted to do that, I'd still be married." She twisted the mirror toward me.

Puffy bags under my eyes reflected in the mirror. Harsh shadows of morning sun were unkind, making me look even worse than I felt.

"You need more sleep. Get to bed early tonight. You know I love ya but I gotta' say, you look like crap."

"You sound like my mother. I've got a dinner meeting so it could be a late night. Besides, I'm getting plenty of sleep, I'm just not getting any rest."

Mother leaving without so much as a goodbye hurt more than I expected. Was it too late to salvage our relationship? She was the only family I had left, now that Dad and Gram were settled in the hereafter. It was reason enough to compromise with Sam. If there was a way for Sam to save face without me weakening my position, I might be able to put everything back the way it was—better than it was. Michael was right. I shouldn't have acted so fast against Sam. I'm an idiot.

There was still this family secret to consider. Only a few weeks had passed since I met the mysterious Emma Collings at Gram's wake. I wondered about Elias Porter, and the fact that I couldn't place his name drove me crazy. "How much do you know about your family?"

"Enough."

"I want to compile a company history."

"Be careful. Family garbage can stink to high hell. The newspaper might cover your plans for the company. Do that instead. People in town want to know what's happening."

"Did the paper send you here?"

"No. People are worried about their jobs. A warm, fuzzy story wouldn't hurt."

"I want to know what's going to happen too, but I don't want publicity right now, not until the dust settles."

"Why not? What's going on?"

"A commemorative book dedicated to my grandmother would be appropriate. More humble than my picture on the front page."

"Yeah, but be ready for anything when you start poking around. I'm warning you."

"Maybe you're right. When one of Gram's cousins lost her husband, I guess I was five or six and curious about death, I asked her why he died, and I wanted to know exactly how he died. She told me he was a bootlegger, and the owner of a speakeasy on Pratt Street stabbed him for watering the whiskey. I never asked about my family again."

"Get out. You made that up."

"I swear it's true."

Marcia made a face.

"With Gram gone, I feel disconnected, so … temporary. I need to establish that I'm part of something with foundation and roots. More grounded. Don't you want to be part of something bigger than yourself?"

"I'm all the big I need." She grabbed and shook her gut. "Talk to your mother."

"That hasn't worked for years so why bother?"

"Because she's all you have."

"Depressing, huh?"

"Then maybe you should think about getting married and having kids. It's time, Del. That's why you're dreaming about little girls."

"I want to have kids someday, but right now I feel the need to make a different mark. I've got to keep the business going for my future children, so I should at least know its history."

Even with Marcia, admitting how little I knew about my ancestors was embarrassing. I knew who my parents were, and my new stepfather, Sam. That much I knew for sure.

Gram was my dad's mother, but I never saw her naked and didn't verify stretch marks on her belly. She was more proper than that. Her name was Margaret Rosa Delito. Great-grandfather Antonio also had a son, Salvatore. Married in Italy. Died young. My own father didn't remember him. Gram didn't seem to have knowledge of being pregnant or giving birth, and she was squeamish when it came to messy stuff. Maybe she never married. Was that her big secret? Bearing a child out of wedlock? Was she not my grandmother? I felt a migraine brewing.

"Again with the history."

Marcia's words startled me. "History before it's forgotten. I'm not sure where to start."

"Your ad agency in New York has copywriters. Call them."

"No, it should be personal, not slick. I thought I'd write it myself."

She shot a queer look at me as if the idea was the strangest she'd ever heard.

"I want to know about Antonio Delito and those men whose portraits hang outside my office. How did they live? What did they believe? I'll sort through the facts. Any ideas?"

"Well, my dad always told me to start at the bottom."

I thought for a few seconds. Then laughed.

"What's so funny?"

"At the bottom is exactly where I should look. You're a genius —well—your dad's a genius. I should start in the basement storage area at the plant with the old company records and the jewelry and the shipping documents and receipts. The place is packed with information. It is our history."

"And you're going to do this in your spare time?"

"Maybe I'll enlist Vinny for the dirty, heavy work."

Marcia handed me another coffee. "I'd better get home and feed Muffin before she chews my new suede boots. I had to pick up dog food, that's why I was out this way."

"Breakfast was great. Come anytime." We walked to the front door, and I helped with her jacket. As her Dodge Omni squealed out of range, I raised my cup to toast her and returned to the den to read the morning paper. Lazy Sundays had been too few, but today became one. Breakfast with a friend who knew when to leave, good coffee, catching the news by the fire, just the way Sunday should be. But it was still early, and anything might happen to screw it up.

KEY PERSONNEL from Delito's New York sales office had gathered in Barrows by Sunday evening—Vice Presidents of Marketing, North American Sales, and International Sales. They'd controlled business a hundred miles from the home office, and until now, they'd answered only to Gram and Sam. They must have been furious when they heard I'd fired him. Tonight would be the first time I'd deal with them from a position of authority. If I had to defend my firings, I would.

I didn't deserve their resistance. Not before and not now. Growing up in the company, working part-time at the plant while in school, full-time summers and vacations wasn't easy. With a Graphic Communications major and Marketing minor, my first job out of the business was with Woburn & Walsh, a small ad agency in Hartford where I worked my butt off and was promoted to Account Executive for a local museum, my first client. I'd work just as hard to earn this, too.

Delito's New York staff could be intimidating, but they didn't own the company. *I did.* And I knew the business as well as anyone. *Who was I kidding?* I knew part of the business. But no matter, their names weren't on the door, mine was. I was coming to terms with that, and it was time to remind them, too.

Pacing in the foyer at High Hill and talking up my confidence, I was determined to arrive in style. I adjusted the long sleeves of a cobalt blue knit dress and slipped on a white cashmere coat to complement the company's white limo. A single strand of pearls and matching earrings from Delito's fall line, Model No. PRL-4864 commanded admiration. "Stunning."

The grandmother clock began seven chimes as Michael arrived in the company car. I secretly relished the beauty of that car but preferred commuting to the office in a compact, five-speed Honda. The Japanese were buying our jewelry so there remained a balance of trade, at least on a personal level. This evening, however, I had insisted on the limo. Besides matching my coat, on rare occasions it served a purpose, and tonight, I definitely had a purpose.

The night air was dry and crisp. Everything sparkled, so visually perfect it could have been a movie set—lighting, props in place, wardrobe, makeup—action.

Enter, Prince Charming.

Michael exited from the rear seat, his overcoat neatly draped over one arm, as always. "Why did you bring your coat inside when you know we're leaving? I'm not moving without an answer." Teasing him was sweet, knowing he'd just die if we were late.

"No mystery." He wrapped the coat around me as he led me out the door. "If stars fell to earth, what would I use to shelter you?"

Michael had been hired a few weeks before Gram strong-armed my return. Being the "new kids," we latched onto each other and had been together professionally for almost a year. Six months ago, friendship evolved into intimacy. Because I was as nervous as any novice employee and had more to prove, I relied too much on him. Maintaining independence was the First Commandment, which both Dad and Gram had preached and because of it, I'd sharpened a cold edge on my relationships. I tried setting boundaries with Michael, but there were times like this, when his presence was crucial not only to my success, but also to my personal happiness, and any walls I'd forged to insulate myself, melted. I could barely look at him without feeling a tingle.

We were still joking about falling stars as we entered the Regency Inn. Vinny met us in the lobby.

Trying to hide my surprise, I said, "I didn't expect to see you here."

"Do you mind? I pressured Michael to invite me. We think I might learn something."

"It's okay. I should have thought of it."

"Is there anything special you want me to do?"

"Just enjoy yourself. We're not discussing business tonight, but if you want to study a master diplomat, watch him." I pointed to Michael.

I approached the three key managers and two associates. "Welcome to Barrows. Thank you for joining me tonight."

The Regency Inn was the best Barrows had to offer. The food was good enough and the staff knew from experience that Delito, Inc. would reward attentive service with generous tips. Each time Michael checked his watch, which was too often, waiters converged on our group like metal filings to a magnet. Dinner was pleasant even though the theme of conversation remained on endings—the war, Nixon's presidency, lines at gas pumps, the pet rock fad, and Delito's "old guard." If only tomorrow's meeting would end so well. Everyone enjoyed themselves, so I was confident it would.

Michael escorted me through the hotel lobby and hailed the car.

"Make sure I have thirty minutes alone with them tomorrow," I said. "If the moment seems right, I want to discuss something I've been working on."

"Want to tell me about it now?"

"Tomorrow I will."

"What have you been doing?" he teased with a playful nudge to a ticklish spot on my right side. "Tell me now."

"One clue—It's a new direction for the business, maybe a new division."

"I'm hooked. Tell me more." The limousine parked at the hotel curb, and Michael opened the rear door.

"Where's your coat? Aren't you coming?" It had been a Cinderella evening and all it needed was a happy ending, not rags and a pumpkin at midnight. And I wouldn't have minded if Michael came home with me, considering last night's puddle of rain at the open door, and my fear that someone had breached High Hill and remained hidden inside. But that excuse seemed desperate and manipulative, even to me.

It wasn't.

"It's late and tomorrow's meeting is important. We both need rest. Our guests will close the bar, so come morning, you and I will be a lot sharper."

"Good plan." I said the words, though my heart disagreed.

"I'm going straight to my room to review my notes, so I'll be ready for anything."

"Even falling stars?"

He kissed my cheek. "Good night, princess. You were great tonight. Very smooth." He closed the car door and twice slapped its roof, indicating to the driver it was safe to leave. He glanced at his watch and returned to the building.

The floor-to-ceiling windows around the lobby clearly displayed the activity within. While the limo paused for an opening in traffic, I looked back to the hotel, debating whether to return. "Use your head, not your heart." Gram's words nagged from her grave. *Call me stupid, but I'd feel more confident in the morning if I spent the night in Michael's arms.*

I watched him move across the lobby, but he didn't turn toward the elevator to his room like he said. Was he settling the bill? No, Vinny did that. This was not good—but not horrible, either. What was horrible was the Lincoln Continental crossing my limo's bright beams. It maneuvered between passing vehicles and nearly nailed an oncoming car as it darted into the Regency's parking lot. Was it his Lincoln? I had to see his face. Beams from a passing car lit behind the wheel. What was most horrible was recognizing Sam Bender.

What the hell was he doing here? Suddenly, I questioned the loyalty of everyone around me, the group from New York, even Vinny, but most of all, Michael, to whom I'd given so much and from whom I needed so much. Now I was forced to doubt their sincerity, his sincerity. Their honesty and his honesty. Their loyalty. And the one thing I craved more than anything—his loyalty. Please. Not Michael.

By the time I returned to High Hill, my anger raged. Why was Michael meeting with Sam? Maybe this wasn't the first time he'd lied. Every occasion when he might have deceived me flashed in my mind as I recalled when I may have misinterpreted a look, a gesture, or a lie.

Quietly sliding something from his hotel's night table into a drawer the night of Gram's wake. Records of a clandestine meeting or merely his notebook? It was he who said firing Sam was "a bit sudden." *He* suggested I concentrate my time with the designers and oversee the new line, which would keep me busy and out of their way. Where was he when Sam grabbed my arm and threatened me at Aaron Schaeffer's office? Where was my trusted guardian then? Why didn't he prevent Emma Collings from leaving the funeral home at Gram's wake? And where the hell was he the night Gram died? Was meeting with the agency so important he had to stay in New York? Why didn't he insist on returning home with me? Why wasn't anyone with me?

~ TEN ~

1899 • May

NURSES HAD REMOVED KATHLEEN'S RESTRAINTS the day after her tantrum, but a week had passed, and she remained in an isolated cell, disciplined with cold-water tubbings. This unfortunate aftermath compelled Maggie to acknowledge that life at the asylum was not the adventure it first seemed. It was a trial of survival.

How did she fall into this dreadful circumstance? Not that Father was abroad, nor that Carlotta loved Uncle Elias. She had seen something she should not have seen. If only she had closed the bedchamber door. Acting on curiosity had endangered her, and though Father had encouraged a spirit of inquiry, he had not warned of consequence. Though she was young, she was more versed in worldly matters than common girls, even more than the women whose charge she had become, yet she was now confined with mad women and controlled by attendants who disciplined by order of a cruel man.

Not much was in her power to change, but she could mind herself and avoid trouble like Matron and Dr. Jameson had instructed. Her habitat had become familiar. The barn was safe in the morn when Emma worked. Matron kept a close eye on the central corridor wards. Most inmate chambers and staff quarters filled two upper floors. The doctor's office, a few isolation cells, and the day room ran the length of the west corridor ending at the dining room, kitchen, and pantries. The scrub room, laundry, and alcoves for water therapies were located east.

The space below had yet to be explored; it must be explored. A harsh scolding was sure to come if she were caught—a small price for a big reward, a safe place to hide, like Father's business lessons had taught.

Maggie paused at the door leading down and scouted the hall to be sure no one watched. Most days she found the door locked, yet today, someone in haste had left the key. A pattern of activity when staff frequented the underground vault was not yet obvious to her, though she suspected it had to do with stocking supplies from additional storage areas like they did at her High Hill home. She twisted the knob and slipped through the opening, dropping the key into her apron pocket to use another day.

The slightest amount of daylight barely filtered through small, grime-encased windows that might be just big enough to squeeze through if she had to. Feeling her way down, she crouched on the bottom step while her sight adjusted to the dark.

Cool and damp, the space held a musty smell that soured in her throat. All was quiet. She tiptoed along a passageway past an arched entrance area where a narrow door led to an intersection of tunnels. Peering right and left, she continued on the widest path straight ahead. Leather soles crunched against the rough stone floor as she eased forward past small rooms and gated areas. Empty coal bins lined both sides and rails for a cart ran down the center and disappeared into the dark. Where drain gutters followed the walls, she nearly lost footing and grabbed a wooden beam to steady her step. Gutters along the walls? What goes on here? For what use are these rooms? She opened each door to see. All were available to her—except one. One door, stronger than the rest, was firmly locked at the end of the tunnel.

Maggie spread her arms and twirled around. She had found a secret place to hide and play. A place where no nurse or orderly would search. An interesting place to explore. Lonesome. Quiet. Order amidst chaos. Her personal asylum beneath a threat of danger. And with the key, she could enter at any time.

~ ELEVEN ~

1974 • November

An undercurrent of evil.
Half dead faces stare.
Drifting numb on an empty sea.
Lost kin. Lost loves. Lost minds.
Eyes that cannot see.

BY MORNING, suspicion that Michael had conspired with Sam roared like fire.

Lost loves.

I hadn't slept well and awoke clutching my sheet so tight, my hand numbed.

At nine sharp, I entered the boardroom feeling neither confident nor in control.

An undercurrent of evil.

How could last night's sweetness have turned so bitter so fast? My internal defenses were pointed as I glanced at Delito's highest executives, and they back at me.

Half dead faces ...

Absorbing the meeting's information caused my eyes to glaze with overload and stare into nothingness. It dragged for hours. Marketing strategy at 11:00. Ad concepts, 12:15. Media schedules, 1:30. A sandwich lunch was served, though I only picked at ham and cheese. Production/Distribution, 4:15. Budgets. Budgets. Notice of a problem must have slipped into my brain by osmosis or something because the incessant drone of one presentation after another became drowned by one prevailing warning. Something was wrong with the numbers. *Act with your head, but listen to your heart. Trust yourself.* Then I tuned out.

The figures and contracts I'd asked for—more than I'd asked for—would take days or weeks to review. Vinny could organize them. He was good with details; no Einstein with original thought, but good with details. And accommodating. Excessively so. Persistently so. Annoyingly so. But he could lighten my burden, and that's what I needed.

Michael had passed several notes asking if I wanted to discuss my new idea. I shook my head offering no explanation.

I couldn't look him in the eye. It would have made me cry.

If I couldn't trust Michael, how could I trust my own judgment? The thought was like acid burning a hole in my heart. Yet without him, the past weeks would have been too difficult to imagine. He'd done everything right. What was going on? He had no idea I saw him return to the hotel lounge or that I was aware of Sam's arrival. Should I confront him? Them? For now, I'd act as if nothing happened, act as I had all day. Wait and watch closely.

By the time the day's agenda had been completed, it was nearly 8:00 p.m. Michael had kept the program on track despite my mood. I walked to where he sat, put my arm around him and whispered, "Thanks for your help. A good night's rest seems to have served you well."

While the others packed their briefcases and prepared to leave, I slipped out of the conference room without notice.

BACK IN MY OFFICE, I felt a quiet peace. A welcome solitude. Asylum.

Vinny had piled mail on my desk. A red and blue striped airmail letter demanded attention. The postmark read Morocco. I grabbed the stack and set it on my lap, placing the foreign letter at the bottom, anticipating its contents, saving it for dessert.

I sifted through memos and notices, then tore through remaining correspondence and heaved each letter, sales pitch, and solicitation into the trash. Why was this junk mail in my inbox anyway? Vinny should be screening this crap.

Instead of my routine cup of coffee, I prepared a glass of hot tea, leaves settled at the bottom, three teaspoons of sugar, like it had been served to me in the desert. I pushed off my pumps and swung my legs onto the sofa, savoring the moment as sweet tea and the Air Mail envelope with exotic postage stamps became a magic carpet to memories of far-off lands.

North Africa in the spring had been like a honeymoon for Michael and me. We'd often traveled to New York and occasionally to Providence and Chicago, but Morocco was our first major buying destination abroad. I believed the trend in fashion would soon swing from the airy filigree styles of the hippie movement toward large, bold, ethnic-looking accessories. After researching designs of Berber tribes in every museum from Boston to Philly and Chicago, I'd insisted on acquiring authentic prototypes, so it was off to Morocco. Gram indulged me.

A Delito family friend, a banker in Rabat, had recommended Hassan Abdella as a reputable trader. I recalled with great fondness his cluttered shop in Tiznit, south of the resort town of Agadir.

The door of Hassan's shop was painted a glaring blue to ward off evil. "The devil will avoid this place because he hates the color blue," I'd told Michael. "I'm not crazy about this shade either; its use should be restricted to swimming pools."

When Michael opened the door, a small spring-bell announced our arrival. Silks and silver and saddles and belts decorated the walls. Brass lanterns and framed mirrors bounced prismatic light around the packed showroom.

The portly proprietor emerged from a hidden room. Michael greeted Hassan in French and presented a letter of introduction from our family friend at the Banque du Maroc.

Hassan stepped out to the street and called into the crowd, "Mohammed. Mohammed." Moments later, a young boy of no more than ten years appeared in the doorway. He dared not enter. "Shey, Mohammed." Hassan waved his hand at the dirty, ragged child to bring tea and be quick about it. "Yalla. Yalla!"

The child soon returned with three small glasses filled with hot tea and sugar, served on a polished brass tray. Hassan closed the door, shutting out the distracting resonance of the bustling bazaar. The tumult of arguing shopkeepers, barking dogs, and bleating goats were instantly muffled. Only the melodic call to prayer on crackling loudspeakers penetrated the quiet refuge. The slow and steady spin of an overhead paddle fan became the pulse of the shop.

Hassan proudly displayed his best Berber jewelry on a square of black velvet. But I was in the market for more than a few select samples and browsed for additional pieces, while Hassan and Michael settled on soft leather floor cushions positioned to haggle. The ritual was more sport than confrontation, but sport I found uncomfortable. I studied Michael's technique, hoping to acquire a taste for the bargaining game he enjoyed. He was at ease in the boardroom, in New York, in Hassan's shop—and in my life.

He and Hassan shifted effortlessly from English to French, and back to whichever language more strongly expressed their argument. At one point, Michael grinned, shrugged his shoulders, and shook his head to reject Hassan's counter offer. I analyzed his body language as he laughed and threw his head back. His throat appeared warm and moist. I watched so intently, I could see his pulse throbbing beneath smooth skin. He said something in French, which delighted Hassan. The price of one more item was agreed on.

Time slowed. The fan's spinning paddles blew Michael's scent toward me. I could almost taste his salt. It was at that exact moment I fell in love, and it was that night we first kissed and everything between us changed.

Maneuvering between stacks of carpets and pillows, I searched the shop for unique pieces—any ornament I could visualize on an American woman with bold fashion sense. My experience in assembly, production, and with raw materials came into play, and I was relieved to have retained that knowledge. A half hour passed, and another, and another. In all, we'd been bargaining with Hassan more than three hours—browsing, negotiating, and drinking sweet

Arab tea. All the while, an eerie sensation gnawed at me. I was being watched.

Not until we were about to leave, did an old man emerge from a rear room hidden by wooden lattice. The man's slippered feet slid in and out of sight from under his gray caftan as he shuffled over knotty floor planks. Prayer beads wrapped his hands, and a white crocheted skullcap topped his sun-darkened head. He looked to be a hundred years old, but he could have been fifty. The old man stared at me, not a stare curious of a foreigner, but one tinged with recognition. He stood in my path. I was certain I didn't know the man, this being my first visit to Morocco, but he was not so sure. The way his head tilted and his brow furrowed, his steady gaze pierced deeper than my eyes as if searching his memory. But despite his best attempt, he was unable to recall.

We had a plane to catch, and I regretted our speedy departure though not nearly as much as I regretted leaving the old man in such a bewildered state, his eyes still fixed on me as I walked out the door.

Hassan happily secured the shutters of his shop as Michael and I packed our bundled acquisitions into the trunk of a rented Peugeot. I kidded that Hassan must be going to the mosque to thank Allah for his good fortune. We left quickly for Agadir and an evening flight. And that was the last time I saw or heard from Hassan or the strange old man.

I was grateful to Hassan for that recollection of a happier time. But recalling how devoted to each other Michael and I had been made my present pain even more insufferable. I wanted us to be like we used to be. So much of my life had come to depend on him. I loved him and hated him for that. Most of all I was angry at myself for allowing dependency to form, and for a split second, I understood Mother's attachment to Sam.

Maybe she did live her life right. She was content, even happy. She wasn't stressed about meetings or proving herself, or sneaking around mental hospitals or lying to her friends, or hiding secret bank accounts to finance her dreams. Who needs this crap? I could sell everything and travel the rest of my life. Buy a small house on a lake. Study painting or sculpting in Florence. Sleep. Read. Live. What was so damned important about the business anyway? It wasn't like Delito fed the hungry or ended war. We made jewelry—mediocre jewelry at that.

Pretending I wasn't going to cry, I sipped tea and read the letter from Morocco:

> *Dear Miss Delito,*
> *My uncle was intrigued by you. It was most*
> *unfortunate your departure was so hasty and his memory*
> *so slow. On my return from the mosque, my uncle asked*
> *for your family name from the record of your purchase.*
> *His mind cleared when I wrote it in block letters and spoke*
> *it aloud.*
>
> *My uncle recalled stories told to him when he was a*
> *small boy. The stories, passed by his father from his father,*
> *were of an Italian merchant from America. Two families*
> *were much alike, my uncle told me, and always when the*
> *merchant visited Agadir and Tiznit, he was a guest in the*
> *home of my uncle's family. The foreigner brought*
> *wonderful gifts for my uncle who was a curious little boy,*
> *and as such, reminded the visitor of his own young*
> *daughter.*
>
> *The merchant was called Delito and my uncle*
> *recognized his face in your face. It is possible he is*
> *mistaken, as you saw he is quite old, but he believes*
> *he has mementos of proof. His package follows this letter.*
> *Watch for it.*
>
> *Good health to you and your family—as Allah wills.*
> *Until we meet again,*
> *I shall remain*
> *Your friend in Morocco,*
> *Hassan Abdella.*

~ TWELVE ~

1899 • August

WEEKS PASSED, THEN MONTHS, and Maggie's hope held strong that Father would come for her one day soon. Maybe today. Perhaps tomorrow. Until then, she followed a set routine, one that she more than anyone had determined. Dr. Jameson allowed her access to his office library where she advanced her studies. On occasion, he took interest in her readings and would offer a book from his personal collection, plus paper and a graphite pencil for her lessons. Some days Old Annie would sit quietly by her side in the day room or on the porch as she read and wrote notes.

In late afternoon, Maggie played and probed and scavenged in the tunnels, then washed for supper followed by kitchen duty and bed, a predictable schedule that forged a degree of security.

Until one horrid day that began like every other.

"Good morning, Miss Cookie."

"In here, dearie." Cookie's voice resonated from the pantry. "What do you fancy?"

"Something with sugar. Yesterday's cake was so yummy it stirred the sweetest dreams, and I didn't want to wake."

Cookie removed a platter from the counter and peeked under the towel that covered it. "Here's a wee bit more."

With her fist wrapped around a fork from the drawer, Maggie climbed onto a stool. "You are the best cook I ever ate for." She took a bite and closed her eyes. "Mmm."

"Don't be sleepin' on me, ya hear."

"I'm not asleep. I was thinking that today my father will come.

I feel it right here that something of great importance will happen."
She rubbed her tummy.

"That ain't a prophesy yur feelin', that's you eatin' too much cake."

Maggie laughed and shook the fork at Cookie. "We'll see. I think he will come."

"You got lots to do, so until he gits here," Cookie said, "you best git busy."

"What shall I do?"

"Emma must hurry home to care for her mum. It don't look good for 'er an' the baby." Cookie shook her head. "Go help 'er with the animals."

"Oh goodness. Poor Emma and her mum. When will the baby come?"

"Can't say. Don't think on it. Best to keep busy. Git."

"Is Emma in the pantry?"

"Gone to the barn. Must be waitin' on ya by now."

Maggie set down the fork without licking it clean. "I'm going. Goodbye, Cookie."

She rushed to the barn worried about Emma's mum and fearing duties at home might cause her to never return. She cherished her friendships with Emma, Cookie, Old Annie, and even Matron Smythe, more than she could have imagined. Their companionship had become more satisfying than days alone at High Hill.

Inside the barn, Emma was nowhere in sight. Cows were secured in their stalls, their udders swelled with milk. Mooing moans begged for relief as black cow eyes strained to see behind. An empty milk bucket lay toppled as if carelessly tossed aside. Maggie searched every corner and beneath each animal as if playing hide and seek, but she didn't find her friend. She returned to the barn door and looked back across the grounds toward the asylum to see if Emma was on her way. She was not.

With a bucket and stool, she sat beside a cow, grasping and tugging its teats, and laughing when milk squirted until she heard the sound of rustling hay. She kept still, her fingers tightly attached to the cow as she labored to hear. Low grunting from the loft. A hardy thump. Dirt and dust glinted with sunlight as it rained down between the floorboards.

Was Emma hiding overhead? Was she playing? Maggie climbed the ladder, slowly and quietly easing upward, hoping to surprise her friend. Her long thin fingers clutched the edge of the loft as she steadied herself, but she saw no one when she peered over the top. Years of climbing her willow tree paid reward as she deftly hoisted herself onto the floor, then crawled toward the corner from where the sounds came. Bales of hay stacked to form a wall. A clever place to hide. She scrambled to the top of the stack and peeked over.

Stunned, her eyes stared. Her mouth fell open, shocked at what she saw.

Heinz knelt over Emma tugging at her dress like a large dog teasing a trapped kitten. Emma's panicked eyes glared at Maggie. Her mouth gaped in terror, yet no sound escaped.

Silent screams.

Fear and outrage hit Maggie like a punch in the stomach or a fall from a tree. Seeing Heinz on Emma made her sick like when she discovered Carlotta with Uncle Elias. The horrible feelings of that wicked day rushed through her. She felt an urge to run for help from Matron Smythe or Dr. Jameson. Why hadn't she moved? The terror in Emma's eyes and her gaping mouth screaming with no sound would be a memory impossible to evade.

Her chest burned inside. Carlotta and Elias. The hurt of their betrayal boiled until her skin grew hot. Frustration over her imprisonment. Anger toward her absent father. Disgust and revulsion. Her heart pounded. Her breaths came faster. Faster. Rage exploded.

She pounced on Heinz and grabbed him from behind. Her arms wrapped tight around his neck, squeezing his throat with all her strength, choking hard. Harder. Stronger. Squeezing and choking—hoping he would die.

Holding tight for life, Maggie struggled against Heinz' attempt to shake her off. His forceful grip on her arms was finally too painful to bear, and she released her hold.

Emma crawled from underneath and crept to the edge of the loft where she sat shivering in August heat.

Maggie scratched at Heinz while she pointed to the ladder and waved her hand directing Emma to flee. The girl didn't move. Maggie screamed, "Run, Emma. Run! Bring help."

Maggie and Heinz wrestled.

He threw her to the floor.

Her head bounced as it struck the wooden boards.

Before she could run, he straddled her and sealed her mouth with his stinking hand. He smelled of sweat and hay.

She kicked hard between his legs, harder than she thought possible.

He rolled off, clutching his groin.

"I'll get you," he groaned.

She scrambled across the loft.

Heinz stumbled after her. "Don't you tell no one, or I'll kill you."

Maggie climbed down after Emma and they raced to the door.

"I'll kill you both. You hear me?"

The girls ran from the barn, Emma to the city gate and Maggie to the asylum. They looked at each other as they ran farther apart, their gaze locked in a silent, secret communication about a perilous ordeal that would forever bind them.

Maggie's feet pounded the earth, her heart pounded her chest. She ran like she did on that dreadful day when Carlotta and Uncle Elias had chased her across the fields. She ran. *I should run with Emma, escape and live in the city with Emma. Her family would help me return home. I might run all the way to High Hill.*

Now it was too late, she was near enough to the main building to capture the attention of Matron and the nurses. She was still trapped at the asylum, confined and locked away like Uncle Elias and Carlotta had locked her in the closet. She stopped at the porch staircase, breathless, her head stunned from its bounce on the barn boards, her thoughts confused and clouded as if in fog. She'd been imprisoned with five months nearly passed. Delusions of security and normalcy had faded long ago. She looked toward the porch to Matron, or anyone older or wiser who might offer comfort.

Father? Was it he who stood at the top of the stairs? Or was she tricked by her light head? She thought he might come. Did he know of Carlotta and Elias? God, she hated them today. She would never forgive Carlotta.

Matron looked down at Maggie. "Milkin' done?"

What should she do? A mind's trick. Father did not come. She had to think quickly. She could tell about Heinz and what he did to Emma, but she was too frightened. She only had to keep herself safe until Father *did* come, for a few more hours, days, or a few more weeks. She said nothing. Did nothing.

Matron shook her head then opened the main doors. An orderly line of attendants and inmates marched to chores at various locations. "Yur barn chores done?"

"No, ma'am. Emma, ah, hurt herself and left for home."

Matron looked across the grounds as Heinz exited the barn and lumbered toward the cottages.

A cold prickle ran down Maggie's neck.

"You feelin' right?" Matron asked.

She nodded.

"Then go. Cows need milkin'. You got to finish."

"Yes, ma'am." She plodded back to the barn, eyes darting from side to side with each cautious step. Even though Heinz had wandered away, she stood at the entrance searching shadows before she entered. Squatting on the milking stool, cringing at every creaking sound, small tears rolled down her cheeks as she reached under the animal.

The sweet morning moments of eating cake and strolling across the lawn to meet Emma seemed a year away. She shuffled down the empty hallway to her room, traded ill-fitting work boots for better shoes, then aimed for the scrub room to wash for afternoon kitchen duties.

Peering through a window into Matron's chamber, she could not believe the sight before her. The door was ajar and Old Annie was sitting on Matron's bed. What spirits possess that woman?

Such a deed could bring severe punishment. Maggie was about to approach, thinking she would rescue Annie before discovery, but Matron's footsteps suddenly resounded from the direction of the washrooms. Matron entered her chamber and closed the door.

Maggie rushed from her ward and back to her spying position. Drat! Matron had drawn the window's privacy curtain, leaving only a sliver of an opening for a squinting eye to observe. The two women sat side by side on the edge of the bed. Matron wrapped her arm around Annie, her head resting against Matron's shoulder while they spoke in soft whispers.

Just then Matron locked eyes with Maggie who understood she should continue on her way. She stood in the washroom, missing home and Father and Sally, and feeling envious of the affection she had witnessed.

~ THIRTEEN ~

1974 • November

AFTER YESTERDAY'S MEETING, I expected to see Michael waiting when I arrived at the office. I paused at the foot of the lobby stairway feeling lightheaded from headache or stress or a fractured heart. When I looked up the stairs, I thought I saw him pass down the hall.

Jack, the security guard, touched my shoulder. "Miss Delito? You okay?"

"Yes, I'm fine."

"Maybe you should sit a while."

"Really. It was ... just that I ... I thought I saw Michael."

"He got a late start. Called a few minutes ago. Should be here later this morning."

But morning passed and the afternoon was nearly gone and Michael hadn't arrived. I was beginning to worry when, finally, I heard him greet several people as he neared my office. The blinking light on my phone alerted me that Vinny must have put a personal call on hold as Michael passed his desk. Vinny did that a lot, but he was the last of my worries.

"Yes, she's in there," I heard him say to Michael.

"Alone?" said the first of my worries.

"All yours."

Michael knocked on my half-open door and leaned in. "Jekyll or Hyde?"

"Funny. Did you want to see me about something?"

"Yes. No. Not about something. I want to see you."

I looked at him without saying a word. What could I say? It would take a week and a day to ask my questions, and after discovering his secret meeting with Sam, I didn't trust his answers anyway. I collected a stack of notes and two packages of jewelry samples and stuffed them into my briefcase.

"Going somewhere?" He asked as if nothing was wrong.

I leaned back in my chair. "No."

"Come on, Del. Don't shut me out."

"Have I?"

"It feels like it. We have to talk."

When I'm good and damn ready. "There's nothing to discuss."

"That's not how I see it. Something's changed since the dinner meeting. We talk all the time. We're good for each other. What the hell happened?"

A silent pause lasted for a while as we sat with arms folded across our chests, staring and holding ground until he finally said, "When you feel like talking, I'll be here."

He left the room.

As late afternoon passed into evening, only two offices remained lighted, Michael's and mine, as we worked into the night at opposite ends of the second floor. Our cars, in the otherwise vacant lot, remained parked side by side as if they had more sense than we did.

THE NEXT MORNING at ten thirty, I was due at Boston's Museum of Fine Art. The two-hour drive passed quickly, but I couldn't get Michael out of my mind. He had never expressed his feelings as openly as he did yesterday. There was no face-to-face conversation about our relationship, what we wanted in our lives, and what we expected from each other. We'd never discussed our future at all. He was right. The past year with him was the best time of my life. We worked well, we were friends, and we were lovers. I wanted him the first time I saw him and wondered if one of Gram's reasons to hire him was to make returning to the business more attractive to me. I would have eventually returned, but meeting Michael that first day hastened my decision. We were soon together ten or more hours a day, every day, and I'd not once felt bored or patronized or smothered.

Enough. I practiced my presentation while I drove. More was riding on my success than people knew. More than I had admitted when I assured the design department, my first day back, that their jobs were safe. Following a decade of steady decline, business had leveled, and we were narrowly keeping pace with the world's mid-size costume jewelry producers, but if my plan came together like I envisioned, Delito's shining role in the industry could be restored. Hell, Delito, Inc. would become its jewel.

Damn you, Michael. I need you now. Can trust ever be restored? Lost innocence remains lost and hurt leaves a scar. But so far, all I had was suspicion. Michael hadn't actually done anything—that I knew of—for sure.

By this time, he had to be wondering where I was, and I was tempted to call from the next highway rest stop and explain, but before I knew it, I was merging onto the Mass. Pike.

The MFA wasn't on my *official* list, but it was a good place to test my proposal for the tough targets ahead, and it was an easy day trip.

My presentation went better than I'd hoped and lasted longer than I'd expected. The Curator of Special Exhibits offered a personal tour, and I couldn't pass on that. It turned out I'd paid a high price. Rush-hour traffic. Argh. By the time I reached Hartford, a milepost marking my extended neighborhood, it was past nine. Too late to drop in at Michael's apartment. Besides, then I'd have to admit where I'd been, and I was too tired to run circles around the truth. But wow, did I do it in Boston. Did I ever.

I hadn't felt this proud of the business since I saw Jackie Kennedy on television wearing a Delito circle brooch. Maybe in the morning I'd tell Michael about my plan and my progress. Or maybe I'd savor the rush by myself. Speeding past the Hartford exits heading south toward home, wind snapped through my hair at seventy miles per hour, and I felt as high as the moon. I tuned the radio, skipping Streisand, Bowie, the Stones—whoa, it was definitely a Bowie moment. Volume blasting, I sang every word of *Space Oddity.*

BACK AT THE OFFICE, the following day, I couldn't have felt better, but didn't realize how much it showed.

"Good morning, Del. Here's your mail," Vinny said. "Wow, you look great today."

When did he start calling me Del?

He handed me two envelopes.

"That's all the mail?"

"I mean it. You look fabulous."

"Vinny, is this the only mail?" I waved the envelopes to get his attention.

"Oh, yes it is. Michael and I took care of everything else because he doesn't want you bothered by piles of junk. That is what you wanted, isn't it?"

I shrugged my shoulders. That's good, I guess. "Please ask him to come in."

"He's at the New York office. He just phoned to see if you were here."

"Right, it's Wednesday. The agency meeting. I lost a day."

"Yes, we noticed. Shall I call him?"

"No, don't interrupt. I'll be in the storeroom."

"Can I help you find something?"

I shot a look. Lately, he was too involved in my affairs. Everyone was. "No, thanks. Maybe later."

"Are you sure? I don't have much to do today."

He was getting way too clingy. Was that my paranoia? No. I was right about this. "I'm sure you really do have a lot to do. Look, if Michael calls, get on the intercom and find me."

I HADN'T BEEN IN THE BASEMENT ARCHIVES since high school when Dad had me organize our vintage pieces—a tedious and lonely task. While my friends camped at Woodstock with Janis Joplin and the Grateful Dead, I was sentenced to the basement for the summer of '69.

The new area was approximately 150 by 400 feet, clean and uncluttered, and well lit by banks of fluorescent tubes. A small, undecorated office space had been walled off in the nearest corner, though it had never been used. I grabbed a flashlight.

A fenced tool crib secured six rows of steel utility shelves that ran the length of the stockroom. Brown corrugated boxes with detailed labels held discontinued samples. A model number marked each box, as well as the quantity, date of first production run, and date of termination from the line. A clear plastic bag stapled to the box displayed a finished sample. I finally understood the value of my summer project, easy identification and so brilliantly simple even a rebellious high school student could do it.

One could trace world history by following the arrangement of product lines. Military uniform buttons and medals from the Great War and WWII, a 1910 hair ornament commemorating the appearance of Halley's Comet, the mass market introduction of plastic, fads and fancy things I'd seen on Gram's dresser or pinned on the gown of an actress in a black and white film. *Must be worth a fortune.* I hoped I'd find the company's old documents as thoroughly recorded. Like I missed Woodstock, maybe Gram had punished Dad when he was a boy, forcing him to organize war buttons rather than allowing him to play stick ball or cool off at the swimming hole with his buddies.

Deeper into the storeroom, I reached the far wall where a single door promised a journey further back in time, and six creaky wooden steps took me there. A straight skirt was not appropriate dress for the task, and with two-inch heels I used extra caution as I wobbled onto the uneven stone floor.

Spider webs and decades of dust coated flat surfaces. It must have been years since anyone ventured here. First sight of a mouse and this would become Vinny's assignment.

Here too, items were displayed outside of sample boxes, more or less in chronological order, but these storage containers were antique tins or hand-carved wood. I followed signposts to the past, occasionally distracted by period pieces as old as 1878. Several items were familiar from my childhood days with Gram at High Hill, and seeing them reminded me of the chore I'd been avoiding —sorting her personal belongings.

Stampings and chains filled burlap sacks and barrels of varying sizes. Jewel cases, music boxes, and chests were stacked on wooden shelves against the wall.

An old steamer trunk rested against the back wall of the darkest room tucked under the shelves as if someone wanted to bury it—though not forever.

With my flashlight set atop a nearby crate, I felt for a handle to drag the trunk into the present. My fingers probed the vaulted top, its cracked surface, and hammered brass corners. A pair of three-inch-wide stiff leather straps looped through sturdy brass buckles. A six-inch gash marred one side as if a heavy object had fallen against it and slashed a permanent scar into its skin.

Pulling the trunk into the light was more of a struggle than I expected. But when I pried the lock from the brittle leather, it easily fell away. Carefully, I lifted the lid. Papers and letters fastened in small bundles filled the shelves and compartments. I removed an armful to carry to my car for later study. Some fell to the floor, fluttering down like autumn leaves.

When I reached to the floor to retrieve them, the area suddenly went dark, and in a split second, the entire basement turned blacker than a moonless midnight. "Oh crap." The dim beam of my small flashlight proved useless and I could almost see the batteries draining weaker before my eyes. Just as my fingers touched the light, it rolled off the crate onto the floor, behind the trunk, and under a low shelf until its last illumination extinguished.

"Dammit!" This was the last place I wanted to be dressed in a tailored suit. I was blind. I stood and reached into the blackness. My hands snagged a spider web. Foul words ran through my mind —words used by drunken sailors, I imagined.

Okay. Don't panic. Where am I? Who knows I'm here? And how long will it take for someone to notice I'm gone? *Hell. The way I've been acting ... could be days.*

There was no chance I could find my way out of here. With the lights on, I narrowly found my way *in here.*

Crash! Something tinny rattled across the floor. My head snapped toward the sound. "Is someone there?" Something clicked against the stone like a rolling glass bead or a scurrying rat. I thought I felt it brush my leg. "Who's there?"

No response. I had spun around and didn't know in which direction to turn. I thought I heard breathing. It wasn't mine.

A dim glow ... then a shadow ... moved toward me. And then a bright sweeping beam of light. A blinding flash. My right arm shielded my eyes. "Who is it?"

"Del, are you okay?"

"Vinny? What are you doing here? What's going on?"

"The lights went out."

"I know that! The power went out?" Just then the elevator rumbled in the new basement. Fluorescent banks flickered on.

"Only this level, I think."

"What?"

"The power. Only this floor went dark. I knew you were here so—"

Vinny flashed his light on the trunk and my stash of papers.

"Help me move this to the stockroom office." We easily pushed it into the space where I'd have privacy with comfort and could research Delito history in peace.

I sent Vinny upstairs. Watched him walk away. My mouth contorted. If he was on the second floor, how did he know the power went out down here?

The trunk was full of historical documents, and who knows what else, most of which had not been seen by anyone who still breathed on earth. Facts, figures, weights, times, and dates. I scanned a few papers. Orders, inventories, shipping lists, and billing vouchers dating to the late 1800s were all here. Everything I hoped for was here. I felt like a kid at Christmas and all the gifts under the tree were mine.

Michael phoned later that afternoon and Vinny told me he'd offered to page me, but he was at the station and rushing to his train. He said he'd call when he arrived in town, but when he did, I'd already left the office, stopped for groceries, and must have missed his call at High Hill. Thursday's telephone tag went about the same way. By the time Michael arrived at the office, I'd left for meetings in Hartford and didn't tell anyone where I was going.

Visiting my old friends at Woburn & Walsh Advertising and lunching in the city was fun and more relaxing than I expected, and by the time I left, I was confident I'd soon have an accurate idea about how much my advertising and media expenses ought to cost.

A four-car pileup in bumper-to-bumper traffic closed two lanes of I-91, stalling traffic for four miles. I didn't return to the office until six. Michael was gone so I went home.

The phone was ringing when I entered High Hill. I ran to answer and stumbled in the dark. The handset bounced to the floor. My knee banged an end table. "Ouch—Hello."

"Del? Are you all right? Vinny said you had a scare in the old basement and—"

"Vinny should mind his own damn business."

"So you're okay?" He laughed.

"Michael, we have to talk."

"I know we do."

"Dinner tomorrow?" I said.

"I can't. How's Saturday?"

"Love to. Oh, no. I promised Marcia. What about Sunday?"

"I have something with the family, but I'll call you."

This shouldn't be so difficult. "Yeah, you do that Michael." I hung up.

A STACK OF PAPERWORK from the steamer trunk lay in my lap. I tried to create a chronological history from orders, invoices, and shipping statements but found it difficult to concentrate. A half full glass of milk sat on the nightstand. Nothing had helped me sleep. For two hours, I'd watched the minutes pass on the clock as fragments of thoughts invaded my mind. The business. Mother. Sam. Dr. Clift's book. And Elias Porter. His name and its connection to me remained elusive.

And then there was Michael—there was always Michael. Our last few days had almost been like good old times, and I reconsidered what had sparked my suspicions. Could his curious behavior be innocent coincidence? Still, I wondered why he was last in my thoughts when not long ago, he had been first.

Dead-of-night quiet stilled the house I'd begun to call home, though some nights it felt less so. Maybe I gave up my apartment too soon. Moving was one more thing that unsettled my world, and it was the one thing over which I had control. Too late now, it was done. And tonight, it was too late to sleep. Waking after two or three hours would make me feel worse, so I brewed coffee, filled a thermos and set out for the office. *I'll work till lunchtime, call it a day, return home, and go to bed.* That's a plan that should work.

It was 3:00 a.m. and not the first time I'd worked through the night. Seeing blocks of failed businesses as I raced through downtown Barrows was like peeking into Delito's future. Delito, Inc. remained at the edge of a precipice, and I was dizzy from looking down. It was time to stop using ropes and start building bridges. Forget the past; we're not headed that way. Focus on the future. Yellow traffic lights flashed caution.

A few spotlights lit the lot nearest the building, but the farthest edges disappeared into darkness as if the world ended there, mostly, my world did end there. I parked near the front door. I couldn't recall the last time I'd had fun, gone to a disco or movie, or enjoyed a good laugh with a friend. I couldn't remember the last time I went out that wasn't related to business or to an asylum. My life was pathetic.

Alongside the building, something rustled in the trees. Must be wind. The lobby's night lights glowed on the entrance. Footsteps squeaked of leather shoes. I walked briskly toward the door.

Hurry. Where's the damn key? Hurry, hurry. Keys jangled. Footsteps in front? Or behind? I was spooked, still spooked by the open door at High Hill and puddle of water. The dark. The nightmares. The basement power failure. The suspicion.

I pressed against the door praying it would open. But it was locked, as it should be. Nowhere to run. I stared into the shadows to my right, to my left. Footsteps closer.

A hand grabbed my shoulder.

I screamed and jerked away.

My keys fell clanking onto the concrete walk.

"Miss Delito?" a deep scratchy voice said.

I turned. "Good God, Jack. You startled me." I gasped, then caught my breath. Argh. I wanted to slap him.

"Something wrong, Miss? What brings you this time of night?" The 40-year old security guard put his hand to his chest. "You scared me half to death."

"You scared me." We laughed. "I couldn't sleep. Thought I'd get an early start."

Jack retrieved my keys from the sidewalk and opened the door.

"What are you doing outside? I thought you made rounds indoors."

"Usually do. Thought I heard something. Maybe a car? Musta' been yours."

"Must have been."

Our footsteps tapped louder than usual with an empty echo against the marble floor as Jack and I crossed the lobby. I was oddly aware of keys jangling on the belt-ring of his uniform as he escorted me down the shadowy hallway from the second floor reception area toward the executive offices. Soft, low lights bathed the purple carpet in a rich, deep hue of cool color, easier on the psyche than the sharp fluorescence of daytime.

As I passed the portrait of my great grandfather, Antonio Delito, his face made me pause. With my new found attention on the past, historical portraits of ancestors and founders, typically taken for granted and rarely noticed, were now front and center.

"Did you say something, Miss?"

"Just thinking."

"I'll go about my rounds if you're okay here."

I entered my office, poured coffee from my thermos, and flipped through a pile of business papers. Cost estimates from the design department sat on my desk along with six samples each of the two Berber pins I'd asked to be replicated. Focus. I wanted to review the estimates and should inspect the samples. I needed to study the budget summaries that since the manager's meeting had been an irritation, but I couldn't.

Instead, I stared at Dr. Clift's book about Brookhaven Farm and the darn thing stared back. I resisted an impulse to fling it across the room. With eyes closed, my fingertips smoothed over the gold lettering imprinted on the cover. Focus. My mind emptied to clear a vacant space, hoping to see the name that eluded, teased, and frustrated me. Until the past was laid to rest, building a solid future seemed a fool's errand.

Information from my earlier reading scrolled in my mind like movie credits—treatments, places, dates. Names. Names. Elias Porter. How do I know you? My memory held the answer, but the closer I came to reeling it in, the faster it snapped away. The book had won. I took a breath and held it, then exhaled. I set it on the desk and stared. Like a sneering child, it taunted, "I know something you don't know."

And suddenly, I knew it, too.

Armed with a penlight from the desk drawer, I raced the corridor outside my office. One by one, I inspected the brass plates identifying the old portraits. The letter style of etching was the same on all—all but one.

The dates were readable on all but one.

The names were legible on all but one.

I crisscrossed the hallway from portrait to portrait, checking dates. Counting in my mind, counting on my fingers, to be sure.

Antonio Delito was the first portrait outside my office. Directly across from him, another man. But the plaque on his frame was different from the others in shape and style. His nameplate had apparently been crafted by another artist and allowed to deteriorate. Not cleaned and polished like the others, and not for mere months or years—but for always.

It was the only plate that was different. Why? I rolled the chair from Vinny's desk and positioned it below the portrait, pressed it against the wall, and held it firmly in place with my knees. I gripped the heavy frame, lifted the portrait off its hook, and let it fall onto the armrests. Without hesitation, I rolled the chair and its cargo down the hall to the elevator lobby. The whole floor rumbled as I steered toward the factory.

I didn't look at the stoic face, but plotted my next move as I waited for the lift to meet the second floor. The mechanical hum grew louder as it neared, especially loud in the stillness of night. I wondered why Jack hadn't come running to investigate the commotion. The wall clock read four fifteen as the elevator clanked to a stop. The doors opened. Michael looked directly into my eyes, and then to the portrait propped on the chair.

"Del. What the hell?"

"Never mind this, what are you doing here?"

"Jack phoned. He was concerned."

"Why would he do a thing like that?"

"My name must be first on the emergency list."

"What emergency!"

"No harm done. What are you doing? Can I help?"

"You're here so you may as well." As the elevator descended, I asked, "How did you get here so fast from Hartford?"

"Vinny said you tried to reach me so I stayed in town at the hotel."

I shot a puzzled look at him.

He removed his coat and draped it over his arm. "I thought I'd get a lead on the day hoping we'd find time to talk."

"And Jack knew you were in town?"

"I left the number with him. I always do." His hip knocked against mine with a playful bump. "Unlike some I know."

The elevator stopped at the first floor where marble and carpeted floors changed to wood planks and concrete. A passage separated offices from the factory. I stopped to flip switches for overhead lights. Row by row, fluorescent banks hummed with flickering brightness as Michael and I proceeded to the plating room.

"Set this portrait over there." The stainless steel worktable resounded with a clanging thud from the frame's weight.

From a nearby toolbox, I collected a small screwdriver, an awl, and tack hammer. I'd worked in every factory department since I was sixteen years old, actually twelve, but no one was supposed to know, and knew my way around the plant as well as anyone. I certainly felt more comfortable here than in the boardroom. Michael clearly did not.

He stood with his hands in his pockets, seeming afraid to touch anything as I pried the brass nameplate from the bottom of the frame.

A dozen spools of wire and chain hung near the table. I snipped about eighteen inches of copper wire and fastened the four-inch plaque to one end, twisting a loop to secure it. Three sinks lined the wall, each with a tray set at its bottom. A painted tin warning sign hung above them: HAZARDOUS MATERIALS! USE SAFETY PRECAUTIONS. An instruction list followed. I didn't need to read it, though it captured Michael's attention. He nervously shifted his eyes as if searching for some hazardous material that might attack him.

"A dip and a swirl in this acid solution cleans the jewelry of oil and grime prior to gold or silver plating." The acid bath had earned my respect when I worked in the plating department during high school. I didn't realize I'd splashed my legs until they stung and I looked down. Acid had sprayed and dissolved holes into my jeans and pantyhose. My skin burned red and raw. The incident took mere seconds, yet spotty scars remained.

I strapped on safety goggles, but didn't bother with a protective apron. Michael shuffled two steps back. I dipped the plaque into the bath until it fizzed like an antacid tablet. The solution instantly devoured decades of corrosion. If left too long, the entire plaque would dissolve. I'd learned about that, also the hard way, so I knew precisely when to remove the metal. After a brief twirl in the second pan holding neutralizer, and in the third pan of rinsing water, I laid it on the counter to inspect.

Pressed into the back surface was the manufacturer's name in Providence, Rhode Island. That's why this one looked different. The others had been manufactured here in the factory.

The name appeared, clearly etched on the front of the plate. I must have seen it long ago before soil camouflaged it. The name, without a doubt, connected Delito, Inc. to the Brookhaven Asylum.

"Elias Porter. We meet again."

Michael's gaze darted from me to the portrait and back. "Who's Elias Porter?"

"Maybe we can talk about it when we have time for each other."

"Come on, don't be like that." It must have been his frustration that spun him around. His arms flapped. "We have time now. I'm trying to help."

"That's not the message I'm getting."

"Then you're getting it wrong. It's the middle of the night and the only reason I'm not asleep is because I thought you were in trouble."

With my hand on my hip, my mouth must have twisted. *Damn. I hate to be wrong.*

He said, "Okay then, we'll talk when we have time."

Ouch. I might have gone too far. Michael slipped on his coat and walked toward the exit.

Oh well. I took the stairway to the basement. Maybe the next stack of documents would implicate Porter. At the very least I now had a name to work with.

I entered the office where I'd begun to organize the contents of the trunk and turned on the light. The neatly ordered stacks I had locked away were now in disarray as if someone had rifled through them before they left in haste. Besides me, who would be interested and who had access? It had to be someone who worked at Delito, but there was no logical reason to search through old documents. I could hardly justify my own curiosity.

~ FOURTEEN ~

1899 • September

MAGGIE AND COOKIE rested on stools at the kitchen worktable like they did every day after serving breakfast. Morning chatter about the previous day's events had long ago become ritual. Cookie spoke of the abundance of late season tomatoes and how she would preserve them for winter. She opened a cabinet door and proudly revealed four dozen new canning jars awaiting the task. Maggie nodded, pretending interest while her thoughts remained bound to last month's incident—the terror in Emma's eyes and her attempt to choke the life out of Heinz. Murder in her heart. That she had done nothing to exact justice and now lived powerless under his threat troubled her most of all.

Cookie's voice broke the silence. "Ain't you speakin' today?"

"Nothing happened, ma'am. I swear." Maggie squirmed on the stool.

Cookie didn't question her response.

"When will Emma come back to her daily chores?"

"Don't you mind her. She's got chores at home, and I got work to do. You goin' milkin'?"

"No, Miss Cookie, I shall not. Not today."

"We start cannin' so you got to git. I can't be worryin' yul get boiled in here."

"I have nowhere to go."

"Walk to the river. Watch for the barge. She'll be comin' today bringin' the last of winter coal."

Maggie jumped off the stool, grabbed an apple from the fruit bowl, and stuffed it into her apron pocket, then scurried toward the rear door.

Cookie called after her. "Take the papers to the fire pit on yur way."

"What's that?"

"Yul know it when ya see it. And take heed, keep outta them tunnels 'cause coal's comin'. Don't go there, you hear?"

"Yes, ma'am." Maggie grabbed the newspapers stacked beside the door and ran outside.

A mound of ashes filled the bottom of a stone pit. She stirred the powder with a stick, dropped in Cookie's newspapers and looked around for bearings to her ward until she spotted her windows with the empty flower vases.

Maggie skipped across the grounds and over the hills until she reached the river. Hot. Humid. The air felt more like August than September, and it was difficult to imagine the need for coal. Her feet dangled off the edge of the pier, far from the water below. She pulled the apple from her pocket and took a bite as she peered downriver. No barge was in sight.

The river flowed slow and lazy from the North to the Sound in endless mesmerizing motion. She wondered if Sally's fear of water had spoiled his first ocean voyage, and if he would ever board another ship. She hoped he and Father had been spared the worst of storms. From what she knew from newspaper reports, the season had been "unremarkable." Father had touted Nellie Bly's bravery when faced with wild seas, and he would tolerate no less courage from his son. Imagining their verbal exchange brought a smile, and she looked forward to hearing the full story. No doubt, their versions would conflict.

She and Father had read Nellie's scathing exposés about child labor and her *Ten Days in a Madhouse*. How ironic was her current predicament. Who could have predicted that she would also find herself among the insane when she promised Father to be as brave as Nellie? At least she could write her own asylum story about the inmates she had come to know, the friends she had come to cherish, and the disturbing acts she had witnessed. Like Nellie, she would record truth in a journal. She would lock it in the chest Father gave her, hide it in a safe place, and map its location—somewhere so safe that Father might find it even if she were to die.

An hour must have passed before a faraway whistle wailed. The barge crawled upriver barely visible in the distance. She left the dock, scrambled to the crest of the nearest hill, and up a good climbing tree between the river and the asylum. Yellow black-eyed Susans and summer garden phlox spotted the grass below. Whistles loudened. A nautical shape appeared more defined. Excitement grew.

The barge moored by midmorning. The captain disembarked and strolled to the asylum's rear entrance where he met Heinz, who unlocked the doors to the underground tunnels. The captain returned to the barge, shouting orders. Six crew members rolled empty carts from a tunnel to the barge, shoveled coal to fill the carts, then pushed the loads onto a rail track just inside the tunnel. They repeated the process for hours, cart after cart after cart.

Maggie watched until long after the afternoon meal had been served, but when her thirst grew too much to ignore, she climbed down the tree to search the kitchen for food and drink.

THOUGH MAGGIE'S CURIOSITY usually prevailed, she heeded Cookie's warning to avoid the tunnels, though she was tempted to sneak in. What a sight it would be to witness the carts rolling down the rails. She imagined the barge crew working below, pushing loads and shoveling coal to fill empty bins. On the front porch, she sat staring across the grounds, winning over temptation to observe below, the dust and the noise and the smell of it.

A nurse startled her when she suddenly appeared at Maggie's side checking her timepiece. "Nearly four o'clock," she said as she stepped down the staircase. She glanced back at Maggie and pointed to the city gate. "Look, here it is."

"Who is coming?"

An ambulance wagon entered the property and stopped where the nurse stood. She greeted the driver, and they chatted while his attendant assisted passengers to unload.

Dressed in what appeared to be their best church clothes, one young woman was likely in her early twenties and another was not much older than Maggie, perhaps fourteen or fifteen. The nurse led the two patients into the main building and to the scrub room where all new patients were introduced to asylum hospitality. Maggie attempted to follow, but the nurse shook her finger, so she diverted to her ward.

Suddenly the floor trembled. A low rumbling belched from below. She now knew it was the carts she once heard and felt, carts heavy with load rolling on rails deep in the asylum's belly. Rumbling, groaning, and shaking the ground. Oh, she had to see it. She tested the door that led below. Locked. Fingers fumbled in her apron pockets. Drat! Her borrowed key was hidden deep in her closet.

She ran outside and crawled behind an overgrown laurel bush to peek at the new patients through the washroom window. The nurse cut the women's hair and inspected their skulls for lice, then scrubbed their bodies in the iron tub. Maggie winced, recalling the day her skin was brushed raw. The women dressed in clean garments, their clothes discarded on newspapers and likely burned in the fire pit.

The barge. The carts. The rumbling. The ambulance with new patients. A day to write about.

THE NEW INMATES sitting across from Maggie were pretty, though thin and unkempt with sloppy table manners, and clearly not accustomed to eating so well. They were as distressed as Maggie had been on her first day.

"The first week is hard," she said to the younger girl. "Then, it's not too bad."

"We fear what happens next." They clutched hands and hid them beneath the table.

"At least you have each other."

The new girls stashed apples and bread in the pockets of their smocks, as if they might never again see good food. A nurse snapped her fingers as she called their names. "Cassidy. Kirby." She led them to Heinz.

We always leave the dining room in an orderly queue while nurses watch. Maggie knew the procedure. *This is wrong. No one goes alone with Heinz.* She hoped she would find them after supper, but they were not in the day room, nor had they been assigned beds.

Every room was searched until there was only one place left to look—the tunnels. But on coal day, no nurse or orderly, not even the doctor was allowed. Heinz saw to it himself.

Recording the disappearance of patients was the first mystery for Maggie's new journal. When bedtime came, she struggled to keep herself from falling asleep for fear that come morning, the Misses Cassidy and Kirby would be gone, like the three women who disappeared on the very day Maggie had first arrived. Frightened faces pressed against glass still haunted her.

Her first day bore its own fear and she had not dwelled on the welfare of others. Not that day. She'd been locked in a closet, stuffed in the rear of a carriage, abandoned at a lunatic asylum— pulled, dragged, and scrubbed raw.

The pieces didn't fit until now. An ambulance delivers the patients who are cleaned, dressed, and fed the evening meal. Never seen again. All this happens when carts rumble below and the building shakes, when the barge is docked. This happens with Heinz in charge and it happens in the tunnels just as Old Annie once warned, "... *Ya go dere ... ya don't come back ....*"

MATRON'S SNORE WAS A LULLABY. As callous as she sometimes was, she excused Maggie from the most difficult physical regimens. Perhaps it was Maggie's youth, or her privileged status that protected her, or that she had become so deft at remaining out of sight and mind. Or maybe it was because she had befriended Matron's favored Old Annie.

Evening passed as she lay in bed considering options as if they were sheep to count. Surrender to sleep was forthcoming. If she didn't rise from bed, she'd miss the only opportunity to discover the fate of the newest patients until it happened again, likely not for months, after ice in the river thawed, and spring floodwaters receded, and the barge sailed. She fetched the door key from her hiding place on the closet floor and tiptoed past Matron's station, careful not to disturb her sleep. Her antics were more like play than treachery with Matron acting the big furry cat, and Maggie, the mischievous little mouse. Her nightdress ruffle swayed behind like a tail.

With so much extraordinary activity during the day, she trembled with a fever of expectation. What goes on down there? Fumbling with the key, the doorknob finally twisted in her hand, and she prayed its groaning squeal would not awake Matron or arouse the staff. She clung to the handrail and stepped down. Faint voices lured her deeper into the dark cold space. Distant murmurs guided her through the tunnel maze. The nearer the voices, the more familiar they became, and she soon recognized one of them belonged to Heinz, who argued with a man she could not yet see.

"My costs have risen," the man said. "My buyers complain the price is too high."

My buyers? The coal was delivered by barge from Pennsylvania and the asylum was the buyer so what did he mean?

"I must have more money for my risk," Heinz snapped.

The other man quarreled about "port charges" and "New York factories" yelling, "I own the damn barges. It is my name on the dockets."

His stunning disrespect of Heinz expressed no fear of him.

"This cargo is young and pleasing to the eye, worth more than the usual fee," Heinz said.

"I have trouble in Brooklyn." The man's voice was known to Maggie.

"Brooklyn, Yonkers, forget about the factories. Sell in the City. For private use. Understand?"

From where Maggie hid, she clearly saw a sliver of Heinz' meaty body. The other man poked Heinz in the chest with his forefinger. Heinz stood like a frightened boy surrendering to a scolding. "Never take me for a fool. Of course I seek buyers in the

City. Mind your business here and be grateful for the payment I give you."

Maggie shifted position for a better view, then stretched to see the other man, the only man who would dare to reprimand Heinz.

"Oh, no. Uncle Elias."

Hands cupped across her mouth muffled her shaky voice so only she could hear. Scrambling away in disbelief, she stumbled backward. A shovel leaning against the wall clanked to the floor. Metal rattled against stone, resounding through the cavern. She ran through the tunnel and up the stairs. Heinz didn't see her, nor did Uncle Elias. She was sure of it.

But perhaps she was wrong.

She rushed to her bed, sliding under the covers and squeezing her eyes shut. If she squeezed hard enough, maybe the truth would change. Only moments passed before a tight hand smothered her mouth, another pressed her legs against the mattress so she could not move. Was this a bad dream? Her eyes shot open. The sun had not yet risen, and the ward was dark, barely lit by a hallway lantern. When Heinz leaned over her, there was no mistaking he was real.

His stinking lips brushed against her ear. "Never speak of what you heard."

Maggie squirmed.

"I know it was you who spied on me. Black powder footprints led to your bed. If I have trouble because of you, you will regret your words. Your time here has been too easy, and that can change on my word." He pressed her knees until she recoiled. "I'll send you downriver to work for men so evil you'll beg to return to me."

Heinz released her legs, and still, she couldn't move. Fear paralyzed her as she stared into his eyes. He stared back as if they both understood that a pact, however reluctant, had been forged.

As long as I mind my boundaries, nothing bad will happen.

MAGGIE WASHED AND DRESSED, ate breakfast, and rushed out the main door. A fine warm day encouraged several inmates to linger on the porch under Matron's watchful eye; one of them was

Old Annie. She sat on one of the reed chair rockers, clothed in a purple chiffon-taffeta shirtwaist suit. White hair was clean and brushed and elegantly piled atop her head. She was clad and groomed as if prepared for a visit from President McKinley, himself. Maggie's mouth gaped at the hallucination that made her question if she herself had at last slipped into madness. She rubbed her eyes, but the vision remained.

"Annie?" Maggie circled to view her from every direction. "You look lovely."

A ringlet fell to rest on Annie's shoulder. Maggie removed a fancy comb from her own hair and returned the curl to its place while Matron observed from the end of the porch.

"Who coiffed your hair?"

Annie's eyes twinkled with a soft smile. "Matron make pretty me."

"Truth?"

"Matron, indeed."

"How did you come by this dress? The color is stunning."

"Matron. From the Cassidy room after she go. Truth."

"Are you sure Miss Cassidy is gone? She arrived only yesterday."

"You the smart girl. All gone now. They come and they go. To where? To where? Nobody knows." Annie bent over as if to reach for something.

"Annie, be attentive to me. Me, Annie." Maggie pointed to her chest with her right forefinger. "Tell me about the Misses Kirby and Cassidy. From yesterday. You must remember."

"Brooklyn by boat. I got her coat."

A tearing sound interrupted, and Annie's fidgeting annoyed Maggie who wanted answers. "When did they go?"

"Why, why, why?"

"You're safe with me. Don't cry." She stroked Annie's back. "Were they sent to a different hospital?"

"No hospital for them. To Brooklyn sent. In the gent. In the gent."

"I don't understand." Maggie puzzled over the riddle and repeated the words in her head while Annie fussed with the hem of the suit skirt. When Maggie looked to see what distracted her, she saw Annie's muddied legs and feet bare of stockings and shoes. From head to waist, she appeared as fine a lady as anyone—her hair styled in a pompadour, her elegant garment decorated with French knots and trimmed with red silk cord. All that was missing was a fancy picture hat and shoes and stockings.

Annie tore away the bottom ruffle of her dress and wrapped the purple taffeta frill around Maggie's neck. It looked like a marabou feather boa she had seen in the Sears, Roebuck Catalogue in Matron's room.

"Pretty color on you, child. You not in the gent. Not Maggie Porter. You fancy child. Annie knows."

Maggie grabbed Annie's shoulder and shook her. "Where did you hear that? How did you hear of Porter? Porter is not my name."

Annie's eyes widened as Maggie withdrew, nearly stumbling down the steps, running as fast as she could, away from Annie's dreadful words. Maggie Porter. The mad had become madder. Uncle Elias with Heinz. What business bound them? About what cargo did they argue? Were the Misses Cassidy and Kirby on the barge, and why did Matron give away their clothes?

She ran behind the hospital to the hill's summit from where the river could be seen. The barge was gone and with it the two new patients. Maggie dropped to her knees; they sank into soft damp grass. Were *they* the boat's cargo?

Oh, Annie, you almost had it right. You told me the missing patients were "in the gent." Yes, they were. Poor patients sent here in their finest garments. Poor. Needy. *Indigent.* Gone to New York with Uncle Elias. Poor indigent souls—about whom no one will inquire.

Maggie didn't speak of the meeting between Heinz and Uncle Elias, nor did she ask about the patients who had disappeared because now she knew. They labored in New York factories or had been sold to wicked men.

And she didn't speak of the incident in the loft, but she met Emma in the barn on those rare days when she came to work, for her company and for their safety.

She almost confided in Matron, coming very close on one of Matron's softer days to telling all, but kept silent. And in return, Heinz did not bother with her or Emma.

Though she protected the asylum's shame, she accurately documented the attacks and the threats, and those who had disappeared. Every name. Every date. Recorded in her journal and locked in her secret box, souvenir from Morocco. Nellie Bly would be proud.

~ FIFTEEN ~
1974 • November

DINNER AT MARCIA'S was starred on my calendar, and I'd
cleared Saturday of professional obligations, if only I could clear
them from my head. My business venture in Boston looked
promising and Chicago was a shoe-in thanks to former colleagues
who didn't even ask to see product. Washington and New York
wouldn't be so easy, but if I could sell the idea to them, the last
three were sure to follow, then all Delito would have to do is write
the orders.

Personal matters proved not as tidy. Because of Henri, I'd
learned something about the antique key, only to face another
mystery. Where was the chest? And what was the significance of
Gram's drawing on the newspaper masthead?

To avoid being rushed, I dressed early. Light, wool tweed
trousers and a loose cotton knit sweater lay on the bed. A cassette
in the tape player played *Songs of the Humpback Whale* while I
showered.

My visit to Brookhaven and readings from Dr. Clift's book
replayed in my mind. Descriptions of treatments. Purges and
bloodletting. Chatter in my head. *Disturbing thoughts breeding
nightmares.* The visions weren't too bad last week, but I had a
feeling the respite wouldn't last.

Elias Porter. The key's diagram matching the torn newspaper
drawing. A family of my own. Time. Treachery. Betrayal. Michael.
Mother. Sam. Hassan. Running.

Nightmares. Their strength was building like a winter storm.
Run the water. Think about water. I lost myself in whale song.

MARCIA WAS A DECENT COOK, and I craved home-cooked
food and simple conversation in an unpretentious home where I
could escape to my old self; not an owner, manager, heiress,
betrayed lover, or estranged daughter.

Early American furnishings filled her split-level ranch. She
must have inherited her decorating taste from her mother. Her
lack of originality disappointed me. I had a pulse on fashion and
worked to be a trendsetter instead of a trend-follower, and that
was the core of my problem with Sam. I was sure about where to
take the business.

Stop thinking about the business.

Several of Marcia's furniture pieces were familiar from our first
apartment, and I felt like I'd passed through a time portal. "Back in
the day, we were so broke, we shopped at thrift stores."

Marcia said, "My parents thought they'd teach the value of a
buck."

"My dad and Gram made me toil for every little thing, but it
worked, didn't it? Look how far we've come. You own your house,
and I run a business."

"I understand the lesson's value, but I'm still broke all the time,
so what was the point?"

I glanced at the dining room table. "*Three* place settings? Who
else—?"

The oven timer buzzed. The doorbell rang.

"You know what to do," she hollered.

"What a surprise." I greeted Jimmy Cassella, and we kissed
cheeks. *Some surprise.* Marcia had been trying to reunite us, and
seeing us at Gram's wake apparently fired up her motivation.
Resisting was pointless, and it was only dinner. Actually, this
might be quite nice. The three of us had a history. I could relax
with them, more than I could with Michael where too much was at
stake. He used to be my solid ground, trust without doubt, but his
secret meeting with Sam—I couldn't get over it. A quiet evening

146

with old friends who had nothing to do with Delito, Inc. was exactly what I needed. Yes, this could be very, very nice.

We gathered in the kitchen to serve the wine Jimmy brought. After a frenzied search of drawers and cupboards, we lobbed glasses and a corkscrew as if choreographed.

Marcia reset the oven timer for a few more minutes. "Don't mess my kitchen. Ya know, you coulda' asked me where that stuff was."

Jimmy picked at a green salad set on the counter. "This was more fun."

She slapped his hand. "Go sit in the living room. Put on some music and leave me alone." That's what she said, but what she clearly meant was—Why don't you two fall in love?

We sat on the carpet beside the turntable and selected The Beatles, Donovan, and Janis Ian from a stack of albums.

Marcia served a prime rib roast, baked potato, and the slightly-picked-at garden salad drizzled with her secret dressing she refused to divulge. Even to me. "Did I forget anything? Just ask. Don't be bashful."

I laughed. "It's a little late for that."

Dinner conversation compared different memories of the same event. We agreed on nothing and laughed about everything. Several hours passed quickly and after dessert we settled at the fireplace. Muffin, her golden retriever, wandered in and snuggled onto Jimmy's lap.

"Animals and kids. They love me." He scratched the dog's stomach.

Marcia blurted, "Jimmy's construction company was awarded the downtown renovation."

"Congratulations. You should feel proud." I raised my glass. He never was driven to lofty heights, but he had knowledge of the industry, and a reputation for being honest and dependable. Still, I'd been more than a little surprised at his success.

"I guess the town council heard about my experience with nineteenth-century architecture. Most anyone who bid on the project would've done a fair job. But you never know what surprises will turn up in those old buildings. That's what I like. They're all different."

"What do you mean by 'surprises'?"

"No, this must be boring for you," he said.

"I wouldn't have asked if I wasn't interested."

"She wouldn't have," Marcia agreed.

"Five years back, I had a project on the river. Underground tunnels connected most of the buildings. The folks there now had no idea how extensive the system was, not until me and my guys checked it out. Some of the staff at The Farm didn't even know the tunnels were there."

I bolted upright, bumping his leg. Muffin stretched and scratched her ear. "The Farm?"

"Yeah, the Brookhaven Center." He leaned toward me. His eyes left mine for only a moment while he refilled my glass. "We demolished an old barn and replaced it with a beautiful period gazebo, then we did a big-time renovation restoring some of the main building and expanding smaller buildings. Ever been there?"

"God, no," Marcia squealed. "Why would we?"

I didn't answer.

"You should go. Pretend you're lost and wander on the grounds. Looks like a park, real pretty. Prime real estate right in the city. Must be worth a fortune. Anyway, the main building was the original hospital. Quality construction. Stuff you don't see anymore, like stained glass transoms, hand-carved banisters, and woodwork—even the trim and borders around the ceilings, all sculpted by master craftsmen. A lot like High Hill. People really took pride then."

"You're right, but I believe most people want to do their best and still take pride in their work if you give them the chance. My people do. But, what about these tunnels?"

"The director warned us of underground passages. But they weren't used anymore, so I had to explore before excavation. Imagine digging for a new foundation and your men and machines get swallowed down a cavern. I had nightmares about it. Anyway, the hospital's maintenance guy gave me old land maps and site drawings that showed entrances and stairways hidden behind newer walls. I found one staircase in great condition behind a locked door off the central corridor. Can you beat that?"

Compelled by his story, I leaned closer to Jimmy. Marcia, however, was well on her way to sleep in the easy-chair.

"Looks like we're losing her. Should we leave?" he asked.

"No, she does that all the time. Finish your story."

"Where was I?"

"The locked door off the central corridor."

"Yeah, right. So we got the door open. First time in fifty years, I figured. We pried it with major damage to the frame, which we fixed like new by the way. It screeched on its hinges like in a horror movie. My guys kidded about it as we went down the steps with our flashlights.

"The whole place was covered with spider webs, all thick and dusty. I gotta say, being underground in the dark really spooked me out."

I cringed and he continued.

"We didn't find where to turn the power on, so our flashlights were the only light we had. We got to the bottom of the steps. They were stone, did I say that? The floor and most of the walls, too. Wooden planks and pieces of old furniture were thrown all over the place. It looked like they might've used the space for storage before it was sealed up." He shook his head then sipped his wine. "What a mess."

"Did you learn what the tunnels were used for?"

"Service tunnels connecting the buildings, coal storage, and lots of little rooms, too. We saw these huge coal bins on both sides. They had to hold eight hundred tons, maybe more. I found out later the coal was hauled on river barges, up from Pennsylvania."

He offered a drink refill, but I declined.

"Did you follow the tunnels to the river?"

"No, we went as far as we could, but the main tunnel dead-ended at a pile of rock and soil, probably a cave-in. We knew we were way beyond the safety area that concerned us. I'd say over a hundred yards beyond." He laughed. "My guys wanted to wander;

that's the only reason we went as far as we did. I'd had enough of the place. I think the river moved from where it was back then, anyway. I have the old maps and building plans at my office. I'll show you if you're really interested. We can pick them up tomorrow."

"On Sunday?"

"Well, yeah, or whenever you want." He smiled. "Anyway, that was one of my more interesting jobs."

His grin abruptly changed. "I didn't like fooling around down there. Made me feel sick. Maybe it was the air or—"

"Or maybe it wasn't?"

"Right, maybe it wasn't. I couldn't shake the feeling that something real bad went on down there."

Jimmy reclined against the sofa. One leg stretched out, the other bent up where he held his glass to balance on his knee. He stared while I tried to poke life back into the smoldering logs.

"You never could leave a fire alone. You haven't changed. You still look like your yearbook picture."

"Yeah, well." I laughed. "It's more likely the sweater you recognize."

He didn't take his eyes off me. Apparently, I'd poked life into more than the embers, because it seemed he'd received a more romantic message than the one I meant to send.

Since Gram's funeral, I'd isolated myself. I was an island where only those who fit into my plan of evolution were invited. Call it independence or a wall of protection.

I had never acted puffy or flaunted family money, but it had made me not need him. Mother had discouraged our dating. No surprise. In the beginning, I saw him just to piss her off. What did any of that matter now? Damage done. Double damage.

I knew him so well I could put myself in his head. *Her skin was hot from the fire. She didn't pull away. She didn't have much to drink, knew what she was doing, and didn't pull away.* He stroked my hand with the back of his fingers. I stared at the flames. Is he in my head?

He moved behind me, pushed aside my hair and brushed his open lips up and down my neck, slowly, barely touching, the heat of his breath warming my skin. Did he fear his next movement would cross a line? That I'd push him away? I wasn't sure I would. The poker fell out of my hand. My head eased backward to rest on his shoulder. His cheek touched mine, and we melted together in the fire's heat. Was he remembering the good that once had been?

I was. Why did we split up? It was getting difficult to recall.

"We can't stay here," he whispered. He took a quilt from the sofa and threw it over Marcia, closed the fireplace screen, and offered his hand. "Come with me."

WE DROVE FORTY-FIVE MINUTES east into the country. He could have taken me home, but when this night was over, there might not be another. That's how he thought. He had to play all in. Best shot. He had to make me fall in love with him.

It was past one when we arrived at his lake house. Only the headlights of his car lit the dirt road, and when he turned them off, everything went black.

"Wait here. The path is rocky and rough." He scrambled up an incline and flipped on deck lights of the contemporary A-frame he had built. I bet he knew every inch of the land.

Moonlight shimmered on the lake's surface, a perfect view of it from inside. Jimmy lit a fire, handed me the poker, and then heated water for cocoa. We sat on the floor and snuggled.

"Is this déjà vu? The way I remember, it goes something like this." He pushed aside my hair. "I still love you, Laura, and I want you."

I caressed his face. "I know you do." Ours was not the kind of attraction you think yourself into. Our passion was raw. I pressed my hands into his thick, long hair and pulled him toward me until his lips pressed against mine. Lust battled with reason. Reason won, and I eased him away. "I can't. Sorry. I just can't."

"Laura, come on. You want to."

He couldn't even call me Del. Delito baggage. Always there. "I can't rush into this."

"What rush? It's not like we're strangers."

"We've changed so much over the years, we are strangers. Don't push me. Not now. I want time with you. I'm just not ready to—"

"Don't say any more. We'll take it slow. Just let me hold you."

"I'd like that." I slept a while in his arms. No nightmares.

Barely speaking over breakfast, I acted more like the Laura he used to know, the one who sulked and kept her mouth shut.

"Eggs that bad?"

"They're perfect." I poured our coffees.

"Is this about last night? I want you, and I think you want me, too."

"I don't know what I want."

He came around the table and took my hand. "I do, but then, I'm not a complicated guy."

"This has nothing to do with you."

"That's a relief." His grip tightened.

"Stop it," I snapped, perhaps too sharply.

My arm wrapped around his waist of its own accord, my face buried itself under his chin. He kissed the top of my head.

"What are you hiding from?"

"I think this all comes down to trust. I don't trust my mother. I sure as hell don't trust Sam. I don't trust the people closest to me at the office. I used to trust Gram and she went and died on me. The worst thing is I don't trust my own judgment."

"There must be someone." He grinned and pointed to himself.

I didn't laugh. He held me through the next moments of silence. It had taken him ten years to get back into my life, and he wasn't about to let go.

The stillness of the isolated cabin was a barricade against the rest of the world. If one chose, there was no TV, radio, or paper. No mail. No phone. Not another living soul. That other life with its problems and pains was arrested somewhere in the distance; far beyond the lake and the trees. In another time. What was real were squirrels jumping from limb to limb stashing food for winter. And clouds racing across the sky. And feeling the heartbeat of a friend against your chest.

I lay in Jimmy's lap. Hushed. He gazed out the slider. I closed my eyes.

"What are you thinking about?" He stroked my head.

"Just for a week or even a day, I need to let go, and let someone else take charge, but I can't be sure of anyone, not positively sure of anyone."

He steadied my trembling hands. "Who is?"

"I suppose you're right, but it makes me paranoid, as if I'm being watched or followed. Even when I awoke during the night, I thought I saw moonlight reflecting on the hood of a car down the road. I figured it must have been kids parking, but I'm not so sure. Could someone have followed us?"

Jimmy closed the fireplace flue and drew the drapes to close the cabin. "Come on, you need a distraction. Let's go to my office, and I'll show you those site plans I told you about."

IT WAS MID-AFTERNOON by the time we arrived at Cassella Construction, which occupied the first floor of an eight-story apartment building.

The work area was cluttered in an organized sort of way; much like Jimmy himself. Stacks of reports, blueprints, and maps littered the floor, covered the desks, and were pinned to the walls. But with little effort, he located Brookhaven's original site plan, along with the hospital blueprints from a flat-file drawer.

He rolled the plans and prepared to place them in a mailing tube. "You can borrow these copies to study."

I couldn't wait and grabbed them from his hand. Unfurling the site drawing on the floor, I anchored the corners with two tape dispensers, a steel ruler, and triangle. Slowly circling the map, I examined it from every angle like a photographer sizing up a shot.

That nagging feeling of something familiar, yet elusive, was back. Something I might have seen but had not noticed, like Elias Porter's name on the portrait plaque. An imprint on my subconscious. I tilted my head and studied the site. A pattern I vaguely recognized during my visit to the Brookhaven Center was becoming clearer.

Jimmy squatted in front of the map. "I told you last night how some of these old buildings seem to have personalities of their own. I don't know how to explain it except that when I go inside and start work, I can almost feel what it must have been like when the place was new. It hits me in my gut. I'm not talking about seeing ghosts or anything like that, but it's definitely a ..."

His words faded as the map mesmerized me.

"Alive. That's the word. They feel alive." He pointed to a building. "I remember this one most of all. My throat tightened. I couldn't swallow. Could hardly catch my breath. But only in the tunnel under that building." He rose to crack open a window. A sudden breeze carried the scent of burning wood.

My hands steadied fluttering papers. "What did you say?"

"It only happened in that tunnel." He pointed on the map.

"I didn't tell the whole truth at Marcia's when you suggested we visit the asylum. I was there last weekend."

His head snapped up from the map. "You what?"

"At Gram's wake, I met this old woman named Emma Collings, and she said something about The Farm that piqued my curiosity, so I arranged a visit. Dr. Clift, the director, showed me around and told me about the tunnels. Where on the map are they?"

His finger traced their location. "See these dashed lines here and here?"

I nodded.

"And they go out this way."

"But when I was there, the river seemed to be farther than this map illustrates."

"It is farther now but it used to be here, like the map shows."

The river. The tunnels. The cottages. The main building.

The solution to my puzzle lay before me. I was sure of it. The map was the key. I grabbed a wide-tip felt marker from a drawing board and popped off the cap. "You said this was a copy, right?"

"Yeah, go ahead."

Kneeling with marker in hand, I scribbled blocks of buildings and their connecting tunnels until they transformed to solid black shapes connected by thick black lines. A distinct and simple diagram emerged.

From my purse, I removed the small paper diagrams, the one drawn on the newspaper masthead and the drawing hidden in the antique key and compared them to my marker strokes. Even to the wavy line of the river—

They were identical!

"I'll be damned. Where'd you get these drawings? Let me see." He juxtaposed them to the site map. "Look, here's the main building and the six original cottages, but what's this X here? Think it's a location map?"

I shrugged my shoulders.

"I've been in these tunnels."

"I've got to see for myself. Will you help me?"

"Sure, I'll take you there. Next Saturday would be best, not so many suits around."

"Great, next Saturday then. You'll pick me up at High Hill?"

"Of course. But I don't understand. Why the tunnels? What do you want to go there for?"

"For something that belongs to me."

~ SIXTEEN ~

1899 • November

CLIFFORD BAINES WAS DETERMINED to be Connecticut's youngest State Treasurer, performing his job better than anyone ever had. As the junior bookkeeper, he aimed to earn a reputation and impress the right people. Following a thorough audit of state accounts, he would soon be prepared to submit his report. Baines dressed in his best worsted suit and a crisp linen pleated shirt. He combed his hair to one side and carved a straight part without flaw. He had labored for months reviewing numbers, then checked them again because he could not believe what he had discovered. How was he to convince the director?

Baines entered the office of his supervisor, the Director of Disbursements. Baines respected the man, his knowledge, and his political acuity. He had no doubt the director would soon be appointed to a position in the government's executive branch, which would present an opportunity for Baines to advance.

He felt comfortable in the director's office and knew in his gut, it would someday be his. He effortlessly imagined himself sitting behind the striped mahogany desk beneath Governor Lounsbury's portrait. A prim expression crossed his face. "Good morning, sir."

"Come in, son. I'm about to leave for the treasurer's office."

"Well, good luck, sir."

The director collected and packed paperwork into his satchel. "How are the audits progressing?"

"Excellent, sir. I'll be finished with them in plenty of time."

"Good man."

"Sir, I've found something that needs immediate attention." He plucked a two-page summary from his report and passed it to the director, then took a seat across the desk.

Baines had invested much time and effort into an audit that should have been routine. If he was right, he would become the hero, but if his work was flawed, he would be the fool. He felt so anxious he chewed on the rubber stem of his Meerschaum pipe as the director reviewed the summary without expression. Surely a man of his experience had seen more shocking accounts. The director handed the report back to Baines and tilted his head as if to say he was not yet convinced. Baines suspected he was also considering the "hero or fool" outcome. He cradled the papers in his arms. "The numbers don't lie, sir."

"Are you suggesting the director of the most renowned asylum in the country perpetrates a fraud against the State?"

Baines stood and stabbed a pointed finger at the bottom line, nearly spilling his papers. "Yes, I am."

"You have my ear."

"If Brookhaven is so highly respected to attract any number of wealthy patients to fill their beds, why are they so agreeable to receive our indigent referrals at minimum financial allotment?"

The director scratched his chin. "It does seem against logic. You checked the figures?"

"I'm confident of my claim and stake my reputation."

"And the reputation of this office?"

Baines replied without hesitation. "I do, sir."

The director shook his head affirmatively. "We need proof."

"Then let me find it, sir. I know I am correct."

"Very well. Proceed with an inquiry, but be careful, son."

Baines enthusiastically shook his hand. "Yes, sir." He grinned and rushed from the office.

That afternoon Clifford Baines enlisted James McPhearson, a young inspector with the State Board of Health, and together they entered the grounds of the Brookhaven Farm Lunatic Asylum. Heinz met them at the main door.

McPhearson announced, "Routine state inspection, Mr. Brudolf."

"We're not due for six months," said Heinz.

Baines skirted around McPhearson and stepped forward. "Are you denying our entry?"

Dr. Jameson emerged from his office and introduced himself. "Gentlemen, what goes on here?"

"These men claim to be with the State Treasury and the Board of Health," Heinz said.

Baines crossed the asylum's threshold and addressed Dr. Jameson. "We are with the State."

McPhearson displayed bona fides.

Dr. Jameson adjusted his spectacles and nodded as he verified credentials.

McPhearson retrieved their documents, and he and Baines began a systematic probe of the hospital. They entered the day room where a matron and several inmates gathered, then they hurriedly looked into the empty dining room. They counted and noted the number of wards and beds and opened wardrobes to confirm the number of patients judged by personal belongings.

Baines totaled his figures and said to McPhearson, "I estimate eighty-five to ninety patients. They claim one hundred and twenty-two. Of their total, we pay for thirty-three."

They returned to Jameson's office where the doctor and Heinz waited. Baines interrupted their conversation. "We need to review your patient registry."

Jameson barked, "Out of the question. You have no authority."

McPhearson answered, "We are merely seeking an accurate count of the patients being housed. Cooperation works to your best interest."

Jameson puffed his chest. "This is the Brookhaven Asylum. We hold information in strictest confidence. Our patients belong to the most important families in the Northeast. I cannot allow this intrusion of privacy."

"I understand perfectly," Baines said.

McPhearson remained where he stood until Baines took his

arm, urging him to leave. As they exited the building and the hospital grounds, McPhearson asked, "Is this where our investigation ends."

"No." Baines smirked. "This is where it begins."

HEINZ'S LIVING CHAMBER was located in the rear of the main building at ground level and though the river was near, grassy hills obscured its view. One northeast window lit the room, but by dusk, the meager space was cast in gloom.

He paced about, glancing toward the river, while he considered this new complication with state inspectors. He suspected he'd not seen the last of Baines and McPhearson. Their surprise visit stunned him into realizing how complaisant he had become. Evidence against him stuffed his cluttered closet. Bureau drawers and shelves spilled with spoils pilfered from inventory and inmates—watches, leather bags and belts, gold and silver jewelry. Cash. His fingers combed through his thin hair as he mumbled foul words.

Heinz first gathered a meager amount of paper money and wrapped it in newspaper. The finest dresses, silks, and fur boas could be safely stashed in the morning. He spread a sheet across the bed, piled on the remaining loot, and tied the sheet's four corners to form a sack.

How careless he had been to retain crucial paper records. Waybills of shipments with incriminating dates coincided with patient relocation and records documenting his partnership with Elias Porter. He formed them into a tight pack, stuffed it into the sheet, and slung the sack over his shoulder.

Heinz carried the sack to the fire pit, dowsed it with kerosene, and set it ablaze.

He circled the building to enter through the main doors, waved to Dr. Jameson in his office, crossed paths with Matron who was escorting an inmate from the day room, and continued down the hall to the kitchen to verify the staff had left. Back past the foyer and down the south hall he paused at Maggie's door. The nosy little gnat seemed to be asleep.

In his chamber with a writing board, Heinz scribbled treatment reports for patients who were no longer there, forging the signature of Matron Smythe. The false reports sat on a bookshelf until the morrow. His nightshirt absorbed his skin's cold sweat, and he lay down to sleep for there was much to remedy at first light.

MAGGIE STOOD AT HER CHAMBER WINDOW to view the sky and identify constellations for her studies as she did each night before sleep. Movement caught her attention. The shadowy figure appeared to be that of St. Nick burning his sack in the fire pit. After first glimpse, she recognized the man was Heinz and wondered what filled his load. He tossed it in the pit, poured kerosene, and lit it. He disappeared into the dark and when she was certain he was gone, she eased open the window sash and climbed outside to investigate.

Tiny embers flew like fireflies as they drifted in an evening breeze. Fire warmed her face as she neared. A white cotton sheet, like those on her bed, burned to ash. Flames licked at a tightly drawn pack of papers. Maggie pushed up the sleeves of her nightdress and reached into the pit, snatching the documents just as the blaze scorched the edges.

She stomped all trace of heat from the charred papers then hurried back through her window and into bed, pinching the covers to her chin, the documents safely clutched in her hand beneath the sheets. Footsteps in the hall approached then paused outside her door. It had to be Heinz. *Will he pull away the bed linens and retrieve his papers?* Her heart pounded as she feigned sleep.

Footsteps continued down the hall until they faded. Maggie exhaled a breath of relief and whispered prayers of thanks. She drifted into sleep thinking of all she must accomplish at first light.

Maggie awoke like every other day except for a smoky memory that lingered like a dream, but the documents under her covers proved it to be fact. The papers had to be important if Heinz meant to destroy them in secret, but their content would have to wait. *Mustn't change my routine.* She wrapped them in a shawl and hid them in her chest at the bottom of the closet. Washed and dressed, she ran to the dining area.

"Good morning, Miss Cookie."

"What's put yur horse to gallop?"

The kitchen ladies roared. "Feed 'er an apple. Tie 'er to a buggy, we'll go for a ride."

"I have much to do this morning." Maggie smeared a dollop of soft butter and bit into a heel of bread just out of the oven. "You're the best cook in the whole world. I'd love to chat, but I must scurry." She waved goodbye, grabbed an apple, and winked at the ladies as she rushed out to their laughter.

Matron's room was vacant when Maggie returned to her ward. With Matron supervising inmates washing and dressing, Maggie had the opportunity to be alone. She pulled her jewelry chest from the closet and shoved it against the front wall where she could not be seen by anyone who passed. The unwrapped rescued papers released the pungent odor of smoke and fire.

The documents were quite ordinary, but two dates held importance—the day she was admitted, and the day she witnessed the argument between Heinz and Elias Porter. On both days, she had seen new inmates arrive, only to disappear. And on both days, the barge had delivered provisions. The papers fell from her hands and scattered on the floor. This meant something, but perhaps a thing she best not know.

She quickly wrapped the stack and shoved it back into her chest. No one knew of these. Heinz believed they were burned. The chest would remain stored on the closet floor for now.

HEINZ DIDN'T HAVE MUCH TIME before the inmates would march outside to their day chores. He raced to the barn, straight to a dark corner cluttered with rusty gadgets and the remains of an old chicken coop. Tools cast aside, he dug into the dirt with a pitchfork until it scraped the top of the wooden box that hid his important stash, his share of cash from business with Elias Porter. He removed hefty bundles of paper money and stuffed them into his trouser pockets. The empty box reburied, he scattered the old tools and chicken wire on top until the area appeared undisturbed.

Just as he exited, the milk girl from the city appeared at the door, but stopped abruptly.

He glared at her. "Chores?"

The girl backed away.

A distant voice called, "Emma."

Maggie was running over the hills toward the barn. He goggled the milk girl. "Go on, git to your tasks." The girl didn't move. "Scat!"

Heinz lumbered toward the asylum looking back once to see the girls enter the barn.

MAGGIE CRIED JOYFUL TEARS and wrapped her arms around the friend she had not seen for a month. "I missed you so much, Emma. I tried to do your chores while you were gone."

"And I missed you."

"Is your mum feeling better?"

"A bit better today. I think she will recover. I pray she will."

"I'm so sorry she lost the baby. It was a black day when we learned of his death. Cookie told me, but I had no way to help you or your mum. I worried I would never see you again."

The girls kept hold at arm's length, talking eye to eye.

"The baby was a boy. Did you hear?"

"Yes, and you so much wanted a brother." They cried together.

"I feared I would lose my mum, too. She near bled to death." Maggie pulled Emma close and let her friend sob on her shoulder while she stroked her head.

"I know, Emma. But every day your mum grows stronger, and I'm here, and we'll always be friends—like sisters."

"Sisters. We are that." Emma's lips turned a limp smile as she wiped her eyes and nose with the sleeves of her dress. "Come, let's get our chores done."

"What did Heinz say to you?"

"He told me to get on with the milking."

"Nothing more? What was he doing when you arrived?"

"I cannot say. He was halfway out the door."

Maggie moved around the barn as deliberately as a stalking cat. Cows stood in their proper stalls, and milk stools and pails remained precisely where she had left them the previous day. The ladder rested against the loft where it belonged, and a net of spider webs remained unbroken. In a corner, the pile of old tools and the broken chicken coop appeared unchanged. She raised her forefinger and tapped her chin. "What was he doing? Maybe he waited for you, or me, to be here alone. What is he up to?"

"Can't say."

"He would not have been waiting for both of us. He can't hurt us together. We must stay together, Emma." She adjusted the milk pail and resumed milking. "It's the only way to be safe."

HEINZ WENT ABOUT HIS WORK, though more deftly than usual. When Dr. Jameson departed for supper in the city, and the inmates and nurses were busy out of the building, he entered the doctor's office, locked the door, and drew the shade. From his waistcoat, he pulled the patient treatment reports he had created the night before and merged them with those of the doctor.

His work was not complete.

During supper when Matron and the nurses tended the dining area, he entered Matron's chamber using his master key to unlock her door. He reached into his trouser pocket and grasped the wad of cash wrapped in newspaper and hid it in the rear of a dresser drawer. Atop her dresser, he arranged a shawl, a brooch, and a purse from a former patient, and covered them with several of Matron's personal items. Heinz grinned. Even if state investigators *did* return, they would find nothing to incriminate him.

MEANWHILE, AT THE STATE OFFICE BUILDING, Baines and McPhearson worked through the night to build their case. Clerks hurried to assemble the names of all the indigents, referred and paid for, over the past ten years. Baines' efficient bookkeeping quickly wrought detailed results—names, ages, and dates of internment, physical descriptions, summaries of symptoms, inventories of personal items, and next of kin. Supported by these facts, Baines, McPhearson, and a small army of investigators from the office of police prepared for their return to the asylum.

~ SEVENTEEN ~

1974 • November

MONDAY CAME TOO SOON. I gazed out my office window in a daydream as I swooned over my weekend with Jimmy. Did he linger in my mind because he showed genuine interest in exploring Brookhaven, or because we shared deeper feelings? No matter, I'd exploit the opportunity.

Someone grabbed my shoulder. I jolted. "God, you startled me."

"What makes you so nervous?" Michael said. "Rough night?"

I resented his sarcastic innuendo. "I don't like it when you sneak up on me."

"I knocked, but apparently you didn't hear. Never mind. We have work to do. Let's get started."

Had I forgotten something urgent? I glanced at the appointment book on my desk. "There's nothing on my calendar."

He glimpsed the book, shook his head, and flipped a handful of pages.

"You're looking at the wrong week. What's with you lately?"

"Oh, please."

"Last Thursday you left for lunch and didn't come back. We look like amateurs to our clients when reception routes calls to your office and Vinny isn't aware you're gone. And where were you the other night? Don't bother, I know. You were here at 3:00 a.m. taking a portrait for a ride around the factory."

"Not now, Michael."

"I tried to reach you over the weekend. Is there something going on I should know?"

"Nothing you should know."

"Talk to me, please. Don't shut me out, Del. I want to help."

"There's nothing to do."

"We have a lot to accomplish over the next few days so let's begin. You may think I'm exaggerating, but Delito's future depends on decisions you make this week."

I ignored him and returned to the window.

"Del!"

"Stop." He could be so annoying.

"If you don't sign off on next year's media buy, we could lose our discount. It might already be too late. You said you'd decide if we'll retain the ad agency, and there are other contracts pending. If we're changing agencies, we should begin the process; it could take months to review presentations. Clients expect disruption after the death of a principal, but honestly Del, they've been patient long enough."

I took a deep breath. "You be patient. You know what our long range plans are. You decide about the media schedule and the ad agency. You decide about everything."

"Good. Fine." He left the office.

"Fine," I snapped as I followed.

A call came in as I passed Vinny's desk. He answered and passed the receiver. "He won't say who he is."

"I'll take it in my office."

"Laura Delito." I immediately recognized the voice of Brian Walsh, an old friend and first employer from Woburn & Walsh Advertising in Hartford.

"Hey, Del, I need to see you."

"Later this week?"

"Can't wait. Our favorite diner on the Silas Deane Highway is half way. Any chance you can meet me in an hour?"

I looked around as if seeking guidance from above, but no one was talking. "Ah, yeah, sure. I'll be there."

AS I DROVE NORTH on the interstate toward the Silas Deane exit, all I thought of was Michael. Our arguments ate at my heart. Part of me was so crazy about him, or at least the man he used to be. He'd been different since Gram died. The new Michael was a stranger to me. His actions were unpredictable. I didn't think it was me that changed, I really didn't.

I was fully aware of the responsibility I'd entrusted to him. My action would have been the same if I had absolute trust in him, which is what I wanted him to believe. And then there was Sam. Before he rose to power, he had served as Delito's Account Supervisor with close ties to the ad agency.

The budget proposal from the New York office was—well—crazy. Woburn & Walsh had agreed to price identical media buys for comparison, but from the sound of Brian's voice and the urgency of our meeting, I guessed the news wasn't good.

Our ad agency's proposal made no sense, and Vinny's notes confused me even more, though I wouldn't admit it. Their fees were excessive, but retaining them had been Sam's decision and maybe they were worth the cost. Was he getting kickbacks? I didn't dare confront him. Was Michael? That would be a stupid move and Michael was not stupid.

There was no decision Michael could make that I couldn't undo, for a price, and this was the only way to know if I could trust him. Our on-again, off-again romance would stop when I forced the truth, and because personal and business relationships had become inseparable, I had to accept that all of it might end—and that would break my heart. My chest felt like the fracture had begun. I took a breath. This whole thing with Michael and Sam had to be resolved, come hell or high water. *Where's my life jacket?*

I pulled into the diner parking lot as Brian arrived.

"Like old times," he said as we hugged.

"I miss this place. It's so ..."

"50s?"

"That too, but I was thinking *uncomplicated.*"

I held his hand and studied his face. "I miss you. How is everyone at the shop?"

He led us to a quiet booth and ordered two coffees. "Very well. I'll tell them you asked."

"What's so urgent?" I nervously smiled. But he didn't. "Brian, you're scaring me."

"You *should* be scared." He pulled papers from his inside jacket pocket. "This is bad." He unfolded the notes and spread them to face me.

The waitress brought a carafe of coffee, mugs, and a small plate of pastries.

He said, "When you came in last week, honestly I thought, hey great, with a slight reduction, we might have a shot at some of your business. So I had my media buyer run the schedule you gave me and this is the number we came up with." He pointed to the total on one of the papers.

"Wow. How much of this did you cut?"

"None. That's the problem. This is the maximum you should be paying with no agency or publication discounts. No one your size pays premium."

I stared at the number, then at him. "And what did the New York agency charge me?"

He pointed to another sheet, and I gasped. "That's almost $200,000! And the schedule I gave you was for half the year. Can you even imagine how many coat pins I have to sell to break even on 200K?"

"Too many. Del, I'm sorry. I'm sure this isn't what you were hoping for."

"As bad as it is, this answers a lot of questions. You have to define the problem before you can fix it, right?"

"Any idea who would do this to you?"

"I'm afraid my suspicions are tainted with personal history."

"We can put together a comparable plan for half of what you're paying. If we can help, we'd love to work with you."

I nodded in agreement. "I have something special in mind for you, but I've got to get out of this mess first. Give me a couple of weeks, and we'll talk. I promise."

"Del, be careful."

"I will."

"No, I mean it. Whoever is involved won't be happy to be exposed. When this much money is at stake, people get desperate. It could turn dangerous."

I shook his hand and held it. "I won't forget you helped me out of a jam."

Brian headed toward Hartford, and I drove back to the plant shocked by what I had learned. With Michael taking charge of our contracts, I wondered—What the hell do I do now?

PRESSURE IN MY CHEST choked me. My stomach churned in a wrenching knot. Maybe Delito, Inc. had been suckered into paying a premium for media and marketing, but I wasn't sure any law had been broken. With briefcase in hand, I left my office and headed down the hall.

"Del?" Vinny called after me.

I hesitated, but kept walking. "I'm going downstairs. Take messages." Maybe he'd assume the design department was my destination. The ruse was intentional. No interruptions. No problems.

Vinny and I had moved the steamer trunk to the storeroom office where I settled in and spread a paper stack from my briefcase. After reviewing notes from letters, newspaper clippings, and photographs, I tackled the daunting organization of decades of information.

Most documents fit into categories that I labeled with name cards—Antonio/Personal, Antonio/Personal-related, Salvatore/Margaret, Delito/Business, Delito/Business-related, Asylum.

Three notable facts stood out. Without exception, Antonio referred to his daughter as Margaret or Maggie, never Rosa. Second, it was impossible to separate Antonio from his business and Porter's name kept popping up to confuse things. And lastly, I had way too many piles.

My second attempt at order reduced six stacks to four. I leaned against the chair and considered key players—Antonio Delito, children Salvatore and Margaret, partner Elias Porter, and finally, the Brookhaven Asylum, even though it remained an empty space on my desk with only a name card.

Great-grandfather Antonio Delito and his first wife had emigrated in 1882, paying passage with dowry money. Salvatore was born in America, his mother died four years later.

Antonio married Carlotta Ferraro and soon after, daughter Margaret was born.

He often traveled to Europe and around the Mediterranean seeking unique items to manufacture in his factory. Records confirmed he would most often sail from New York harbor on ships owned by Elias Porter, to ports in Spain, Italy, Turkey, Egypt, and Morocco. He and Porter seemed to be a compatible business match, though I found no photographs of them together, and nothing indicated they had been friends. Antonio was well-liked and respected by his contemporaries. But, Porter....

During Antonio and Grandfather Salvatore's first voyage, Margaret suddenly died.

What! That can't be. If she died, I had wrongly assumed Rosa and Maggie were one and the same. Could they be two different people? There was no record of Maggie's death, but I did discover a dated receipt for the purchase of her grave marker, which I figured would have put her at age twelve. Was Gram not Salvatore's sister or his wife? Was she married at all? Did she bear a child, my dad, out of wedlock? The biggest mystery was that all birth and death records were missing. This was getting too complicated, and I couldn't get sloppy with the facts. *Slow down.*

A thorough search produced nothing about Antonio's second wife as if someone had removed selective histories. But who would do that? And why? Salvatore and Margaret were brother and sister. Weren't they? Could Rosa have been a second sister? By which mother? It was possible, but too fantastic to be believed. And if so, who were my grandparents? And who was Maggie? Everything I knew, or thought I knew, about my family was a deception. *Who the hell was I?* I was never so confused and angry with Gram as I was at this moment—angry that she died and left this mess.

Among the newspaper announcements, an advertisement surprised me. The headline read:

PORTER CARGO TRANSPORT CO.

TRANSATLANTIC TO EUROPEAN AND MEDITERRANEAN PORTS.

AMERICAN EAST COASTAL, CANAL AND RIVER DESTINATIONS.

Cargo transport to river destinations. Now *that* was interesting. And it made sense that once Porter expanded overseas trade to include shipments up and down the East Coast, he'd have the transport business locked. His barges likely carried fruit and raw cotton from the South to cities and mills in the North, and Pennsylvania coal to colder locations in New England.

I'd have to investigate this new twist because river transport had to lead to the asylum—*it had to*—yet, there was no record of a single shipment to the asylum by Elias Porter.

"Del, do you want some help with that?"

The sudden interruption startled and annoyed me. "Vinny. What are you doing here?"

"You're late for a meeting in the design department." He tapped his fingers on the table as he studied my papers. "They've been calling."

I shoved the papers and notes in my case. "Who's been calling?"

"Henri, ah, then that junior designer." His gaze darted around the office and the trunks.

"What the hell is wrong with you?"

He glared at me. "Nothing is wrong. What do you mean?"

"You've been acting weird. Fidgety. I don't know … just get it together."

We left the storeroom and headed up. I exited the elevator at the main floor and turned to Vinny. "I need you to be sharp."

I think he nodded in agreement, but the doors closed too fast to be sure.

THE DESIGN MEETING lasted just short of an hour, and when I returned to the second floor offices, my head was still reeling with questions about my family's personal history, and lack of it, and I remembered Marcia's earlier warning I may not want to turn on the lights in all my closets.

Though the trunk contained complete and careful documentation, not one paper mentioned the asylum. Why all the damn secrecy? What a stupid waste of time and effort.

I grabbed my mail from Vinny's desk. A small package postmarked Morocco was set conspicuously on top of the pile—the package promised by Hassan. I tore open the tightly sealed parcel to reveal gifts and souvenirs Antonio Delito had once given to his Moroccan friends. Painstaking care over the years had preserved the mementos, each pristine item now a valuable antique.

Especially precious to me were the early pieces manufactured during Delito's infancy—a nickel and silver lip salve and powder box, several enamel and silver brooches, a leather money purse and four shell hair combs. I shivered when I saw a gold-plated hand mirror and hairbrush, identical to the one Gram had in the hospital the night of her death.

Black velvet wrapped a Florentine silver frame like the mirror frame in Gram's kitchen—this one held a photograph of what looked like a desert oasis. Several men and boys, dressed in djellabas, posed on flat sand against a backdrop of dusty palm trees and distant minarets. Antonio Delito stood in their midst.

Even in window light, it was difficult to identify the object cradled in his hands, so I rushed back to the design department. A light box used for viewing product transparencies emitted the brightest light in the building, and a jeweler's loupe magnified the object Antonio proudly held. "Henri. Come quick."

He focused the glass and after cautious consideration, turned to me. I twirled the old key from Emma Collings—the key that inspired my search into the past.

After a long hesitation, he said, "The image is small. It is difficult to be sure."

"Is it the chest?" I demanded.

"It is possible."

~ EIGHTEEN ~

1899 • December

THE BEGINNINGS of several intriguing mysteries in Maggie's journal begged investigation. The tunnels with the secret room and the missing patients were most alarming. She had compiled a list of nearly a dozen names, some she knew, and some were merely whispered in tales.

Rumors of a state investigation rippled through the asylum, and everyone sensed a time of great change. Strict order and discipline soon ruled. Schedules followed precisely. Procedures executed to perfection. Patients were deprived of privileges. Hospital workers were forbidden to sit, read, or write while on any post of duty. The staff was troubled, the nurses brash, and the patients agitated. Something profound was bound to happen—and soon.

The double doors of the asylum slammed open. The crashing noise startled Maggie. She slipped into the day room just inside its doors where she could listen and observe without being discovered. Two police officers remained stationed at the main entrance while six others filed through. Police dispersed down the south and west hallways that intersected at Dr. Jameson's office. One officer sauntered toward the day room, turning his gaze from side to side as he passed closed doors, knocking with his fist, and checking the locks. He nearly reached the day room before he halted. She pressed into the shadows as she assessed the officer. He wore a bell-shaped hat with a slight brim and a handsome, taut uniform of navy wool. A revolver, a club, and a twister of wood and cat gut were fixed to his belt. He stood firm and fierce, his gaze directed down the hall as he stood guard.

The head constable, James McPhearson, an inspector from the Connecticut Board of Health, and Clifford Baines, the state bookkeeper, presented identification and served papers to Dr. Jameson as they confiscated his patient records.

The constable said, "We insist on seeing the following patients —Geraldine Cassidy, Victoria Kirby, Mrs. Caroline White…."

Thirty more names were called, some entrusted as long as seven years ago. Two young women admitted last month were Eleanor Grist and Catherine Lerner, Maggie recalled seeing them, though their names had been unknown to her until now.

Heinz rushed from the dining area toward the commotion outside Jameson's office. He flew past the spot where Maggie hid, but when the officer blocked his way, he called to the constable, "None of those patients are available."

The constable waved Heinz closer and the officer released him.

Baines pushed his way to the front of the group. "Not one? Where in hell are they?"

The constable shouted orders to search every room. They began in the director's office.

Maggie clasped her mouth and nose to prevent her breaths from being heard. The officer near her, along with two others, aimed toward the rear rooms and charged into the dining hall. Maggie followed them and quickly merged with an assembly of patients.

An officer grabbed Matron's arm. The color of her cheeks paled to match her white apron. Patients stared up from their meals; some cried, some crawled under tables or gathered in small groups clutching each other.

Maggie feared for Old Annie who trembled in her seat. A stream of urine formed a puddle beneath her bench. Maggie patted Annie's hand, pretending she was not aware of the old woman's accident.

"It will all be made right, Annie. I'm leaving you now to see what happens."

Annie held tight to her sleeve, but Maggie pulled away. She followed Matron, Heinz, and the police down the corridor—far enough behind, she hoped, that they would not notice her. She crept into her ward across from Matron's quarters and settled under her bed where she hid to watch the search of Matron's chamber.

The police rifled through stacks of papers, then emptied Matron's shelves and drawers and hurled her belongings on the bed. She stood silent with Heinz beside her while police inspected each item and flung it aside. An officer tore open a small package wrapped in newspaper. A wad of paper money fluttered to the bed. Matron appeared bewildered. Maggie had often seen her anxious, even fearful because of Heinz, but she had never seen Matron as frightened as she was now.

"What is this?" Baines waved the money in her face.

The constable pointed at Heinz. "Take him away." An officer hauled him from the room.

With Heinz gone, Matron matched eyes to eyes with Mr. Baines. "I swear by God's wrath I've never laid me eyes on it."

Several items roused the attention of Clifford Baines—a brooch, purse, and a shawl that matched the purple chiffon-taffeta dress that Matron had given to Annie. He held them longer with more thorough inspection than other items while repeatedly referring to his list. "This property belongs to Geraldine Cassidy. Her sister described it to me." He clenched the shawl and said to the constable, "Take the matron to jail."

An officer restrained her with his twister and the constable bellowed, "Put her in shackles."

Maggie gasped and squirmed deeper under the bed while police stood outside her door. Heinz whispered to Matron as she was dragged past him toward the transport wagon.

What shall I do? Maggie shivered because she also possessed a piece of that purple chiffon-taffeta, the ruffle Annie had torn from the dress. *Will I, too, be accused? Will they take me to jail with Matron? I didn't harm Miss Cassidy. I didn't steal.* And she thought it incredible that Matron had.

Maggie followed as Baines and McPhearson positioned themselves outside the dining hall where every patient had been gathered. Heinz identified each by name as they exited to return to their chambers. Baines crossed off names from both his list and the asylum's registry. When Heinz explained some patients may be off the grounds, in town with an orderly, or visiting family, Baines eliminated asylum names because the state had no financial interest in them.

The false name of Margaret Porter from Providence, and her absence, went unnoticed. The state had no interest in her.

THE ASYLUM had become more strange and unpredictable than the day Maggie arrived. Patients vanished. Matron jailed. And of late, Heinz became more fiendish, more devious, and more desperate. Too much had changed too fast, but one thing was certain. Maggie needed to move her journal to a more secure hiding place, to preserve the documents she had rescued from the fire pit—and she needed to protect herself.

She secured her journal pages with red cord trim and wrapped them with the purple chiffon-taffeta ruffle from Miss Cassidy's dress. A light silk scarf bound the charred documents. Her coins, combs, and dancing doll were all safe. She kept favorite poems, scraps of paper, and a bottle of ink, then collected candles and a box of wooden matches she had borrowed from the kitchen and hidden in the drawer of her night table.

In the chaos, Maggie scatted down the hall and down to the tunnels, hugging her jewelry box to her chest as she searched for a spot to conceal it.

In the main tunnel, what once might have been a small storage closet was nearly closed off except for a crevice between a vertical wooden beam and a boulder. Wider on top, the opening narrowed near the floor.

Balanced on a nearby crate, her candle lit behind the wall. The small open space was just a few feet deep with a stone floor. Perfect.

She gripped the chest, stretched her arm through the crevice, and squeezed to the floor, gently setting the box on the bottom stone. With the box safely hidden, she found an equally secret hiding place for herself where she crouched in the dark, listening to the ruckus above—footsteps, chattering, police and investigators shouting orders, patients whining and crying.

She held her breath waiting for them to find her—*hoping* they would find her.

~ NINETEEN ~

1974 • November

A GRAY VAN lettered with CASSELLA CONSTRUCTION & RESTORATION turned onto the grounds of the Delito estate. A week had passed since Jimmy and I matched Gram's newspaper diagram to Brookhaven's site map, and he was taking me to the tunnels as promised.

"Hey, the place looks great. It's been years. I always loved this High Hill house. You've changed it some." Before I knew it, I was in his arms being kissed.

He'd drifted in and out of my thoughts all week, more so when Michael ticked me off, and part of me wanted to cancel Brookhaven and discover where passion might take us. But I couldn't cheat on Michael even though technically I wouldn't be guilty. I nudged him away.

He unzipped a tote bag. "This should fit." Navy overalls with straps matched the uniform coverall he wore. Yellow thread on a front pocket spelled CASSELLA CONSTRUCTION.

"Nice touch." I rushed upstairs returning moments later. Sleeves furled to my elbows, rolled cuffs and bright yellow socks. "So, where's my hard hat?"

"On the front seat." He pointed to the van.

"I was kidding."

"I'm not. You'll need it to hide your hair, and it might save your head. Ready?"

I grabbed my copies of the maps and packed them into the tote along with a small purse. "Ready." I slipped on a down vest.

"Are you confident they'll let us in?"

"When Brookhaven hired me, I included an inspection clause in the contract. Couple times a year, I check adjoining structures and advise on repairs. I confirmed this appointment a few days ago. Told them I'd be checking several tunnels."

JIMMY DROVE THE VAN along the tree-lined drive and stopped at the guardhouse gate. "Mornin' Danny."

A young attendant in a burgundy wool blazer leaned out of a sliding window. "Hey, Mr. C." He rubbed his hands. "Gettin' nippy out here. Time for our checkup?"

"Thought I'd finish underground before the freeze."

"Under all that muscle you're a weather wimp?" He bent lower, checking inside the van. "I see you got company."

Twisting my head toward the passenger window concealed my face from his line of sight.

"Training a new kid." Jimmy waved and drove off, veering from the main entrance to a service road and the rear of the complex.

"A new kid?"

"I know Danny. He remembers every guy on my crew." Jimmy gently squeezed my knee. "I don't want him remembering you."

Parked at a narrow, unmarked door at the back of the building, he opened the van's rear doors while I studied the landscape. "Beautiful view from here. Wow, huge fire pit. I wouldn't mind having one at High Hill."

"I happen to know an excellent contractor who can help with that." He grabbed a small pick axe, a crowbar, and two flashlights and handed one to me. "Grab your bag, Toto. We're off to see the wizard."

Warped and stuck shut, the old door finally opened after several hardy yanks. A musty smell escaped. I flipped a nearby light switch, but nothing happened. Stone grades, moist and slick, descended below ground level. We turned on flashlights and Jimmy led the way through the first small room. Barely wider than a hallway, it ended at an arched doorway.

"Great stone work." He ran his hand over the surface and poked the mortar with the awl.

Iron hinges and a thumb latch handle adorned the wooden door that was crafted like those in the old section of Delito's factory basement. My hard hat bumped the wall. I shifted it back in place.

Our passageway split in three directions. I checked the site plan and shrugged. "I don't know where we are. From my visit a few weeks ago, I remember the director's office was located left of the main entrance. Can you get us to the main hallway?"

He pointed ahead. "Follow me, but be careful. And don't touch anything."

All this time. The questions, the wondering, the searching. At last, it was real. Clues were beginning to fit. The irony was, that after the sleepless nights plagued by nightmares, the days of delusion and paranoia, the first time I was not feeling crazed was inside an asylum.

We reached the front wall shown on Gram's drawing. Wide steps worn to a shine curved in the middle and slanted downward at least ten degrees. Beyond the blackness, I sensed history. If I was alone, and could concentrate, I might walk into yesterday as easily as taking the next step. Small mounds of coal remained as evidence of a functional past. Muffled voices on the first floor demonstrated that people were near, perhaps mere feet away. I imagined their voices fading, replaced by the busy chatter of kitchen or maintenance staff scurrying through tunnels like worker ants. Housekeepers gowned in aprons and bonnets. Groundsmen covered in...

Jimmy tapped his flashlight against my hardhat. "You with me?" The beam fanned to mark our choices. "Which way?"

I navigated with Jimmy in front, brushing away dusty cobwebs.

"This is exciting." When our path intersected another tunnel, I nudged from behind and took the lead. "Turn right." Groping along the wall, stepping over shards of wood and rocks, my foot slid into a curved ditch. Cold, damp, and slippery. I lost balance.

"Whoa, what was that?"

He caught my arm. "Careful."

"I'm good."

Our beams traced the gutter until it vanished into a far room where a strong, heavy door hung precariously on a single rusted hinge. We peered in. Shelves stored haphazard piles of rags and tools. Ropes and chains spilled from drawers. Pieces of broken furniture littered the floor. Several tables and chairs with wide leather straps dominated the space. *What went on in that room?* I couldn't imagine.

Jimmy crumpled against the wall like a deflating balloon, his head drooping toward his knees. "Let's get what we came for and get the hell outta here."

"What's wrong?"

"I can't breathe. It feels dead in here."

"Yes, let's go on."

We reached the intersection marked on my diagram by an X. "This is it." I flapped the map.

"Yup. Looks like this is the place. Right here." He compared Gram's drawing to the site map and stomped the heel of his work boot against the floor. "Feels solid. Nothing unusual."

We felt the wall for loose stone and picked at its joints. After testing it to be secure, Jimmy forced his arm into a crevice between a vertical wooden beam and a boulder, and panned his light inside. "There's an open space behind this wall."

"Can you see anything?" I searched for something to stand on, but only splintered slats of an old crate littered the area, so I stretched on my tiptoes straining to peek. "I feel like Howard Carter."

"Who?"

"The English archaeologist who discovered …. Never mind."

"Well, the space goes back only a few feet. Maybe eight feet across." He checked the tunnel ceiling and pounded the old beam with his fist. "They must have doubled the wall here for more support."

"What's in there?"

"Nothing. But most of the floor is outside my sight line."

"Give me a boost. My head can fit through the wider opening up top." I stepped onto his cupped hands and steadied myself against the wall until he raised me high enough to see. With my right arm swung over my head, my beam aimed at the floor in a wiggling movement as he compensated for my swaying. "There's something down there!"

"What is it?"

"I'm not sure. A small box. About a foot wide. Ick."

"What's wrong?"

"A shriveled rat. I've seen enough." I stepped off his hands.

"I'll try to reach the box." He secured his footing then forced his arm into the fissure, grunting as he pressed harder into the slim opening.

Eager and impatient, I nervously tapped my light against my leg. "Can you reach it?"

Jimmy bent his knees and felt deeper into the space, squeezing his arm into the crack where it narrowed near the floor. "Not yet, but it's at the tip of my fingers."

My legs trembled from excitement or cold.

"Yeah, I feel something. I think it's wood. Can't quite reach it." His moans dropped to a baritone pitch as he stretched.

"Let me try," I insisted.

He eased out his arm and massaged where it had been pinched.

My bulky vest offered comfortable padding but cost the inch or two I might need, so I stripped it off and handed it to Jimmy, rolled up my shirt sleeve and stretched my bare arm into the rift. "I'm not thrilled about this part. You didn't feel any live rats, did you?" My fingers were my eyes, defining the shape of the object. "Rectangular box. Carved wood. Metal hardware. Hinges. Keyhole." I accidentally pushed it farther away. Something that had rested against the box clanked to the floor. I patted the area to locate it, catching a dirty substance under my fingernails. A handle and a corroded blade, it felt like a knife. I slid it toward the crevice to retrieve later. My hard hat crunched against the wall and spewed stone grit past my face. With my eyes tightly closed, my head jerked to avoid the raining granules, but its sudden movement dislodged even more debris. "Didn't you bring a sledge hammer?" Dirt spilled onto my open lips.

"To break down the wall?" He chuckled. "Forget it."

"Get this silly hat off me." My head tipped backward as he removed it.

"Oh, yuk." I spit out dirt and wiped my mouth on my sleeve. "That's better." The crevice seemed a living thing, devouring my limb deeper into its dark self. The narrowing crack pinched the tender skin under my arm until I had a firm hold of the box. "I have it!"

"Don't drop it."

I rose cautiously, gripping the box tighter than was necessary, then freed my arm and my treasure at the wider opening. "Wow, look at this. We did it. I can't believe it's in my hands."

Jimmy took the chest and stuffed it into the tote bag. "Let's go."

I slipped into my vest and followed him to the exit. "Wait. Wait. The knife." I ran back and grabbed it from behind the wall. "Whoa. This is no kitchen knife. It's a dagger." I bounced it several times. "Heavy. Looks like it's been there as long as the box." Jimmy slid it into the tote. I grabbed him by his coveralls, pulled him against me, and planted a hard kiss on his lips. "Thank you. I couldn't have done this without you."

We loaded the van and drove toward his lake house. For miles, I checked the rear view mirror expecting to see police cars in pursuit.

"Aren't you going to open that thing?"

Picking at the dirt under my nails, it looked and felt like candle wax. "I can wait another half hour." Opening it now would be like sloppy sex in the back seat of a car.

My excitement piqued. The box I embraced held answers to my questions. Hidden all these years. Preserved for only me. Emma had safeguarded the key. The chest must have belonged to Gram, but why did she hide it behind the wall or ask Emma to guard the key "with her life?" At last, I'd know the secret that had saddened her, what ghosts had seeped into her life, her nights—and into my dreams. I wanted more than anything to free them from their dismal graves, but deliverance must be properly executed. Respectfully. Almost ritually. Sure, I could wait. I savored the wait.

I clutched my prize to my chest where my heart hammered against it.

THE DRIVE FROM THE ASYLUM seemed to take hours. I didn't want to risk Michael or Marcia dropping in at High Hill, so we drove to Jimmy's lake house. As soon as we arrived he poured two half glasses of Yukon Jack, which surprised me since I expected cocoa, but sipped the drink nonetheless.

"I told you how sometimes I feel the soul of a building. I swear that one has no soul. I hope you got what you wanted because I don't want to do that again." He threw the drink down his throat. "That's better. So let's see about this chest." Following a quick assessment of the lock, he gathered tools and set them beside the chest.

I reached into the neckline of my shirt, revealing the necklace and key.

"Right. You have a key." Jimmy unhooked the clasp when I lifted my hair.

The key fit perfectly into the lock, but the rusted mechanism didn't budge. After some jiggling and whispered prayers, the latch clicked, and my eyes shot open. Jimmy also looked surprised. We didn't speak while I hesitated, wondering if I was about to open Pandora's Box. Shaking tension from my hands, I gripped and raised the lid while Jimmy watched, his chin bracing my shoulder. My open palm pressed against my heart as if preventing it from bursting out.

The lid creaked open revealing the contents—colors, textures, shapes—neatly packed like the suitcase of a seasoned traveler. One by one, I removed the treasures:

A handful of coins, the oldest dated 1885—the newest, 1899.

A glass bottle of ink, contents dried and cracked into pieces. I rattled the bottle and set it on the table.

Two shell hair combs identical to those I'd seen inventoried and stapled on sample boxes in the factory basement.

A tattered doll that twirled on a wooden stick.

A stack of scorched papers wrapped in a light silk scarf.

A candle and boxed wooden matches.

Several pages torn from a book of poems by Elizabeth Barrett Browning.

A package, wrapped in purple chiffon-taffeta and tied with red cord, wedged into the bottom of the chest. I eased it out.

A scrap of paper was folded into the fabric like an amulet tucked into mummy wrappings. An invitation or a curse? The verse read:

> *Will you come? When I am gone*
> *Where all sweetnesses are hid —*
> *Where thy voice beside the stone*
> *Will not lift up either lid*
> *E.B.B.*

Jimmy briskly rubbed his arms. I shivered.

We moved closer together, drawn to the parcel by the prophetic message—Gram's voice hidden behind the stones. I unfurled the ruffled fabric as carefully as undressing a newborn baby, or disarming a bomb.

Red silk cord tied what appeared to be a journal written on scraps of paper. I wanted to run home to read in privacy as if a best friend was about to confess a secret held too long.

~ TWENTY ~

1899 • December

THE ASYLUM was in such a state. Matron Smythe's sudden absence created an emptiness as if its heart had been torn away. Maggie huddled in bed under a blanket with eyes open and ears sharp. Peaceful sleep would not come easy now that her protection was gone. At least her jewelry chest of treasures was safely hidden.

No light burned from Matron's room leaving the entire floor darker than the outside night. The halls were silent. Suddenly, the latch clicked and her door eased open with a tiny squeak. Who would dare enter? Surely, not Heinz. That would be reckless when caution would be his wiser course. A shadowy figure circled her bed. A gentle hand touched her face.

"Good God. Annie! You mustn't be here."

"Scared." Annie wept.

"Yes, I'm scared too. You scared me. What do you want?"

"Sleep near Maggie." She crawled onto the bed and lay atop the blankets.

"Only for a short while, then I'll take you to your room and tuck you in."

Annie snuggled close and released a quiet sigh as Maggie stretched her arm around her old new friend.

Sleep came faster than Maggie had expected and the sun was rising when she opened her eyes. Annie was gone. She washed, dressed, and hurried to the kitchen where she grabbed a round bread spread with raspberry jam.

What was it about Annie and Matron and their improbable rapport? And what of Heinz? He had become more dangerous than before. Shouldn't Father be home by now? Frustrated and angry, Maggie rushed to the barn.

"Why are you late? Milking's near done," Emma scolded.

"Something happened last night. Did you hear about the police raid and Matron's arrest?"

"Yes, of course. And by tomorrow, everyone in the state will have heard."

"They *should* know. They should know everything that goes on here."

Emma gripped Maggie's arm. "You mustn't say such things."

"Perhaps it's time we tell all." Maggie set her stool beside the last cow.

"Imagination or facts? What is it you really know? And who would you tell?"

Maggie reluctantly confessed. "Merely suspicion."

"Then how can you say?"

"How can I *not*?"

"Best to keep those thoughts to yourself. Be sure of what is true."

"I have concerns for Annie. I've not seen her since the night." They strolled away from the barn. "She's quite frightened."

Emma waved as she veered toward the city gate. "Maggie, we're *all* frightened."

"That we are, Emma. But at least we've got our wits about us." Maggie knew that much to be true.

IT WAS RARE for Maggie to venture to the cottages, but she felt compelled to search for answers. She roamed an hour in and out of the small, simple houses where inmates lived and worked a bit more independently, yet unfit to live freely in the community. Their faces were solemn and weighed with concern. None of them was Annie's.

The tone at the midday meal was tense. Maggie ate alone at the table she'd shared with Matron and Annie. She lingered long after the others returned to chores, hoping Annie would appear, but she did not and Maggie worried.

"What's you doin' 'ere?" Cookie asked.

"Sitting."

"Waitin'?"

Maggie nodded.

"Well, I ain't seen 'er. You should go before Heinz comes lookin'."

"Yes, ma'am." Maggie pushed her chair from the table as Cookie removed her plate.

"You come early tonight, you hear? I got somethin' special planned. Gonna make everyone feel better."

Maggie ran to Matron's vacant room. Bed linens remained disheveled, drawers open with contents scattered, like the police had left them. Something shiny beneath the bed glinted of sunlight. She crawled under and snatched it. No one had taken possession of Matron's master keys, those that jangled when she walked. Now she could go anywhere—now she could open the door of that one mysterious room at the far end of the tunnel.

She had to find Annie and searched every ward, cottage, and path, all the while knowing Annie would never enter the underground realm where something terrified her.

"The dog he gonna git ya ...

Ya go dere ... ya don't come back."

Yet Maggie *did* go there. It was her respite from the madness. She retrieved her jewelry chest from behind the wall and recorded her thoughts and suspicions in her journal. She wrote of Matron's arrest and of Annie's fear.

Humming the notes of Sally's piano music, she removed familiar objects from home and dwelled on memories they invoked. The doll, with the fancy dress like the one Maggie had worn, danced on a stick like Maggie and Father had danced on holidays past. Christmas, mere days away, would be a bleak day already difficult to endure. Sally's piano melodies and High Hill memories faded as her sobs grew louder.

Hours passed and Maggie woke with a shiver on the cold stone floor, the dancing doll still gripped in her hand. With her treasures packed and the chest stashed behind the wall, she wiped grit off her face and raced to the washroom to freshen for supper, because that's what a fine lady did.

HOT CIDER, WARM CAKE, AND COOKIES. Maggie had entered an aromatic dreamscape or lingered in a Christmas trance from her afternoon nap. The toasty warmth of the dining room was a soft blanket, a homey comfort so different from the dank tunnel where she had passed her day.

"There's me girl," Cookie said. "Come in." She waved Maggie into the kitchen where she had removed a pan of sugared cookies fresh from the oven. "Come close."

Cookie bent down until their eyes met.

"Don't be afraid, little one. What happened last night with Matron and the police ain't nothin' to do with you." Cookie patted her head with all the kindness and care that would turn anyone's pout to smile. "Wipe them tea plates and set 'em on the table in the day room."

With a honeycomb towel from the cupboard drawer, Maggie wiped the plates and carried them to the parlor where Emma was arranging chairs. She set down the dishes and looked around. "We can dress this room to look more festive. Shall we?"

"Oh yes, let's. That would be lovely."

They set to their task and found damask napkins and seasonal trimmings in the linen drawers of a carved oak sideboard. Bells and candles, spools of red satin ribbon, and wreaths of silk poppies soon transformed the parlor into a holiday fantasy.

Cookie soon entered with two platters of fancy cookies and teacakes. "Ain't you the clever ones?" She called the kitchen ladies, then the nurses, who squealed with praise and delight. A nurse sat at the piano and played cheerful music.

The patients soon wandered in; the witch lady and even Kathleen appeared, and finally Old Annie. What a relief to see her! The patients chattered, sang, and laughed. Nurses watched and smiled. The kitchen ladies giggled like young girls. Hot cider with cinnamon and cloves, music and decorations. A joyful party had indeed begun.

Maggie placed pastries on a plate and offered them to Annie who sat alone on the sofa. "Do you feel better? Why did you leave in the night? I would have returned you to your room. Where have you been all day? I looked everywhere. I worried about you."

The rapid interrogation agitated Annie. Her muscles tensed. Her eyes darted as if she searched for someone, perhaps for Matron.

"Matron went away. Remember?"

"I saw her today."

"No, Annie, the police arrested her last night. She's not here."

"I go there."

No point arguing, she simply nodded and bit into a teacake.

Annie leaned close until her face brushed Maggie's hair. "I see Matron in the jail." Her statement was not at all confused. "Matron in the jail. Matron in the jail." She suddenly screeched and pointed toward the door.

Maggie looked toward the hallway exit. There stood Heinz, his arms folded across his chest, his gaze targeting Old Annie. He then backed into the hall and disappeared. Annie whined and sobbed and seemed to lose her breath.

"Calm yourself." Maggie put her arm around her and rocked until she no longer cried.

In fact, Annie was completely lucid when she said, "Matron asked me to convey a message to you."

The woman's skillful use of language sent Maggie close to fainting, and she wondered where the smelling salts were stored. "Do not fool with me."

"Matron says you must escape."

Maggie removed her arm from around Annie and slid to the other end of the sofa, staring eyes to eyes. "Escape? How can you suggest such a thing? Don't you understand that Father will soon come? I must remain here."

Annie reached for Maggie's hand and held tight. "He is not coming. Matron told me. If you do not run away..."

She squirmed to release her hand from Annie's grip. Her crazy friend never looked so sane, or so sincere as she warned...

"…You will die here."

THE DAY ROOM had been cleaned and restored from yesterday's party, and Cookie was pleased. With breakfast served and morning duties finished, the kitchen staff relaxed before beginning lunch preparations. Cookie spread *The Hartford Courant* on the worktable and the ladies gathered around as she read:

STATE INVESTIGATES FRAUD AT NOTED ASYLUM

The Brookhaven Farm Lunatic Asylum is accused of denying the State's indigent citizens the treatment that had been contracted. The State of Connecticut immediately ceased payment for those inmates who had not been accounted for, and the Department of Police began an investigation to determine the whereabouts of the missing inmates.

The investigation originated at the behest of the State's Director of Disbursements, following a routine audit by Clifford Baines, a bookkeeper in the department.

State investigators led by the chief constable, James McPhearson from the Connecticut Board of Health, and assisted by Baines, have discovered the asylum accepted stipends for care of inmates no longer in residence. The asylum also faces the criminal charge of fraud and may be indicted for additional offenses.

"Collectively, the monthly amount paid to the hospital was substantial," said Baines.

In an interview with McPhearson, he stated that head Matron Smythe was in police custody and held at the Hartford jail. "She's not talking," he said.

The investigation continues with focus on Director Dr. Jameson and Chief Steward Heinz Brudolf, though evidence of their involvement is lacking.

"Bloody hell," Cookie said.

"Not Matron," one woman called.

"What kind o' dumb writin' is that?" another said. "The doc ain't a criminal."

"We know who is," Cookie said and the ladies agreed. "But keep yur tongues in yur mouths if ya know what's good for ya."

"That's what Matron's doin'. Ain't she?"

The ladies understood their long-held suspicions were true, and it was best to keep secrets as they had for years. They began preparation of the midday meal in an uneasy silence.

Cookie folded the newspaper, carried it out back and threw it into the fire pit. She stood by the pit inhaling scents of burning paper and old ash. Her arms folded across her chest, wondering if a sudden chill was due to winter's first snow—or an omen of things to come.

MATRON'S ARREST and Heinz' threats. Annie's warning to escape or die. Bad thoughts. Terrible thoughts. Sleep lasted a short while until screams woke Maggie.

Nightmare or illusion? No. The screams were real. Howling from far below. Maggie buried her head under the pillow and squeezed it tight against her ears. She tried to shove the awful sounds back into the darkness. While medicine made the others sleep through the night as if they were dead, screams beckoned her.

She crawled from under her feather blanket and tiptoed out of the ward. No one heard.

Gaslights lit the hallway, hissing like snakes when she passed. Darting in and out of shadows, Maggie crept toward the door that led below, pausing to check the corridor like she had so many times. No one stirred. With Matron's set of master keys she'd found under the bed after her arrest, she unlocked the door and pulled it only enough to squeeze through before iron hinges squealed her location. She hesitated on the top step, afraid to enter the place where she must never be at night.

… Ya go dere … ya don't come back …

Old Annie's rhyme taunted her as she felt her way down the

dark stairway. Gripping the handrail, her fingers cramped, and her knuckles drained white. Her long, cotton nightdress trailed behind, sweeping the stone steps clean. She stooped at the head of the main tunnel, her hands groping the coarse cold wall. Spider webs, like silken hairnets worn by nurses, snared her fingers.

On both sides of her path, bins overflowed with coal delivered only days ago. The smell of it masked the cellar's dampness. Coal day was the one day even she would not play in the tunnels. Black dust hung in the air for hours—sometimes days—and when it finally settled, it was a blanket of black snow fallen on her black world.

Of all the vault's hiding places, only one remained closed to her—one secret room, secured by a padlock. She had often tried to remove it, but had failed. It was from this room at the far end of the tunnel that a line of light flared from the door cracked open.

The lump in Maggie's throat thickened with the bitter taste of coal and fear, yet weakening cries drew her closer. For months, she had wondered about that room, imagining horrid images about its use. There was no backing away now. She must know the truth and she blindly followed the path of a sunken drain gutter. Her bare feet felt the way on the cold curved stone. Her eyes squeezed shut, and her hands cupped her ears. *Make the cries go away.*

Maggie cowered beside the door, out of the light, too frightened to look—

Then her feet touched something.

Not cold stone, but something warm and wet. Trickling thick between her toes, like a stagnant puddle of rain turned tepid by summer's sun. She stretched her leg from under her gown into the shaft of light and glared at her foot.

Oh God, it's red. It's red.

Her body wrenched as if her gut lost its wind like when she fell from her tree, the fall that led her here. She felt faint as if her soul were sliding away, refusing to participate in this hell. *Look if you must*, it said.

The stream oozed from the room and followed the gutter. Warm red blood soaked Maggie's feet. She stood in horror as it touched her. Shivering. Cold.

Shivering. Warm.

Screams had replaced lullabies far too long, and she could not bear more of it. She must look into that room. Could she live with herself if she did not? Could she ever face a mirror and not feel shame, if she did not? Nellie Bly would look and she'd drag the truth into light for all to see because it was right. It didn't matter that she was young, and young girls should not have to see bad things, nor should they be the charge of big, bad men.

Crouching low and making herself small, she leaned forward where the door cracked open.

She peeked inside.

Dr. Jameson and Heinz stood on each side ... and there ... there sat Old Annie.

Oh God, oh God, oh God.

Maggie's hands sealed her mouth. Her eyes locked open.

Leather straps at Annie's chest secured her to the straight back of a large wooden chair, her arms and legs bound to its arms and legs, bound so tight they pinched her skin to pleats.

Blood pulsed from a slice in Annie's arm.

No diseased blood needed to be released from Old Annie. She muttered her riddles and caused no harm.

... Ya go dere ... ya don't come back ...

Matted hair fell in gray strands across her face, moist with blood and spit. A thin cotton nightdress, soiled with urine, splattered with blood, and wet with sweat, clung to her body like the translucent skin of a gray ghost—as if she were already dead.

Her near nakedness embarrassed Maggie. She was probably the last person—the only person since Matron's arrest—to have hugged Annie, or held hands, or offered a bed to sway her fear. As lost as Annie's mind was at times, her empathy had soothed Maggie. Like a granny or auntie, the old woman had watched for her safety.

Annie's eyes rolled wildly, then closed as her blood pumped out to the drain gutter.

A tube, like a thin pipe or a fine hose, pierced Annie's other arm. Maggie traced the tube upward.

Beside the chair, a dog hung by his neck from a pole. His head flopped to one side, his long tongue dripped from a gaping mouth. Four once powerful legs, his male part, and his tail dangled as still as the tendrils of Maggie's weeping willow on a windless day. The dog—dead, or nearly dead.

She had not seen dogs at the asylum though she'd heard them in the night, yapping at the moon even when none shined.

... The dog go dere ... he don't come back ...

This dog was golden brown, a powerful breed bound to a gray ghost. What Heinz and the doctor were doing was insane—they were filling Old Annie with the dog's blood.

... The dog he gonna git ya ... ya go dere ... ya don't come back.

For an instant, Annie caught sight of Maggie, or somehow knew she was near. Maggie hoped she did, because it would mean at least, that Annie would not die alone. Annie glanced out the door. The slightest upward turn of the corners of her mouth veiled her face with an aura of peace at the moment of her death.

Annie's head slumped to her chest. Her eyes fixed open. Her blood no longer flowed.

Maggie inched backward into the first small room she came upon. Her back pressed against the stone wall seeking comfort, needing protection as she sank to the floor. Curled like an unborn child in a damp, dark womb. Her arms wrapped around her knees. She remained through the night.

Helpless. Hopeless.

Glazed eyes staring into enduring gloom.

The image of the dog hanging on the pole and Old Annie's lifeless face burned forever in her mind.

~ TWENTY-ONE ~

1974 • November

THIS QUIET SUNDAY AT HIGH HILL had all the makings of becoming one of my favorite days. The stage was set. The den was prepared with a bucket of kindling and a stack of firewood, long wooden matches, reading glasses, and a quilt. A plate of chocolate chip cookies, a cup of hot cocoa topped with Cool Whip, and the chest buried at the asylum sat on an end table beside the recliner. I unfurled the purple chiffon-taffeta and untied the red cord that fastened the loose paper sheets that were stuffed in the chest.

The handwriting in Maggie's journal could have been Gram's when she was a girl, but proof of authorship would come in the words. I read how a worldly but lonely little girl had discovered her mother in bed with her father's business partner, and how that accidental discovery had changed the course of her life.

I expected to be reading in the chair for hours, or at least until the cookies ran out, but I couldn't resist running to the second floor and staring into the bedroom at the top of the stairs—like Maggie had done—to imagine what she had seen.

When I returned downstairs, I opened the closet door and saw the frightened girl cowering on the floor. I wondered if the fireplace kindling now filled the same old bucket it had back then. I stretched my arms, shook my hair, and scratched my head.

Maggie wrote about a witch-looking inmate and about her guilt for causing an incident with a knife. But she also wrote of cherished friendships with Old Annie and Matron Smythe, the cook and Emma Collings, and her colorful description of milking cows.

I read about Heinz and his failed assault on Emma, never imagining Gram to be so brave in a physical way.

She listed names of patients who had disappeared.

Reading no more than a few pages at a time was all I could bear. Each episode commanded consideration. Emotions craved release. So many of Gram's quirky behaviors and convictions suddenly made sense.

I read of Annie's death.

Oh my God! I was reading my own nightmare. Fragments of scenes drawn from Gram's hellish experience, bleeding through time ... *My feet walk cold on stone floors.* The damp tunnels and the smell of coal. The secret room. A gray ghost. *Gray ghosts. Gray ghosts.*

AN UNEARTHLY SCREAM echoes in my head. Looming figures surround me, dark silhouettes in a dimly lit chamber. Musty air wraps my face like a widow's veil. Faint whimpers escape from a dog who could not bark. Limbs twitch until the dog hangs limp.

I cannot move. My arms, bound at my sides. My legs, restrained. Red pulses from a dark door as if the nightmare has a beating heart. I hear it in my head. The pulsing. Throbbing.

I try to scream, but no sound comes. I'm spinning. Spinning, while piano music plays and red dolls dance. I'm screaming.

I scream.

"Del. Del!" I heard my name called from afar, distorted as if I were under water.

Drowning. Drowning.

My lips parted as I tried to speak. I was lost from my body like a severed soul.

"Del, wake up."

My mouth gaped. My throat contracted. I screamed for help with silent screams.

"Dammit, Del. Wake up!"

A few minutes passed. I collected my scattered atoms and recreated myself. I was back and alert. Grounded again in the present.

Marcia rose from the lounge chair and hovered over me, staring into my eyes as if looking for someone she recognized. Scared me half to death. "What are you doing here? What's wrong?"

"You're what's wrong. What was that about? Nightmares getting worse?"

I nodded. Shivered.

"Don't you think it's time you saw somebody about them? Like a doctor?"

"I don't need a doctor."

"You didn't see the look on your face while you were dreaming. You're scaring me, Del."

I'm scaring myself. "I fell asleep reading a chilling story, that's all. Forget about it." I rolled on my side yearning for another hour or a few minutes in a pleasant dream to dilute the bad taste.

"Oh, no you don't." She opened the drapes. "Why are you sleeping in the den? Wake up and tell me about it." She returned to the lounge chair and nudged me with her knee. "Tell me."

Fighting her determination seemed futile. "There was a dog. I'm not sure if the animal was in my dream or in my yard."

"You look pale."

"I'm exhausted and my throat is sore."

She felt my forehead for fever. "Nah, you're okay." Her red wool scarf brushed against my cheek.

"Get off me." My hands slapped at my face in a frenzy.

She backed away. "What the hell is wrong with you?"

"Is it on me?" I brushed my cheeks. "Is it on my face?" I wiped my chin and inspected my hands as if I expected to see them stained with— I bolted to the nearest mirror. *I'm okay. I'm fine.* Pale, except for the slapped cheeks. Eyes puffy. Hair messed. Clothes wrinkled.

Marcia remained at safe distance, wary of my every move and poised for a quick escape.

"Your scarf startled me. It's nothing," I reassured her. I reassured myself.

The clock read almost nine thirty. "The office expects me by noon. Would you please start coffee while I dress? You're staying for breakfast, aren't you?"

"Yeah, I'm stayin'."

Twenty minutes later, I entered the kitchen feeling more like myself.

"When I called your office, Vinny didn't know where you were."

"He's never supposed to say that. Half the time he impresses me, then he does something stupid like that. I can't trust him."

"You don't trust anyone. Maybe it's not them. Maybe it's you."

I poured a cup of coffee and added cream. "You should have called here."

"I did. When I got here the receiver was off the hook. Sooo, what did you do this weekend? Were you with Jimmy?"

"Nothing happened." Her interrogation continued over breakfast. I reluctantly described my visit to Brookhaven with Jimmy, and she nagged about being obsessed with the past.

"That's what you did? You do need to see someone."

"I've got to get to work."

"Maybe you should call Vinny first. He said if I found you, to tell you everyone's in New York."

"Why didn't you say so? Who? Michael?"

"What the hell. It's *your* office. He said 'everyone.'"

Why was I the last to know? Why would Michael meet the New York executives without me? If Sam was behind this— "There's something going on and I don't like it." The clock said 10:10. "I need a ride to the station. Get your coat. If we hurry I can make the 11:05." I snatched her car keys from the table and tossed them to her.

When we turned off the downtown New Haven exit of I-91, I checked my billfold. "Twenty-three dollars. That's just great."

"Don't look at *me*. I'm broke."

"Call Vinny to have the New York receptionist draw a couple of hundred dollars in cash." She parked curbside at the station entrance. I stepped out then leaned back in. "The receptionist must not tell anyone I'm on my way. Can you do that for me?"

"Okay. Go."

"You're a lifesaver."

She gripped the stick shift and shoved it into first gear. "Get outta here."

She left the drop-off area and parked near a bank of pay phones.

I ran through the station's underground tunnel that led to the tracks.

In and out of shadows.
Dark tunnels. Musty smells.
Running. Running.

Numbered track signs blurred as I rushed past and up the stairs to the southbound train. I fell into a window seat in the center of the car, facing forward, just as the train left the station. My nightmare hung in my memory like a bad hangover, but the haunting images would have to wait their turn. The troublesome here and now demanded I deal with my future with or without Jimmy or Michael or ghosts from the past.

~ TWENTY-TWO ~

1900 • March

IN THE SHADOW OF A GREAT SHIP docked in New York's harbor, two ragged boys hoisted the last of nine trunks onto a coach. Antonio Delito charged Salvatore to pay the boys while he assisted Gisella, his son's bride, into the passenger compartment. The noise and congestion faded as they rode toward the railroad station to board a train to Connecticut.

At last, the horse-drawn-carriage from New Haven Station neared High Hill. As his property came into view, Antonio could hardly contain his joy. A great and prosperous future for the Delito family was about to begin.

He patted Salvatore's knee with a proud smile. Not even the long journey had diminished Gisella's glow as she stroked her belly, swollen with child. Salvatore clearly cherished his bride, a bright and opinionated girl of good temper. The couple loved each other as much as Antonio and his first wife had loved. His first grandchild had been conceived, and he was about to reunite with the whole of his family. How happy he was! After nearly a year of travel, returning to his country lifestyle was too wonderful for words.

Maggie was sure to pout about his extended absence, but with his son's future settled, he could now devote attention to molding his daughter into a fine, young lady. Her tutored education would continue, and her travels to the continent would begin. Oh, what a grand time was to come.

When the carriage arrived at High Hill, Antonio jumped from inside, ran to the house, and burst into the foyer. Gisella followed, carrying her two small personal satchels, while Salvatore unloaded the trunks.

"Where's my Maggie?" He had been anticipating their reunion for months and playfully searched from room to room. "Maggie. Papa has returned and he needs a big hug." He leaped up the stairs, three at a time. He thought he heard footsteps below and leaned over the banister to see Salvatore struggling with one of the trunks. A cast-iron plant stand wobbled and crashed to the floor spilling soil from a potted fern and gouging a six-inch scar into the trunk's skin. Salvatore glanced up to his father as if expecting a reaction to the damage, but nothing so petty could alter Antonio's excited state.

"Run to the field and get your sister down from that damned tree. And check the barn for the groundsman." A wild spin punctuated his frustration.

Salvatore bolted from the house and returned a few minutes later. "I looked for her, Papa. She's not there."

"You looked high?"

"Sì, Papa. I called for her, but she's not there."

Nor was Carlotta, nor were the servants anywhere to be found.

"They must be in the town," Salvatore said. "Don't worry, they'll come soon. Before dark, you'll see."

Two hours passed. Tired from the day's overland journey, Gisella fell into sleep in an upstairs bedroom. Salvatore had emptied the carriage of satchels and trunks and prepared a simple evening meal.

Antonio paced from library to foyer and back, until the sound of hoofs on hard ground broke the quiet. He rushed to greet the carriage that carried his daughter and wife. Carlotta stepped out first. A fine chambray dress perfectly fit her curves, its sequined neckline glistening against her creamy skin. She smelled like roses. Antonio kissed her cheek while he eyed the carriage interior.

"Is Maggie not with you?"

"Antonio, you look thin. The sea was not good to you? Come inside. You'll catch a death. Where is Salvatore? Salvatore, come, I have bad news to tell."

Antonio demanded, "Where is she?"

Carlotta dropped her packages beside the door and entered the library. She filled two glasses with apricot brandy from the spirit cabinet, handing one to Antonio and gulping the other.

He hurled his drink. The glass splintered against the fireplace wall. Grasping her shoulders, he shouted, "Tell me."

"Sit down, my love. The news is tragic."

He shook her.

She planted her hands against Antonio's chest and pushed until he released her.

"Fever and consumption plagued Margaret and she died."

Antonio stood silent as Carlotta's words struck his heart, and his fist struck his chest. "It is not possible. I would have felt it in my soul."

"I tried to care for her, but she refused to rest. I told her to stay in bed, but you know how the girl was ... out all the time. I found her one night, lying in ice and snow. She passed before Christmastime."

He braced himself at the door leading to the fields, staring through leaded glass panes into the night. I cannot believe this lie. "Why do you not wear mourning clothes? Where is your veil?" He grabbed Carlotta's shoulders and shook her hard. "Speak the truth."

Salvatore ran into the room and separated them. "What happens here?"

"She wouldn't let me care for her. She wished to be with you."

"Why did you not send a wire when she fell ill?"

"When? At her first sneeze? Would you return? Her first fever? Would you have come?"

"What's happened to Maggie?" Salvatore asked.

Antonio turned away.

Carlotta said, "Your sister lives no more."

Salvatore stumbled against the fireplace, his hands cupping his mouth.

The guilt of his absence gripped Antonio. Had he been home, he would have engaged the finest physicians. "Which doctor cared for her? I wish to speak with him."

"None. I cared for her."

Anger boiled. He punched open the double doors and staggered into the fields.

"Antonio, she passed quickly." Carlotta called after him as he disappeared near the stone wall. "Be thankful she didn't suffer."

A SMALL, BLACK, RIDING CARRIAGE came to a halt at the graveyard gate. The sun rose over mountains across the valley promising a beautiful day. Mist drifted from graves like spirits drawn to heaven. Antonio Delito cut through fog as he searched the burial ground, a lone rider dressed in a long flowing coat, its sleeve cinched by a black armband, a declaration of his grief.

He prayed that Carlotta's account of Maggie's death was a cruel deception. Perhaps she had been sent to stay with distant family. He would read every name and verse to prove to himself that Maggie lived. But as he stood before a grave mound, with his eyes locked on an unadorned stone marker, his last hope dissipated faster than mist.

> *Here Lies the Body of*
> *Margaret Rosa Delito,*
> *Beloved Daughter.*

No threat of danger nor storm at sea had been as disturbing to Antonio as was this day. He slumped to the ground. Winter's frozen loam had thawed, and a thin layer of wet mud cushioned his knees and soaked through his trousers as he fell closer to his buried child.

The day would have been splendid had he and Salvatore reunited with Maggie, or if they had shared a morning meal, or if he had shared her excitement as she opened his gifts to her. It would have been a beautiful day if Maggie had gone to the factory to see workers welcome him. It might have become a perfect day were he not kneeling at his daughter's grave, if he did not need to purchase an angel of stone, nor contract a mason to carve a weeping willow on the base of the monument above his daughter's name—Margaret Rosa Delito, Beloved Daughter.

He imagined her before his voyage with dry leaves snagged in the curls of her auburn hair. Her cheeks turned red like maple leaves in late October as he reprimanded her for some trivial reason he no longer recalled. He remembered choking his laughter as she clutched her dress, attempting to hide the tatter from his sight. She had often played at mimicking Carlotta, dabbing perfume behind her ears, or donning a bride's lace veil while dreaming of the dashing man she would marry one day. Antonio would never have a grandchild by her, to be like her, to share his business or fulfill his aspirations. Gone were those dreams, all dreams.

Antonio Delito had never felt as alone as he did at that moment. He knew he would never be free enough of this sorrow to permit himself to laugh or to weep for any reason as he wept now. God or demon had reached into his life and stolen his soul. He would walk the rest of his days in a gutted shell, more dead than alive, more dead than the bodies buried beneath him—more dead than Margaret Rosa Delito, Beloved Daughter.

~ TWENTY-THREE ~

1974 • November

THE NEW YORK OFFICE of Delito, Inc. occupied a suite on the twentieth floor of its Fifth Avenue address. Hurried men and women dashed through the modest lobby of the turn-of-the-century structure seated on the fringe of the fashion district. Occasional business trips allowed me to squeeze in a visit to the Metropolitan, treasure hunt for period jewelry at neighborhood flea markets, or savor cannoli and cappuccino at an outdoor cafe in the Village. Though I preferred my Connecticut country lifestyle, I held great fondness for the City, but not today.

The elevator slowly creaked upward, carrying young men at the threshold of their careers, meticulously adorned in designer suits. I imagined their hunger for success might drive them to do anything. Lie. Cheat. Steal. Anything. Would Michael do anything? He'd met with Sam in secret and he'd lied about it. Did he also steal? Someone had taken my money, enough to put the business at risk. That it could be Michael didn't ring with truth, nonetheless, the money was gone and the business teetered on the brink of failure. And here I was, surrounded by sharks. Just then, one of the men glanced at me and grinned. And they read minds? I shuddered at the possibility.

Dementia with delusions of persecution ...

Recent polishing intensified the regal red of our mahogany door. Three-dimensional brass letters gleamed—Delito, Inc. I shined a smudge with my suit jacket sleeve.

Asylum.

The middle-aged receptionist, dressed in a pink suit, sat discomfited, apologetic, and apparently embarrassed by the argument festering in the conference room. She handed me a plain white envelope stuffed with cash. I thanked her but didn't engage in small talk. Jamming the pack into my purse and rolling my eyes, I ventured toward the fracas.

Yelling. Cursing. Raving.

I felt trapped in a state of déjà vu.

The volume of the squabble increased as I passed empty offices. The lights dimmed as I peered down the hallway.

Dark tunnel.

Leaning against the wall around the corner, I remained out of sight.

I had to look into that room.

What was going on? I gripped my head, my confused thoughts were like fragile pieces spilling to the floor, rolling into dark corners. Composure became more difficult to maintain. Alone and exposed, everything hinged on my next move. I had to go into that room.

Men arguing ... fighting.

Every voice was familiar to me—Vice Presidents of Marketing, North American Sales, International Sales—the managing staff I'd come to mistrust, senior executives who scrutinized my every move, hoping for a big mistake, believing I "should be married by now" and hosting fancy parties. "She'll be a suitable figurehead with public relations value, but keep her out of decision-making." Office gossip was an anchor hanging around my neck.

The dispute sounded as if they were close to blows, and I didn't have a clue who was on my side. I peeked in. Everyone shouted at Michael. Anger colored his face. Composed and confident for all the time we'd worked together, I had never, never, seen him like this. I stepped into the doorway.

Red.

Delito, Inc. was bleeding to death. Money. Kickbacks. Greed. Charges flung so fast I couldn't keep up. *Be quiet, I need to think.* "Quiet," I said. "Quiet!"

No one heard. Few people had ever heard me speak louder than a demure tone. "What the hell is going on?" I shouted and threw my purse on the conference table. It slid six feet and in an instant, the row ceased.

Michael's voice cracked as he tried to be calm while addressing me. "I've just fired them. All of them."

Seething, teeth grating, I searched his eyes for explanation but saw only rage.

I felt no alliance with the others. Intuition said any one of them would just as easily cross to Monet, Napier, or Trifari, as work for Delito. Loyalty was what I needed most and there was not a trace of it in this room. Michael's action would stand, at least for now. Yes, they were fired.

All eyes fixed on me. "All of you ... clear the room." They stormed out, except for Michael. He and I remained. Still and quiet. Eye of the storm. Several minutes passed as I paced. "God, Michael. What were you thinking?"

"Oh there's more," he said without hesitation. "This morning I fired the ad agency."

I turned my back to him. Couldn't bear to face him. Looking at him tore me apart. Half of me wanted to scream. The other half yearned for his touch. "We hadn't decided about the agency. Now, we don't even have sales staff. How could you do this?"

"You *did* tell me to make these decisions. And even with that said, I tried to find you. I looked everywhere, and you were playing house with that construction worker."

"Is *that* what this is about? You're sinking my business because of jealousy?"

"Del, I've done everything for you. I've kept the business going and Sam out of your way. And I've engineered the transition of ownership." He slammed his fist on the table. "I've been available to you, twenty-four hours a day. Damn, I even arranged Rosa's funeral. I've been nothing but dedicated to you. What the hell more do you want?"

My legs wobbled. Looking deep into his eyes, I felt a shift. He carried my burden, so I could mourn. I could sit in the big chair without worry, free to create a new product line. And because he handled daily business, my special project received attention. All of this was possible because Michael was there to pick up the pieces—my fragile pieces. He cleaned the mess and put me to bed at night.

I had misinterpreted so much and now realized my error. Everything he did that had appeared suspicious, in retrospect, could have been on my behalf—was on my behalf. Even his secret meetings with Sam? The lump in my throat was choking me. Life was choking me. I wanted to love him. At this moment, all I wanted was to fall into his arms and cry, and for the first time in my life, allow him to be close to me without secrets between us.

"I did everything for you, Del, and you took another lover."

"Damn you, Michael! It's more complicated than that."

"You spent the night with him. I was worried about you, so I drove to his cabin at the lake the night you claimed to be dining with Marcia. I parked down the road. I know you stayed all night. I saw it myself."

"How did you know I ran into Jimmy? Marcia wouldn't have told you."

"She didn't. *He* did. Geezus, Del, I would never follow and check on you unless provoked. He called to tell me you were back together. He warned me to back off. I didn't believe him, but it wasn't the first time."

"He's called you before?"

"The day after Rosa's funeral. I started to tell you, but you were just back to work and in a firing mood. I didn't want to add fuel."

"I interrupted to tell you I'd fired Sam. I remember. You don't have to say more. I'll take care of it. Michael, you know I didn't sleep with him, right?"

"If you say so, I'll believe you. So, say so."

"We didn't make love. There was no sex. He wanted to. I didn't." I'm not sure Michael believed me. The pounding in my heart slowed to a near-normal beat, but my nerves burned raw about the business. "Explain what you did here, today."

"Someone had to stop them. By tomorrow you wouldn't have a business. You'd be out of a job—and so would I—one I like very much. I had a future here, too—at least I thought I did."

"Just give me your reasons."

"You don't trust me?" He removed his jacket and threw it over his arm. He tore at his tie to loosen it. "I don't have any more to give."

He didn't look back as he disappeared down the hallway. I barely heard the front doors close as he rushed from the office. He was gone. Really gone. Possibly for good. I collapsed into a chair and shook my head in disbelief of what had just happened. *Damn.*

A BITING WIND ripped through skyscraper canyons. The sun gave little relief. "Parkview Hotel," I said to the cab driver. Finding Virginia Bender in New York was too easy. She'd stayed at the same hotel twice a month, reserving the same private retreat for as long as I could recall. They may as well have named it the Virginia Suite. I called from a lobby house phone and hung up when Mother answered.

Ninth floor. Suite 9060. I knocked.

"Is Sam with you?" Not waiting for an invitation, I dashed from room to room as if hunting a cheating lover.

"It's lovely to see you too, dear." Mother was dressed in a celery-green robe that hid her steps as she floated over the carpet. "He'll return shortly." She massaged hand lotion onto her skin. "No one said you were in New York. What brings you to the City?"

"This isn't a social call. It's serious."

"Don't start with your drama. I'm not in the mood."

I turned my back to her as I stood at the balcony door overlooking Central Park. After several deep breaths I collected my thoughts. With my hands firmly planted on my hips, I turned. "I need the truth. Are you aware that Sam remains involved with the business?"

"He told me he had resigned."

"He hasn't said anything more? About Michael? Or me? Or agency friends?"

Virginia shook her head. "I don't know any more than what I've told you." She sat on the sofa to show me a bottle of nail polish she'd selected from several on the coffee table.

"Mother!" I snatched it and slammed it so hard it bounced, hit the wall, and landed on the floor. "Forget about the freaking color. Don't you care anything about the business?"

"No. I don't." She retrieved the polish and set it on the table. "I couldn't give a damn. Why would you ask? I've been saying it for twenty years." She paced to the window and back. "Look honey, I've devoted most of my life to you and your father. I wanted to, then. Now, I need my own life. I want to know who I am."

She reached for me, but I pulled away.

"I was willing to turn the blasted thing over to Sam after we married, but Rosa fixed that with proof of controlling interest. I don't understand why the two of you can't work together; you want the same thing. Just leave me out of it."

She may as well have said the words—Don't ask me to choose between you and my husband, you might not like the result. My stomach clenched like it took a punch, like when the high school public address system interrupted civics class and the principal's shaky voice announced the President had been assassinated, or when I learned my father had died, or that I'd inherited the family business. Or that my mother had less interest in me than the color of nail polish. It was the stop-me-dead-realization that all I was, and all I had, was me, and it had nothing to do with accountants or attorneys or lovers.

"I need to see Sam. Will you at least tell him I'm looking for him?"

I was half way to the elevator when I heard her say, "Of course I will, dear."

The hotel doorman hailed a taxi for me. I slipped him a five and stepped into the car. Just as I settled into the seat, a white limousine with Connecticut plates, my company limousine, pulled in front of the cab. Michael stepped out.

"Good day, Mr. Bryce," the doorman said.

This couldn't get worse. As I watched him disappear into the lobby, I felt sick. "They know him by name!" The slowing spin of the revolving door made me feel even sicker.

The cabbie looked at me through the rear view mirror.

"Grand Central."

He nodded and set the meter.

MICHAEL CROSSED THE HOTEL LOBBY and entered the lounge. Floor-to-ceiling drapes blocked most outdoor light. He paused for a moment while his eyes adjusted. Candles in brass lanterns lit a dozen square tables set on a red and gold plush carpet. A middle-aged couple cuddled, barely visible in a private corner. Three men and a woman dressed in business suits chatted over documents. At the bar, Sam waved.

"I ordered a Heineken for you. Need something stronger?" Sam asked.

Michael chuckled. "Thanks for meeting on such short notice."

"I was in town with Virginia. I wouldn't miss this. So what happened?"

"Well, it could have gone better. Del arrived for the finale. She knows how it ended but not how we got here."

"Did any of the VPs come clean?"

"Tried to implicate the agency. Claimed they didn't know, so it must be the agency."

"They know. Marketing and sales? They're in it to their necks. International is in Europe more than half the time so he's probably okay."

"I fired him anyway, but we'll get him back when this shakes out." Michael sipped his beer. "I'll call him tonight and tell him to hang in for a few days."

"I met with the auditors this morning," Sam said. "They say it may not be as bad as we thought. Maybe only two hundred thou' through the second quarter. We stopped a quarterly media payment that saved us sixty."

"Good. We should put the brakes on everything until we figure out what's going on."

"If Rosa hadn't died when she did, they could have sucked the place dry. Laura was clever to ask for those contracts."

"We have to tell her," Michael said.

"We should wait. A police investigation will take a while. We don't have exact numbers, and we're not sure who the players are. She's been through so much, I'd like to present solutions when we explain the problem."

"You're right about that, but not knowing is making her crazy, then she makes me crazy. She's thinking the worst and suspecting the wrong people."

"I see your point. Besides, after today's stunts, what's left to keep from her?"

"You should have seen her. We could have done better with that."

"Well, it's over now. I'll take care of it. I'll explain everything when I return home."

"We're right about this, aren't we, Sam?"

"What do you mean?"

"We got the right people. We got everyone, didn't we? This is really over, isn't it?"

~ TWENTY-FOUR ~

1900 • March

MAGGIE SCREAMED, twisting and kicking, as if struggling to free herself from binding leather straps. A stinging slap crossed her face.

"Wake up," a nurse snapped.

Her eyes shot open. "Ouch." She rubbed her cheek and glared at the nurse.

"Stop. It was only a dream." The nurse's unblinking stare probed deeper than her eyes.

The hideous, horrible nightmare had Maggie strapped to a chair like Old Annie, her limbs bound. Her arm sliced. Her blood spilling down the stone drain until it ran cold.

She gazed at the nurse who had rescued her from the dream with her big green eyes … *dead, black eyes* … eyes void of the sparkle born to every child … eyes that had come to stare cold like Kathleen's and the witch lady's, and every other inmate—but Maggie could never, would never, speak of what she had witnessed that night in the tunnel. "Only a dream," she muttered as she turned her stare to safety, turned it to the window because the window didn't stare back wondering where little Maggie had gone.

Matron Smythe's arrest and Annie's death maimed more than the soul of the Brookhaven Asylum. It was the beginning of events that cut the hearts of those who lived and worked there. Three months had passed and Old Annie's presence remained as vivid as the night she died—as did Annie's spirit that walked the halls and rocked on the porch in her favorite reed chair.

Kathleen often spoke to Annie, and Emma claimed to see her, but most often her spirit haunted Maggie. Her ghost was the last thing Maggie saw before sleep. A gray ghost with matted hair, dressed in a cotton nightdress soiled with urine and blood—a gray ghost sitting on Matron Smythe's bed as if she awaited her return.

Maggie remained in her bed feeling faint as if her spirit was fleeing through the window. *Let go. Be free.* She curled into a fetal ball, her blanket tucked against her chin. Her arms wrapped tight around her knees as if she prevented her soul's escape. Dreams of Annie and the dog hanging on the pole repeated night after night after night … "It's only a dream … only a dream."

GROUNDSMEN KNOCKED AROUND and by the time Maggie awoke, washed, and dressed, they had cleared the old mattress and wardrobe from Matron's chamber and had begun to paint the walls a clean cream color that matched other wards. Perhaps finally changing up Matron's room would help Annie's spirit move to a better place. Perhaps finally a new matron had been hired.

Still dazed from a wicked sleep, Maggie sat on her bed as proper as sitting at the opera. Dangling legs crossed at her ankles. She straightened the folds of her smock, set her hands in her lap, and waited for performers to appear across the hall. Her mind had returned to normal, for now. But she was slipping toward a hellish place and feared next time, her mind may not return.

A workman soon arrived and unfurled a lovely carpet patterned with green and oak scroll, then left. Groundsmen came and went. Two nurses from down the hall chattered and cackled. Each held lace fabric folded over her arms. One nurse pointed and smiled at Maggie when she waved to them.

"Who is she?" Maggie asked.

"Are you feeling better today?"

Maggie nodded. "When is the new matron coming? What do we know of her?"

"Seems everyone's feelin' better. Matron should arrive today," one nurse said.

"Mid-afternoon I expect," the other added.

Maggie inched off the bed and stood in her doorway. "Did you meet her? Is she pleasant?"

The nurses laughed. "We will know her soon enough."

She entered the new matron's room with the nurses as they admired the carpet. They hung lace curtains on washed windows and Maggie helped.

A nurse stroked her head. "You do seem more like yourself."

The main door at the end of the hall slammed open. Maggie and the nurses looked toward the noise of wheels rolling toward them.

"Now, scoot." A nurse guided Maggie back to her ward.

The nurses waited in the hall, stretching their necks to see what came their way.

Soon the groundsmen returned, pushing a flat wagon stacked with new furniture and a mattress. They unloaded and set aside a fine chair with neatly shaped arms and a saddle seat that rotated like the one in Dr. Jameson's office. Maggie sneaked to sit on it, rested her arms, and spun around.

The men next delivered a desk with shelves, drawers, and cupboards for books, documents, and writing paper. A small parlor table, a divan, and armchair with removable cushions completed the furnishings. Maggie tucked the office chair under the desk to complete the room arrangement. "It's lovely. Matron should be pleased."

The groundsmen rolled away the cart and the nurses followed toward the main entrance. With a wool shawl wrapped around her shoulders, Maggie rushed down the hall, through the kitchen and to the pantry where she found scissors.

She raced past Cookie, ignoring her caution. "Where ya goin' with that? Don't run ... yul poke yur eye out." Cookie's words faded before she was out the back door.

Evergreens bordered the fire pit area. Maggie clipped a few low branches and returned the scissors. She searched the day room sideboard for a fancy lace doily, brought the greens and doily to her room, and set them on her bed. In a vase from her window sill, she arranged the greens, then spread the doily on the parlor table in the new matron's office, and set the vase on top. Not much to do now but wait.

The transformation of Matron Smythe's chamber was so thorough, Maggie wondered if she would ever again see Old Annie's ghost.

MAGGIE ROCKED on the front porch. Not even the crisp March wind deterred her from welcoming the new matron. A carriage appeared within an hour. Maggie opened the main door, leaned inside and hollered, "She's here! The new matron has arrived."

Dr. Jameson, Heinz, and the floor nurse met the carriage. Maggie stood on the porch, her body braced against the wall, her insides bristling with excitement. Jameson opened the carriage door and the new matron stepped out. Her dress was simple, clean, and neatly pressed, a bit out of fashion but suitable to her station. Her stride was benign, as if she were familiar with creature behavior and had learned to approach even human animals with caution and reservation.

The doctor walked alongside the matron and up to the porch. Matron smiled. "Hello, Margaret."

What! A big grin crossed her face. "How do you know my name?"

"I told her."

Maggie's head snapped toward the carriage from where the small voice came. There stood Emma carrying a small satchel in each hand. Maggie ran toward her. "Emma! What happens here?"

Emma dropped her bags and hugged her friend, swaying side to side as if they danced. "Mum made me promise not to tell."

"Your mum is the new matron? The room across the hall had remained vacant for months, and I wondered why the position had not been filled."

"They waited for my mum's return to good health. It troubled me to hide the secret, but I couldn't risk her job. We're going to live in an upstairs apartment."

"I'm so happy." Maggie sobbed. "This is the best day of my life."

The girls sat on the porch and talked and watched the

groundskeeper remove two trunks from the carriage and carry them inside.

"Come and meet my mum."

"This is truly a glorious day. Everything will be different now."

WITH THE CASE AGAINST MATRON SMYTHE stalled, and the state's fraud investigation of the asylum at an impasse, it was clear to her not a soul had divulged the asylum's impregnable secrets. And as the only suspect, neither had she. The women's jail proved to be not as miserable as rumored. Well lit and ventilated, her cell was no less spacious than her chamber at the asylum. Good, plain food was served three times daily, though not as cheerfully or proficiently as did the asylum's kitchen ladies, and she was permitted fresh air for one half hour per day.

The section door of the women's lockup squealed open when the jail keeper entered. Matron's pacing stopped as she listened. A ring of keys fastened to his belt jangled with each step. She scolded and shook her fists when the guard finally appeared. "Where you been with my food? Sleepin'? I been waitin'."

"You got to be somewhere?" The guard laughed so hard his belly wiggled. "You got no place to go. Step back if you want your meal."

Matron moved from the bars and leaned against the far wall. Her arms folded across her chest; one foot impatiently tapped against the wood floor.

The guard unlocked the cell door and eased it open. "I heard about your old haunt." Locking eyes with her, he set a supper tray on a small table and backed out of her cell. "You was matron at the lunatic asylum, weren't ya?"

Squirming on her bench, Matron gulped a spoonful of beans and pork fat. "What if I was?"

"Been some doins' there. Been some real doins'."

"What 'ave ya heard of it?"

"Maybe there been a murder."

"Murder?" She stifled a snicker and nearly spit her beans. "Been more than one. Folks been vanishin' for a long time. Ain't you heard?" Bolting up and scrambling toward the iron bars, she said, "That's why I'm here, you dumb fool."

"Easy. Easy." The jail keeper backed away. "They say someone's been killed havin' one of them 'speriments. Happened a few months back."

Matron laughed. "And yur just hearin' 'bout it?"

"Maybe there was good reason to keep news of this one quiet."

"Great learnin' used 'round the world comes from the doctor's research." She bit into a heel of bread. "Some folks die."

"Well, this time the one what died made the governor madder than the patients."

"Annie." Matron kicked her table. The bowl bounced. Beans and gravy splashed across the jail cell floor.

"You crazy old woman. You sure you was matron and not one of them damn lunatics. Look what you done here." He locked the cell door and disappeared down the hall.

"I got to speak to someone better than you. Get the constable."

Moments later, the jail keeper returned with an old rag and threw it into the cell.

"Get the constable. Bring the governor." Matron screamed after him. "I know who killed her." She slammed her empty tray against the cell bars. "I'll see 'im hang. I swear, I'll see 'im dead if I have to kill 'im myself."

Matron crawled on her hands and knees, wiping the mess from the floor, too angry to cry for her friend Annie, sister of the governor's best friend. "She was like a child. Never hurt no one. Good Old Annie. Good old soul."

THE DAYS PLAYING WITH EMMA were nearly joyful, and their friendship numbed the misery of Maggie's dreadful state. Staring out the window of her ward room, Maggie pondered her situation. Most recently it had become peaceful, predictable, and certainly tolerable, yet she feared she had become too complaisant. Keen wits were losing their luster. A deep breath escaped.

The new matron's boundaries were reasonable and discipline fair. She tutored the girls' studies and introduced a balanced orderliness that included chores, schooling, and play. Matron's wisdom about love and life had been born of her own recent tragedy, the loss of her baby, which she freely discussed if questioned. Yet Maggie could not bring herself to speak of the events that most troubled her—her wrongful detention at the asylum, Carlotta with Uncle Elias, Emma's attack and Heinz' threats, the vanished patients—Annie's gruesome death. Her list of villainies grew each month. In actuality, Maggie's joyful facade masked a bleak spirit and watching tender moments between Emma and her mum made her miss Father and Sally all the more. Emma's mother could never be the mother Maggie longed for. Truth was, Maggie couldn't bear to watch her tuck Emma into bed.

She blinked away moisture puddling in her eyes and wandered toward the dining area to find Cookie and the kitchen ladies, friends she needn't share. Mummers of astonishment and bewilderment came clear as Maggie swung the kitchen door.

"Special provisions? What's that?" someone asked.

"Serve meals in bed. I ain't no maid servant."

Chatter stopped when the ladies saw her in the doorway.

"Come in," Cookie said. "We ain't talkin' 'bout nothin' you can't know."

Maggie perched on a stool and picked morsels off a muffin. "What troubles you?"

Cookie poured a cup of milk and set it in front of her. "We're lookin' at a new food list."

"May I see?" She took the paper from Cookie's hand and read aloud. "Extra water, broth, fruit juice." Puzzled, she glanced at Cookie.

"Do you see the look on 'er face?"

"It ain't for you." One of the ladies laughed. She raised her hand to hide her toothless mouth. "We know you can't live without yur sweets.

Maggie laughed, too.

"Doctor has new orders for patients after bad blood is released. They got to stay in bed with meals served for a day and a night," a cook said.

"And more, till their strength returns," another interrupted. "Doctor expects their manner to remain solemn."

"Doc's been to a medical conference in Albany. He says he'll be solving this problem of weak blood ... expectin' to find a cure, he is."

"His last idea was to replace the bad blood with the blood of a dog."

"And we know what happened to Annie," Maggie said.

Dead silence set in as all eyes aimed at her.

"What is it? We all know, don't we?" Maggie asked.

"Shhh." Each turned to the doorways to see if anyone else heard the accusation.

"It hurt you hard, didn't it?" Cookie said.

"Yes, ma'am."

"Best you git ready for bed. Go on now."

But Maggie was too upset to sleep.

RAGE WAS THE BARRIER holding back Maggie's tears. Anger as raw as new spilled onto the pages of her journal as she reviewed and expanded the details of Annie's death—the slice in her arm, the dead dog hanging from a pole, Annie's near-naked body bound by leather straps—her own feet painted with blood. She added, pressing so hard, her pen tore the paper, *I have seen these things myself.*

Red silk cord bound the journal pages. She tucked them into her chest and prepared for another restless sleep filled with haunting images. Even with the new Matron Collings, she no longer felt immune to peril like she did when Matron Smythe patrolled the halls. The day's last thoughts were now of death that she feared would soil her dreams for the whole of her life.

She tried to hold the memory of the last happy Christmas when Father handed her a key. Salvatore sat at the piano playing faster and faster as she scurried closer to find the jewel chest Father had hidden. The chest, he'd said, contained wonderful souvenirs from the continent—hair combs and coins, and a dancing doll from London. The doll hung on a stick like the dead dog hung on the pole.

Another dream damaged. Another sleep disturbed. Dogs and ghosts replaced music and dance. Then everything washed away— Annie, Heinz, the doctor, and the dog—washed away by a flood of blood. Swept into a river and carried to the sea. Her own screams woke her. Her legs ached as if she were treading water. She choked as if drowning and recalled Annie's warning from Matron Smythe, "Your father is not coming. If you stay here, you will die."

She drew a simple map on a three-inch square scrap—the river, main building and cottages, and the tunnels. An X marked the spot where the crevice broke the wall—where she hid the chest. With her little map tightly rolled, she squeezed it into the key's secret shank.

Maggie would twirl the dancing doll no more. She couldn't bear the sight of it. She slipped it inside her chest, with the journal's ragged pages, on top of the charred documents Heinz had attempted to burn. She tucked it in as if putting it to bed and locked the chest.

With no one in sight, she raced to the tunnels where she stashed it through the crevice, behind the wall where its bloodstained memory and that of Old Annie would remain hidden.

Where all sweetnesses are hid—

WITH THE DAY'S WORK COMPLETE, evening meals consumed, and inmates in their wards, Matron Prudence Collings climbed the steps to the third floor. Window nooks and sloped ceilings lined narrow passages that led to her apartment.

Emma emerged from the bedroom to meet her mother in the front room. "Mama, Maggie is here." She pointed into the bedroom's cramped space. "She wishes to speak with you."

"Hush." She snatched Emma by the arm and led her into the bedroom where she found Maggie hiding in a closet. "Margaret, what are you doing in there?"

"I'm so awfully frightened. I've come to trouble with Steward Brudolf."

"And you bring this trouble to me? You must not be here."

"Mama, please listen."

Prudence Collings sat on the bed to hear the girl's story.

"I fear I am in great danger."

"Child, that's a ridiculous thought. Nothing can hurt you here. I won't allow it. We must get you to your ward." She extended her hand to the girl.

Emma fidgeted. "Mama, listen to her."

"Heinz makes the patients disappear," Maggie blurted. "He puts them on the barge that brings provisions and coal, and they're not seen again. I don't know where they go. Matron Smythe was jailed for his crimes, then Old Annie went to the jail to visit Matron so Heinz killed her, too. He will kill me."

"Annie was a sick old woman. She didn't know what she was saying."

"No. Annie was not confused. She repeated to me, 'Matron in the jail. Matron in the jail,' then she screamed and pointed at Heinz. He stared at her and the next day … she was dead."

"But she was mixed up in her mind."

"Annie told me, 'Matron asked me to pass a message to you. Matron says you must escape.' She wasn't crazy at that moment. She said Father was not coming for me, and if I did not escape…"

"Shhh. Do not speak of escape. You're safe here with me."

"You can't protect me from him. No one can. You don't know what he can do."

"What are you talking about?" Matron stooped to Maggie's eye level and affectionately held her arms as she listened.

"He's the devil. I've seen his evil face. He'll make me disappear like the others. They're all dead now. I know they are. Annie's ghost tells me so." Maggie glanced at Emma. "If you try to stop him, he'll take Emma and hurt her like he tried to hurt her in the barn. He'll take her and keep her, and he'll force you to do anything he wants. If I do not escape…"

"Stop. You sound like a lunatic. Come, I'll take you to bed."

"… I'll die here."

Maggie reached into the neckline of her blouse and ripped out the key to her treasure chest. "Keep this safe. If I disappear, if *anything* happens to me, give this to Father when he comes for me. He will come. And he'll know what to do."

Maggie handed the key to Matron who studied it in the palm of her hand, and then placed it in the top drawer of her dresser.

"I'll keep it safe, dear, just like I'll keep you safe."

Maggie pleaded with Emma. "Guard it with your life."

Matron Collings tiptoed to Maggie's ward and tucked her in. "Sleep now. I'll sit in the office until then. Don't worry, dear, everything is going to be just fine."

After a short while, Matron checked the girl. She lay still with her eyes open.

AWAITING HER MOTHER'S RETURN, Emma pulled her nightdress from the dresser drawer and slipped it over her head. Maggie's key fell from the folds onto the floor. She was about to return it to the drawer when she heard her mother enter their quarters. Jumping into bed, the key remained clutched in her hand as she considered what Maggie said. Heinz frightened her too, but for now, she and her friend were safe. She pulled the blanket to her neck and fell into sleep.

When Emma awoke in the morn, she strung Maggie's key onto the chain she wore around her neck close to her heart—a keepsake of their friendship. She knew Maggie wouldn't mind.

~ TWENTY-FIVE ~

1974 • November

WORKING BACK AT THE HOME OFFICE was good for me. Anywhere else was good after yesterday's mess in New York. My life had been heaved off the cliff, and I wondered how far the fall. Most others were gone by 6:40 p.m. when I descended the stairs to the lobby. Sam Bender was the last person I expected to see. The mere sight of him at Delito headquarters messed with my mood. After a pause, I continued. No reaction. No hysterics. Good for me.

He stood to greet me. "Laura, we need to talk."

"Nothing you say can change how I feel."

"Virginia said you wanted to see me. There's more to what happened in New York than what you stepped into. Mike was forced into that confrontation."

"What are you talking about? And don't bullshit me, Sam. I saw him at your hotel."

"Sit down, please." His gesture toward the sofa expressed more of an invitation than a demand.

My briefcase served as a barricade on the center cushion between us.

His hand swiped across his forehead. "Where do I begin?"

"Tell me why you're still involved in my business."

He looked me straight in the eye. "Mike asked me to help. He suspected a problem and didn't know who to trust."

"So he called you? That fries it."

"Listen, here's the short story. Someone's been stealing for at least a year, and it seems $900,000 is gone."

"Geezus Sam, that's almost a million dollars."

"Last week, we renegotiated one contract that saved sixty grand, but if Mike had waited, tomorrow's hit might have cost another three hundred thou. That's why he acted fast."

Gram had held such a tight rein, it didn't occur to me to probe too far. But Michael and Sam did. My stomach didn't churn. My throat didn't tighten. My mind kicked into a controlled state that took me by surprise. I became an automaton, reviewing past events faster than the computer on Star Trek's *Enterprise*. Reassessing every suspicion I'd had from an opposite viewpoint, only bolstered his version of events. I wanted to believe him. "I've been doing my own digging. Remember my first real job at that small ad agency in Hartford?"

"Sure. Woburn & Walsh. I hear good things about them."

"We've been in discussions. Their media people reviewed our contracts and invoices. They found discrepancies. Who did this?"

"We suspect either marketing, legal, or both."

"The scale of betrayal is too hard to accept. Both VPs have been with us over fifteen years. Do you have proof?"

"No. We would have involved the police if we did, and we would have come to you. Mike couldn't stand to see how this affected you. We didn't anticipate you'd read so much into my involvement."

Sam explained how their investigation had evolved over the weeks since Gram's death. He explained every one of my misgivings about their conspiracy and answered my questions without reservation. Each word or look or action that had appeared so threatening, now proved innocuous. My paranoia wasn't foolish, it was legitimate because something was wrong, but I had focused on the wrong people. My artistic ego had dictated business choices, just what Gram had warned against. There'd be no reason Sam and I couldn't make a go of it if we could tame our egos. Besides, everyone was now clear about who was in charge. "So what do we do next?"

"Mike and I believe we'll find evidence if we track the money. I'll start tomorrow if that's okay with you."

"Of course. Your office remains exactly how you left it. I need you to come back. Sam, I'm sorry about the way I acted. I regret that I blamed you."

"Never mind. I underestimated how close you were to Rosa and how her death affected you. And I apologize for underestimating your ability."

"Thanks, your opinion means a lot. It always did, you know. If it didn't matter, I wouldn't have been so angry."

I had come close to shooting myself in the foot, but I was still walking, even if I did have a limp. "What about Michael? Will he ever speak to me again?"

"I couldn't say, but I wouldn't wait too long to find out."

I HAD TO SET THINGS RIGHT with Michael. Never had I hurt anyone so badly. Never had a man been so important to me. He was half of me, even while I worked to build my independence. That was difficult to admit, but it felt right, more right than anything. Not because I needed him to make me whole, but because I wanted him by my side.

Before I set my life straight, I had two or three closets to clean.

Conflicting emotions muddied what had to be done. The romantic illusion of the Jimmy I'd conjured in the past no longer existed, and it was unlikely it ever did. I waited until morning to settle with him and entered his office a little after eight.

"Hey Laura, come in. Give us a minute alone." He motioned for two office clerks to leave the room. "What a nice surprise."

"You won't think so when I'm finished."

"Sounds serious."

"It is. Michael told me something that disturbs me."

He moved closer. "Let's talk about it."

I backed away. "That's the problem. We don't talk. You talk. I listen. When I talk, you don't hear a word I say."

"Laura, I *do* listen. Sit down."

"You phoned Michael. How dare you interfere."

He shrugged his shoulders.

"You told him we were involved, so he should back off and give space for our relationship to develop."

"What's wrong with that?"

"You called him the day after Gram's funeral. We had no relationship."

"We've always had one. I knew when I saw you at Rosa's wake that you wanted me. You looked so damned helpless. I can take care of you. Look around, I built this for you. I can give you everything you need."

"Whether I want it or not?"

"Don't talk crazy. I know what you want, and I can give it to you. You needed to go to Brookhaven, I took you. Did anyone else listen to you about that? Anyone at all? No. But I did."

"That's true. You did."

He reached toward me. "Let me hold you. Don't be so uptight." He stepped closer.

"How could I have been so stupid?" I pushed him away. "I thought you'd changed. You don't understand that I want to run my business."

"If it's that important to you, I'll let you do that."

Frustration and disbelief propelled me toward the exit. "You'll *let* me!" I turned back to him. "Listen. For once. This is over. I never want to see you again." Slamming the door behind me served as punctuation. He didn't chase after me.

Next victim? Marcia. Before I lost steam.

IT WASN'T EVERY DAY that a Delito boldly strutted into the offices of the *Barrows Record-Journal*, so I shouldn't have been surprised when employees whispered as I passed. I found my way to Advertising Sales and to Marcia's office though it had been over two years since I'd visited. I closed the door behind me and took a seat.

"I don't believe my own damn freakin' eyes. What are you doing here? Want coffee?"

"I can't stay. I came to say one thing."

Marcia leaned over her desk. "What's up?"

"Don't ever again try to push me and Jimmy together."

"Oops, what'd he do?"

"It doesn't matter, because I'm telling you what I want. It's over, so keep out of it. Understand?"

"Okay, I hear you. It's over."

"Well, that's all. I have to run. Maybe we'll talk about it another time."

When I reached the door I glanced back at her. She rubbed her eyes as if she wasn't sure she had seen me.

I got in my car and drove onto the highway to see Mother.

Two down. One to go.

ONCE A FARMER'S FIELD, the new condominium development boasted a private neighborhood of attached townhouses and luxurious individual homes, all located beside a golf course. The setting was idyllic and hospitable, even on a gray November day. I parked in a visitor space and knocked on Mother's door. She greeted me with a smile. Had I never before noticed how my surprise visits lit her face? "I'm glad you're here, Mother."

"Come in honey, I made a fresh pot of coffee."

"Is Sam here?"

"No, but he'll be back in about an hour and a half."

"I can't stay that long." My hands trembled.

"Are you okay?"

"Not really."

She set down two cups in the kitchen's breakfast nook. "Would you prefer herbal tea?"

"Coffee's fine." I took two teaspoons from a drawer. "Sam was waiting in the lobby when I left the office last night."

"If this is going to be—"

"It's going to be an apology, Mother."

She poured and sat across from me. I added cream and sugar and stirred my drink more than it needed. "He told me everything that's been going on."

"What's that?"

"You really don't know? All this time, I thought you did." Our eyes met.

"I didn't want to be in the middle of your feud, but that's where I seem to be."

"It's my fault. I'm sorry if I made you feel uncomfortable."

"So tell me now. What's this problem you thought I knew about?"

"Inheriting the business was difficult for me. I was as surprised as anyone. That Gram had skipped over you made me feel awkward, but it wasn't my choice, it was hers."

"I know it was. We had discussed her intentions and her will, so I didn't anticipate anything more. Rosa knew I had no interest in the business."

"But how did Sam feel?"

"He never expected she'd leave it to him. Why would he? We both were shocked when you fired him. He felt you didn't give him a chance to show he could work with you, or prove his loyalty to you, to the business, and to the family."

"What I did was premature, and I've settled with Sam. He'll resume work tomorrow. Anyway, I'm here to explain this mess. I want you to hear it from me and not second or third hand. I reviewed the books with an accounting firm Attorney Aaron Schaeffer recommended."

"That was a smart thing to do. Aaron remains a good friend and has always been loyal to the family."

"I knew something was wrong. And it had gone on for some time. I'm ashamed to say Sam was the first person I suspected. I'm sorry about that."

"Don't apologize to me. Tell him."

"I did, but we'll soon air our feelings in a nice long talk. It's overdue. About the same time I became aware of the problem, Michael's suspicions also grew. He brought it to Sam's attention and the two of them began their investigation and discovered nearly a million dollars had been embezzled."

Her mouth gaped. "Why didn't anyone catch this earlier? Why didn't Rosa? Who did this?"

"There was a lot going on with Gram's health, worse than she let on. Sam was in charge, yet not privy to all he needed, and with the geography of two offices in two states, country and city, well, misconduct was inevitable. When Michael took over some of my responsibilities, he saw the broader picture and his suspicions were confirmed. I didn't know he and Sam were helping me. I thought they were conspiring against me."

She laughed a little. "Oh, honey, I'm sorry, but that's so typical of you. I can see why you became paranoid about Mike and Sam, but what made you wary about the money?"

"Early on, the day of the will, Aaron set me up with a reputable accounting firm and their audit exposed numbers. No one knew who was responsible and no one imagined it was ongoing. I looked for blame and because I was uneasy with Sam's old ad agency connections and wanted to work with my own people, I contacted friends who run a small shop in Hartford where I used to work."

"I remember. They helped you begin your career."

"We had fun, too. Well, when I compared their costs to what we've been paying, it was clear something was out of whack, and their report pointed me in the right direction."

"Why didn't you do something immediately?"

"Honestly, I felt out of my element. If I'd known what to do right then, I'd have done it, but there was something else on my mind."

"Then it's fortunate that Mike and Sam got to the bottom of it."

"Yes, but in suspecting Michael and making a complete idiot of myself in New York in front of the VPs, I'm afraid I may have hurt him beyond forgiveness. He was angry when he walked out."

"Mike is too smart not to know that he and Sam fueled your distrust. And I think he loves you too much not to forgive you."

"You know we're seeing each other?"

She laughed, "Sweetheart, everyone knows."

"Everyone?" Shaking my head, I buried my face in my hands. *Of course they know. Probably from day one.* "Anyway, I hope you're right about him forgiving me. I'd better find him and get this straightened out. If we're going to stabilize the business, I need his help more than ever. And Sam's too."

"Sam needs to be back on the team." A subtle smile crossed her face. "I need him back on the team."

I rose from the chair and took a last sip of coffee. "I'd better get going."

"You started to say that something else was on your mind?"

"It's nothing."

"What is it?" She refilled my cup and suggested I sit beside her.

"Well, do you remember if Daddy or Gram ever talked about her childhood?"

After a moment, she said, "Not that I recall." Her eyes squinted with a curious look.

"That in itself is odd, isn't it?"

"Yes, it is. Laura, if you want to know more about the old days, look in the basement of the plant. Your father mentioned trunks of old paperwork. I wanted him to trash it all, concerned it was a fire hazard, but he insisted on keeping it. He planned to sort it someday, but then—there must be something down there, if not valuable, at least sentimental."

"I did that already and found most of what I was looking for, except for birth and death certificates. I wanted to see Gram's marriage certificate, but I didn't find it."

"Oh honey, I thought she told you."

"Told me what?"

"Sweetheart, she was never married."

I fell back into the chair. "Oh, my God. Why wouldn't she tell me?"

"She would have, but sometimes it's difficult to find the right moment."

"Clearing all doubt from my mind, do we know, as fact, she and Salvatore were brother and sister and not husband and wife?"

Mother chuckled. "Honey, they were not husband and wife."

"There's no chance?"

"None at all. They were brother and sister, well, technically half. Your father was Salvatore's son and when Salvatore died, Rosa raised him as her own." Mother stretched her memory. "I don't know the details of his death, but you should be able to find out. Back then everything related to Delitos would have been headline news. Anyway, Salvatore was your dad's father and when he died, his widow left your dad in Antonio's care. She returned to Italy, remarried several years later, had three more children, and lived happily ever after."

"You mean Aunt Gisella?"

"Yes, she was your dad's mother, your blood grandmother."

"Oh, my God! Gram visited her in Italy. She often invited me to go, but I never did, and when Aunt Gisella died, she was quite insistent that I accompany her to the old country for funeral services, but I was starting college … and … oh, I feel horrible."

"Honey, I'd have told you, but honestly, I thought you knew."

"What do you know about Great-grandpa Antonio? Did he really die of a heart attack?"

"He did. Your father and Rosa were both with him when he passed. They were walking in the fields at High Hill. His death was as peaceful as a heart attack can be."

"What happened to Great-grandma?"

"Well, you know Great-grandpa's first wife died so young we hardly counted her. And his second wife, Rosa's mother, Carlotta … hmmm. I don't know." She shrugged. "She may have returned to Providence, but your dad never spoke of her. I guess she remains a mystery."

"I guess so. Thanks, Mom."

Mother smiled, perhaps because of the easy sound of Mom instead of the sharpness when I usually snapped *Mother*.

"Maybe now you'll put all the pieces together. Keep looking through the basement documents; search newspaper accounts. And talk to Aaron Schaeffer. He knew Rosa longer than any of us. You'll figure it out."

"Yes, maybe I will."

~ TWENTY-SIX ~

1900 • April

THE SKY AT SUNRISE appeared as somber as Antonio Delito when he tramped to the east field's hilltop summit. In the valley below, gray mills and brick factories with towering smokestacks were scattered throughout the thriving village his business had helped to build. White-washed church spires dotted the landscape but failed to deliver serenity to his soul. High Hill was not the family Utopia he had hoped to create; neither did a prosperous business bring success to his life.

Mount Higby was clearly visible in the distance beyond his fields where nature emerged from the winter he did not know— the winter he lived abroad. The old willow stood alone in the west field. He strolled along the stone wall, tugging the ends of his mustache as he neared the great tree, each step a hesitation. Leaning against its trunk, tilting his good ear, neither trailing branch nor single fragile leaf rustled. The lifeless landscape was more of a painted mural than natural vista. Shivers ran through his bones.

Resting on the largest boulder of the stone wall, he thought to that day he told Maggie of his journey. No wind stirred the fields, but on that day, it roared like a storm at sea and the swaying grass changed to ocean swells. Stories about Nellie Bly's courageous travels calmed Maggie, yet he wondered now if her inexplicable fear had been a premonition of tragedy.

He relished the open space in the fields, his secret place. His mind cleared in its vastness, creating an opening for novel ideas.

Some might say High Hill was closer to heaven, though as of late, his anger at God resulted in few conversations between them. But perhaps he would try.

ANTONIO RODE TO THE VILLAGE CENTER and entered the church his hands had helped to construct. He traced the sign of the cross and eased toward the altar. In God's house, neither kneeling nor praying, he stood strong and poised for a fight.

A voice whispered from behind, "Mr. Delito?"

He turned. "Good day, Reverend."

The priest suggested they talk, and he led Antonio to the front pew. "I have missed your presence at mass, and I thank God to see you in good health."

"I have returned from abroad only days ago. Salvatore traveled with me."

"How is the boy?"

"He left a boy, but returned a man. He married in Italy, a lovely girl named Gisella who carries his child."

"Praise God."

Antonio nodded as he rose to leave. He was halfway down the aisle when the priest called out, "When will Margaret return?"

Antonio's heart nearly stopped. Blood rushed from his head and he steadied himself on a nearby pew.

The Reverend hastened to his side. "Antonio, what is wrong? Are you ill?"

Unfounded speculation about Maggie's mysterious death had been rampant, yet he had scrutinized every frivolous rumor to no avail. Gaping at the priest like a man facing God, his voice cracked. "What did you say?"

"I wondered when little Margaret will return. I saw your wife in town at Christmastime. They had not been to church, and when I inquired about your daughter, she told me Margaret was visiting family."

"What family? Where?"

"Oh, sir, 'twas too many months ago. Springfield? Providence? I cannot recall."

Antonio ran from the church stoked by joy. Fueled by rage. Was it possible Maggie lived?

He rode hard toward High Hill and to Carlotta, but he digressed to seek the groundskeeper who tended Maggie's grave. The priest's words stunned him into hoping for the impossible, but similar talk and speculation had led to disappointment and he would not dwell on that path again. He ran between headstones to the chantey where he found the man who took care of the cemetery.

"Was it you who dug my daughter's grave?"

"I did, sir."

"Were you present at the ceremony?"

"I was."

"Who attended?"

The man appeared puzzled by the direction of his inquiry. "Your wife."

Frustrated, Antonio asked, "Yes, yes, but who from the congregation?"

"Congregation? No one came."

"Was it you who lowered the coffin?"

He nodded with a curious expression. "It was."

"Did you see my daughter's body in the coffin?"

"No sir, the box was sealed when your wife brought it."

Antonio threw up his hands and seized his head as if the idea was too big to be contained in his skull. His footsteps stomped between grave mounds in a boiling rampage.

His search for Maggie was about to begin. He did not go to High Hill.

Were he to see Carlotta, he would kill her.

ANTONIO EMBARKED on a journey to Hartford where friends in the state government were sure to assist with his search. He arranged for a private coach and purchased turnpike tickets for a route through the valley, mapping roads between the majestic West Peak and Mount Lamentation and through Green Swamp and Kensington Parish. Sullen skies gave way to bright orange as the sun's last rays lit church spires to glow as if they burned. Along the way he made inquiries at every tabernacle, tavern, and town center where he showed Maggie's photograph tucked in his compass. Despite interest in his story and sympathy to his plight, the townspeople knew nothing of her whereabouts. All he could do was leave his calling card.

Night fell with a full moon and a starless sky and by the time Antonio reached Rocky Hill, the landscape was too dark to travel. He entered Granny Griswold's Place, a tavern visited by travelers from distant parts who came for good food, hospitality, and bit of merriment. He brushed his clothes, scraped his boots, and washed road dust from his face and hands before joining those who gathered 'round the fireplace. With a mug of ale, he told his story to a group of peddlers who studied the photograph of his missing daughter.

"I have not seen her," one said.

"No, sir," said another.

Then another offered, "I've not seen nor heard of your daughter, but I've come from Hartford where scandal brews. They have jailed a crazy woman who claims the vanishings of women and girls. If your girl has disappeared, perhaps someone at the lockup knows more."

"I thank you, sir. I will go there in the morn." Antonio did not place much value in the peddler's incredible tale of a jailed suspect, but the Hartford jail was as befitting a place as any to continue his search.

ANTONIO WAITED at a small, round table in the office of the Hartford jail. When the warden entered, he offered his card and told the man of his absence abroad and his wife's tale of Maggie's death.

"My deepest regrets, but I question why you are here, and I fear your trip was for naught."

"My daughter is alive."

"The loss of a child must be impossible to accept."

"I could accept that she is lost if I had proof she was, but I know she lives." He struck his breast and told the warden his wife had lied to their priest, their personal physician knew nothing of her illness or her death, and no one—not even the grave keeper—had seen her body. "She lives somewhere and waits for me. You must help me, sir."

"The circumstances do appear suspicious, but what can I do?"

"I have heard you hold a woman who knows about the disappearances of young women and girls, and I wish to speak with her."

The warden said, "It is true we are holding a suspect by the name of Smythe who was employed at the asylum. She has been imprisoned for four months." He rose from the table, pulled a registry from his desk drawer, and flipped back several pages. "Been here since December." He snickered. "Yes, I remember the night they dragged her in. Screaming and kicking, she was. Damn near broke the place apart. She had calmed a bit of late, until—" The warden looked from his records and closed the book.

"She calmed a bit until when? What set her off?"

"When she heard one of the lunatics was killed. Claims the woman was murdered by the steward."

"Was she? Murdered?"

"Smythe blames every crime on the steward. No one accepts her words as truth."

"I would like to see her, nonetheless. I have nowhere else to go. Perhaps she has news of my daughter."

"Smythe was matron at the Brookhaven Farm Lunatic Asylum. How is it possible she would know your daughter?"

"I do not know, sir. However, I am here. She is here." Antonio raised his hands.

"Very well, but I would not believe a word that spills from her lips. Her lies are likely to disrespect your daughter's memory. You may wait in the holding room. I will bring her to you."

Antonio stood, straightened his posture, and tugged the front of his coat with a snap. The warden led him to a secure room, empty of all but two matching armchairs on each side of a sturdy mahogany table.

In a few minutes, the warden appeared with a middle-aged

woman. Her gray apron stretched tight across a hefty midriff, her graying brown hair pulled taut into a bun at the nape of her neck. She appeared clean and healthy with good color. And well-fed.

The warden ordered Matron Smythe to sit across the table from Mr. Antonio Delito. "She is not a violent criminal, but I will chain her if you wish."

Antonio waved his right hand in a gesture indicating he did not. "Please leave us."

With the warden gone, Matron eased. She stared at Antonio's face, slightly rocking forward and back. "May the saints sin, if she doesn't have yur bones."

Determined to be cautious, Antonio maintained his relaxed position. His back rested against the chair's wooden slats, his legs crossed at his knees, his left arm lay on the table. His face held no expression when he asked, "Do you know of my daughter, Margaret Rosa Delito?"

"Aye sir, I know 'er well. Cared for 'er better part of a year."

"How can this be when I am not certain she lives?"

"Names are often confused. And some lie. But I swear my eyes see truth. I know your daughter, sir. And she is alive. She came to the asylum when I was Matron, and there she remained till the day I was jailed." Her hand stretched across the table to touch his arm. "She's no more dead than I am."

More than anything he wanted to believe. "I am a man of wealth. How can I know you have not concocted an extortion?"

"I didn't come lookin' for you. It's not money I desire, but revenge …" Her gaze turned toward the doorway as she hollered to the warden, "… And my due freedom."

Antonio's fingers tapped on the table while mistrust tempered elation. He stared at a vacant wall with pensive posture. He had been lost on this false road of speculation and rumor, only to fall into despair. Dare he lose himself again? He felt inside his coat where he kept his compass and recalled what he had told Maggie —When I am lost, yours is the face I see. He pulled his compass from inside his coat and searched for the truth in Matron's eyes as she viewed the photograph. "Do you know Margaret?"

"Not Margaret Rosa Delito. I know this girl. Margaret Porter from Providence. She prefers the name Maggie."

Antonio leaned forward. "Go on."

"She would vanish quite often to a 'secret place,' she called it."

Hope filled him.

"The lofts in the barn ... Well, sir, she's a climber, ain't she." Matron chuckled.

Antonio's hands cupped his nose and mouth as if holding hope inside.

"Oh, yes. Maggie," he whispered as if his normal voice would rouse him from this dream. His arms stretched, and he grasped Matron's hands. "Tell me all."

"I was charged to clean the girls, scrub 'em, and check for vermin. The day she came to me, I saw 'er hands and knees was hurt. To stop any man from accusin' me o' hurtin' the girl, I asked about the wounds. I tended to them as best I could, cleanin' the dirt that was left for a day. Had to scrape her scabbed skin till she bled. She never cried. Can ya fancy that?"

Antonio nodded with a quiet smile.

"She told me she'd fallen from a tree. Said she ran for 'er mum and found 'er in yur bed with a man she called Uncle. They locked 'er in a closet, not feedin' 'er for a day and night, only a plain bucket to relieve 'erself."

Antonio's teeth clenched. His chest tightened as Matron Smythe spoke.

"The following day, yur wife and the uncle brought 'er to the asylum. We assumed they was 'er parents. The man paid the steward a hefty purse of silver for the care of 'er. I guessed the girl's story was born of 'er imagination, or it was a 'delusion spun by a lunatic plagued with paranoia,' like what the doctor said."

"I've heard enough." He twisted in the chair. "Warden!"

The warden entered.

"This woman speaks the truth." Antonio assured Matron, "My solicitor will handle your defense. He is most competent, from New York City, and he assists with my legal matters. You will soon be free. I give my word."

Matron looked quite smug as her glare struck the warden.

"Are you certain?" the warden asked.

"Yes, sir. This woman knows my Maggie. I now know what I must do."

The only words that Antonio had retained were that Maggie was alive. The sorry details of Matron's story had not yet settled in him, but they soon would.

NOTHING COULD DIMINISH Antonio's joy, not even the knowledge that his wife and his partner had sold his Maggie. He returned to High Hill where Carlotta's laughter ripped from the parlor as she conversed with Salvatore and Gisella. Antonio directed his son to come to the foyer and leaned to his ear. "Take Gisella out."

"But Father ..."

"Leave the house." He handed Salvatore his coat.

"What's wrong, Papa?"

"Ask your wife to wait with you outside for a short while. Go. Prepare the carriage and hold the horses until I join you."

"Antonio, come," Carlotta beckoned from the next room. "Salvatore told the most wonderful story. Salvatore? Where did he go?"

Antonio climbed to the master chamber, Carlotta's footsteps trailing behind him. Scowling at the bed, he tore the linens off the mattress and hurled it from its frame.

Carlotta gripped his arm and spun him around to face her. "What are you doing?"

Her face incited his fury. Anger rattled his body. He pushed and she fell to the floor.

Fear crossed her face as she scrambled to her feet. "Have you gone mad?"

In a small satchel, he jammed two dresses and several undergarments, grabbed the bag with his left hand, and with his right, he snatched Carlotta and pulled her down the stairs and out the door.

Shoving her onto the carriage floor, he tossed in the satchel. "Salvatore. Come. Sit with me."

Seated high on the driver's boot, Antonio grabbed the reins. He glanced back at Gisella, hugging her belly, standing still as a statue at High Hill's front door. Mouth gaping. Eyes wide. He called out, "Remain inside and wait for our return. I will send a neighbor to chaperone."

As the carriage left the grounds, Antonio assured his son, "Gisella will be well cared for and Carlotta has not been harmed."

At four in the afternoon, Antonio and Salvatore with Carlotta inside the coach, arrived in the town center. He tied the horse to a hitching post at the village green in front of the church where he and Carlotta had married.

When he pulled Carlotta from the carriage, a small crowd gathered. Private coaches carrying other prominent citizens stopped to witness the spectacle. The Reverend ran from the church and stood among his congregation and other village residents.

"This whore has brought shame upon me and my family." His voice cracked. "She lured a man to my home and to my bed and gave herself to him, then imprisoned our only daughter in a lunatic asylum to protect her scandal."

The crowd gasped. Women shuddered and reared back.

Salvatore glared at Carlotta huddled on the ground. His hands fell away from her satchel as Antonio snatched it from him. He affectionately squeezed his son's arm, then threw the bag onto the road. "This woman is a lying pig. She invented my daughter's death and left my son and me to mourn her. I can never forgive her for causing our unbearable grief.

"I say before the God that joined us in this church that she is no longer my wife, and my family has no obligation to her. I will remove her from business interests and will strike her name and all history of her life from family records."

Lunging from the carriage, Salvatore poised to strike her, but Antonio stopped him.

Carlotta scrambled to the base of the church steps, her torn clothes soiled with the gutter's dirt. A young couple cautiously moved closer to verify the woman to indeed be Barrows' most elite, Carlotta Delito. The woman clutched her man's arm and pulled her shawl over her mouth to mask her shock.

Antonio pulled aside the priest. "Please send church ladies to High Hill to help Gisella until we return. The baby may soon come. The family of my solicitor can also help. They own property on High Hill's west border."

The priest agreed.

Returning to the carriage, Antonio called a warning to all. "Do not help her. If you honor what is just, you will shun this woman."

As he and his son rode off, they looked back. The crowd stepped farther and farther away until Carlotta was alone, kneeling in filth at the deserted village green.

~ TWENTY-SEVEN ~

1974 • November

A LITTLE PAST EIGHT in the evening, I knocked on the door of Michael's apartment on the tenth floor of a Hartford high-rise overlooking Bushnell Park. My life-changing closet-cleaning began a mere twelve hours ago, and I'd even managed a few quick stops at the office. Jimmy was history. Marcia had been warned. And relationships with my mom and stepdad aimed at recovery. Even the business showed promise. I only had to fix things with Michael and life would be headed toward perfection. My screw-up, so I might have to grovel.

"Michael, it's me. Let me in." I should have taken the spare key when he offered. To protect my knuckles, I tapped my key ring, knocking harder. My ear pressed against the door. Nothing. I rifled through my purse for paper and pen and wrote a note to slide under the door. *Sorry I missed you. I was a jerk. Let me apologize. Love, Del.*

Forty minutes later I was back at the plant. The lights in Michael's office were clearly visible from the parking lot. I parked my car next to his.

"Don't you have a home?" Jack asked as he held open the door.

I smiled, and pointed to the second floor. "How long has he been here?"

"Half hour. Be careful. He's cranky."

"Cranky, huh? Not much gets past you."

"Will you two be needing a referee?"

"I hope not. But if I'm not back in a week, call the police."

"Yes, ma'am." He grinned and winked. "A week it shall be."

From my office, I attached a handkerchief to a pencil, then walked the long hallway to the far end of the building and tapped twice on Michael's door.

"Come."

I stuck my hand inside, waving the little white flag I'd just crafted.

"Get in here." His attempt to stifle a smile failed. "I don't want to fight with you." A cardboard box from the shipping department balanced on his bookcase.

"What are you doing?"

"Deciding if I should pack my things."

"Please don't." I grabbed the empty box and hurled it down the hallway. "I was an idiot. I hurt the people who mean the most to me. You, most of all."

"You *did* hurt me. A lot. If you had suspicions, you should have asked."

"My mistakes are obvious to me now. I should have trusted you, but I was afraid."

"Of what?"

It took all my will to keep my eyes from tearing. "I was scared I might be right."

"Did Sam tell you everything? We waited too long."

"Seeing the two of you meet in secret at the Regency Inn set me off."

"You knew?"

"Ever since I spotted his car, I've been reading your actions through tainted glass."

"No wonder you thought the worst. Had I known, I would have come clean immediately." He offered his hand.

I looked deep into his eyes. "Is this something we can get through?"

"I can forgive you. But I hope we learned something."

"We did. No surprises. No secrets."

"Deal," he said.

"I hate secrets. I've had it up to here with goddamn secrets.

One thing I've learned for sure is how much I miss you, and I'm sure I want you in every part of my life."

"So, tell me where you've been disappearing to. What's this mysterious project you're working on?"

"It's not really secret ... well maybe a little, and I'm not being secretive with you now, I just don't want to talk about work."

"Let's go away for the weekend." He put his finger on the light switch.

"The Cape?"

"I'm all for that. Should we tell anyone?"

"No." I grasped his forearm, moved his hand from the switch, and turned his wrist to see his watch. "It's close to ten."

"It would be 2:00 a.m. by the time we arrived. Off-season though, we might find a hotel."

"Let's leave tomorrow. I should work a couple of hours anyway."

He agreed. "Around noon. A lobster lunch at the shore, Old Saybrook or Mystic, then drive to Chatham or Wellfleet."

"Sounds like a plan." My hand slid under his suit jacket, followed the contour of his waist, and pulled him close until our bodies pressed together. "We feel good." I caressed the side of his face. His eyes held no judgment, no need to control, no scheming. And in his arms, I felt secure.

"I've missed this ... missed you. A perfect fit. I can't wait until tomorrow to be with you." He kissed my forehead, my eyes, cheeks, and my lips. "Never leave me."

My walls fell away. "I hope this feeling never ends."

"I'll follow you to High Hill to see that you get home safely."

"I'll be okay. You should go home to pack and rest."

We walked arm in arm, down the stairs and across the lobby. As long as he was at my side, I felt I could handle rough waters. I could even dive into the deep end.

Jack rose from the reception desk to unlock the door. "You two all right? Miss Delito?"

No reply from me, as I snuggled my head against Michael's chest.

"Mr. B, everything okay?"

Michael silently signaled a thumbs-up as we exited the building.

Jack stood in the doorway and watched us enter our cars. I waved to him, and he smiled, as if he remembered how magnificent it felt to be young and in love.

MY OVERNIGHT BAG was packed and in the trunk of my car. A beautiful autumn morning dawned at High Hill as I drove away, daydreaming of walking and talking with Michael on a Cape Cod beach, waves lapping at our feet. First, I had to make a quick stop at the hardware store, clean up a few things at the office, check on Vinny, then I'd be free to leave.

By the time I arrived at the office it was nearly nine. A production meeting with the designers finished later than expected. Okay, so our drive to the Cape would start later because I was delayed. Guilty. I scanned the mail and assigned a few projects to Vinny, enough to keep him productive for a few days. I had hoped to spend time in the basement sorting old documents, but time ran out when Michael announced we were leaving.

With my trunk popped open, I tossed in my briefcase and Michael grabbed my weekend bag to stow in his back seat. I slipped my car keys into my coat pocket and they jangled against the package from the hardware store. "Almost forgot. Be right back."

I rushed to the lobby and said to Jack, "We're taking off for the weekend, and I'm leaving my car here."

"I'll keep my eye on it."

Michael called out, "Jack, remind Vinny to go to the thing Sunday night. He'll know what I mean."

"Will do, Mr. Bryce."

"Thanks for your help," I said. "Can I ask a personal favor?" I reached into my pocket and pulled out a brown paper bag. "You know that small office in the basement where I've been working?"

"Sure thing. Everyone's been wondering what you do down there."

"Please put this padlock on the door right away. Have someone from maintenance or the plant take care of it, just get it done fast. Today. Now. Okay?"

"Sure. Happy to help."

"Great. The combination is set, so I leave the rest to you. I really appreciate all you've done for me. I don't say that enough."

"Have a wonderful time. Don't give another thought to things here."

As Michael opened the passenger door, I asked, "What's the Sunday night thing?"

"Chamber of Commerce banquet. I didn't think we'd be back in time, so…"

"So you supposed Vinny would clean up nicely, and you lent him a tux?"

"That's about right. He'll be a good company representative. I think he has a great future with us."

"I'm not convinced. Something about him bugs the hell out of me."

"Yeah, he tries too hard, and he's a bit too slick, but I can fix that. Leave him to me."

"Maybe that's it. We'll see." I opened the window a few inches. "Beautiful day."

"All set?"

"All yours for three glorious days."

THE CASTLE INN had enjoyed better years a decade ago. Set at the edge of Long Island Sound, its rock and concrete seawall had endured hurricanes, pounding surf, and relentless tides. Slightly run down, the inn was cozy with the warmth and smell of burning logs crackling in a six-foot fireplace. There wasn't a better indoor view of the sea for fifty miles.

Sturdy, rough-hewn tables and chairs dotted the main dining room though few diners remained. Michael and I lingered after lunch in the glassed-in porch. Our plates, piled high with cracked lobster shells, sat longer than the empty dining room warranted. He flagged a waiter and pointed to the dishes. "Two coffees, extra cream, no dessert."

Coffee was immediately served.

"There may be a thunderstorm today," I said.

"I didn't hear the forecast, but the windows are rattling more than when we arrived."

"Look at the waves." White-capped swells battered the wall below. The wind gusted through a single open window in the corner of the porch and toppled a blush wine promotional tent card on a nearby table. I shivered.

"Would you rather not go to the Cape? We can aim for an inn in Vermont."

"No, I love this weather. We weren't going to swim anyway."

"No, we weren't." He grinned.

I set elbows on the table and rested my chin atop laced fingers as I stared out to sea.

"What are you thinking?"

"Remember that old woman at Gram's wake?"

"Yes. Emma Collings."

"That's right. I'd like to see her again."

"Why?" He paid the check and scooped two after-dinner mints from a clear glass bowl beside the register, offering one to me, and popping the other into his mouth. "Why her?"

"It's a long story."

He wrapped his coat around my shoulders as we crossed the parking lot. The scent of sea salt filled the air. Waves crashed below though they were beyond our view.

"It's a long drive," he said. "A long story might be very nice."

~ TWENTY-EIGHT ~

1900 • April

THE SUN HAD LONG SET by the time Antonio and Salvatore arrived at the asylum. Matron Smythe's fantastic tale became less of a fable when they read the etching beside the door—*Brookhaven Farm Lunatic Asylum.*

A young matron, Prudence Collings, explained the director attended a conference in Boston, but the steward was likely on the grounds though she hadn't seen him since midday.

"I have heard rumor my daughter Maggie is kept here."

"Maggie! Good Lord, of course she's here. I put her to bed myself not an hour ago."

An excited chill flushed through Antonio, and he nearly collapsed with joy. He crisscrossed the corridor surveying every room.

Matron called after him. "Come this way. This is her ward."

"Maggie!" Antonio rushed into the room. But it was empty. Her bed had been turned down and appeared to have been slept in. He felt the mattress, but it did not hold the warmth of her body.

Matron Collings opened the wardrobe and spun with surprise toward Antonio. "Some of her belongings are gone."

He rifled through the familiar articles left behind. "These are Maggie's clothes." Weeping at the sight of them, he held them to his face. "Where can she be?"

"Emma." Matron called up the stairs and again louder. "Emma, come quickly."

A small girl, rubbing her eyes, appeared on the landing above them.

"Where's Maggie?"

"I haven't seen her since after supper when she went to bed."

"Go back to sleep, sweetheart."

Emma remained crouched on the steps against the rail banister staring below. "Mama, who are these men? What do they want with Maggie?"

"Scoot. Back to bed." Matron Collings looked to Antonio. "She cannot have gone far."

Salvatore interrupted, "We'll search the entire grounds. Where does this door lead?"

"The underground storage area, treatment rooms, service tunnels ..."

"I'll begin at my top floor apartment to be sure the girls aren't playing with us."

"We will search down there and proceed up." Antonio ran toward the door that led below.

Matron said, "Steward Brudolf might be in the tunnels, and he may know where she is."

ANTONIO FOLLOWED HIS SON'S DESCENT on stone steps into the basement. Salvatore lit one of several lanterns that hung at the base of the stairway and swung the light to illuminate an intersection of tunnels.

"Shhh." Antonio raised his forefinger to his lips. "I hear someone ahead. Maggie, is that you?" He bolted forward in near darkness. "It is Father. Where are you?"

"Papa. Papa, wait for me."

Heedless of Salvatore's fading warning, Antonio turned to a wider tunnel guided by the sound of crisp footsteps against stone.

Just ahead, the slight figure of a man was barely visible in shadow. Antonio slowed his pace, reached into his belt and withdrew a dagger from its sheath. He stepped into the light toward the man and tightened his grip on the knife—poised to kill anyone who stood in his way.

Hauling the man from the shadows, he was stunned and shocked by the face he saw. His partner and ally—a man he had welcomed to his home to share meals, personal tales, and business plans; a man he had trusted with the safety of his children and his wife. Elias Porter—the villain who had betrayed him.

"You did this to my family!"

"Antonio. What are you ... why ..." Porter stared aghast, his cheeks dimming to ghost-pale, his expression riddled with fear and desperation.

"What have you to do with Maggie? Where is she?"

"I tried to keep her safe until your return. I brought her here where the best doctors care for her."

Antonio grabbed his collar and thrust the knife to his throat, nicking his skin.

Porter shuttered. "She's safe. Put down the bloody knife. I'm sorry about Lottie. A foolish mistake. I don't know what you imagine happened to Maggie, but you're wrong. Come, let's find her, and I'll explain."

With the knife moved only a fraction from Porter's skin, he gained enough leeway to wiggle free. A fight ensued and grew fierce as they grappled over the weapon, its polished blade glinting with light from nearby lanterns. Possession shifted from one to the other until Porter won control.

Antonio backed away, grabbed a wooden plank, and slammed it against Porter's arm. The dagger snapped from his hand and soared across the tunnel where it glanced against the facing wall, disappeared into a dark crevice, and clattered to the floor.

The blow sent Porter reeling against stone where he lay stunned.

Scrambling to the wall, his arm stretched into the crevice, Antonio's fingertips barely felt where the knife had come to rest against a carved box. He lay outstretched on the floor with the tight crevice pinching his arm, the dagger just beyond his grip. Porter struggled to his feet and stomped Antonio's exposed torso. Pain seared as each kick blasted his breath.

Footsteps faded down the tunnel as Porter made his escape. A distant door banged shut. The snap of a whip and galloping horses sounded from the same bearing.

With his arm freed, Antonio staggered to his feet and hurried down the tunnel in the opposing direction to where he had last seen his son.

Two men wrestled in a rumpus of smacks and grunts. When the burly man caught sight of Antonio, he slid his fingers into the boy's thick curly hair and smashed his head against the stone wall. Salvatore collapsed to the floor.

The man fled, disappearing toward the building's rear where Porter had also escaped.

Antonio rushed to his son.

Salvatore groaned and touched his forehead's torn skin. Blood wet his fingers. "I'm good, Papa. It's just a bump."

Antonio helped him to his feet.

"His name is Brudolf. Heinz Brudolf," Salvatore said between gasping breaths. "The hospital matron told us. Why did he attack me?"

"He has escaped. As has Elias."

"Elias Porter is here? I don't understand. Papa, Matron said Steward Brudolf may know where Maggie is."

"I heard Porter's carriage leave in haste. Something stinks here. Bad deeds." Antonio snatched a lantern and raced through the tunnel where both Porter and Heinz had run. A stone stairway exited the building.

As the light of a full moon pierced a rift in the clouds, grassy fields with tree silhouettes stretched before Antonio and Salvatore. They scanned the horizon for Heinz Brudolf.

"There." Salvatore pointed to a distant hill. "Can you see?"

His eyes not as keen as they once were, Antonio said nothing. A cloud now masked the moon, darkening the land. With Salvatore leading the way, they both ran across the field toward the spot where Heinz had been. Clutching his chest where Porter's forceful kicks had struck, Antonio trailed behind with growing distance, yet his pursuit was determined even as Heinz fled farther away.

At the horizon, Heinz disappeared over a crest as if he had run off the edge of the earth. Salvatore glanced back at his father.

Antonio struggled, but could no longer match his son's speed. "Don't wait for me. Run, Salvatore. Run."

SALVATORE FLEW THROUGH THE NIGHT and was halfway across the low ground when his father finally reached the hill.

"Salvatore, I can run no more." The cool night breeze carried his plea. "Catch him. Make him tell you of Maggie."

Salvatore waved to acknowledge his father's request.

Just as he gained ground, Heinz cleared another ridge and when Salvatore arrived there, Heinz was again almost out of sight. If not for moonlight breaking through the clouds, he might have vanished, but his white blouse shone like a beacon for Salvatore to follow.

Spring rains and melting northern snow had swelled the river. Cold water flooded lowlands where it should not be. Hair bristled on Salvatore's neck. All sounds ceased except for the steady roar of the monster before him. The vision paralyzed him. He imagined the slithering river snatching him from shore and lobbing him like one of Maggie's dolls. Dirty water filling his lungs. Mud snuffing his breath. A net of debris binding broken limbs until his body was forever trapped on a murky bottom. His rotted carcass stolen from Christian burial.

A branch snapped. Salvatore turned. The illusion faded, but the terror remained.

Heinz jumped onto the deck of a barge with a loud thud. Engines cranked to full power as he yelped orders at the crew and the barge moved.

Following the footpath was like walking on glass marbles. Salvatore stumbled down the embankment, slid to the bottom, and ran along the water's edge. Ink-black waves licked smooth stones with cold tongues. The current ran fast, and each time he reached the barge, it slipped away.

From the top of the bank, but out of sight, his father bellowed a last appeal. "Catch him, Salvatore. Make him tell you where Maggie is."

Salvatore signed himself. "In the name of the Father, Son, and Holy Spirit." He took a deep breath. "God help me."

He leaped into the water.

DEEP INSIDE THE BARGE, a squalid cargo hold stank of human waste. Maggie huddled in a corner drifting in and out of sleep—in and out of truth. Her dream was so real. Father's voice calling her name until the motor jolted her awake. As she listened, she heard nothing except the river slapping against the hull.

Father's dream voice was a lullaby replaced by Heinz' barking at the crew. When had he boarded? And where were the other girls? Nothing, but being alone, could be more frightening than sailing on the barge to unknown destinations; nothing—except that Heinz was also on board.

Maggie closed her eyes hoping to retrieve Father's voice, but the only sounds she heard were the coarse hum of the engine, the roar of the river—and a strange heavy thumping against the wooden hull.

SALVATORE CLUNG TO A ROPE dangling from the deck. He pulled himself closer to the boat, hand over hand, his fingers numbed by the cold. He tried to climb aboard, but could not secure his footing on the slimy wood. The barge's wake bounced him against the hull. Thump. Thump. Thump.

Water-laden garments added weight to his burden. Thoughts of his little sister, his father, and his pregnant wife, soon to give birth, lifted him. His honor and his life depended on his next moves.

Damn the cold and damn the water. This was not how he would die. Not this night.

His hands became claws gripping wood until he reached the deck. He rolled to a dark place where he hid under a canvas, lying still amidst empty crates until he caught his breath, wary of the movements of the crew working at the bow.

In the murky light of nearby lanterns, Salvatore felt his way to a cargo hatch, climbed over the edge, and dropped to the floor. The thud resounded in an open space. He remained where he fell, huddled on the floor, expecting to be discovered. Cautiously he rose. Nothing broken. Nothing sprained. Cold wet clothes clung to his shivering body.

MAGGIE AWOKE WITH A START. Fresh night air from the open hatch was a perfume of spring blossoms. A faint shaft of moonlight beamed on a figure with an ethereal glow. She studied the man who must have dropped or been tossed from the deck. His presence comforted her. Could it be his familiar shape? The gentle fullness of his hair? Though darkness and doubt honed her vigilance, he did not seem strange to her. If her eyes deceived, a pinch to her cheek would wake her, but all she felt was the sting of her fingernails.

Maggie had lost confidence in her sense of recognition. Hope had often fooled her. It had conjured Annie's ghost to roam the halls, and Father's image on the asylum's porch. Sweeping hair from her eyes, she blinked, leaning out of the darkness. She quietly studied the silhouetted figure of a man, the cut of his clothes, and the rhythm of his movements. Could it be? Dare she call his name? She whispered, "Salvatore?"

He froze at the sound, looking like a deer in the forest hearing a hunter's footstep snap a twig.

She spoke a bit louder. "Salvatore."

He scampered into the darkest shadows.

Silence.

No one had held her for so long, it almost didn't matter if she was wrong. Rising slowly with cautious steps, Maggie approached him. "Sally, it's me, Maggie."

He lunged from the dark with outstretched arms poised to catch her. She sustained their embrace, afraid if she let go, the illusion would end. Weeping in his hold, her body shuddered as if a year's worth of despair had finally escaped.

Sally brushed aside her hair and wiped her tears. He had grown in stature to be like Father. "What's all this sobbing about? You're going to wet my coat."

"Silly." Water splashed their faces when she slapped his river-drenched garment.

"Stop crying now. I've had enough water for one night."

"Sally, you're hurt." Though her touch of a bleeding bump on his forehead was soft, he cringed.

"I ran into a wall. Come. Tell me all you know of this boat."

"We're sailing to New York. I'm almost sure of it."

"How many crew? Did you see?"

"Just a few, maybe four, five, or six at most, but I can't say for sure."

"Does the barge stop anywhere? Did you hear anything about that?"

"No, Sally. I don't know. What shall we do?"

"I have to think." He scanned the cargo area as if searching for an idea.

"It's empty down here. They delivered supplies so nothing is left but the empty crates. Other times they had stolen several women, but tonight, I'm the only one."

"Perhaps their plan changed because Papa came to rescue you."

"Father? He's with you?"

"No, but we were together at the asylum. He fought with Elias."

"It was Uncle Elias who put me here."

"I know he did."

"And Carlotta …"

"Papa knows."

Relief overwhelmed Maggie. Another soul believed her story at last. "A dangerous man said he'd kill me if I tried to escape, and he'll kill you, too."

"Heinz Brudolf?"

"You know of him?"

"I was chasing him when he jumped on board."

"I heard Heinz. I thought I heard Father's voice, too."

"You did, Maggie. He was screaming at me to catch Heinz. Papa called your name."

"I *did* hear him." Hope and joy made her dizzy. "Sally, please take me home."

"I will. We must get off this barge. Are you ready?"

She squeezed his hand.

Salvatore hoisted her over his head and she sat on his shoulders with her legs wrapped around his neck like they had played so many times. She raised one leg at a time, balancing herself to stand on him until she was high enough to climb onto the deck.

Several crates stacked in a wobbly pile formed his stairway to the hatch.

Maggie hid under the canvas where her brother had instructed her to wait for him.

"Listen to me. This is what we must do," he said.

"I'm ready."

"This will be dangerous and scary, but if you do exactly as I say, we *will* return home. Do you promise you will?"

"I promise, Sally."

~ TWENTY-NINE ~
1974 • November

"HELL OF A STORY, DEL," Michael said. "And all that was in Maggie's journal?"

"Most. Up to Old Annie's death. That's when she hid the journal. She must have been so frightened. How much that incident must have haunted her." The road hugged the shoreline. Waves crashed nearby in a startling spectacle of power. "I always wondered why Gram seemed so troubled. The journal explains a lot. Scenes flash in my mind. Maybe Gram told me more than I consciously recall. Maybe she talked to me when I was a baby. Maybe her spirit still tells stories. It's difficult to separate what I've heard or read from what I've seen in nightmares."

"I'm so sorry, babe. I wish I could help put this behind you."

"I know you do. It would be easier if I could talk to Emma Collings, but without her to light the way, all I've got is old newspapers and books, and our visit to Brookhaven."

"Oh, that. I wasn't much help, was I?"

"Your exact words were—If you keep acting weird, I may send you back there myself."

"That wasn't encouraging."

"It didn't encourage *me*. I haven't sorted what I found in the basement rooms."

"Did you bring anything with you?"

"No. I brought *you* with me. This break is for us and it's too brief for other distractions."

His hand rested on my leg and gently squeezed above my knee.

"How far up the Cape do you want to go?"

"If I say higher, we could be in trouble here."

He laughed and patted my leg, then returned his hand to the steering wheel.

"We're coming up on Dennis Port," I said.

"I know a cozy resort hotel on the water just a few miles from here."

"Sounds perfect." We took the next exit.

After checking into our suite, we changed into jeans and sweaters for a sunset walk along the shore.

"My mom and I met for coffee the other day. Things will be different between us."

"Good for you. I'm glad."

"I told her I'm okay with Sam, too."

"That must have been a relief to her, not that they need the money, but getting back to work will restore Sam's need to be needed."

"And I get the feeling she prefers her space. Sam and I have more in common than I thought."

Pressing closer together, we were the only people in the world walking on a beach created just for us. I said, "Margaret Rosa Delito. Never married. Raised her dead brother's son—my father. I was stunned when mom told me my Delito heritage was born of Salvatore and my 'Aunt' Giselle and not Rosa. Do you think that's why she never told me?"

"Maybe she was afraid it would change how you felt about her."

"Or the subject was too sad because she didn't have children of her own."

"We live with our choices, Del."

"I want children someday. Do you?"

Michael pulled me tighter against him. "Yes, I do. Two or three, I think."

"If only she'd told me the truth, I'd have assured her none of it mattered. I couldn't have loved her more."

"She knew how you felt, and she was so proud of you."

"Thinking about her death doesn't make me cry anymore. Maybe some days I will. But not today. Maybe not ever." We snuggled closer, my arms wrapped around his waist. "Sometimes I wonder if everyone for whom I would have cried for has already died. I worry I'm becoming too hard."

His arms wrapped me in a tight hug. "Won't happen."

"I miss her."

"I know. I miss her, too." He kissed my head and cradled it against his chest. "Margaret Rosa Delito. Who would have guessed? When we get home, if there are any loose ends, we'll figure them out. But for now, wow, look at that sky."

Dark clouds directly overhead dissipated. The setting sun slashed the horizon, refusing to die without a blaze of color. Orange. Purple. Red. Tomorrow promised to be a beautiful autumn day. Sailor's delight. We walked toward the bright gold light. Long shadows stretched behind us.

"It looks as if the storm will miss us after all. I've never seen the water so calm."

~ THIRTY ~

1900 • April

BENEATH THE CANVAS TARP where Maggie and Sally hid, odors reeked of wet wood, river muck, and sea salt. She listened for the crew, then peeked out. The barge cut through a thin layer of mist that hovered above the river's surface. The sun had just risen and bathed the valley with that soft light between the dark unknown and the promise of every dream, but dark unknowns had become commonplace and dreams had been scarce. She huddled against her brother.

"We must go now," he said. "Keep beside me like a shadow. Don't question me and don't move away, no matter what happens."

He shoved out a sturdy crate from under the canvas and stooped to hide behind it. Maggie followed. Crawling side by side, they slid the crate across the deck until they reached the stern, closer to starboard.

The river rushed wild and Maggie saw Sally's fear of it in every muscle of his body. Her brother had never acted as bravely as he did now. "I love you, Sally."

"Ready, Maggie?"

"Ready."

He made the sign of the cross. She did, too. In one smooth motion, he threw the crate overboard, snatched her in his arms and jumped into the river.

Icy cold from northern snows in the full, fast waters nearly knocked her unconscious.

Her limbs kicked and flailed to keep her head above water until she found her strength and reined her panic.

Sally surfaced from the river's depths and they swam toward the floating crate, she clinging to him, mirroring every stroke like a newborn dolphin beside its mother. The current propelled them and they swam hard, yet the crate remained out of reach. For the first time, the power of the water frightened her.

"You must reach it. I'll help," he said.

Maggie bobbed in the waves, spit out water, and gulped a breath of air.

He gripped her arm and pulled her forward. Strong hands and long fingers clutched her waist, then her leg, as he thrust her in front of him. She steered herself and stretched, but missed the crate by mere inches.

A fierce push against her feet and— "I have it, Sally." Adjusting her grip until her hold was firm, she looked behind. Her brother was nowhere in sight. "Where are you? Come up, Sally."

The barge had vanished around a bend, its engine long silenced. At least they were safe from that. Searching the surface for signs of her brother, she called his name again and again. Water filled her mouth and flooded her nose. She choked it up, still clenching the crate. Then something snagged her ankle and tugged, a familiar hold that was Salvatore's. Stiffening her body, she became his rope; hand over hand, he pulled himself closer until he, too, clung to the wooden lifesaver.

He coughed up water. "Aim toward the bank. Don't fight the current, let it drive us." Laughter signaled relief. "We're going to make it."

"I knew we would."

Salvatore scouted the shore as they veered toward it. "I'll push you toward that bush where branches hang to the water. Do you see?"

"I do."

"As soon as you're near enough, let go and reach for a branch. Hold tight. The river will pull you so you must hold tight. Do you understand?"

"Yes."

As they advanced toward the bank, Sally yelled, "Let go of the crate."

Maggie snatched a branch and used it to pull herself out of the water. Sally also seized a nearby limb and hauled himself toward the bank. She watched as the crate drifted away. Hammered by broken logs until it shattered, the crate splintered against the rocks and disappeared.

Then a creak. A snap. A jolt, as Sally's branch cracked. His lifeline to land, a weak string of bark.

A bold and proud expression changed to one of surprise and fear. And when Maggie realized how tenuous his hold was, his terror became hers. While her right hand held the branch, her left hand stretched to her brother. His left hand grabbed hers. The roots of his thin connection broke from the earth and his right hand stabbed the air as if seeking another.

The river pulled at them. Maggie's branch stretched taut and creaked with his added weight. Its roots threatened to snap. Sally released her hand and began to slip away.

White knuckles. Ice cold. Numb. Maggie clutched his coat sleeve, and held on for his life. The look of surrender on his face frightened her. His teeth chattered. His body went limp. She tried to pull him toward her, but he was heavy and she was small. His added weight and wet woolen garments strained her fingers to cramp with unbearable pain, yet she held his sleeve.

The branch that was her lifeline creaked again. He kicked trying to catch a foothold on slick stones as she helplessly watched.

"Maggie, let me go." Sally pleaded with her.

Her grip tightened. The branch snapped, bending farther into the water.

"Do as I say. Let go of me."

Maggie cried. "I can't Sally. I won't."

"You promised to do what I asked. Papa says we must never break a promise."

"Please don't ask."

Stretching her arms to their maximum reach, tension wrenched both shoulders. The strain increased with each strike of wood and debris against Salvatore's body. She cried for his pain. His coat sleeve nearly torn away, his arm jerked free. He was now farther from the bank, tangled in his twisted garment.

As Maggie exerted to brace herself against earth, her feet carved troughs in the mud and slid on rotted leaves and slimy stones. The branch that she clutched cut deep into her palm. Her feet slipped into the water.

One of her frozen fingers suddenly released its grip. The others compensated.

Salvatore screamed. "Let go!"

The intensity of his voice alarmed her, yet she didn't flinch.

"I won't. You saved me."

Something hard and sharp struck Maggie's hand. She yelped with the worst pain she'd ever known. Her blood splashed into the water. Broken timbers freed from northern shores rushed forward. Shards of lumber hammered her hand and her finger, and another, and another. And she screamed.

Cold and smashed. Another finger released her brother's sleeve. And then another.

"Sally, it hurts. Help me. Try harder."

Salvatore made a desperate lunge toward shore. His hand brushed against hers. She tried to catch it, but her crushed fingers no longer moved. She stared at her digits hanging limp from her useless hand. The sight of the damage shocked her—and she knew she would fail.

A sturdy wooden plank struck Salvatore's head. His eyes rolled. He slid beneath the surface. All tension and weight dispelled in an instant as Maggie clenched his empty coat.

The branch she had so tightly held finally snapped off the bush. She scrambled to higher ground.

A string of logs bounced downriver. Maggie ran along the bank, her hand still gripping Salvatore's coat, dragging it behind her. She peered to see if he had drifted toward the shore or away from it, squeezing tears until they no longer blurred her sight.

She thought she saw his head bob at the surface. Once or twice.

"Sally. Sally!" She stumbled along the bank watching her brother struggle toward shore, but the logs obstructed his course, and the current forced him faster and farther away.

Salvatore disappeared under the water, but Maggie still ran, hoping he would surface again—hoping he would wash ashore. She ran though her legs cramped, though her chest ached, though her breath labored.

She ran and she hoped—even though she knew that hope was futile.

She ran until she could run no more. She fell to the ground. Her knees pressed into the muddy earth.

"No! Sally!" she screamed. Kneeling in the muck, staring downriver, mesmerized by rushing water, her body and her spirit numbed.

She could not release the cold wet coat clutched in her battered, bleeding hand.

~ THIRTY-ONE ~

1974 • November

DENNIS PORT, CAPE COD—In the restaurant dining room across the street from our hotel, sea-green ribbons tied dried flower bouquets and candles. A couple silently studied menus at a corner table. A family with two children seemed out of place. And across the room, three women in their fifties laughed recklessly.

The waiter chuckled as he approached. "Good evening. What'll you folks have to drink?"

Free and safe, far from responsibility, and alone with Michael, an occasion worthy of celebration, I ordered champagne.

"Champagne it is," Michael said. The waiter left dinner menus and Michael passed one to me.

"I know what I want."

"I'm sure you do." He studied the selection. "What is it?"

"Something honest like meat and potatoes, milk and cookies...."

"Champagne for two." The waiter set the bottle into a bucket of ice. "Ready to order?"

"Spaghetti and meatballs for the lady. I'll have Veal Francaise with ziti. Garlic bread. House dressing on our salads and Chianti with dinner. We're not in a hurry so don't rush."

"Yes, sir."

Michael raised his glass. "To honesty."

"To us. A most interesting combination."

"It's good to see you like this again." Candle flames sparkled in his eyes. "I don't recall when I've seen you so effervescent." He took my hand. "There's something a little mischievous about you, tonight."

"You're right. I know we said we wouldn't talk about work, but I can't wait until Monday. I'm too excited about this project I've been working on, and I want to tell you about it."

"It's about time." Leaning into the chair back, he crossed his legs and folded his hands in his lap. "Please continue, my dear."

"You know how we've been adapting the Berber designs?"

"Yes, that's going well. Buyers in New York are excited over the samples. Macy's is considering a special display with Moorish fabrics, music, incense, the whole deal."

"Well, I thought, why not expand the idea with a series. Bold, exotic styles reflect where trends are heading. So I thought we'd go not merely international, but historical as well. Like the Lost Jewelry of Pompeii, early Rome and Persia, the Grandeur of Ancient Egypt."

"Easy to research, plenty of reference available. Fun to develop. I like it. I like it a lot. Would we market the line as 'inspired by'?"

"Not inspired. Replicated. Jewelry of the Queens. I don't know, something like that."

"Wow, Del. The possibilities." He patted his chest out of habit, checking for a pen."

"Stop."

"Just a couple of notes. We'd have to do something big to kick it off, and we'd have to put enough money into advertising and P.R."

"That's the best part. Our introduction is a once-in-a-lifetime opportunity."

"Go on."

"The King Tutankhamun exhibit in Washington, D.C."

His mouth gaped. "Oh yes. Too perfect."

"The deal is done. I've already been to the National Gallery."

"You're kidding."

"Not kidding. I've been there. And to Chicago and New York."

Without saying a word, he stepped around the table, lifted me from my seat and twirled me around. "You did all this yourself? I am so proud of you, I can't even speak. Do you know what this could mean for the business?"

"I'm hoping." I laughed aloud.

He released me and paced around the table. "The Louvre, Uffizi... I can't wait to get started."

Excitement about my project bubbled more than my champagne. I had a true partner in life and in love—something Jimmy never was, nor could ever be.

The young girl at the nearby table with her family pointed and stared at Michael. When he waved to her, she shied behind her mother, and in that moment, I saw him as the father of my children.

Though oblivious to Michael's antics, the three ladies across the room roared with an infectious laughter that spread to me. Maybe it was getting away from the office and the freedom from responsibility. Or perhaps it was unburdening my secrets and reuniting with Michael. I laughed so hard my eyes teared. "Michael, sit down. The exhibit doesn't open until November."

"That's only a year from now. We have to leave."

"We're not leaving until Sunday night. And that's November after next, in '76. We have two years."

"Okay, but we should go to London, to Cairo, to ... I'll arrange ..."

"Calm down. We have time. I know people at the top, remember?"

"Where else does the exhibit travel? I should follow up?"

"New Orleans, L.A., Seattle."

"They should be an easy sell with New York and Chicago on board. How much traffic are they expecting?"

"Ticket lines to the streets."

"Wow. Where's our dinner? What's taking so long?"

"Michael, remember why we came here."

"To get away from work and spend time together like two normal people. How could you keep this to yourself for so long?"

"It wasn't easy, I almost told you once or twice."

"I can't wait to tell Sam." He paused. "Are we going to tell Sam?"

"Definitely. We need his help. But I don't want our New York agency working on this. I want to keep my hands on it; it's my baby—our baby."

"Maybe it's time to give Vinny more responsibility?"

"I'm not so sure about Vinny. He's up to something, and I'm going to get to the bottom of it when I get back."

He raised his glass. "I'm so happy."

"And I couldn't be happier." Though I grinned as I thought of a half dozen ways we might try later tonight.

THE HOTEL'S COZY ARMCHAIR was angled in the corner beside slider doors that opened to a small deck overlooking Nantucket Sound. Up at sunrise, I wrapped myself in a white chenille robe and propped my legs on the ottoman. Though the outside air was chilly, I slid open the door just an inch to hear the gulls and smell the sea. Michael's shower stopped running and a moment later, he appeared barefoot and shaking his hair dry, a bath towel tied around his hips. A satisfied grin crossed my face— about the day, the sunrise, the soft robe against my skin, and the beautiful man standing before me.

His steps abruptly stopped and he stared at me.

"Michael? What?"

"It's just that you look so … relaxed … lovely … enchanting. I don't know … the way the light falls on you, like a Vermeer painting, or Raphael … a masterpiece."

"What a sweet thing to say. Thank you for this wonderful weekend, and this cozy suite, and for being you." That much was truly heartfelt, but under the surface of my tranquil facade, my insides seared with anxiety, and I didn't know why.

He blew a kiss. "I'm going out for a paper."

My hand waved, urging him to approach. "Give me a real kiss."

"We'll end up in bed all day."

"We certainly would." I laughed. "Don't be long."

"Call room service, and I'll be back before breakfast arrives. Sausage, eggs, and French toast for me."

"Got it."

Dressed and out the door in a flash, he soon returned with several Sunday papers.

"One wasn't enough?"

"I don't want to miss anything. This is how I relax. Here, check out what's going on today in town." He tossed the local paper on the table beside me while he kept the Boston paper and *The New York Times*.

We hadn't been here twenty-four hours, and I was restless. When I wasn't on some private mission, letting go of responsibility came easy to me. Reading, watching a TV movie, or sitting by the sea, and staring for hours at the waves would be just fine. I didn't need to be engaged in activity every minute, so my unease made me wonder what was brewing in my deeper thoughts. I trusted my feelings, and if my personal and business problems were close to being resolved, why was I so edgy?

Michael glanced up from the headlines, winked, and returned to his reading. At least I was certain about my feelings for him and no matter what happened, I was sure of our love.

"After breakfast let's wander around the village," I said.

"Sounds good. We can walk to the docks from here and comb the beach along the way. I know a great little clam shack for a late lunch."

As I passed him to shower and dress, he raised his fingers to brush against my hand.

HOLDING HANDS OR ARM IN ARM, we wandered through the village pausing at quaint shops where windows displayed hand-crafted pottery, stained glass and hippie jewelry. Michael bought me a pair of one-of-a-kind filigree earrings with lapis beads, handmade by a local woman, a souvenir of our weekend escape.

We arrived at the clam shack at mid-afternoon and sat at a weathered picnic table. A determined breeze carried the aroma of shellfish and corn on the cob. Halyards clanked against the masts of boats bobbing at dockside. My appetite grew as I brushed off sand from a handful of colored sea glass chips I had discovered on the beach. We talked a bit over our food, but mostly we sat in contented silence, mesmerized by ocean and sunset views.

"I miss Daylight Savings Time," he said.

"Me too. I feel like I work every hour of the day."

"Del, we do work every hour of the day. And into night. That's got to change."

"Hey, what's that?" I pointed out to sea.

"I don't see anything."

"The light has to hit just right, I guess." We both stood to see better, then I asked a teenage boy who passed by with a take-out bag. "Do you know what that thing is?"

"Rough water grounded a small barge on a sand bar 'bout a week ago."

I thanked the boy and he continued toward the parking lot.

Michael laughed.

"What's so funny?"

"I was thinking that we didn't see a story about the grounded barge in the paper. It proves my theory of everything."

"What theory is that?"

"It goes like this: Today it's news. Tomorrow it becomes rumor and speculation. And after a week, it's a tourist attraction."

"You're right." I laughed. "And we're the tourists. Now what?"

"Depends." He shrugged. "Obscurity. Or tourists will line up even after three thousand years."

"Point taken." Clear images raced too fast through my mind. Ticket holders. King Tut's golden death mask. New York. Grounded barges. River currents. Gulls soaring over a rotted carcass. Waves crashing.

My mind must have drifted longer than I was aware. Michael's fingers were combing through my hair, and I didn't realize it.

"Del, where are you?"

"Thinking about your theory. I'm okay. I love it ... the theory."

"Yeah? Well, don't flip out on me." Straightening my hair where he'd messed it, his ring snagged my new dangling earring. A lapis bead popped off and clattered to the table. His forehead furrowed with apparent remorse as he handed it to me. "Is it broken?"

I laughed and reassured him it was not. The bead easily hooked back onto the filigree stamping. "See, good as new."

"They *are* new." He laughed. "You usually wear Delito jewelry, and you should. But I want these earrings to remind us there is life outside the business. I meant what I said before, we have to curb our hours and live … enjoy each other."

"That's a sweet thought. They're so pretty, I'll wear them often." I kissed him. "I'm ready to go to the hotel. Are you?"

"Sure. Once the sun's down, it'll cool fast. We can bundle up on the deck and star gaze."

"Mmm. Sounds good."

We walked along the water huddled together. Keeping warm. Staying close. Still, I felt something important had yet to be resolved. I faced rough waters. I just knew it.

~ THIRTY-TWO ~

1900 • April

WHEN BRIGHT SUN CUT THROUGH leafless branches, Maggie squinted and raised her hand to shade her eyes. Pain burned with the motion. A bandage crudely formed from the ruffled hem of her dress wrapped her hand and fingers. Cloth strips torn from her apron protected her feet, replacing the boots she had lost to the river. She had no recollection of bundling her limbs, though the ties appeared to be her doing.

Where am I? Had she trekked downriver or inland in search of a road or her home? Wandered dazed in circles? Her damp dress clung to her skin like Old Annie's nightdress on the night she died. *What had happened?* A fog whirled in her head, her memory confused. She must have collapsed on the riverbank, though the river was nowhere in sight.

She lifted her head ... tried to stand. *Is that a farmer's field? A mirage of High Hill?* She strained to rise on weak limbs while scanning the landscape for her willow tree. Her head felt light ... her body heavy. Thirst. Hunger. And oh, so cold. Her hand throbbed. She lay back onto the ground, scooping dried leaves against her body like a feather blanket. Her eyes closed as she drifted into sleep until God or devil woke her.

Minutes or hours passed in clouded awareness. A dog barked. A faint pleasant voice called. Footsteps crunched leaves and twigs.

... Spared wildflowers if he could ...

A dog's wet nose sniffed her face, first startling her, then feeling like a playful tickle. A long, rough tongue licked her cheeks. Her body stiffened and though her stomach was empty, it churned with angst. A wave of disgust surged. The smell of the dog's coat swept a flood of vile debris—a dead dog hanging, limp legs, black eyes. Gray ghosts.

"Good boy. Good boy. Good God, what did you find?"

Father? Sally? Angel of God?

Strong male arms lifted her battered body. He pressed his ear to her chest and held her tight as he ran. Her eyes blinked open to see his work coat. It held the scent of barn and cow, as did her apron after milking.

Maggie bounced in his arms as he raced across the field toward a modest farmhouse. The dog ran ahead of them, crisscrossing their path, urging them on, frequently glancing back as if to confirm they followed.

"Jane! Jane, come quick."

The dog barked, punctuating the man's plea.

A rugged, fair-haired woman stepped from the house, returned inside, then reappeared with a blanket and charged toward Maggie and the man who carried her.

"Where did you find her?" The woman covered her, tucking the blanket against her body while they entered the house, dashed through the parlor, past a kitchen to a bedroom. The woman pulled down the quilt and the man laid her on the bed. She told her name when the man asked.

"What happened to you? Where is your home? Who are your kin?"

"Andrew." The woman scolded, "Leave her be."

Maggie rolled her head to one side, closed her eyes, and listened.

"Leave the room," Jane said. "I need to put her in a clean nightdress, then we'll see how she fares. Poor little thing. What trouble has found you?" Her sympathetic voice was a comfort. "Get into this."

She slipped off Maggie's dress and undergarments, patted her skin and her hair with a cotton towel, and slid a nightdress over her head, guiding her small arms into delicate sleeves. "Bring hot water."

Jane unwrapped Maggie's feet and replaced the muddy rags with wool stockings from a dresser drawer, then lifted her hair like Matron hunting vermin, though Jane likely searched for wounds.

With a light knock on the door, Andrew returned with a bowl of water and clean, white cloths and placed them on a bedside table next to a wood-framed wedding photograph.

"Let me see this." Andrew sat on the bed and raised Maggie's injured hand to his lap.

Maggie said, "I wrapped it like a mummy I saw in a picture book."

"You did a fine job."

Maggie winced at his touch, locked eyes with his, and nodded her permission.

Cautiously loosening her wrappings, his brow furrowed when he saw the damage.

She also winced at the sight of her hand, bruised yellow and blue, scraped and covered with dried blood with three mangled fingers she did not recognize—the smallest nearly torn from the larger joint. Her eyes teared from the pain. She bit her lip.

Andrew showed the injury to his wife. "We must clean this wound. Get vinegar from the pantry."

Jane shook her head in disagreement. "Fetch Doc Farrell. I'll clean her while you're gone."

Andrew looked at Maggie. "Don't worry. I'll be back in short time with a physician. My wife will look after you."

"Yes. Hurry," Jane said.

A door slammed. A horse galloped. Jane loosely covered Maggie's hand with clean dressings, then served her hot tea and two biscuits. "He is my husband."

Maggie nodded and glanced at the wedding photograph beside the bed. "Where am I?"

"Bell's Farm, west of the river. A half day's ride from Hartford. You must be hungry."

"Yes, Ma'am."

"Eat this biscuit. I will heat last night's soup." She pulled the blanket to Maggie's chin and stroked her head while offering a compassionate smile.

The dog lay quietly beside Maggie's bed, its head resting on crossed front paws. She wanted to love the animal, but everything in her abhorred the sight of it. "Please, will you move the dog? He stirs a dreadful thought."

The aroma of boiled onions wafted into the room and Mrs. Bell left for the kitchen taking the dog with her.

Maggie felt more secure than she had in a long time. Luck had not followed her through the past year, but it found her this day in the form of a gentle farmer and his kindly wife, who was a model of what a mother's caring touch should be. She was asleep before the soup warmed.

MAGGIE AWOKE to the slam of a door, footsteps, and voices in the next room.

"Good day, Mrs. Bell."

"Thank you for coming, Doc."

"How is the girl?"

"Sleeping since my husband left. She didn't eat more than a few bites of a biscuit."

"Best to wake her or risk coma. Did she state what injured her?"

"No. She seems a bit dazed, not confused. Cautious, perhaps."

"I'll treat her injuries, but lest we upset her, I think it best we delay further inquiry."

Maggie raised her head as Jane entered. "My husband has returned with the doctor. I'll bring them in."

"Ma'am, I put no faith in doctors. The truth is, I have a fear."

"He's a good doctor, the best around these parts. I'll stay by your side."

The doctor slowly approached. "Hello, Maggie. I'm Dr. Farrell. I would like to examine you, and I'll do my best to make you well."

She viewed the long, lean man and his kindly smile and nodded her permission.

Andrew cleared the bedside table and the doctor set down his medical bag. He removed a stethoscope and listened to her heart. "A bit fast, but strong and steady." He inspected her eyes, then her head. "No cuts. No lumps." He felt her limbs, her ribs, and pressed her stomach with rigid fingertips. "Good. Good." His reassuring smile comforted her, but when he unwrapped the bandage on her hand, his expression soured.

Andrew asked the question Maggie was thinking, but was reluctant to say aloud. "Can you save her fingers?"

The doctor looked her straight in the eye. "Your head, heart, and lungs seem to be healthy. I see no evidence of injury inside you, but we'll watch closely for several days to be sure."

Maggie focused on every word.

"You are well nourished and your muscles seem strong. I feel no broken bones in your arms or legs. Your feet and your right hand suffered scrapes, cuts, and bruises. Keep them clean and they should heal to normal in a week or two." The doctor took a breath. "Three fingers on your left hand are badly damaged. I believe the middle finger will heal. The ring finger will heal, but its function may be limited. The small finger ..." He glanced toward Andrew, then Jane, and back to Maggie. "The small finger is crushed beyond repair."

Maggie's eyes shot wide open. Her brow rose.

"If you lay in the best hospital in the country instead of this farmhouse, the damage could not be fixed. Do you understand?"

She nodded and he continued. "Were it to remain as it is, the infection would put your life at risk." He swallowed hard. "The finger must be removed. Immediately."

His words rang as if they were the only sound in the world. Emotion overcame her, not that her finger was to be taken, but that it was the climax of all that had happened to her. Anger. Fear. Guilt. Quelled feelings rose to surface. And she was about to be branded with a permanent reminder. She locked eyes with Doc Farrell. "Do it."

"I can take you to hospital," he said.

Jane interrupted, "I can care for her here."

Maggie looked at her then to her husband who agreed. Her body shrinking, she offered her hand to the doctor.

He opened his drug cabinet as he explained, "First, I'll administer morphine to ease the pain. The cuts on your hand and on the damaged fingers will be thoroughly cleaned, then I'll remove the little finger and bandage your hand. I can leave medicine to help you sleep."

"Do it now."

Doc Farrell tapped a soft finger on her chest. "You are a brave little girl."

Andrew agreed. "That she is. Braver than most men I know."

Jane took a seat beside Maggie, across the bed from the doctor. Doc Farrell sterilized his instruments while the drug began its work. The last thing Maggie clearly saw was a brown glass bottle labeled IODINE. She turned to her right where Jane sat holding her hand, then everything blurred. Jane's silhouette faded like a ghost. The bedroom disappeared. Her head felt light, then her body … like hovering over water. Maggie saw things as if she were perched in her tree at High Hill. Green fields. Floating on air. Slamming to earth. Carlotta and Uncle Elias. Kathleen waving a knife. Heinz attacking Emma.

Her mind followed the potent sanitary smell. Cool liquid poured over her skin … she drifted … warm wet feet. *Red.* She was outside the room where a dog hung limp. Old Annie's eyes staring. A gray ghost. *Gray ghosts.*

As Andrew steadied her left arm, she squirmed but could not move … *as if wide leather straps secured her … as if they bound her limb so tight they pinched her skin to pleat.*

Past and present battled in her head.

Where am I? What happened to me?

"Hold her tight now." The doctor's voice sounded supernatural as it rippled through a netherworld.

Grab a branch and hold tight. Do you understand?

"I understand," Andrew said.

"I understand, Sally," Maggie called out. She was back in the river, swimming hard, struggling to keep her head above water, steering the wooden crate toward shore. She grabbed a branch and held tight, clutching Sally with her left hand.

Doc Farrell pinched her finger and pulled it taut.

"Let go of me ..." She mimicked Salvatore's demand.

Stretched taut ... the branch would soon snap from its roots ... something sharp, hard, and swift banged against Maggie's hand.

The doctor's instrument creaked as it opened. He positioned it near the knuckle joint.

White knuckles. Ice cold. Numb.

Let go of me. Salvatore's plea haunted her.

The instrument closed around her finger, tighter and tighter, cutting skin and muscle.

The branch snapped.

She cried out, "Sally, it hurts."

Salvatore drifted away.

The doctor cut until the bone severed from the joint. "It's done."

Maggie drifted away.

~ THIRTY-THREE ~
1974 • November

I COULDN'T GET BACK TO THE PLANT fast enough. Seeing the grounded barge in Nantucket Sound triggered an idea, and I knew I'd find answers in the old trunk. They *had* to be there. Porter's shipping business and his association with the asylum. Coal and supplies delivered by barge. Young female patients gone missing. It had to be connected. I missed something, must have overlooked it when I didn't know what to look for. Michael would be half way to Hartford by the time I parked my car at the main entrance around eleven. I'd have called to say goodnight if I wasn't so excited to collect the documents I needed. I flipped on spotlights at several storage shelves as I passed through the basement.

The small office had been padlocked like I'd asked Jack, the security guard, to do, but the lock had been cut and lay on the floor, the door left ajar. I eased it open and turned on the desk lamp. My papers were in disarray, shelves ransacked, and my tidy document stacks had been shuffled. *Who would do this?* I collected all that remained for safekeeping and would complete my investigation at High Hill.

The letters. The newspaper articles. *Where are they? I need them.* A headline I'd not noticed, a photo I'd not seen, a story I'd not read. The past three days opened my eyes—traveling along the shoreline, crossing the Connecticut River, stumbling on the grounded barge. I emptied every paper from the old trunk.

I brushed loose hair away from my eyes and fastened a sloppy ponytail with a rubber band from the desk drawer, accidentally knocking off an earring. I didn't hear it hit concrete and waved the light around. Michael would be so disappointed if I lost it so soon. If it wasn't on the floor, it had to be in the trunk. My fingers searched the base with smooth strokes until I found it. "Dammit!" The lapis bead was missing, again, likely popped off when the earring hit bottom. I scanned the flashlight beam, but it wasn't there. Stooping to the floor, I checked again. The beam glinted on the bead, fallen through a crack in the trunk. *Where did it go?* Not underneath. It's sitting on wood, not the concrete floor. I pressed hard on a corner and the bottom wobbled. "What the hell!"

I set down the flashlight and emptied the trunk, lifting small piles and stacking them on the desk. "Mmm, nice antique paper." One letter stood out, from some priest or reverend, but I would read it later.

My finger squeezed into the board's corner and tugged for leverage, but the piece broke off. "Ouch, that hurt." A splinter pierced my left pinky with a long narrow shard. Small price to pay. With the corner broken, I was able to retrieve the bead. I wanted to leave this stupid basement before I killed myself. *But what was this space beneath the bottom?* The very tip of my finger touched the edges of brittle pages, newspapers—important enough to hide. What *news was so vital?* The time for gentle coaxing was over. I shimmied and shattered the board and tossed aside its pieces, revealing a secret compartment where a neat pack was tightly tucked. Anticipation matched that of opening the chest and finding the journal.

The New York Times, The Hartford Courant, Providence and local papers from shoreline towns, spread across the desktop, organized by publication date. I hung my jacket over the chair and settled in to browse the headlines:

State Investigates Fraud at Brookhaven Asylum

Delito Girl Missing—Family Seeks Information

Barrows Man Disappears. Asylum Steward Sought.

**New York Police Nab Asylum Steward Brudolf—
Matron Smythe Released**

Matron's Testimony Aides Prosecution in Asylum Fraud Case
Asylum Steward Convicted in New York Labor Scandal
Shipping Magnate Elias Porter Jailed
for Trafficking Human Cargo

If journalists had been diligent in their investigations, the details of Gram's past would finally come to light. The headlines indicated a complete story that no longer required secrecy, and I was eager to share what I'd found with Michael. I packed a cardboard shipping carton and was about to leave when a small article fluttered to the floor.

Clipped from the Providence paper, its masthead was torn ... oh my God ... the tear exactly matched the scrap Gram had stuffed in her purse. The headline read:

Connecticut Socialite Convicted of Theft

What the hell was this about? What does this have to do with Gram? Was she the "socialite"? Nothing relevant was on the paper's back side, only an ad for farm machinery. *Why save this?* I pulled the desk lamp closer. The damp chill that typically filled the back area of the basement was nothing compared to the chill that rolled down my spine when I read:

> Carlotta Ferraro Delito, formerly of Barrows, Connecticut, was sentenced...

> Her son and his pregnant wife, both Providence natives, attended the hearing but were reluctant to comment...

What's Carlotta got to do Gram? The individuals involved in this mess were coming into focus, but I wasn't close to seeing the whole picture. Delito. Ferraro. Barrows. Providence.

My head was spinning with confusion and clutter—past, present, and future.

Glancing over my shoulders, my eyes darted into the basement, affirming I was alone. *Damn!* Alone down here was the last place I should be.

~ THIRTY-FOUR ~

1900 • April

NEARLY A WEEK HAD PASSED since Antonio, with Salvatore, first scoured the asylum in search of Maggie, and on that night his son also went missing. Irony could not have been more cruel when it delivered baby Joseph Delito on the very day Salvatore disappeared. Antonio embraced Gisella and baby Joseph as his new family. However, Maggie and Salvatore were gone.

Matron Prudence Collings had assured Antonio she would contact him if she heard of his daughter. Meanwhile, he distributed photographs to newspapers, police departments, and parishes throughout the state.

Police informed Antonio they had stopped the barge downriver, but their search uncovered neither Maggie, Salvatore, nor Heinz Brudolf, and suspicion leaned to an act of abduction and flight beyond state borders.

Antonio divided his days between his High Hill home with Salvatore's wife and child and his business, where he pressed for rumor of Porter's whereabouts, perhaps his best chance to recover his daughter and son. He hoped for the best, but feared the worst, and once or twice, he prayed to the God he had deserted when he dumped Carlotta at his front door.

THE CONNECTICUT RIVER spilled into Long Island Sound at Old Saybrook where four local boys surveyed their strip of the shoreline as they had nearly every day of their lives. The boys, ten to fourteen years of age, knew the sands, and the sea and its tides, as well as they knew their homes … as well as they knew each other.

The boys darted back and forth attempting to elude the cold lick of ocean waves while they searched moist sand for telltale bubbles of buried clams. Low tide with its robust odor was ideal for clamming and for scavenging treasures and oddities washed ashore.

Two years ago, they had discovered the broken mast of a schooner. Their find had dominated the news for a week. Mariners and townspeople had assembled near the lighthouse at day's end to speculate. Which ship? British or Dutch? Yankee or Rebel? What caused it to sink?

Over the years, the boys had collected driftwood, shells, sea glass, polished stones, coins, tinware, and bottles. They searched at water's edge, lined side by side, poking at seaweed clumps. Talking. Laughing. Daring. Each one hoping he would be first to spot the next great find.

"Whew!" One boy's face contorted. "Do you smell that?"

"Stinks bad. Dead fish?"

"Look there." One boy pointed ahead at a low dark mound veiled in seaweed.

They approached with caution. "Too big for a fish."

"Could be a big fish." They laughed.

"Maybe a dolphin."

"Or a whale?"

The boys, each one poised with his stick, surrounded the mound like compass points. One pulled his sweater over his nose to filter the stench of rotting flesh. Another poked his stick at the pile. Three crabs scattered. The boys jumped a step back and glanced at each other when nothing more stirred.

"I dare *you* to look," one boy said.

"I dare you," said another.

A flock of gulls soared overhead as the boys inched closer to the mound.

One by one their sticks picked off seaweed strands and tossed them aside. Flies buzzed. Lots of flies.

First the boys revealed a human leg.

"Bloody hell."

"Geezus. It's a man."

"A boy, I think."

Further prodding uncovered an arm. Its hand was gone.

The boys peeled layers of weed like sheaths of an onion. Shredded skin rimmed a cavity in the body's torso.

"Shark bite."

"That's a fine suit he wore."

At last they uncovered the head. Battered. Bruised. Swollen to distortion.

"What happened to this poor fellow?"

"Could be a turtle nipped his lips."

"Look, his clothes caught tree branches."

"Must have washed down the river."

"Yup, that would bang 'im up."

"Who could he be?"

A boy shrugged his shoulders. "How can we know? His own mum wouldn't know him."

In a short while, townsfolk had gathered and summoned police.

Detectives investigated.

A journalist interviewed the boys while a photographer posed them for a portrait. The stranger's identity was soon revealed and news spread statewide with headlines that read:

Local Boys Find Drowned Body
of Missing Barrows Man

The sea had spit up a battered body cocooned in a seaweed shroud.

The boys had discovered the remains of Salvatore Delito.

DOC FARRELL RETURNED to Bell's Farm to examine his patient and instruct Jane and Andrew how to clean the girl's wounds and change her wrapping. He inspected the point of amputation. "This looks fine."

Maggie swooned and her head settled against her pillow, her eyes half closed.

"She sleeps a lot," Jane said. "Perhaps not so much from her injury as from her experience before we found her."

"Has she told you what happened? Who she is? How she came to be here?"

"No," Andrew said. "But in her sleep, her bad hand reaches out and she calls for a girl named Sally."

"Perhaps a sister or a friend?" He rubbed his chin. "She also called for Sally when I took her finger. When she was affected by the drug."

"Perhaps Sally is also lost. I'll search my land for her."

"A good idea." Doc Farrell thought for a moment. "I know of no one by that name among my patients, but I will ask."

"We're grateful for any assistance," Jane said.

"Don't worry. She's young and strong, and she's been well-fed. Her overall health is excellent, so I don't foresee complications."

Andrew nodded. "Thanks Doc, I'll walk out with you."

Doc Farrell waved to Maggie and Jane who sat at her bedside. "We'll see how she feels by week's end. I believe she'll recover from all that ails her."

Outside, Andrew said to him, "My wife has taken a liking to the girl."

"It's natural."

"I'm afraid that time will forge too strong a bond, and Jane will grieve when the girl's family comes for her."

The doctor shrugged his shoulders. "It can't be avoided. I'll ride to the parish and speak with Reverend Thomas. We'll make immediate inquiries." He placed his hand on Andrew's back in a reassuring gesture. "We'll get to the bottom of this."

The next day, when Doc Farrell, accompanied by Reverend Thomas, arrived at Bell's Farm, Maggie was up and sitting at the dining table while Jane scrubbed potatoes. Maggie spoke of her past months at the asylum, and he attempted to sway her from her story, but the girl remained steadfast with her particulars. "That's a mighty tall tale."

"And every word is true," she insisted.

"I've heard enough. It won't be long before we know the facts. I can promise that." He suggested Maggie remain at Bell's Farm until then.

He and the Reverend stepped into their carriage.

"What do you think, Doc? Is the girl an escaped lunatic?" the Reverend asked.

"She has her wits about her."

"That she does."

"What can you do to help her?"

The Reverend grinned. "I believe I know her identity. I will send a letter to her father."

A GRAND AND PROPER CHRISTIAN BURIAL had been arranged for Salvatore Delito with internment on the cemetery's highest hill, far from the false grave of Margaret Rosa Delito, Beloved Daughter.

Black wreaths of laurel leaves, placed by townspeople, adorned his plot. Visitors paid respects then returned to their homes and families, leaving Antonio alone amidst grave markers silhouetted against the most intensely blue sky he had ever seen.

Antonio visited the grave of his first wife, the only woman he'd ever loved. Her loss remained an unhealed wound. Now their firstborn child, his only son, had passed to heaven to reunite with her. And Maggie? Only God knew of her, but once again, Antonio's conversations with God had stopped. *What kind of God gives you every beautiful thing, then takes it from you?* He had been tested and he had lost—lost everyone he had loved and everything important to him—even his faith.

The next day during supper, Antonio and Gisella barely spoke. He feared she would return to Italy and he would never see his grandchild again. What could he say? She had sampled the small town of Barrows where the Delito name meant respect and wealth. Life would be easy, but would it be the life she wanted. Family, friends, and everyone she had ever known lived an ocean away.

He assured her they would continue to live as kin. He would provide for her and Joseph. And he would help her preserve a closeness with her people in the old country.

She buried her face in her hands and wept.

"I am sorry, dear Gisella. My loss has so overwhelmed me I had no regard for yours." He held her like a father would hold a daughter and guided her toward the warmth of the fireplace where they silently huddled until the flames died.

The following morning, Gisella informed Antonio of her desire to return to her family. At eighteen, she was young enough to begin her life anew. They wept as she confided, in bold truth, her dreams of a different future. "My homeland continues to draw me. The idea to return did not suddenly come in the night, to the contrary," she said, "It has consumed me since the night you returned without Salvatore. I care for and respect you and am more sure than ever of my decision."

He offered to pay for her voyage and assist with securing passage.

"Though returning to Italy may be best for me, I do not believe it best for Joseph."

"What do you mean, daughter?"

"If you agree, I trust my son to your care."

Antonio fell into the chair behind him, his hands too shaky to grip its arms.

"I have given this much thought and know it is the most difficult decision I will ever make. There will be times I will regret my choice." She sat beside Antonio and held his hands. "Knowing you will be a generous and responsible guardian to my son will be my solace, and as he grows in America with you, he will have opportunities I cannot imagine."

"I will give him everything I have."

They visited Antonio's solicitor that afternoon. And in only two days, she left for New York to visit family and friends and prepare for her ocean voyage.

GISELLA'S DEPARTURE AFFECTED ANTONIO more than he'd imagined. He had come to love her as his own and regretted that was not the role she wished to fill. Her absence became another

loss he must endure, yet he had Joseph, his only reason to live—
until the letter arrived by courier:

> *Dear Mr. Delito,*
>
> *We met when you visited my parish in search of your missing daughter, Margaret Rosa. I believe I have seen the girl in the photograph you carry in your compass.*
>
> *Several days ago a member of my congregation found a young girl on the edge of his property. She had suffered cold and hunger. Scratches and bruises marked her skin.*
>
> *He carried her to his home where he and his wife care for her. A physician has cleaned and dressed her wounds.*
>
> *The girl is approximately twelve years of age and fifty inches in height with auburn hair. Her only distinguishing mark is a missing finger, though it is a recent injury.*
>
> *The girl tells an incredible story of unjust confinement and escape from the Brookhaven Farm Lunatic Asylum, yet she seems to have sharp wits about her.*
>
> *Mr. Delito, I believe your daughter has been found.*
> *I advise you come at once.*
> > *In God, I am*
> > > *The Reverend Colin Thomas*

~ THIRTY-FIVE ~

1974 • November

I HAD TO GET OUT OF THIS BASEMENT and tell Michael what I'd found. I threw the Reverend's letter and the newspapers into the carton, tossing the Carlotta Delito article on top. I ran across the basement toward the exit, and clutching the carton, flew up the stairs to the factory assembly area. The basement had never been so dark. On the landing, the fire door had been propped open and marked by a line of light. I froze and checked up and down the stairwell and set down my box of documents. Not the slightest noise resounded. The back of my neck prickled. Someone had braced the door and admitting who, would be too terrifying.

I had to get out or get help. The nearest phone was across the factory floor and the only way out was through the fire door. I inched it open and gasped.

Vinny Ferro posed on the other side dressed in the black tuxedo he'd borrowed for the Chamber of Commerce event. Tall, strong, and confident. Waiting. Lurking. A sterling flask in his left hand. Smug satisfaction on his face as if he'd won something big.

Vinny.

Can it be? ... I fit the pieces together, saw the letters in my mind floating like puzzle pieces as I always did when committing names to memory like Gram had taught me. "Spell the name in your head." F E R R A R O. Ferraro. So similar to Ferro. What are the chances? Did Carlotta dissociate from all things Delito? Did Antonio force her isolation? Would she have reverted to her maiden name? Vinny moved here from Providence and this newspaper is from Providence where the Ferraro family lived. It's no wonder Gram avoided Rhode Island. Maybe Antonio did too, to keep distance between him and Carlotta. Wow, he must have learned about her affair with Porter. It would explain why Delito, Inc. really remained a hundred miles from the center of jewelry manufacturing, and not the fable I'd been told. I'd been pursuing clues around the world, hoping smoke would lead to fire, while Vinny's rage smoldered down the hall.

Everything I'd uncovered led to this. And I now had proof. A seventy-year-old news story explained everything—and it was worse than imagined.

The danger I faced was wrapped in a fancy tuxedo. I didn't *feel* trapped in a savage nightmare—I *knew* I was.

But unlike the others, this nightmare was all mine.

Mine and Vinny's.

My heart pounded. Pounded as if I'd been startled by a stranger in my home. Pounded as if I'd been running, been chased, like in my nightmares. Suffocated and paralyzed, I was literally scared stiff as my mind planned possible moves.

I couldn't talk my way out of this. Should I fight? Too small. With what weapon? Beads, chains, pliers? Not much to choose from in a jewelry assembly plant. Or I could run like in my nightmares, run like hell, run as if my life depended on it ... for a phone ... for an exit ... or forever.

My lips finally parted. "What are you doing here?" My foot braced as I readied to bolt.

With every little twitch and each hesitant step, Vinny moved to block my way. My back pressed against the wall. Across the aisle, eight feet away, he leaned against a steel worktable. His skin reeked of cheap aftershave. His breath smelled of liquor.

"What do you want?"

"You've been digging into Delito secrets for a month. You know what I want."

"There's no way out of this for you." Inching away from the stairwell door, hoping he wouldn't notice I was changing direction, but he paced in a cocky way, mirroring my movement, adjusting the barrier between me and escape.

"Lay it out, Del. You think you know the whole story. Lay. It. Out." He sipped from his flask. "Start with our favorite granny."

"What's Rosa got to do with this?"

"Do you think she knew who I was or where I came from? When she hired me on the spot, I wondered if she recognized family blood. Do you think she knew it was I who left the newspaper on her desk the day she died?" His fingers wiggled and he smirked. "Hey, you don't think the shock of seeing it caused her heart to flutter? Do you?"

"Whatever happened to you and your family didn't start with Gram, has nothing to do with Gram, and nothing to do with me."

"Whatever happened? What the hell do you think happened? My crappy life happened."

Where he was headed was obvious, but the longer he talked, the more time I had to devise an escape. "I have no idea what you're talking about. All I know for sure is someone's been stealing from the business, and I can't prove who."

"No kidding. Let me clear it up." He slapped his open hand against his chest. "It's me. I've been moving money since I got here, creating phony media buys, faking paperwork, diverting checks—collecting my share."

"Who was in it with you?"

"See, Del, now you're pissing me off. You don't give me the credit I deserve. Always underestimating. This is all me. None of those ancient assholes in New York had a clue."

"I don't understand. Why did you target me?"

"Delito money is mine."

"And you came to that conclusion ... How?"

"Del, Del, Del. You're a smart girl. Didn't you figure out the best part?"

I scanned the area, searching for a way around him, any way out of this mess.

"The great Antonio Delito tossed Carlotta Delito—my great-grandmother—like stinking garbage. All the while I worked here, I sat across from his portrait wondering how a man like him could dump his wife in the street and ride away."

"From what I know, she had it coming."

"My mother and her mother didn't. I damn sure didn't. We didn't deserve this shit life forever."

"No, you didn't."

"When Carlotta made her way back to Providence, men couldn't resist her beauty. The old girl had a talent, you know. She survived on her back, picking one useless piece of trash after another, taking everything she could from them—a lifestyle that would not end with her."

"I don't know anything about that."

"No, I don't imagine Rosa told you that bedtime story."

Ha. If only he knew Rosa told me nothing. "What do you want from me?"

His arms stretched in a sweeping motion. A few drops from his flask that smelled like bourbon splashed into the air. "You and I share the same lineage. I should own half of this and I don't. I should be living at High Hill and I'm not." He gulped from the flask. "My damn name should be Delito," he shouted. "And it isn't."

"That sounds reasonable ... complicated and worth discussing, but we're both tired ...."

He wriggled like a little boy.

My suggestion was absurd. I knew it was. But I was getting more desperate because he was getting more drunk, angry, and aggressive.

"Vinny please, let's sit down tomorrow and have a long talk. We can compare what we know and figure out the rest."

"Nope. Nothing more to talk about. See, I think you're still confused, so I'll sum it up. Carlotta Delito was your great-grandmother and mine, too."

I couldn't tell him what I'd discovered. It would be suicide to tell him he was wrong about his lineage and it had nothing to do with Carlotta. "She was a curse on my family. This whole horrible mess began with her."

"If you had just let it go ... I only wanted enough cash for a fresh start."

"Then, what."

"I'd have left the state. Settled somewhere more suited to me. L.A., Miami, maybe Vegas. Far from New England and this tired old town."

He looked away for a second as if he were imagining his better life. I bolted for the exit and he chased after me.

As I raced down an aisle toward the door to the main lobby, assembly stations blurred by. I flew past workbenches, overturning boxes of beads, hoping Vinny would slide on spilled debris.

I ran and ran and glanced behind. Nothing had slowed him. He kept pace. Driven by revenge. Angry and drunk. Running faster. Closer. Like a nightmare that wouldn't end—a nightmare that began too long ago.

I could almost feel his breath on my neck.

Maybe this was the night the nightmares would end.

Vinny's arms wrapped around my knees in a lunging tackle. I fell forward.

My body bounced and slammed against wooden boards. The impact forced the wind from my chest. My head hit the floor. Time slowed. Sound faded. Light dimmed. My eyes closed as I lay stunned.

Dizzy. Spinning. Stinging. I'd been here before.

I gasped for air. It tore into my lungs like a breath from
God raising the dead. Dust in my mouth. Blood on my lip.
My body wrenched with pain as I waited for my limbs
to move—prayed that they would move.

Vinny lay still.

Blood smeared the leg of the steel workbench where his head must have hit. A gash oozed and dripped down his forehead.

His arms held me tight against him—hugging me like a lover.

He whispered. "We had nothing. A small, dirty room. Sharing a filthy toilet. My old man went out one night and never came back." His fingers slid into my hair and jerked my head until our eyes met. "Against my grandmother's wishes, my mother appealed to Rosa for help. Did you know that?"

My whimper said no.

"She was desperate when the old man left. Swallowed her pride. Begged for help ... but Rosa refused."

"Can you blame her? Carlotta had her committed to an asylum and told Antonio she was dead."

"My mother had nothing to do with that. Hell, my mother's mother had nothing to do with that." His whisper was a confession. "You have everything and I have nothing. My mother whored for rent money. I was her johns' second choice." He squeezed me closer and nuzzled his face against my neck. "So tell me, Del, how was it where you grew up?"

The sound of his voice faded until I could no longer hear.

"I'm sorry you had it so tough, but none of that was my fault or Gram's." Half hoping he wouldn't hear, I whispered, "You don't have Delito blood. And your name was never Delito."

His tight grip slowly, maybe unconsciously, released. I caught my breath. Lifted my fingers, one by one. Shifted my arms, then my legs. His hold on me loosened as his arms went limp. Barely conscious. His steel broken.

I rose with caution, feeling where I hurt, spitting dust and grit from my mouth. My lip bled. My legs ached. My knees burned. I leaned against a bank of sinks and gained my balance, forcing myself to examine my wounds. Slivers had pierced my arms and knees when he tackled me to the floor. Sliding across rough floor planks had scraped my hands. Blood oozed from shredded, swelling skin. But I was free of his grasp. *Safe* ...

... Safe until his hand seized my ankle and he used my body to pull himself up. His strength was greater than I anticipated. His voice softened, "My name ... it could have been Delito. I could have had ..." His head tilted during a long pause. "... Everything." His eyes fixed on mine with an expression of defeat as if he'd come to realize his better life would never happen.

"Vinny, stop this. Let me go. You don't want to hurt me."

"What else can I do?" His free hand braced against the sinks until he lifted himself off the floor. "You said it yourself." His demeanor changed. "There's no way out of this." He stared with wild eyes. Vengeance ablaze in crazy eyes. Eyes resigned to kill.

I returned his stare. I hated him for turning me into a monster. I hated him for what I was about to do.

From the sink behind me, I reached for the pan. Gripping it firmly. Careful not to spill. "I'm sorry."

The pan I hurled hit his legs. Acid fired through the trousers of Michael's borrowed tuxedo with smoking holes growing larger as it consumed the fabric—and melted flesh.

A low groan erupted to a squeal as he fell to the floor writhing in pain and reaching for his burning legs.

"Don't touch them!" I shouted. "You'll burn your hands."

Hanging on the wall, spools of decorative link chain we used for belts made for good bindings, and I wrapped his arms and ankles until confident he could not move.

My hands and forearms thrashed in the neutralizer pan, rinsing splashed acid from my skin before pouring the solution on his legs to stop the damage.

By the time first shift employees arrived at seven, the ambulance was long gone, yet police cruisers remained in the parking lot. I sent factory workers home until the next day and asked the shop foreman to phone and cancel those scheduled to work the next shifts.

Michael soon arrived and insisted on taking me to the emergency room to have my hands examined and bandaged. Though I'd treated my burns with proper first aid, I appreciated and accepted the extra care, and saw an opportunity to tell him what happened without curbing my emotions because employees were near. I hadn't slept for twenty-four straight hours, since we awoke at our Cape Cod hotel, and in that time I rode across New England, uncovered my family's past, discovered who stole from the business—and saved my own life.

Michael and I waited in the emergency room where I fell asleep in his arms.

~ THIRTY-SIX ~

1900 • April

ANTONIO DELITO RODE his small carriage hard through the night, an unusually warm night lit by a nearly full moon in a cloudless sky, a perfect night to find his daughter. The letter from Reverend Thomas seemed too good to be true, but surely, such a man would not be frivolous with words regarding a matter of such importance.

Antonio had left baby Joseph down the road from High Hill in the care of his solicitor's family, who had become his most trusted friends. He rode fast for nearly three hours until he arrived at the parish, pounding every door until the Reverend appeared.

"I knew you would come. Welcome, sir."

"It is good to see you again, Reverend Thomas."

"Come inside while I dress. I will take you to your daughter."

They left a few minutes later. Antonio followed the Reverend's carriage and they arrived at Bell's Farm within the hour. There, he was introduced to Jane and Andrew Bell.

MAGGIE STIRRED IN THE BED Jane had prepared in a second bedroom. She thought she'd heard horses, the dog barking a warning of visitors, and the squeal of the door when it opened— the quiet and familiar voices of Jane and Andrew, Reverend Thomas and— Could it be? Her mind had tricked her before.

Father!

She ran from the room and paused in the doorway, watching and waiting for him to see her. Donned in a white nightdress, she stood with arms straight at her sides. Her heart nearly bursting from her chest.

Father turned. His head tilted. His hand swiped his forehead as if wiping sweat. His arms unfurled as she ran to him. It seemed she would run forever. She ran like she had at High Hill when Carlotta and Uncle Elias chased her, and like she ran after their carriage when they discarded her at the asylum. She ran like she had run alongside the river witnessing Salvatore fight for his life—wondering if he would live.

She jumped into her father's arms and buried her face in his coat as he kissed the top of her head and stroked her hair.

"My Sunshine." His voice cracked. "We are going home."

There was much to speak of, but it would wait. At this joyous moment, she couldn't bring herself to ask—where is Sally?

Andrew offered his home to rest, and at daybreak, Jane served breakfast. She and Maggie packed a travel sack with water, biscuits, and a blanket. Jane helped her dress and wrapped a light wool shawl around her head and shoulders.

"Andrew and I will miss you terribly. Take care of yourself." Jane kissed her forehead. "Be careful with your hand until it is healed. Come and visit us anytime."

Father thanked Reverend Thomas and promised the Bells he and Maggie would return when her injuries healed. They boarded the carriage and began their journey home.

Maggie waited until they reached the main road. She stared straight ahead when she asked, "Where is Sally?"

Father's gaze locked on the road like a horse wearing blinders.

"He was in the river. Did you find him?" She looked at her father with tear-filled eyes, knowing the river had taken him, yet as long as Father didn't speak, she could believe her brother had saved himself. She held onto hope like the lifesaving branch rooted in the river's bank. She held her breath. "Father, where is he?"

His arm wrapped around her and held tight. Would he tell her now? She wept when she realized her beloved brother was dead—and Father could not say the words.

Relief came with silence. If she didn't make him tell her about

Sally's death, maybe he wouldn't ask what happened on the river. Maybe he wouldn't ask how it was that she lived and Salvatore died. She would never have to tell him her brother drowned because she let him go.

Her weak useless finger deserved to be cut off.

HIGH HILL NEVER LOOKED AS MAJESTIC as it did on the day Antonio brought his daughter home. Sunlight filtered through stained glass transoms, splashing vivid color on the parlor's polished floor. Rich fabrics on fine furniture. Sparkling crystal candlesticks and vases of fresh cut lilacs. Silver service and Florentine picture frames. Perhaps its beauty was born in its aura of safety, and at this moment, Antonio thought he and his family might never venture beyond these lavish walls. But of course, they would.

Maggie left the library, stepping slow and steady down the hallway. She stopped at the closet and kicked its door, then kicked it again and again.

He let her.

A fearful look up the stairway suggested something dreadful awaited.

Eventually they would have to revisit the upstairs chambers, and he knew it must be now. He climbed halfway up, but she didn't follow. "Maggie." His voice was firm when he extended his hand. "Come with me."

She leaned against the bannister, gripping it with both hands as she slid to the floor and sat on the bottom step, shaking her head.

"Margaret Rosa. Let go of that railing and come upstairs."

Her hold relaxed, and she hunched with her face buried in her arms crossed on top of her knees.

He sat beside her and wrapped his arm around her. "Look at me."

She raised her head. "I can't go there with you. I don't want to feel bad again."

"You feel bad now, don't you?"

Maggie agreed.

"You will tell me all that happened to you. We will get these secrets out of ourselves and be done with it."

"No. I don't want to, Father."

"I will not allow this stain to soil the rest of our days. We ask and tell everything tonight."

Maggie told him about the last bad days at High Hill and how she fell from the tree, and hobbled to the house. She raised her dress to her knees to reveal her scars. A thumping noise had lured her up the stairs where she found Carlotta with Uncle Elias naked in his bed.

The more she talked, the easier her telling became. They held hands and climbed to the second floor where she reenacted pulling open the doors to his chamber where she watched his bed shake and bang against the wall.

She ran downstairs to the library, pointing outside and describing how Carlotta and Elias had chased her across the fields, then locked her in the closet overnight with only a bucket to relieve herself. At the closet, she demonstrated how she pressed herself into the corner because she was afraid. Then she described the best and the worst of her days at the asylum, and they laughed and cried together.

"I have friends at the asylum, Emma and her mum and Cookie. I want to visit them."

"Never. I forbid it. This ends tonight."

"But Father, they will worry about my welfare."

"I will send word of your safe return, but you will not maintain friendships from that past."

"But my jewelry chest with my secret things, and I wrote a journal and—"

"Where is it?"

"Hidden behind a wall in the tunnel. No one will find it."

"There it shall remain. Come, I have something to show you." In the parlor, he pulled a steamer trunk to the center of the floor, the same trunk Salvatore had damaged when the cast-iron plant stand wobbled, fell against it, and gouged a scar into its skin.

"All reminders of these events will leave our home." He raised the lid of the trunk. "I packed Carlotta's photographs and records from my dealings with Elias Porter. Give those newspapers to me."

A broadsheet with a photo of four boys on a beach lay on top of the pile. Salvatore's body had been found. Her face paled as she read the story. "I asked Salvatore's wife to remain with our family, but it was her desire to return to her life in Italy. You and I will visit her one day. We will survive this." He pried up the trunk's false bottom and tucked the newspapers underneath it. If you have anything to say about Salvatore, say it now."

Maggie shook her head. "No, Father."

"Good. Come with me. We will dispose of this trash." Antonio and his daughter loaded the trunk into the carriage and rode to the factory where they stashed it in the depths of the basement, where in privacy he might add remaining documents should they surface.

Back at High Hill he asked, "Will you be all right with this?"

"This catastrophe ends tonight," she mimicked his words. "We will never speak of these dark days again."

"Good girl."

MAGGIE SLEPT UNTIL EARLY AFTERNOON when her father woke her. She felt as gutted as a huntsman's catch, yet strangely relieved, cleansed somehow, like the air after a storm. Perhaps Father was right. Clear all reminders.

"Maggie," he called from the bottom of the stairs. "Get dressed and come down. We are going out for supper." By four o'clock, they arrived at the nearest homestead.

"Father, who lives here? I don't know them."

"The family name is Schaeffer. They arrived from New York City some eight months ago. A fine family who have become good friends to me."

"What's his business?"

"Solicitor. He has helped with several legal matters regarding the business, as well as in Hartford where he defends a new friend of mine, a common woman accused of fraud against the state, but never mind that. Come, let us go inside." He helped her step down from the carriage.

"Do they have children?"

"Yes, one son named Aaron, Aaron Schaeffer, and another child due in summer. The boy is smart, well-read, and well-traveled. I think you will take a liking to him."

"It will be wonderful to find a new friendship close to home."

"Margaret, there is one more thing. I am going to hire a housekeeper and a nanny."

"Father." She giggled. "I'm too grown to need a nanny. I can care for myself."

"That you can, girl." He laughed as he knocked on the Schaeffer's door.

Young Aaron greeted them. A pregnant Mrs. Schaeffer holding a newborn baby confused Maggie as her eyes darted from the woman's belly to the baby in her arms and up to Father.

He laughed. "The nanny is not for you. She will be minding Joseph Salvatore Delito. This is Salvatore's son."

Maggie's mouth dropped. She laughed and cried and felt the whole of her fill with joy.

Mrs. Schaeffer handed the baby to Maggie and properly positioned him in her arms. "Hold on to him."

Cradling the baby, she rocked him until he found her eyes and smiled at her and reached for her. His tiny hand curled around her fingers and held them tight—like Sally had held them in the river.

She swayed from side to side and softly sobbed. "I will never let you go."

~ THIRTY-SEVEN ~

1974 • November

THE HOSPITAL STAFF had transferred Vinny to a Boston burn center by the time Michael and I left the ER four hours after we'd arrived. We were both relieved to learn my acid burns weren't as serious as they first looked. My quick reaction to slosh my arms in neutralizer had prevented deep burns. Damaged skin would heal with minimal scarring.

The police needed my statement, and I made an appointment for the following day.

While I indulged in a nap, Michael moved the old trunk from the plant to High Hill then returned to the office to ensure that the mess of my fight in the factory would be properly cleaned.

Later, I browsed through several newspapers from the trunk and came upon the letter I had previously set aside. A Reverend Thomas had written Antonio Delito that Margaret Rosa had been found on a farmer's property where she told a story of escape and rescue from a lunatic asylum.

Gram's legacy had been redeemed, and I had no doubt of her trials and accomplishments. The memory of her life and her triumph over adversity was better than that which I had known. For all my excitement, curiosity, and persistence regarding my family's past, I felt more satisfied by my present, and more tantalized by possibilities in my future.

Michael called to say he was working on our travel itinerary. We were leaving for Cairo in less than three weeks. Anticipation and enthusiasm had me packing in my mind.

After the next day's meeting with detectives and a prosecutor from the District Attorney's office, Michael and I relaxed in the den at High Hill. He pulled me close. "So this is done? No more scraping around the factory basement? No more asylums, hospitals, or police?"

"It's done. I swear. At least until Vinny's trial. And all this crap was for nothing."

"What do you mean?"

"Well, I was thinking, I checked old birth records and learned Vinny's grandmother was born to Carlotta only months after she resettled in Providence."

"Yeah, we assumed that much. So?"

"So who got her pregnant if Antonio was in Italy for a year? That's the kicker; Vinny and I have no shared bloodline. He doesn't have a drop of Delito blood in him."

Michael was taken aback. "What?"

"Try to follow." My bandaged hands scribbled as I put pen to paper on my unstable lap. Starting at the bottom of the sheet, I wrote one name above the other. "There's me and my dad Joseph, Joseph and his dad Salvatore, Salvatore and his dad Antonio. But Salvatore was born of Antonio's first wife. Salvatore's mother was not Carlotta. You with me?"

"So far."

"Okay, new column. Enter Carlotta, so let's add Gram's name, Rosa, in parentheses next to Salvatore because they're the same generation." I glanced at Michael. "Then Carlotta is banished."

"I get it. Put her in a third column."

"And she's carrying Elias Porter's child, Vinny's grandmother, same generation as Gram and Salvatore, but not related. Then we have Vinny's mother, then Vinny. See? Vinny and I aren't even related. I am Salvatore's granddaughter. The only child of Carlotta's union with Antonio Delito was Gram, and Gram had no children —end of the line."

I drew a long loop around column three. "Carlotta Ferraro and Elias Porter began a new line that ends with Vinny."

"Poor Vinny," he laughed and shook his head.

Half his attention shifted to his newspaper and half remained with me, but I didn't mind. I was relishing security and contentment simply being a normal couple.

Michael didn't even look up when he said, "Aaron Schaeffer phoned yesterday afternoon."

"Really? How is he? What did he want?"

"Couldn't believe what happened at the plant. Asked how you were, if you needed anything, and could you call sometime soon. Said he had a great story to tell."

"A great story, huh? I bet he does, and I need to hear it. I'll call him early next week. Let him know, would you?"

The phone rang. Michael answered. I looked up, but he raised his hand indicating the call was for him.

"Now?" He took his notebook from the table and jotted a few words before he hung up.

"Get your coat," he said.

"Where are we going?"

"Hartford Hospital."

"Why? My hand will be okay."

Michael turned me to face him, brimming with pride and self-satisfaction. "I found her."

"Found who?"

"Emma Collings."

I slipped on a sweater and grabbed my purse. Hartford Hospital was an easy drive up the highway, not far from Michael's apartment. I must have looked dazed as a million questions ran through my mind. I wasn't aware of the ride nor did I realize we had parked the car, and before I knew it, we were in the hospital gift shop buying flowers and my attention had returned. "How did you locate her?"

"Friends in low places." He grinned.

We stepped off the elevator. "Seriously, how?"

"Since Rosa's funeral, I've had every hospital and rest home in Connecticut watching for her."

"What a sweet thing to do."

He handed me the flower bouquet and checked the room number he'd written on his pad.

"How sick is she? Does she know I'm coming?"

"Fractured hip. She should be okay, but her age is a factor. She's expecting you." He pointed to Emma's room, then leaned by the door as I moved inside.

The old woman smiled when she saw me. "Maggie."

"No, Emma. It's Laura Delito. We met at my grandmother's wake." I set the flowers on the tray table beside her bed.

Daylight from a bank of windows illuminated the white bed sheets, casting soft reflective light on Emma's face. "They're lovely. And you also appear to be in better spirits than when we last met. You do look like Maggie when she was young."

"Her spirit remained young and vital, so her death was a shock. I miss her. I always will. But I'm moving on with my life. It gets easier as I look to the future."

"She was a kind friend, and I'm proud to have known her."

I inched toward the bed, sat on the edge, and held her hand. "Emma, I know all about the asylum."

Sobbing like a baby, she blurted, "I'm so sorry. Please forgive me."

I cradled her in my arms. "What is it? There's nothing to forgive. I know the whole story, and there was nothing you could have done to alter events."

"It was my fault. I stole her key."

"The key didn't matter."

"But it would have, if I left it in the drawer where my mother hid it. Maggie's father would have known to look for her chest. Then he would have found Maggie. And Salvatore wouldn't have died."

"Oh, no. No, no, no. It wouldn't have made a difference."

"Maggie trusted my mum and me to keep the key safe. She knew her father would come. No one believed her. Not even me. Yet her hope never wavered. I didn't mean any harm. I wanted a keepsake, so I took the key from the drawer, fully intending to put it back. But with so much happening so fast, I forgot, and my mum didn't give it another thought."

"Emma, the key wasn't important, not then. Only a journal was in the chest. Even if your mother gave it to Maggie's father, do you think he would have paused to search for the chest, read the journal, and investigate her story?"

Emma shook her head.

"Of course, not. He and Salvatore would have pursued Heinz and Mr. Porter, just like they did. It couldn't happen any other way."

"After Salvatore drowned, I couldn't face her. Did she speak of me? I never saw her again. Maybe she looked for me, but I moved out of state for a while, then I kept to myself when I returned. Will you forgive me, now?"

"My grandmother never spoke of her childhood, but I suspect she often thought of it. She said she wouldn't tell me because she didn't want me saddened by events so long past. I wish I had known. How can you love and be close to someone and not share all of their life, even when knowing about them hurts you?"

Michael heard every word, and his quiet smile made me realize the importance of what I'd said. I'd been so secretive with him and my mom, but my suspicions created problems that weren't there. "That's what makes losing Gram so painful. As close as we were, I feel robbed of knowing her."

Emma wiped her eyes and a peace came over her. "I've carried this pain for more than seventy years. What a horrible waste. Maggie and I could have been lifelong friends."

"Emma, if you had not kept that key and troubled yourself to bring it to me, I wouldn't have learned the truth about her life and for that I am grateful."

I held Emma just as I had held Gram on the night she died. "May I visit again? I'd like to know more about your good times with my grandmother."

"There were many, and I remember as if they happened yesterday." She pulled me near and whispered in my ear.

Michael curled my hand around his arm as we left the room. "What did she whisper to you?"

"She said, 'Your young man is a good man. Hold on to him.' And I plan to." Glancing up, I leaned against him.

He nodded with a subtle smile. "Good advice."

My grip on his arm tightened, tighter than an affectionate hold, and I didn't know why, except that knowing Gram's childhood and easing Emma's guilt had boosted my strength and cleared my vision of Delito, Gram, and me. We'd been lost on a dismal path, but had finally found our road home. As Michael and I walked the hospital corridor, dream images flashed before me.

I would direct Delito's business success. Michael and I would marry. We would raise three children together. I could see them playing in High Hill's fields. I knew Gram approved of everything leading to my life's joyful and contented end.

I knew this because a new angel named Maggie had sent snapshots of my fate from heaven—and she would light the way.

Delito's dark days were history.

I knew this because I had a sense about things like that.

~ Discussion Topics & Questions ~

Asylum is set in 1899 and the mid-1970s, when the rise and fall of manufacturing, changing mores and folkways, and struggles for equal rights, prompted discussion of social issues that remain relevant today.

Confinement & Times of Danger

Asylums, Retreats & Prisons

Asylums often served as storage for unwanted women, children, and those who had become burdensome to family or society due to finances or behavior. More socially acceptable than divorce, asylums were the prisons for non-compliant and disobedient wives who were declared insane by their husbands.

- Can you imagine your life under such control?
- Can you imagine being compliant?
- Discuss similarities between asylums of the past and today's prisons?

Safety & Security

In 1899 when twelve-year-old Maggie unwittingly witnessed a shocking scandal, she ran. When she discovered a wicked villainy at the asylum, she had little choice but to record it. In our time, we are often urged if we "See Something. Say Something."

- If you witnessed wrongdoing, would you most likely report it, ignore it, or run for your life?
- Have you been in that situation? What was your response and why?

Relationships

Family & Genealogy

Laura and her grandmother are as close as two people can be and they have a psychic connection, even sharing the same dreams. Laura and Marcia are closer than most sisters, yet they're not related.

- In your opinion, is blood thicker than water?
- Is your ancestry important to you?
- Have you visited a genealogy website?

Friends, Best Friends & Lovers

Though best friends, Laura and Marcia don't share common interests, social standing, or financial status. Shared values, common history, reliability, and trust cement their bond, and individual strengths and weaknesses balance a non-competitive and durable friendship.

Friends ... contd.

- What qualities do you value in a "best" friendship?
- Would you date your best friend's ex (lover, husband, partner)?
- Would you borrow money from, or lend to, your best friend?
- Have you been betrayed by a close friend?

Loss & Grief

Maggie, Antonio, and Laura react differently to the tragic loss of loved ones. Laura must navigate new responsibilities, shifting relationships, and settling in her High Hill home. Grief leads to feelings of guilt, inadequacy, and self-doubt, all of which interfere with progress.

- Have you lost someone close?
- Has time eased your grief?

Society & Community Life

From Town Greens & Parishes to Shopping Malls & Social Media

In his desperate search for his daughter, Antonio Delito queries parish priests who would be aware of the comings and goings of their flock.

- What is today's version of "one who knows"?
- How do you learn what's happening in your community?
  In your neighborhood? In your family or household?
- Have you relinquished too much privacy?

What's Trending

Fashion Trends & Fads

As Laura plans a radical new product line for Delito, Inc., her personal style remains conservative. She wears "... neat classic clothes. ... not satin or velvet—and definitely not polyester."

- Does your personal style accurately reflect who you are?
- Which fashion trends, products or services from the past would you like to see return?
- Which fashion fads from the past deserve an unmarked grave?

Communication & Technology

Without cell phones, a 24-hour period of "telephone tag" between Laura and Michael forced time for ideas to incubate, resulting in more effective communication.

- Have modern devices make life easier or more stressful?
- Do modern devices help or hinder meaningful communication?

- How do you prefer to communicate? With family? Friends? Lovers?
- How do you communicate with co-workers?
- Do you, or does your employer, set limits on work-related texts or other forms of communication during off-hours?
- Are you addicted to your devices?
- For how long can you tolerate separation from your devices?

The Art & Necessity of Letter Writing

In 1900, Antonio's life changes when an urgent letter arrives by courier. In 1974, a stack of mail on Laura's desk includes "A red and blue striped airmail letter ... The postmark reads Morocco. ..." She places the foreign letter at the bottom of the stack, "... anticipating its contents, saving it for dessert." She prepares a glass of Arab-style tea, creates a ritual around reading the letter.

- Do you value receiving handwritten letters?
- Do you write letters? How often?
- After decades of decline, more states support teaching cursive. Should cursive be taught in schools?

Social Issues, Workplace Culture & Women's Rights

Women in the Workplace

Happy to be living far from family scrutiny, Laura Delito's independent career was at the brink of success when her grandmother urged her return to the family jewelry business. Male executives preferred the status quo and resisted her return.

- Have you had to work harder than male coworkers to advance in pay and position?
- Are all positions in the company open to you?
- Does being female in the workplace offer any advantage?

Workplace Troubles & Harassment

Laura was offended by a pinup calendar hanging in the factory assembly room. She said, "It's crude and vulgar and it disrespects me." At first opportunity, she tore it down.

- What did you think of Laura's strong reaction to the girlie calendar?
- Have you been offended by sexual displays or jokes at work?
- Have you witnessed or been sexually harassed in the workplace?
- How did it make you feel? What did you do about it?

* * *

~ About the Author ~

Kathryn Orzech is a seasoned world traveler, avid film fan, and self-proclaimed news nerd, who writes mystery, suspense, and thrillers. Female protagonists confront heart-pounding situations, flirt with romance, and brush with the supernatural.

Online since the 1990s with visitors from every U.S. state and more than 50 countries, her *DreamWatch* website inspired the novel *Premonition of Terror* when she wondered, What if...?

Also by Kathryn Orzech

Premonition of Terror
a psychic thriller

Globetrotting suspense strikes close to home

DreamWatch.com, true paranormal experiences of ordinary people, began as a hobby. It was *supposed* to be fun—until premonitions from around the world predict the same catastrophic attack.

The last time reluctant psychic Kate Kasabian revealed a prediction, people close to her were hurt. But with thousands of lives at risk, she has no choice but to badger her FBI brother to investigate. He refuses to help until the legendary Matt Chase from Counterterrorism alerts agents to a credible threat—eerily similar to Kate's warnings.

Tracking clues from Prague to New England, Kate trusts dreams and premonitions, while Chase relies on technology and global intelligence. Can their unlikely alliance stop the U.S. plot?

Counting Souls
a contemporary mystery thriller
(a work in progress)

A quiet valley town in Connecticut seems to be the target of an enigmatic serial killer—but not one body has been found at the bloody crime scenes. Citizens are frightened. Police are frustrated. Detectives are baffled. Only two sisters see the signs in ancient writings the killer left behind.

To learn more about Kathryn Orzech and her writing,
and to connect online, visit her official website:
www.DreamWatch.com